DOGSTAR RISING

PARKER BILAL is the pseudonym of Jamal Mahjoub. Mahjoub has published seven critically acclaimed literary novels, which have been widely translated. *Dogstar Rising* is his second Makana Mystery. Born in London, Mahjoub has lived at various times in the UK, Sudan, Cairo and Denmark. He currently lives in Barcelona.

DOGSTAR RISING

PARKER BILAL

BLOOMSBURY
LONDON · NEW DELHI · NEW YORK · SYDNEY

First published in Great Britain 2013
This paperback edition published 2014

Copyright © 2013 by Jamal Mahjoub

The moral right of the author has been asserted

Bloomsbury Publishing, London, New Delhi, New York and Sydney

50 Bedford Square, London WC1B 3DP

A CIP catalogue record for this book is available from the British Library

ISBN 978 1 4088 4256 0
10 9 8 7 6 5 4 3 2 1

Typeset by Hewer Text UK Ltd, Edinburgh

Printed and bound in Great Britain by CPI Group (UK) Ltd, Croydon CR0 4YY

www.bloomsbury.com/parkerbilal

Apocalypse:

From the Greek ἀποκαλύπτω, apokalupto,

meaning to uncover or reveal – to remove the veil;

the revelation of what was hidden from mankind;

the end of a long dark age ruled by corruption and dishonesty.

Prologue

Cairo, 2001

At first no one really noticed. Everyone was too busy with the daily struggle. Nobody had time to lift their eyes from the uneven road in front of them to look skywards for fear of stumbling. The lighting in that part of town was poor anyway and you had to keep your wits about you if you didn't want to get knocked down by an impatient driver. To make things worse, the sightings took place at night, when the street was one long vale of frustration: motorcycles popping, minibuses beeping, bicycle bells and sirens, vendors calling out their wares, horses protesting. There was no time to notice anything, least of all a figure perched high above the street.

The mysterious figure rarely showed itself in the same place more than once. It would appear high up on the corner of a building, or perched on the balustrade of a darkened balcony, with no explanation of how it got there, nor where it disappeared to when it went. '*Malaika!*' cried one woman. An angel. She fell to her knees, much to the amusement of onlookers on either side of the crowded street. Gruff men threw back their heads and laughed. But then someone else pointed and soon a whole crowd was peering up into the gloomy shadows of the jumbled walls high above, trying to make out what it was that seemed to be poised there, halfway between heaven and earth.

It was a bad time for anything out of the ordinary. Nerves were on edge, tempers frayed easily. The appearance of this 'angel' had coincided with the murder of a number of young children in the area. How could anyone kill a child, people asked, and where were the police when you needed them? Three bodies had turned up so far, and every day brought the possibility of more.

The sighting of the angel was taken as a sign, that God had not abandoned them. A small group of devotees formed a loyal cult. They would meet every evening to hold a candlelit vigil on bended knees in front of the church, hands clutched together in supplication, praying for a miracle. As they waited, their eyes sought out any sign of movement above. Reports naturally varied. It was quite a slight figure some said, while others claimed it was tall. Some said it was as rigid as a statue, others swore that it had wings that glittered like silver or gold. It glowed as if it was burning.

'It is a sign,' they whispered. 'Things are going to change soon.'

'Good will prevail. Our suffering will come to an end.'

'We will be released from this trial.'

The angel, many were heard to say, had been sent to protect the young ones in this dangerous time. Soon there were avid watchers posted on every corner, craning their necks to see if it would show. The word spread. Christians in particular took this as a message meant for them: an angel had descended from heaven to bring them comfort in these difficult times. To guide them through this trial of persecution. The newspapers and the radio stations chattered eagerly on the subject, with everyone adding their own interpretation of the facts. There were suggestions that it was a trick, a hoax, but no one could prove who or what might be behind it and nobody stepped forward to claim responsibility. Was it a government plot to take people's minds off the hardships? Or had the Israelis started putting hallucinogenic substances in the drinking water?

The sightings continued. Whenever it was spotted the message went out and within minutes a group of Christians would arrive, hands held together in prayer, rosaries pressed to their lips. They ignored the jeering, the obscenities and rotten vegetables thrown in their direction. The newspapers and television stations began to take an interest and soon the Angel of Imbaba was being discussed on chat shows and talked about in the papers.

And while there were those who saw the angel as a benevolent presence, a sign of God's protective hand, there were just as many who viewed it as a bad omen. Why had its appearance coincided with the murder of those young boys? What connection could there be between one event and the other? People became fearful of letting their children out of sight. The police, whose presence was rarely anything but scarce, made little effort to find the brutes responsible. The death of a child in these parts was hardly worthy of their attention. But this was different. The children were murdered, their bodies mutilated in the most awful way. Now if the child had been rich, it would have been another matter.

The weather was unusually hot for this time of year. The nights brought little relief since the temperature barely cooled down at all. People behaved like dogs, barking at the moon, going mad in the sun. Fights broke out between brothers, between people who had been friends for years. The neighbourhood was like a tinderbox, ready to explode at any minute. Over all of this the angel seemed to float, as if biding its time, waiting for what was to come.

I

Dog Days

Chapter One

The offices of Blue Ibis Tours were perched on a concrete ledge that constituted the third floor of a crumbling building downtown, a stone's throw from Al-Ubra Square, named after the old opera house that once stood on that spot until it was burned down in the riots of January 1952 and eventually replaced by a multi-storey car park. Blue Ibis flew tourists down to the Valley of the Kings on whirlwind tours of the hot and dusty resting places of long-dead pharaohs. They took them on camel treks into the Sinai Desert in the footsteps of Moses, before depositing them on a beach by the Red Sea where they could roast nicely for a few days and feed themselves on lavish buffets or dive in clear blue water among the coral reefs. The nights shook to the uninhibited pulse of dance music that provided them with the hedonistic lifestyles they associated with being on holiday. They ran them up and down the Nile in luxury boats with belly dancers and live folklore shows every evening. The food was all prepared to European standards so that nothing as inconvenient as indigestion might come between them and their once in a lifetime experience.

Makana learned most of this from a stack of brochures resting on the table next to the chair by the door, while he waited for Mr Farouk Faragalla to turn up for their appointment. He had plenty of time to study them because Mr Faragalla kept him waiting for over an hour. Makana was not in the best of moods to begin with, suspecting that he was wasting his time. He might even have left but for the fact that work had been slow, and that he was doing a favour for the son of an old friend.

Having gleaned a lifetime of information about the travel business, Makana tossed the brochure aside and kicked himself for being so soft-headed. Talal's father had been a highly respected lawyer in the old days in Sudan, one of the few who dared to challenge the regime on a legal front, for which he paid a price. When his father died in prison, Talal and his mother fled to Cairo, where Makana had taken it upon himself to provide whatever help he could. Talal was a bright young man trying to make a life for himself in his adopted home. He wasn't doing too badly and had turned himself into a respectable tourist guide and interpreter. He now unravelled the arcane mysteries of the pharaohs for eager visitors in Chinese and Spanish. Others did the same in Japanese, Russian and German. Curiosity about the Ancient Egyptians was unlimited. People came from all over the world. They saw the same mess that Makana saw, but they paid a lot more for it. Talal's real problem was that he was a hopeless romantic. To begin with he secretly ached to be, of all things, a composer of classical music. It was an ambition Makana had not quite managed to grasp but he put it down to the boy having an Egyptian mother of a certain social class and no particular talents, channelling all her failed ambitions into her only son from an early age. His father's death had brought mother and child closer together than was probably healthy, and so Talal was struggling. Being a tour guide was, as far as he was concerned,

4

just a temporary station along the way to composing and conducting his own orchestra. Becoming an African Mozart seemed like an odd kind of ambition to Makana, but then again everyone needed a dream to hold on to.

Talal's ambitions had become further entangled by his romantic involvement with Butheyna, commonly known to her friends as Bunny. Talal, being the muddle-headed and soft-hearted kid that he was, had convinced himself that his life would be incomplete without this woman. Love's arrow had struck its fatal wound while they were studying the complexities of the tourist trade together. In this area, she had a distinct advantage over him as her father happened to be the very same Faragalla that Makana was now waiting for. Talal thought he might improve his standing with the girl's father by persuading him to enlist Makana's services to solve a problem that had been worrying him.

With a glance at his watch to see if the minute hand was still doing its job, Makana picked up a creased and well-read newspaper. He had ignored it at first, noting that it was several days old, but the appeal had started to grow as his interest in the tourist business waned. On an inside page he found a double spread about a recent spate of attacks on churches. It was not the first time the Coptic community had been targeted and in all likelihood it would not be the last. Every now and then somebody would get it into their mind that a 14 per cent minority posed a deadly threat to the way of life of the other 86 per cent. Violence towards Christians had been going on for centuries. The response from those on high had been the usual murmurs of consolation and promises of change to come. *Al-Raïs* himself, the president, was pictured shaking hands with the Coptic pope, always a useful gesture even if it signified little in the way of real change. The

Minister of the Interior claimed confidently that such events were the result of a criminal element which was trying to undermine the country, and called on everyone to help fight this attack on the nation's security. At the bottom of one page, tucked into the corner, there appeared a brief mention of a church in Imbaba which was battling against the threat of closure due to the building having been declared unsafe. There was a blurred photograph of a fierce-looking priest declaring he would fight until his last breath to keep the church open. In the closing lines of the article, the journalist noted that the priest, Father Macarius, was regarded as a controversial figure, accused by some locals of conducting satanic rituals, which may or may not have been related to the recent spate of young boys being murdered in the area.

Tiring swiftly of this nonsense, Makana tossed aside the paper with a sigh and got to his feet to begin pacing. There wasn't much room for pacing, most of the office being cluttered with desks, all of which, bar one, were empty at this hour. Talal had led him to believe that Blue Ibis Tours was a fairly successful operation. It now seemed obvious that Talal's eyes were clouded, firstly because he was employed by the company, and secondly, and probably more significantly, by the fact that he was infatuated with the owner's daughter. Makana decided he would hold on a little longer, for the boy's sake if for nothing else, but his first impressions were not encouraging. Either they were doing so well the owner didn't need to be on time, or, more likely, there was so little to do nobody could be bothered to be behind their desks at nine in the morning.

The only occupied desk was the one closest to the door, facing the entrance. The woman who sat behind it was the person who had let him in. She certainly didn't seem short of work.

'I don't have any record of an appointment,' she had said,

looking him over and coming up short of conviction. 'Can you tell me what it concerns?'

'Mr Faragalla would not thank me for discussing his business without his permission.'

To her credit she did not show annoyance at this. Instead she tried calling her boss a couple of times without luck. Obviously Faragalla had better things to do with his time than answering the telephone. Now the woman seemed to take pity on Makana. She ceased the clicking of her keyboard and reached for the telephone again.

'I'm sorry,' she said, listening for a time before replacing the receiver. 'Are you sure I can't get you something to drink? Coffee or tea?'

Makana reconsidered his options and decided a cup of coffee would not be out of place. 'Have you worked for Sayyid Faragalla for long?'

'Almost a year,' she smiled briefly. 'How time flies.'

Makana was beginning to warm to her. He smiled back.

'And how is business these days?'

'You don't really expect an honest answer to a question like that, do you?'

'I was just wondering why you are the only person who seems to be working.'

'Oh, the others usually turn up just before it's time for them to go for breakfast.'

'You talk as if you were responsible. Are you Faragalla's assistant?'

She laughed aloud at that. 'Oh, no. I don't know what made you think that.'

There was something about her which didn't quite fit into this environment. In her late thirties, he guessed. She had a narrow face and eyebrows whose arch betrayed a keen intelligence. Her clothes had been selected with practicality in mind and not towards enhancing her slim figure. Indeed, the long skirt and jacket made her look somewhat drab, and certainly older than her years. She chose to blend in, not to stand out. The ring told him she was a married woman. The tips of her collar and cuffs showed slight wear. A woman who lived frugally and was careful with her money. Whatever Faragalla was paying her it obviously wasn't enough to refresh her wardrobe too often. Either that or she was unconcerned about her appearance, except that she was not a mess. Her long dark hair was clean and neatly tied back with a simple black ribbon. She wore little make-up and on the inside of her wrist she had a pale-blue tattoo of a cross.

The building's *bawab*, a grey-haired man with a hunched back, limped in carrying a tray in one hand. He saluted Makana like an old soldier as he set down cups of coffee and glasses of water with trembling hands, managing not to spill too much.

'*Ya Madame*, you work harder than all the others put together. Give your fingers a rest and drink some coffee to give you strength.' He winked at Makana.

The woman laughed, which made her look about ten years younger. Then the light faded from her eyes and her normal reserve returned.

'Abu Salem is quite a character,' she said when he had gone. 'I think he keeps us all going.'

She might have been about to say more when the glass door flew open and the first of the day's arrivals finally made an appearance. A young man in his twenties entered. Wearing a brown suit and a white shirt with pleats down the front. His hair was slicked back heavily with oil and he trailed an overpowering scent of aftershave behind him.

'Ah, there she is, the light of my eye,' he breezed as he swept by, the heavy bag slung over his arm thumping into the door as it swung back. A young man heading firmly towards an overweight life, he had the plump, well-fed look of a proud mother's pampered son. The suit bulged tightly around midriff and thighs.

'Good morning, Wael.'

'What's new, *ya habibti*? Any pyramids fall down overnight?'

'Not that I've heard of, but then I've been so busy working . . .'

'Yeah,' he said, slipping into English. 'Always the busy bee. Well, all that gonna change now, darling.' He broke off as he noticed Makana and reverted back to Arabic to address him formally. 'Are you waiting for someone?'

'He has an appointment with Mr Faragalla.'

'*Marhaba*, welcome, *bienvenue*. Is he not here yet?'

'Not yet,' the woman said. As she caught Makana's eye a brief look of complicity passed between them. The others began arriving soon after that. There were six in all, including the woman behind the front desk, whose name Makana gathered was Meera. There was a general assistant with a club foot who shuttled around between the desks running errands and carrying papers back and forth from the photocopier. The three main players were the plump young man, Wael, then Yousef and Arwa. Yousef was a small wiry man in a leather jacket. His eyes were cold chips of stone deeply sunk into their sockets. He muttered a brief greeting as he entered and then hurried across to his desk on the far side of the room where he threw himself down into his chair, spun towards the window and reached for the telephone. He smoked incessantly with his back to the room, glancing round from time to time to keep an eye on things. The vain and energetic Wael seemed to have boundless energy. He spoke to clients on the phone in a confused babble of English, Arabic and French, with a word of Spanish or German thrown in here and there for good measure, though by the sound of it his knowledge of these languages did not extend much beyond the odd compliment or greeting. Despite this, he carried himself with the weight of a man who was negotiating world peace or brokering million-dollar deals on the stock exchange rather than arranging a few holidays. The final member of this happy family was Arwa. Short and somewhat overweight, she was buttoned down inside a heavy black coat that came down to her ankles and wrists and turned her into a shapeless creature of indeterminate gender. She wore a leopard-skin hijab and chewed gum like it was an Olympic sport. She shuffled across the room to her workspace with barely a nod to anyone.

Faragalla himself finally turned up. A bluff, clumsy figure of a man on skittish legs. His features were blurred by loose, hanging folds of flesh which gave his face a puffy, indistinct look. His eyes were jaundiced and swollen. Dressed in a shapeless two-piece suit that looked as if he had slept in it for a week, he wandered by like a man under heavy sedation, a handful of newspapers under one arm, and nothing more than a brief nod to Meera on the reception desk.

'This is Mr Makana,' she announced, leaping to her feet. 'He's been waiting for some time.'

'Waiting?' frowned Faragalla. 'Whatever for?'

'He says he has an appointment.'

'An appointment?' Faragalla peered at Makana. 'What appointment?'

'I believe Talal had a word with you, sir?'

It took a while for the clouds to lift from the other man's brows, but then he gave a start. He brushed a hand over his grey moustache and nodded his head.

'Ah, yes. Yes, of course. You'd better come in.'

Faragalla's office was the most chaotic mess Makana had seen in a long time. It was hard enough working out where the desk was. Finding anything in the heaps of folders and files and papers that were stacked up in every conceivable spot around the room would have been an impossible task. A row of shelves had collapsed under the pressure and now slumped at an alarming angle into the far corner like a paper landslide. Faragalla fiddled with the air-conditioner switch, flipping it back and forth and thumping the unit with his hand until finally it wheezed into life, filling the room with an unhappy grinding sound and a faint current of warm, dusty air.

'Have a seat, please.' Faragalla disappeared behind a wall of paper as he sat down. He got up again and shifted an armful of files to the top of a filing cabinet, where they perched precariously, and began to go through his pockets. 'Of course, Talal told me all about you.' He finally found the pipe he was looking for. 'He said you were an old friend of his father's?'

Back in the days when Makana was a police inspector in Khartoum, he had worked together with Talal's father on a number of cases. Abdel Aziz fell foul of the authorities long before Makana did. He protested frequently and, being an intelligent man, managed on a number of occasions to outwit the regime's legal goons, most of whom, he proclaimed indignantly, would never have managed to get into the Faculty of Law in his day, let alone graduate. Makana had tried but failed to persuade him to flee. Despite his being a prominent figure it was only a matter of time before the regime decided to rid themselves of him. Eventually he was charged with conspiring to overthrow the state and sentenced to death.

'Talal tells me you were in some kind of trouble yourself.'

Faragalla was stuffing the bowl of his pipe with large, clumsy fingers. Flakes of tobacco fluttered left and right like insects scurrying to safety.

'They were difficult times for everyone.' Makana shifted in his seat and reached for his cigarettes. It was ten years since he had landed in this city and he wasn't keen on going over all of that here and now. It all seemed a long time ago and far away. 'Why don't you tell me what is bothering you?'

Faragalla had a match going by now and the big fleshy head nodded up and down like a baggy elephant as the flame veered sideways before being sucked into the bowl. In a few moments he had a forest fire going with clouds of smoke filling the room.

'Yes. Well, it's not as simple as all that. You see. A man in my business has to be discreet. You understand that? Reputation is everything and I don't mind telling you there are a few people out there who would not shed a tear if I was to go out of business tomorrow.'

'I can imagine.'

Faragalla's eyes flickered up from the bowl of his pipe as if he detected a faint note of what might have been sarcasm. He let it go.

'The point is I need a man who knows how to keep his mouth shut. Have you had coffee? I wouldn't mind some myself.' He reached for the telephone and Makana suppressed the desire to reach over and hit him with it. Instead he waited while Faragalla ordered his coffee and stoked his pipe some more and then rocked himself back in his chair.

'It would help if I had some idea of what exactly we are talking about.'

'I'm getting to that. The point is that we must have an agreement.'

12

'What kind of agreement?'

'You would answer directly to me. Anything you find, you tell me. Nothing goes outside this office unless I say so.'

It was always something of a miracle to Makana that anyone ever hired him at all. A good deal of his job often involved actually working out why it was he had been chosen in the first place. Of course, nobody had much faith in the police, which didn't hurt his cause. You don't involve officialdom in any of your business because there was always a risk it might attract the wrong kind of attention. It was a system that was true only to itself, faithful to maintaining its own existence, to feeding its needs, its appetite for power. It wasn't a place you went to for justice. On the other hand, it was also true that in most cases the kind of people who needed his services usually had something of their own to hide: a weakness, a character flaw, a crime – sometimes serious, usually minor. Enough, in any case, for them to turn to somebody who was outside the circle of influence. Someone who could be relied on to be quiet. Someone like Makana.

'Discretion, that's the key to this.'

'I could use a little more information if you can spare it.'

Faragalla stoked his pipe up some more, taking long puffs to keep the flame from going out, before plucking the stem out of his mouth and staring into the bowl as if he expected it to speak.

'My grandfather started this business in the days of King Farouk. I grew up hearing tales of the glamour of the golden age, when tourists were gentlemen and ladies. Things have changed. The kind of client we deal with has changed, but our reputation goes back to those days.'

It went some way towards explaining the air of decay that hung over the place. By the looks of things they were surviving on the last gasp of those glory days.

13

'Talal said that maybe you could help to put my mind at ease. He said you have some . . . expertise in these matters?'

'In what matters?' Makana's patience was being slowly drained. 'Exactly what kind of threat are we talking about?'

'Perhaps it is best if I show you.' Faragalla produced a set of keys from his jacket pocket and opened a drawer in front of him. He rummaged around for a moment before producing a sheet of paper which he handed across to Makana. It contained a few lines, printed close together in a block at the centre of the page. Makana read slowly: '*Have you considered him who turns his back upon the Faith, giving little at first and then nothing at all? Does he know, and can he see, what is hidden?*'

'What makes you think this is a threat?'

'Well, it's obvious, isn't it?'

'Is it?'

'Of course. It's from the Quran. I looked it up. The Sura of *The Star*.'

'That still doesn't make it a threat.' Makana looked down at the letter again. 'I mean, there's no actual mention of a threat here. Nobody is explicitly saying they wish to do you harm.'

Faragalla's hand wavered in the air, a lit match flickering at his fingertips. 'Talal led me to believe that you had dealt with these fanatical types and that you would immediately spot the danger.' The match was burning perilously close to Faragalla's fingers.

'Fanatics?'

'You know, Islamists. Jihadists. People who want to lead us back to the eleventh century.'

'You think they sent this letter to you as a threat, because it contains a quote from the Quran?'

'Isn't that enough?' Faragalla blew out the match before

placing the charred remains carefully in the ashtray. 'Let me explain something to you. This is a travel agency. We have been bringing Westerners into this country for years.'

'Since the days of King Farouk,' murmured Makana.

'Exactly.' Faragalla fixed Makana with a beady eye. 'So they come here, they visit the museum, take a few pictures of the pyramids, ride on a camel, and then what?'

Makana waited.

'They go back to their hotels where they drink wine and beer, and they sleep together in hotels, even when they are not married, mark you. During the day they throw off their clothes and display themselves publicly to the world as naked as the day they were born. Now I have nothing against them doing what they like in the privacy of their rooms, but I'm sure I don't have to tell you that some people do not take such a liberal view of things.'

'So, someone is targeting you because of your involvement with tourism?'

'Isn't it obvious?' Faragalla stared at Makana, temporarily lost for words. He started to speak, then stopped. Makana reached again for his cigarettes.

'Let us assume for a moment you are right, that someone is threatening you. What do you think they want? I mean, the letter makes no demands. They are not saying shut your company down, they are not asking you to impose rules of behaviour on your foreign clients. So the question is, do they want to harm you personally? You follow me? Maybe it's about you? Aside from the possibility that someone with a religious sensibility might be offended by how your guests behave, is there anything else, any other reason someone might want to harm you?'

'Something like what? Isn't that enough? Only a few years ago they were gunning tourists down in Luxor, taking potshots at trains. There have been kidnappings in the Sinai. I'm not invent-ing this!'

'I meant, you personally, your company in particular.'

'What difference does it make?' Faragalla brandished the letter. 'This makes it personal.'

'Can you think of anyone who might have a reason to try and hurt you personally, or your company? Has anyone threatened to close you down?'

Faragalla pulled a face. 'These people don't need reasons, they have divine right on their side. They are fanatics.'

'Yes, you already said that.' Makana examined the letter again. It was printed on cheap, low-quality paper full of imper-fections. A couple of the letters were smudged around the edges and there were faint but regular ink spatters consistent with an old-fashioned printing press. He tossed the paper back on the desk. 'It could simply be a joke. Not a very good one, perhaps, and in bad taste, but nevertheless . . .'

'A joke? Who would dare such a thing?' Faragalla's jaw went slack.

'A rival company perhaps? Someone who would like to scare you out of the business?'

'Who?'

'That's what I'm asking you,' said Makana patiently. 'How many people have seen this?'

'Nobody apart from myself and Meera, the girl in reception. She usually opens the mail.'

'Could she have spoken to anyone?'

'No, she is very discreet. Coptic. Well educated.' Faragalla seemed to grow exasperated. 'Look, will you investigate this thing or not?'

'How many of these have you actually received?'

'That's the only one.'

'You haven't told me about your competitors. Who might profit from closing you down?'

'Of course we have rivals, but quite frankly there are other ways for them to steal our business, this isn't one of them.' Faragalla reached for a glass of water on his desk and gulped it down like a man who had just made it across the desert. 'Look, I really don't understand why you refuse to take this seriously. It is clear to me that someone is trying to scare me. Why, I cannot say, but I would ask you to treat this matter with the respect it deserves.'

'Very well. How easy would it be to put you out of business?'

'You are asking me to be frank with you, so I shall ask you to keep this to yourself.'

'Not a word outside this office.'

'Exactly.' Faragalla rested his hands on the desk between them. 'Now, the fact is that things have not been going well for some time. To be honest, we cannot survive another bad season.'

'In other words, you hardly represent a threat to other travel companies.'

'There is our reputation to consider. Our name is a respectable one. We have been running since—'

'Since the days of King Farouk, yes, you mentioned it.' Makana drew a deep breath. 'If I am to investigate this I'll need an alibi, a cover story. People out there have to think that I am here to work for you.'

'That will never work,' Faragalla snorted. 'I've been letting people go, refusing to raise salaries. I could never explain taking on another person.'

'Tell them I am assessing the company to come up with ways of improving efficiency.'

'That might work.' Faragalla seemed to cheer up for a moment. 'How much do you charge?'

'Sixty a day, plus expenses, of course.'

'You don't come cheap.'

'If you want the job done cheaply, I'm sure you can find someone else.' Makana made as if to rise.

'Don't be so hasty.' Faragalla flapped a hand in the air. 'All right. I don't believe in cutting corners when it comes to matters of life and death. How long do you think it will take you?'

Life and death seemed like an exaggeration to Makana. 'If I knew that I would be better off making a living as a fortune teller. And I'll need some expense money to start out with.'

'Naturally.' Faragalla nodded, reaching into his jacket for his wallet and began counting out notes onto the desk. 'Just so long as we are clear,' he said softly. 'Anything that you find which is, shall we say, out of the ordinary, you will come to me directly, and to no one else.'

'Any information I turn up is provided to the client, that is you. Nobody else.'

'Good.' Faragalla pushed the heap of notes across the desk.

Makana picked a brown envelope, tipped the contents out onto the heap of disorder, and slipped the letter and the money inside.

'Then I think we have an understanding.'

Chapter Two

The two of them went out to face the office. As agreed, Makana was introduced as an assessor whose job was to come up with new ways of improving efficiency. If anyone had difficulty believing the story they made no outward sign of it. There was scepticism on some faces, apart from Wael, the young man with the eager-to-please smile on his face, who actually stood up and applauded rather self-consciously, as if hoping this would improve his chances of surviving any imminent cull of existing staff. With a quick, dismissive wave, Faragalla disappeared back inside his own office and closed the door, leaving Makana to face the stares.

'And there was me thinking we were in trouble,' muttered Arwa, the woman in the leopard-skin headscarf, just loud enough for everyone to hear. The others went back to work one by one. Makana became aware of Yousef watching him closely from across the room, but he said nothing and after a time reached for his telephone and began speaking again.

'Well, I suppose you're eager to get to work.'

Makana turned to find Meera, who now seemed unsure exactly what note to strike with him now. She led him along a narrow, gloomy corridor past a bathroom to a small room. They leaned in through the doorway. A row of old metal filing cabinets stood guard along one wall, suggesting that once upon a time some semblance of order had existed here. Now it was almost impossible to even get over the threshold due to a mound of folders and files stacked on the floor, climbing perilously in tottering heaps that looked dusty, forgotten and just about ready to keel over the moment anyone touched them.

'This is our archive room,' Meera explained. 'There are files here dating back to the days of Ramses II. Just kidding. I mean, Mr Faragalla's grandfather – Mustapha Bey.' She pointed to a black-and-white picture of a man wearing a fez that hung at a lopsided angle on the far wall. 'In those days it was rather a grand operation,' she sighed, gazing at a poster on another wall which displayed the elegant old train carriages that used to transport travellers up the Nile. 'People used to travel in style. Not any more, I'm afraid.'

'But there are more tourists than ever.'

'Everyone wants to see the world,' she nodded, 'but there's only so much world to go round.'

Opposite the archive room was a small kitchen. A picture of the company employees was stuck to the front of one of the cupboards with yellowed Sellotape. It showed a group of about twenty people, all lined up alongside a boat on the Nile. It looked like Upper Egypt.

'Where was this taken?'

'Oh, that's Luxor. We have part of our operation there.'

Makana leaned closer to the picture. 'You're not here.'

'No,' said Meera. 'Before my time.'

Makana peered at the photograph. He picked out Yousef and Arwa. Standing next to Faragalla was a young man in his twenties.

'That's Ramy. Mr Faragalla's nephew. He is running our Luxor office.'

'You seem to know your way about this place. How long have you been working here?'

'About a year.'

'What did you do before this?'

'Oh, this and that,' she brushed a hand through her hair. 'Why do you ask?'

'Somehow you don't strike me as someone who belongs in the tourist business.'

She met his gaze evenly. 'And you don't strike me as a management consultant.'

'Fair enough. How does anyone ever manage to make sense of all this?' he asked, gesturing at the archive room and the heaps of paper.

'They don't. This is the age of mass travel. The name of the game is speed. Get as many people into and out of the country as fast as possible. You have to push the prices down as far as they can go. The big foreign agencies demand huge discounts. So the only way to keep going is to increase the volume. People come to Egypt for the trip of a lifetime, but they don't want to pay more than is absolutely necessary.'

'You sound like you know a lot about it.'

'I'm a fast learner, as I hope are you.' Meera picked up a ledger and began to explain how their accounting system worked. There was a series of categories and codes. Hotels and resorts each had their own sub-headings, as did locations – Sinai, Aswan, Luxor, Valley of the Kings. Then there were packages – Nile cruises, adventure sports, diving, etc. Another set of codes applied to the tourists' country of origin. Makana had never imagined how complex this business was. They needed interpreters who had fluent Korean, Japanese, Chinese and Russian, as well as English, French, German and Spanish.

'You'll excuse me if I say that this doesn't look like the most efficient way of counting money in the world. How do you square all the accounts?'

'Well, I'll be honest with you, since you are here to help the company,' Meera said, looking him in the eye. 'That worried me at first, then I realised they just make it up.'

'So that all the pieces fit?'

'Exactly.'

Back in the main office the woman in the hijab, Arwa, muttered loudly: 'This place is like a prison sentence.' It wasn't clear who the comment was aimed at exactly. She rummaged in an enormous handbag that took up most of her desk and produced a bottle of perfume which she proceeded to spray in a halo around her head, as if warding off evil spirits. 'Did I tell you they took my nephew away? Nothing. No charges, no idea where he was or why. He just vanished.'

'You'll have to excuse her,' Wael addressed Makana. 'Arwa has her own special way of expressing herself.' He ended with a chirpy giggle.

'You can laugh, you don't have responsibilities. They beat that boy so badly he still doesn't walk properly. And for what? For wearing a beard? For declaring his love for Allah?'

Wael was still laughing, although it wasn't clear why. Arwa made a dismissive gesture.

'If you had a family you might understand. Or maybe you're not interested in marriage?' A sneer twisted her features. 'Is that it?' Wael suddenly took a great interest in rooting through a heap of paperwork in front of him. Arwa chuckled, her fat fingers crunching the stapler as they might an insect.

'Why don't you give your overworked tongue a rest,' snarled Yousef. His face had a rodent-like quality to it and he carried himself with the assurance of a man who is not afraid of much. He certainly commanded authority in that office. The others were silenced. When he smiled, a thin-lipped leer crossed the pockmarked face. 'Mr Makana is here to help us. Isn't that right?'

'I'm certainly going to try.'

'He's going to try.' The idea seemed to amuse Yousef. 'You hear that? He's going to show us the error of our ways. So why don't you all stop complaining and get to work before he decides the solution lies in throwing you to the dogs.'

Suddenly everyone had something else to do. The chatter of conversation died as if cut off by a knife. Yousef gave Makana one last look before turning away.

By the time Talal turned up late that afternoon, Makana had already concluded that his love for Faragalla's youngest daughter was a hopeless quest. He was also convinced that nothing but divine intervention could improve the fortunes of Blue Ibis Tours. What Faragalla really needed was a decent accountant with a sharp pencil. The company records were in a chaotic state. They were in such a hurry to take on new business they tossed aside old files the minute the tourists were on their plane home. He was willing to bet there was a small fortune buried there in outstanding debts and duplicate bills.

Talal's tall, bony frame was topped by a wild bush that he probably imagined made him look like a mad conductor. To most people, of course, he just looked mad. Cheerful by nature, he was greeted by the others with surprising warmth. Everyone seemed not only to know him but to be glad to see him. Makana watched from his corner of the room as Talal drifted round, perching himself on a desk here, sharing a joke there. He seemed capable of lifting everyone's mood, even Arwa appeared to lighten.

'Have you met our latest recruit?' Wael asked, waving a hand in Makana's direction. 'He's going to save us all from ruin.'

'Of course he knows him,' snapped Arwa. 'They are compatriots, after all.'

'Not all Sudanese are born knowing one another,' Wael countered bravely.

'We do actually know each other,' Talal smiled. 'In fact, I recommended him to Sayyid Faragalla.' For a moment Makana wondered if he was going to get carried away and tell all.

'You see?' Arwa shook her head and Wael rolled his eyes.

'In fact, I was hoping he was going to show his gratitude by buying me a cup of coffee.'

Which was music to Makana's ears. He was already on his feet reaching for his jacket.

On the ground floor a sad trail of lifeless shops lined a passage leading into the building from the street. The crumbling stucco around the entrance arch had been covered over by tacky sheets of chromed plastic adorned with gaudy kaleidoscopic tassels that fluttered in the occasional gust of wind. Somewhere an architect was turning over slowly in his grave. The dim arcade was lifted from the gloom by the white neon strip lighting covered in cobwebs that illuminated the shop displays. Cracks in the floor stood out like veins on the worn marble. Hijabbed mannequins stared glassily at Makana and Talal as they passed down to a narrow café set so far back that daylight barely reached it from the street. The distorted screech of excited music greeted them and the door appeared to be permanently jammed halfway open. Inside there was barely room for a grubby counter and a couple of tables that might once have been bright orange in colour but were now a shade of mud. Talal's arrival was met by a brief nod of recognition from a heavy-set man whose right eye drooped severely to one side. He leered at them from behind the counter.

'Look,' Talal said as they sat down, 'I know you are doing this as a favour to me, or to my father really, and I can't tell you how grateful I am.'

'Don't mention it,' said Makana, idly watching the man behind the bar fishing a couple of cups out of a sink of dirty water. 'Your father was a good friend.'

'If you could only meet her, you would understand how much she means to me.' Talal grinned like a schoolboy.

'I'd love to meet her.' Makana didn't have the heart to tell Talal that to judge from the look on Faragalla's face when his name came up, Talal had as much chance of impressing the girl's father as the sphinx had of flying.

'You would? When?'

'I don't know, anytime.'

Makana had never had a son himself. He had hoped, of course, but when Muna delivered a girl he contented himself with that and Nasra was as dear to him as any son could ever have been, more so even. Muna used to tease him about it. Men always talk about sons, she used to say, but what they dream about is a daughter who will take care of them and admire them more than any son could ever do. But they were both gone now. Talal had lost his father and seemed to have turned to Makana to fill that absence in some way.

'That would be great. I mean, I don't have any family here, really, apart from my mother. I want her to know where I come from. You understand?'

Makana looked into the earnest young man's face and nodded. 'I understand,' he said, reaching for his cigarettes. 'Don't worry about it.'

A boy of about thirteen came in through the door carrying a heavy bag. As he went behind the counter the man grabbed hold of him by the neck and dragged him out through a back door where he began to shout at him. Having finished shouting at the boy, the man came out and walked straight towards the door.

'Hey, what about our coffee?'

'The boy will see to it,' muttered the man, who paused then and took his time to look Talal over as he lit a cigarette. 'Muhammed,' he called, raising his voice, his eyes still on Talal, 'hurry up, people are waiting.' Smiling, he then turned and walked out.

'I understand you had more important things to talk about,' the afro bobbed up and down energetically. 'So now you're on the case, right? You're working?'

'Actually, I'm not sure how much I can do here.'

Talal looked pained. 'I told him you were the best.'

'It's okay. I'll take care of it.' Makana had already decided he would give the Blue Ibis four days, a week at the most, and if nothing came up he would quietly break it off. That would give him enough money to get to the end of the month, if he was careful. As for Talal's chances of marriage, he didn't want to even think about how he was going to break the news to the young man.

'You have to solve this one, really. My life depends on it.'

'I'll keep that in mind. Tell me about the company. How long have you worked for them?'

'Oh, a couple of years now. On and off. It's all temporary. In my position I have to move around from company to company, taking any work I can find.'

'Go on.'

'I suppose I charge less than most interpreters. Well, I know I do. I have to. It's the only way to have an edge. Nine times out of ten they would rather not hire a foreigner.'

'You're not a foreigner, your mother is from here.'

'They take one look at your skin.' Talal shook his head. 'You know how it is.'

'I get the impression business is not going too well upstairs.' Makana lit a cigarette as the boy came out from the narrow space behind the counter to place two small glasses of coffee down on the table. As he straightened up he felt Makana's gaze on him and his eyes darted away. Talal was still talking.

'They live on their name, which is not bad. It still has some leverage. But you know, loyalty to hotels that had a good reputation twenty years ago doesn't make much sense nowadays . . .'

'Faragalla is slow to change. Who takes over when he goes? Your young lady?'

'Bunny?' Talal winced. 'No, I don't see her taking over. She hates the business.'

'Who else is there, any sons?'

'No sons. There is a nephew, Ramy.'

'The one who is running the office in Luxor.'

'Ah, you heard.' Talal stopped stirring his coffee. 'He's a strange one. He didn't tell anyone he was going, just disappeared from one day to the next. There was a story he was mixed up with some of the clients. Women. You know . . .' The eyebrows bounced up to meet the afro. 'I'd better be going. I have a piano lesson.'

'Really, you're learning to play the piano?' It was lame, but it raised a laugh.

'Very funny. No, I give lessons.' The wiry young man turned

his attention to the device in his shirt pocket. The wires on the earplugs had become tangled and he suddenly became interested in unravelling them, as if this was the most important task in the world. 'Have you ever heard of the Conservatory in Vienna?' Talal looked up to see the blank look on Makana's face before going on. 'Well, it's simply the best school of its kind in the world.'

'I'll take your word for it.'

'They invited me to audition. If they like my work I'll get a scholarship to attend for a year.'

'That's wonderful.'

Vienna seemed as far away as Mars. Why he should want to go there was beyond Makana.

'There's only one problem. To get a visa I need to prove I have enough money to live there for a year. Can you imagine how much that is?' Talal waited for Makana's response. 'I would need to rob a bank to get that kind of money.'

'Things work themselves out.' Which was another way of saying that Makana had no spare cash to lend. He had barely enough to live on himself. Talal nodded solemnly, as if he never expected anything different. After a time he said:

'Do you ever, you know, think about going back?'

'Back?'

'Back home I mean.'

'There's nothing for me to go back to,' Makana said. He peered into his glass. The coffee had tasted faintly of detergent, which he found oddly reassuring.

'And if there was a reason, would you do it?'

'You're full of questions today.'

'*Maalish*,' said Talal, bouncing to his feet again. 'I probably shouldn't have asked.'

Makana watched him go, the long, slim figure loping along in a loose-limbed way through the arcades towards the opening and the tangle of hooting, nervous traffic beyond. In a way he envied him. The boy moved in a different world to him. He was doing all right. If it didn't work out with Bunny, or whatever her name was, that would be all right too. He was still young. He had ambitions and he clearly had talent of some kind.

With a glance towards the counter Makana got to his feet. The boy, who was barely visible, was busy furiously scrubbing something out of sight. In a gesture of sympathy, Makana dropped an extra note on the table.

Chapter Three

In the street Makana raised a hand and instantly retracted it as two taxi cabs veered alarmingly towards him. The first was a stately old Peugeot driven by a grey-haired man who was lost behind the huge wheel. The second was a small, battered, and somewhat lopsided 1970s Datsun that careered wildly across three lanes before skidding to a halt at his feet. The small car shuddered on its springs as the ensuing hooting and shouting match unfolded around it. The driver was the size of a small gorilla. As he hung out of the window the other man realised he had met his match and drove off with a dismissive wave over his shoulder.

'*Yallah, ya bey!*' the driver leaned over and called up. 'Don't anger me by making me wait.' Without further prompting Makana dragged open the rear door and climbed inside, only to be thrown backwards as the car took off. The interior was badly beaten up and so torn the upholstery looked like it had been mauled by hungry dogs.

'You were a bit hasty back there.'

'I am truly sorry, sir,' the driver sought his eyes in the rearview mirror, though his tone suggested he wasn't in the least repentant. 'I meant no offence, believe me, but in this business one has to fight. I swear by Allah that every morning I tell myself I'm a warrior going to battle. I have five children to feed.'

'Take me to Imbaba.'

'Hadir, ya bey.' The driver wrestled the protesting gearstick and pinned it squealing in place so that Makana actually felt sorry for it. 'I'll get you there faster than lightning.'

'Just get me there in one piece.'

As they drove, Makana wondered about Faragalla. The more he thought back over their meeting the more it seemed to him that the man's bumbling incompetence was no more than a convenient shield to hide behind. Even if the letter contained a threat, it was of such a veiled nature that it would take a guilty conscience to see anything there at all.

As the car scraped and coughed its way along, Makana became aware of the giant watching him in the mirror.

'The brother is here on business?'

Makana was used to being taken for a visitor. If his dark skin didn't do it, his accent gave him away immediately.

'I live here,' he said wearily.

'Ya ahlan wa sahlan, you are very welcome, *Effendim.* If you ever need a car . . .' With a speed and dexterity remarkable for his size, the driver flourished a business card from under the strip of artificial black-and-white Dalmatian fur that ran across the dashboard. 'Twenty-four hours a day,' he added, raising a thick index finger towards the sky. 'Allah and mechanics permitting.' Makana glanced idly at the card as they crossed to the west bank of the river. Above a telephone number ran the words, *Sindebad Car & Limoseen Servise – 24hrs anytime.* Makana leaned over the front seat to take a better look at the big man's profile.

'Is that you, Sindbad?'

'Ah, of course it's me, who else would it be?' Irritated, the driver glanced back and then stopped. A frown puckered up the fleshy features as his eyes widened. For a moment their journey risked coming to an abrupt and unpleasant end as the car drifted across several lanes and back again, like a duck sailing over a flooded field. He was oblivious to the hooting and swearing that followed him.

'Is it really you, *ya basha*?'

'How are you doing, Sindbad?'

'I ask you,' the big man lamented. 'See how I have come down in the world. You knew me when I was working for Saad Hanafi. Those were the days.' He indicated the grubby shirt and trousers he wore. 'I am a sorry figure compared to that proud man.'

Sindbad had once had a promising career as a boxer. They had met a couple of years ago when he had been working as a chauffeur for one of the wealthiest men in Cairo. In those days he had worn a suit when he drove.

'You never really liked wearing those clothes, did you?'

'To be honest, no, *ya basha*. It made me feel stiff, like one of those figures in the shop windows in Talat Harb Street. I still have it, though. Some days I think about wearing it to work, just to remember what it was like.' Sindbad shook his head. 'But it's not the same. Nothing ever is.'

'You lost your job, then?'

'When the old man died everything went to pieces. They let us all go.'

'I'm sorry to hear that.'

'Well, to tell you the truth, it was a blessing. The money they gave me was enough to buy this car and now I am my own boss. There's nothing like it in the world. I can tell you, I wouldn't go back for anything. Not now. No matter how bad things are. Working for yourself, a man can keep his dignity. You understand what I mean?'

'I think so.'

Sindbad tapped the wheel gently, the way you might pet a cat with a furious and unpredictable temper. 'Actually, I bought it from my brother-in-law who is always in trouble with money. I was doing him a favour.'

'I see,' said Makana. It explained a lot. 'So now you're a free agent.'

'*Al Hamdoulilah!*'

'Do you have other people to help you, or do you work alone?'

'Just me, *Effendim*.'

'Then how do you manage to work twenty-four hours a day?'

A cloud descended over Sindbad's face. 'I have a wife and five children. When the Lord gives you a life like that he doesn't intend for you to sleep.'

The traffic was the usual snarl of hot metal and smoke, but Sindbad had a good eye. Restlessly grinding the gearstick and twisting the wheel, he darted into openings, carving a swift line through the clogged obstructions. Before long they were pulling up under the twisted eucalyptus tree that leaned precariously out over the riverbank. Down below the *awama* waited, as regal as an emissary from a long-forgotten kingdom.

'What are you doing tomorrow?' Makana asked, as he climbed out.

'I am at your service, *ya basha*. All you have to do is call.'

Makana watched the black-and-white taxi clatter away under a cloud of exhaust, then he turned and made his way down the path towards the river. At this time of day, as evening was falling, the *awama* seemed to lose all her blemishes and defects. As the light grew faint, the houseboat seemed to loom out of the shadows in all her former glory, or at least it seemed that way to Makana.

A large, untidy man missing most of his front teeth stood in the doorway of Umm Ali's hut chewing a piece of sugar cane. This was Bassam, her useless brother, who had turned up about a month ago and seemed in no hurry to return to the home village in the Delta. The story was that his wife had left him. 'First sensible thing that woman has done in her life.' Umm Ali was not the type to mince her words. 'Now if only she had poisoned him before she left . . .'

Spitting a wad of chewed-up pulp on the ground, Bassam wagged a finger as Makana went by. 'And don't forget about the rent this month. My sister is too soft, but don't think you can play those games with me.' The finger disappeared inside his mouth to fish out something caught between his few remaining teeth.

'Why doesn't he just go home?' Aziza, Umm Ali's youngest daughter, lay sprawled on Makana's sofa where she regularly hid when she wanted to get away. Locking the place was a waste of time. He had the idea that Aziza climbed along and through the window on the riverside. It didn't matter how carefully he locked the shutters, she still managed to get in without any trouble at all. Now she was reading one of his books, or pretending to do so. The cross-eyed Aziza was the sharpest tool in the box. Her voluptuous elder sister was as slovenly as she was lazy and wouldn't lift a finger if she wasn't forced to. And at the ripe old age of eleven, her little brother Saif was already a veteran delinquent. He'd already been through Makana's belongings and deemed there to be nothing worth his time to be found. Aziza guarded the place with a fierce sense of propriety. She cleaned up without being asked. In return Makana would slip her some money when her mother and siblings were not looking.

'If a stone accidentally fell on his stupid head while he was sleeping, would I go to prison?'

'He's your uncle. He's family.'

'There's no law that says you can't hate your family.'

Makana had to concede she had a point. No doubt Bassam would sooner or later get bored with life on the riverbank and decide to go home to get his wife back, or, failing that, find some other idiot to marry him.

'He says we should throw you out and move in here ourselves.'

'Does he?'

'Will you kill him now?' Aziza sat up eagerly. Makana shook his head as he went into the kitchen to make coffee.

'Go home. I have work to do.'

Grudgingly, she got to her feet and walked towards the door. 'Well, if you find me dead tomorrow don't come complaining to me.'

Makana listened to her go, singing to herself softly, the wooden boards creaking under her feet. It was impossible for him to look at her and not think of his own daughter, Nasra. How old would she have been now?

Hardly a day went by when he didn't think back to that night on the bridge. He played it out in his mind over and over. It seemed to him that he was compelled to keep asking the same questions again and again. Their lives had been in danger. There had been no other option but to flee, he knew that. But could he have played it differently? And if he had done, would they still be alive now? These were questions to which he knew he would never find answers.

The last rays of light were draining from the sky as he climbed the stairs to the upper floor. Makana threw off his jacket and lit a cigarette before settling down into the old armchair to watch the sun going down. This was his favourite time, when the fury of the day had worn itself out and the world seemed to roll onto its back and breathe a sigh of relief before the evening started in earnest. Up on the bridge the familiar honking of horns heralded the sunset, punctuated by the occasional bleating of a musical interlude on a siren. It was always impossible to tell the jokers from the real thing, an ambulance on a hopeless mission to get through the gridlock. He finished his coffee and lit his second cigarette as he turned his attention to the letter Faragalla had given him.

In another life one might have resorted to sophisticated forensic techniques to search for fingerprints, or even DNA identification, but no such technical option was open to him. There was also no telling how useful it would be since he had no idea how many people had already touched the letter. Which meant, finally, that the only clues he could hope to find would be in the content of the letter itself. By now the light had almost gone. He moved over to the large table that stretched along one wall and constituted his office. Switching on the desk lamp he rummaged around in a drawer for a large magnifying glass. The letter was clearly printed not on a simple office printer but with ink and typeface. Putting aside the magnifying glass Makana dug about for a copy of the Quran and looked up Sura number 53: *Surat al-Nejm*. The Star. Here he read:

The Unbelievers follow vain conjectures and the whims of their own souls, although the guidance of their Lord has long since come to them.

Have you considered him who turns his back upon the Faith, giving little at first and then nothing at all? Does he know, and can he see, what is hidden?

The stack of reference books and encyclopaedias he had accumulated over the years from a variety of bookshops and the second-hand stalls around Ezbekieh market now formed a pillar by the side of the table. Here he learned that the star in the Quranic text referred to Sirius, the brightest fixed star in the sky, that it was the first to appear, which explained its Arabic name, *al-Shiara*, which meant 'The Leader'.

In Ancient Egypt the star was known as Sothis or Sopdet and was associated with Anubis, the god who appears at times with the head of a jackal, at others with that of a dog. It was found on the tombs of the dead and guarded the way into the Underworld. This explained its Latin name, *Canis major*, or the Dogstar. Sothis represented change. The regeneration of the earth. The solar year began with the first appearance of the Dogstar on the eastern horizon shortly before sunrise and marked the start of the annual floods, which were vital to the country's agriculture. Its absence from the sky was believed to coincide with Osiris' journey through the Land of the Dead and so it was associated with the resurrection of the deceased. To the Greeks the star was a gate into hell, out of which fire poured – the cause of anxiety in the so-called dog days prior to the flood, when the rising heat drove people to madness.

Makana pushed the books aside finally and lit another cigarette. Astronomy. Ancient Egyptians. He got to his feet and went over to the railing. He felt unsettled and couldn't work out why. The lights of Zamalek swirled in the water at his feet. The sound of cheerful music came from a small boat that sailed by below. The passengers were strobe-lit by the disco beat pulsating through a string of lights whose colour reverberated against the dark water. When they spotted him the young men and women began to wave and cheer wildly. If it went on like this, Makana thought, he would be in danger of becoming a landmark.

One line in the Sura kept turning over in his head: *Does he know, and can he see, what is hidden?*

Chapter Four

Arwa was wearing a gold lamé hijab covered in palm trees in shimmering Islamic green. Otherwise the Blue Ibis offices looked pretty much the same. The same air of dysfunctional chaos reigned as on the previous day. Telephones rang unanswered; queries were yelled across the room to no response; people appeared at the door and then eventually left when no one attended to them. It was hard to comprehend that the Blue Ibis actually managed to function at all.

'Your people in Quseir,' Arwa cupped the mouthpiece of the telephone as she called across to Wael. 'What happened to them?'

'What people?' Wael didn't even bother to lift his feet down from the desk in front of him.

'There was supposed to be a bus to pick them up yesterday.'

'Who is that on the phone?'

'The hotel.' The receiver was dropped on the desk as she went back to typing a letter. 'They want to know what happened to them.'

'How should I know?' Wael held his hands up in the air.

'Just speak to them, will you?'

'Is it always like this?' Makana asked as Meera went by on her way to the filing cabinet next to him. She lifted her shoulders. It was more like a gesture of resignation than an answer. She pointed out a table in the corner.

'That's your desk.'

No sooner had he sat down than a thickening cloud of cloying scent settled over him and he looked up to see Arwa approaching with an armful of files.

'Here we were expecting you to be setting an example for us, and you sit there waiting for work to be brought to you?' She dumped the heap of folders in front of him and flipped the first one open to reveal a sheet of accounts. 'What matters is the final figure at the bottom. Understand? The boss never looks any further. As long as the final tally shows a profit you don't have to worry.'

Makana raised his eyebrows. 'Even if it doesn't match the receipts?'

The crown of palms shook. 'Don't even think about trying to straighten it out. The last person who tried is buried under the pyramids. All that matters,' she went on, enunciating every word slowly, as if addressing an idiot, 'is that the two figures match. That is all you have to do. A small child could manage it.' She swivelled on her heels and was about to march away when a thought occurred. 'I know nothing about improving efficiency, or management, but if the boss sees you lazing around you'll be fired before you even have time to settle in.' Arwa clucked at her own humour. 'Now that might improve our situation.' She marched off before he had time to respond.

'I got the same lecture when I first started here,' Meera said. 'The mess goes back as far as you can imagine and many of the figures are inaccurate or illegible.'

Intrigued, Makana went through the heap of files trying to get an idea of how this firm managed to operate. The problem was that nothing really matched. Even the names of places seemed to vary. Makana didn't need to be a trained accountant to understand that the Blue Ibis administrative system was in such disarray it was hard to understand how a company could manage to function in such a state of disorder. Money was seeping out of the company like a leaky boat. Nobody really had any idea how much came in or went out. There was a trail of unfamiliar names too, the mention of which elicited only blank looks, or remarks like 'Oh, she doesn't work here any more' or 'He left years ago!' The high turnover of employees might also have explained the variety of filing methods. Each new person appeared to have brought their own system with them which would then be abandoned when it came time for them to leave. Some were alphabetical, others numerical, some by year, others by month, one was even based on country of origin. And someone had come up with an innovative method of classifying tourists according to their dietary requests. Makana's head was spinning when he looked up to find Yousef standing in front of him wearing a thin, cunning smile.

'So, how are you getting on?'

'Well, you know. It takes time to get the measure of things.'

'Yeah, I'll bet it does.' Perching himself on the corner of Makana's desk, Yousef produced a green-and-white packet of LM menthol cigarettes from his breast pocket and shook one out. Makana declined, preferring his own Cleopatras. Yousef then lit both of them with a gold lighter.

'So you're here to clean things up for us, eh?'

'Sayyid Faragalla thought I might be able to help.'

'I'm sure he did.'

Yousef wore a gold chain around his neck that matched the watch on his wrist. There was something about him that was hard and cheap. It made you want to count your fingers after shaking hands. But he was also at ease. Makana had met his type before. He was used to giving orders, to being in charge.

'Maybe you want to take a break from all that?'

'I could do, I suppose.' Makana stretched his arms above his head.

'I have an errand to run. I thought maybe you could help me. Get some fresh air.'

'Why not?'

Nobody in the room seemed to pay any notice. On the reception desk, Meera's attention was focussed firmly on the typewriter in front of her. As they started to descend the stairs, Yousef turned to him.

'You don't have to play games with me. Faragalla told me you just got out of prison.'

'It was a misunderstanding,' Makana improvised, wondering what else Faragalla might have dreamed up.

'It always is,' Yousef said knowingly. 'I understand you are distantly related to him?'

'A distant cousin, on his mother's side.'

'I didn't know he had relatives abroad.' Yousef paused, then dismissed the matter. 'Still, you learn something new every day.' He drew on his cigarette, examining Makana carefully. 'You can drive, right? I need someone who can take me around.'

'I thought Faragalla wanted me to work here?'

'You'll find out that Faragalla leaves most decisions to me. Come on.'

Yousef led the way downstairs and out into a side street where

41

an Opel Rekord, the brown colour of rotting bananas, was parked. The cars were all tightly packed in a row, nose to tail all the way down the street. A couple of street boys, no more than twelve years old, ran up and started rolling the cars back to allow them to get out. Yousef called them over and handed them each a few crumpled notes.

'You were in the army?'

'I did my military service,' Makana replied, which was true. He omitted the part about going from the army into the police.

'I did fifteen years in the Military Police. It does something to a man, don't you think?' Yousef tossed the car keys across to Makana. 'You drive.'

'Where are we going?'

'I'll tell you on the way.'

The traffic was heavy. When a car cut in front of them Yousef leaned out of the window to hurl insults at the driver before slumping into his seat, overcome by a dark, morose mood.

'I hate this city. People here are as dumb as shit.'

'It's not all that different from anywhere else.'

Yousef snorted and examined Makana with a wary eye. 'What did you do to get yourself locked up?'

'I'd rather not talk about it, if it's all the same.'

'Sure, I understand.' Yousef smirked. 'I don't like to judge people.' He directed Makana down Ghamhouria Street to park in front of a small hotel.

'I'll get into trouble if I stay here.'

'Don't worry,' Yousef grinned, revealing a gold eye tooth, 'everyone round here knows me.'

Not only did they know Yousef, they knew his car. Makana sat behind the wheel and watched uniformed policemen walk by as if the Opel were invisible. After that they toured more of the city's hotels, coming to a close at the Sheraton in Dokki. This time, Makana watched Yousef disappear through the door, waited a moment, and followed him inside.

The lobby was a vast marble hall broken by partitions and thick pillars. There were lounge areas, a restaurant and café. Sinking into a chair behind a screen, Makana picked up a discarded newspaper from the table. For a moment he thought he had lost Yousef completely, and then he reappeared on the other side of the reception area where he was shaking hands with a man in a dull brown suit bearing a name tag in case he forgot who he was.

The paper contained a story by Sami Barakat on the murders in Imbaba. Another body had been found. Makana had known Sami for a number of years now, ever since he had been investigating the disappearance of footballer Adil Romario. Since then they had become friends. Sami was one of a small number of journalists who was openly critical of the government.

Sami's article gave the impression there was more to the case of the murdered boys than was obvious. The latest victim had been badly disfigured. Sami gave few details, no doubt at the request of the police investigators. A number of factors pointed to the possibility that the young boy had been living rough, one of the thousands of homeless children eking out an existence on the streets. This, Sami suggested, was one reason so few resources were being allocated to the case. The child's body showed signs of extensive torture over a long period of time. 'All the evidence points to someone exploiting these children for their own foul purposes,' Sami concluded. 'There are those who appear to want to use these killings to spread irresponsible talk of rituals and stir the flames of sectarian hatred.'

'Makana, isn't it?'

He looked up to see a tall, uncertain man standing awkwardly before him. His prematurely thinning hair was combed back from his narrow forehead. His clothes while neat were too big for him. The eyes were a shade of grey, clouded with some murkiness that Makana could not quite decipher. In his hand he clutched a paper napkin. A spot of cream dotted the corner of his mouth.

'It is you, isn't it?'

The eyes widened and the smile revealed teeth that were yellow and uneven. They stood out against his pale skin like discordant notes on a sheet of music.

'I said to my wife, I was sure it was you.'

The woman standing behind him hovered uncertainly. She was a rather plain young woman wearing make-up and clutching a shiny plastic handbag adorned with gold buckles big enough to sink a small boat. They made an odd couple, confused and out of tune with their surroundings. Gentle music was playing in the background over the clink and clatter of plates and glasses.

'You don't remember me, do you? Ghalib Samsara?'

Makana did remember. A little over a year ago he had been hired by Samsara's father. A long-time civil servant as honest as the day was long, but struggling to make ends meet. The family had once been wealthy, but over the years they had slipped down the scale and now lived in a building that was not only falling into ruin, but was about to be taken over by an unscrupulous speculator who was bribing local officials. Makana dug around until he found enough evidence to make the speculator back off. It had been a slow case but Makana could not recall having met the son on more than one occasion.

Makana, on his feet now, folded the newspaper and stepped towards the tall man, trying to edge him away. Ghalib Samsara took offence, sensing that Makana was trying to get rid of him. His face reddened and his jaw clamped tightly.

'How is your father doing?' Makana enquired, edging around him, until he could see over Samsara's shoulder.

'He's much the same, thank you.' Samsara's voice was flat with disappointment. Makana realised he had wanted something from him, recognition perhaps. Was he trying to show off to his wife? Now his voice took on another tone. He regarded Makana stonily.

'I've been abroad,' he said, 'studying. In Germany.'

'That's nice for you. Where in Germany?'

'Hamburg. I studied engineering.'

The door through which Yousef had disappeared was now opening.

'There's no work here. You know how it is.' The smile flashed with complicity, quick and far too bright. 'It all depends on who you know.'

'It's not easy,' Makana conceded.

'Are you here alone?' Samsara's head turned to follow Makana's gaze.

'Actually, no, I'm meeting someone.'

The woman was tugging his arm, but Samsara hung on, his eyes widening with realisation.

'I understand!' he whispered. 'You are working on a case.'

'I really have to be going,' Makana said. The door yawned open to reveal Yousef and the man in the suit shaking hands.

'Of course. I just wanted to . . .' Samsara smiled his crooked smile. What he wanted remained unclear. 'Perhaps, when it is convenient . . . I am sure there is much for us to talk about.'

'I'm sure,' Makana said, without much conviction. He began moving towards the exit. Samsara shadowed him, walking sideways, still talking. If he had waved a flag over his head he couldn't have looked more conspicuous.

'Corruption. You must understand what I mean. A man like yourself.'

'Corruption?'

'Society,' Samsara nodded. 'We have sold our souls to the West, allowed them to turn this country into their playground. They do what they like. They walk through the old bazaar half-naked. Within sight of the mosque of Hussein. There is no respect.'

Makana turned and hurriedly handed the man his card. 'Let's meet and talk. Give me a call.'

'She says I never stop talking.' Samsara clutched the card as if it were a sacred gift. His eyes glowed. 'I am learning to fly. Soon I shall go to America.'

Makana made a mental note to find out which airline would be mad enough to employ a man like this to fly their planes. Samsara beamed at him, amused. Then, like an actor leaving the stage, he bowed his head slightly and stepped back.

'Fate has brought us together at this time.'

Makana watched him go, wondering absently what it was that was ailing the man. When he looked round again Yousef stood before him.

'I told you to stay in the car.'

'I wanted to get a newspaper.'

'If I tell you to do something I expect you to do it.'

'I was never any good at taking orders.'

'Yeah, I can see that.'

Outside, Yousef lit a cigarette. A cool breeze swept up from the river. 'In this business there are plenty of opportunities. If you play your cards right I will show you.' He blew smoke into the air above Makana's head. 'But first you have to learn to do what you're told.'

Chapter Five

The rest of the day proved a fruitless waste of time. At around six Makana decided that enough was enough. He waited until he saw Meera begin to pack up her things and then, with a loud yawn, he got to his feet and said goodbye to everyone, receiving barely a murmur in return. Downstairs in the arcade he lingered outside a shop selling ladies' footwear, shoes of the most extravagant and impractical styles he had ever seen. Lacquered and adorned with shiny buckles and spiked heels, they resembled medieval torture instruments. The young woman arranging the window display glanced nervously at Makana as if to ask what he was staring at. Makana ignored her and took his time lighting a cigarette. If high heels had been around in the time of the Prophet, they would no doubt have been designated haram, but then so would many aspects of modern life, including cigarettes, and then where would we be? he wondered. When he glanced round he saw Meera appear at the foot of the staircase. When she spotted him she gave a start, then carried on towards the entrance.

'You were waiting for me,' she said flatly. It was an observation, not a question.

'Do you mind? I just thought we might be able to speak more freely away from the office.'

She looked at him for a long time before making up her mind.

'Very well,' she said, then led the way down to the street and raised her hand for a cab. A moment later they were driving in the direction of Tahrir Square and the river. Meera sighed. She shook her hair free as she settled back in her seat, letting the warm air blow through the open window into her face.

'There are days when I can't breathe in there, when I just want to scream.' She was looking out of the window as she spoke, as if she had forgotten he was there. 'It's stifling. Everyone is afraid of losing their job, of being replaced. That's why they don't trust you. They think you are there to fire them.'

'And you're not worried?'

She brought her gaze round to him. 'I know your real reason for being there. I heard Faragalla talking on the telephone. You're a detective. You're here to find out about the letters.'

The late-afternoon traffic surged forward in spurts. The cars rolled like loose cogs in a slow-moving mechanism, jamming and freeing themselves according to their own built-in logic. People were hungry and tired, and ahead of them was a long journey home. The horns like discordant trumpets sounding the retreat from battle.

'You said letters. I've only seen one.'

'There are more.'

'Why did Faragalla only show me one?'

'Because he doesn't know about the others.'

'But you do?'

She nodded as they crossed the river to Zamalek which lies in the middle of the Nile. Meera directed the driver to let them out under the 26th July bridge.

'Did you know that this island was once a marshy plot of land with a handful of fisherman living on it?'

'I had no idea,' Makana confessed.

'Well, it's true. Nobody is completely sure, but the name Zamalek may derive from the Armenian word for straw hut. Khedive Ismail built a summer palace here to get away from the heat and now look at it,' she gestured at the stylish, crumbling buildings clinging together for comfort as more cement blocks rose up, eating away the remaining fields and villas.

'Palaces are overrated. You don't belong in a place like the Blue Ibis.'

'Am I supposed to take that as a compliment?' She met his gaze evenly, leaving Makana momentarily lost for words. On Ahmed Sabri Street they passed St Joseph's Church founded by the Catholic Fathers of Verona.

'My father taught in a school they built in Khartoum,' said Makana without thinking. 'Bishop Comboni.'

'They fled here when your Mahdi decided to persecute them.'

'You certainly know your history.'

'If we don't learn from the mistakes of the past we are condemned to repeat them.'

'Karl Marx?'

'George Santayana. Spanish philosopher. Now why would someone like you know Marx?'

'Someone like me?'

'You know what I mean.'

She led him down tree-lined streets to a chic café called the Alhambra. Modern and bright, it was filled with students from the design school carrying outsize folders and plastic document rolls. Meera seemed to be quite at home here, as if this was her natural environment. The café's proprietors, a jovial couple in their thirties, both greeted her with the familiarity of a regular visitor. She ordered something called a latté and Makana, feeling out of his depth, agreed to have the same. He followed her across the room to a table by the window.

He watched her as she lit a cigarette. He hadn't seen her smoke all day. Freed from the confines of her job she handled herself with a confidence he hadn't witnessed at the Blue Ibis offices. Makana allowed his eyes to rest on her hands. They were slim, elegant hands, with slender wrists and long fingers that tapped impatiently on the table.

'Why are you working at the Blue Ibis?'

'The oldest reason in the world – I need the money. We need the money.' She tapped ash with the tip of her index finger. 'Three years ago I taught English Literature at Cairo University. My husband had a good post. Then one day he was fired. Just like that. It was a huge scandal, but there was no going back. He lost his job, everything. My contract was due to be renewed and it wasn't. As simple as that.' Meera paused and looked up, a smile on her face for the woman who brought over the tall cups of coffee, waiting until they were alone again before resuming her story.

'My husband was denounced as an apostate. The evidence, they claimed, lay in his writings, which were an insult to Islam, and in the fact that he had married a Christian.'

'Your husband is Ridwan Hilal?'

Makana was familiar with the story, which had been the cause of much debate at the time. It had created a huge stir, even in the international press. Considered a landmark case in the fight to keep Cairo University secular, it had failed spectacularly. Hilal was effectively ostracised, thrown to the wolves. A sign of just how conservative things had become. The attention from around the world only made his case all the more hopeless. He was seen not only as an apostate but as being in the pay of those secular forces in the West determined to bring down Islam.

'Nobody at the Blue Ibis offices knows your real identity?'

'No, and that's how I want to keep it.' Her eyes flickered upwards to meet his.

'Your lives were in danger. Why did you never go abroad?'

'Running away is not my husband's style.' Meera stared out of the window at the young people going by. 'It's not that we were short of opportunities. There were offers of refuge from all kinds of institutions.'

'But you decided to stay.'

'Up until now, yes. My husband's work is about uncovering truth in all those old texts. He couldn't hide if he wanted to.'

'Truth comes at a heavy price these days.'

'I know,' she said quietly, leaning her elbows on the table. 'And besides, this is our home. We both believe in this country. Somehow, despite everything, there is something here that is unique and worth fighting for. We've always believed that . . .'

'Until now?'

'Now I'm no longer sure. I used to think it's what you do with your life that counts, not how long you live.'

'And now you think that perhaps it might be smarter to live a little longer.'

'If these letters are really a threat.'

'You said there were more than one. How many exactly?'

'I'll come to that.' Meera let the air out of her lungs slowly as she stubbed out her cigarette. 'You haven't touched your coffee.'

Makana lifted the tall glass and examined the frothy substance. He preferred his coffee plain and black. Still, out of courtesy he sipped.

'Tell me about your husband, what does he do nowadays?'

'He does what he has always done. He works. Night and day. He's writing a book. It will probably be published abroad, where it will be highly acclaimed. Here, naturally, it will be banned. It doesn't matter to him. What matters is the work.'

'That's quite a sacrifice for anyone to make. I mean, it's not your fight.'

'Of course it's my fight,' she retorted angrily. 'It's everyone's fight. It is about the soul of this country. The complex diversity that makes us who we are. If we lose that, we lose everything.'

'But you choose to hide your identity at work.'

'For obvious reasons. I'm a Christian, Mr Makana. When you are part of a minority you learn to avoid making yourself a target. How long do you think Faragalla would hold out? There would be complaints from the others about having to work alongside an apostate.'

'Aren't you exaggerating just a little? How can you be sure the others would object?'

'Faragalla would run a mile at the mere hint of scandal. He would fire me for sure. You have no idea how long it took me to find that job.' Meera paused, studying him for a moment. 'You must come and meet Ridwan. We live just around the corner. It's a small flat that used to belong to his grandmother. It's all we have. We can't afford to move out.'

After that she talked about her family. Her great-grandfather used to run a provisions shop around the corner on 26th July Street. They specialised in wine and imported delicacies from Greece, France and Italy. Back in the fifties and sixties they used to supply the big hotels. 'It was a different world,' she smiled. 'When you see the pictures, it all looks so glamorous. They had style in those days.' Eventually the family business folded. The clientele of old Greeks, Copts, Syrians and Europeans vanished into the woodwork or out of the country. The shop was turned into a snack bar for a time and then sold on, eventually becoming a currency exchange. Makana knew the place, where bearded men counted out banknotes, their fingers a blur.

'On the bad days I think, what is the point? Why risk our lives for something that so few seem to believe in any more?'

'You must have had opportunities to leave.'

'We did. The Dutch, for example, offered to give us refugee status in Holland. A new life. Comfortable and safe. But what would we become? Stateless, homeless. Unable to come back. Who would we be? Have you any idea what that would be like?'

'I think I can imagine.'

Meera smiled and bowed her head. 'I'm sorry. That was thoughtless of me. I should have guessed you are in exile. Can't you go back?'

'It wouldn't be a good move.'

'Then maybe you do understand,' she said slowly. 'I can't bear the thought of leaving. If we were to turn our backs on this country it would end up in the hands of pious brothers and corrupt businessmen. Greed and piety, the two crosses we have to bear, if you will forgive me a little joke.'

'You forget the army.'

'Once you take off their uniforms they fall into one category or the other.' Meera stirred the dregs in the bottom of her coffee cup. 'Don't you wish you could go home?'

'I lost my wife and daughter,' said Makana. 'There's nothing to go back to.'

'I'm sorry,' she said. For a time neither of them said anything. A noisy group of youngsters came in and made a big fuss moving tables together and scraping chairs. They had the look of soft, comfortably-off kids without a care in the world.

'I feel like telling them to enjoy themselves while they can,' she said. 'In a few years' time they will finish their studies and find themselves out of work.'

'You miss teaching?'

'Your students become a form of hope. It's a shame, all that energy and enthusiasm going to waste. Don't you like your coffee? I can ask for something else.'

'No, thank you, it's fine.' Makana reached for another ciga-rette. 'Why don't you tell me about these letters. How many are there?'

'Three. They arrived in the morning post. No stamp. No address. But there's nothing odd about that. People drop letters off with Abu Salem downstairs. Everyone knows I open the post.'

'And they all contained the same passage from the Quran?'

'No, all of them are different, but from the same Sura.'

In the context of what Meera had just told him, about who she was and who her husband was, the idea of the letters being a threat addressed to her made more sense.

'And you are convinced they were meant for you?'

'Oh, yes. I mean, if I hadn't been late that day Faragalla would never have seen them. Look,' Meera said, 'the Sura is addressed to the Arabs of the Jahiliyya, the age of ignorance before the coming of Muhammed and his message. It is addressed to pagans, idolaters, worshippers of stars.'

'People like your husband.'

She nodded. 'Someone must have found out my identity.'

'But there is no specific threat, or demand in any of the letters.'

'No.' She hesitated.

'Is there something more, something you're not telling me?'

'No, it's nothing.'

'Look, it sounds like you are in some kind of trouble. I can't help you if you don't tell me everything.'

Meera nodded, her eyes on the table. She reached for another cigarette and he lit it for her. She exhaled slowly. 'Things are about to change. I can't explain it all right now but . . .' Her eyes lifted to meet his. 'Perhaps if you talked to Ridwan. You could come to the flat, we could talk, all of us together. I might be able to persuade him.' She sighed, staring out of the window. 'This place, after a while it just closes in on you. You forget there is a world out there full of life.'

Chapter Six

Makana had no trouble finding another taxi to take him home. As he climbed out under the big eucalyptus tree and descended the path, the sun was setting and the water was streaked with change, purple and blue. There was no sign of Bassam today, but the smell of food frying came from behind the wooden shack where Umm Ali and her little brood lived, and although she couldn't see him she called out a greeting as he went by.

'Good evening, *ya bash muhandis*.'

'Good evening, Umm Ali.'

Filling a bucket, Makana bathed in the timeless manner of pouring water over himself with a large plastic beaker. He watched the soap suds swirling through a hole in the bathroom floor to vanish downstream to the sea. Having washed and changed his clothes, he walked back up the incline to the road and joined the glowing red stream that slid like molten metal back into the city.

Since getting married, Sami Barakat had settled down in a small flat with his wife Rania who was also a journalist. The story went that they had known one another for years before love had struck its fateful chords. They now lived in an old red brick building on Adly Street, not far from the synagogue. From the outside it was an impressive, stylish affair from the turn of the last century. Inside it had high ceilings and an old elevator that Makana avoided, preferring to walk the five flights of stairs instead. There was a large living room/dining room that gave onto a narrow kitchen. Like most young couples, they never had time to cook and an invitation to supper implied they would be ordering in from one of the many takeaway places nearby. The low table was, as usual, laden with reading material: newspapers, magazines, journals of every description, which Sami proceeded to clear away in preparation for their meal. Rania came into the room carrying a tray of glasses, plates and cutlery. Her face broke into a beaming smile when she saw Makana.

'We were wondering if you had forgotten us.'

Rania was easy-going and lively. When Sami had first found this place it had been dark and dingy as a monk's cell. The brown walls were scarred with cracks and the air fetid. If it had been left to Sami nothing would have changed, not even the furniture, which looked as if someone had died in it. Now the room was bright with colour, with white walls on which a few prints, mostly done by Rania's artist friends, had been hung. The two sofas and table, and the rug underneath it, were all new.

'Why don't we see you more often?' she asked. 'You're working all the time.'

'I had the impression it was you two who never have a spare moment,' said Makana.

'It's true,' she laughed, pushing her long black curls behind her shoulder. 'If we were left to our own devices neither of us would probably come home at all. We would entirely forget about the existence of this marriage.'

'What nonsense are you telling him now, *ya habibti*?' Sami appeared bearing an armful of Stella bottles. 'Would it be that easy to forget me?'

'If you weren't reminded from time to time that you had a wife to come home to you would completely forget my existence.'

'Imagine, if this is married life after only one year, what will we be like after fifty years?'

Domestication seemed to agree with Sami. He had put on a little weight which made him cut an older and somewhat more dignified presence, although the hair was still a wild nest. He had become something of a celebrity. Publishing a couple of successful books had turned him into not only a well-respected investigative journalist, but a spokesman for political integrity. His weekly column in a satirical magazine, *Abul-Houl* (The Sphinx), had brought him a younger generation of readers. Nevertheless, he remained just as disorganised as ever, opening beer bottles with his teeth, having been unable to locate an opener. Handing Makana a foaming glass he settled down on the sofa opposite and prodded his spectacles back up his nose with a stubby finger.

'*Saha*,' he said, raising his glass in health before launching back into a speech on the state of the world which had begun on the way up the stairs. 'We're going backwards in time. This country used to be the vanguard of the Arab world. Books, movies, we made the best. Dissidents from less fortunate places flocked here in search of freedom. Not any more. You know how many books were published in this country last year? Less than four hundred. And the movies are the same romantic trash designed to keep our minds occupied while telling us nothing. Diversions.'

'Tell him what Safwat said,' Rania encouraged from across the room where she was calling in their order.

Sami leaned over the coffee table and reached for his cigarettes. 'I wrote a piece about how the courts are dominated by judges who see themselves as religious figures. They even come to court dressed like imams. Okay, that fool Sadat amended the constitution to make Sharia the basis of Egyptian law, whatever that means, but we still have a constitution, we still have, in principle, secular courts, right? Wrong. Even the Supreme Court is bowing to this madness.'

'Sometimes I worry,' whispered Rania, coming to sit beside him. 'It's like the Spanish Inquisition. They judge us for our ideas. Who gives them the right?'

'It's not that bad yet,' Sami said, trying to comfort her, 'but it's getting serious. Even good colleagues start to look for ways around it. They don't come right out with it, of course. They say something like, Islam is the only way to resist Western decadence.' He threw his head back and laughed. 'What kind of a statement is that?'

'They are afraid,' said Rania, 'that if they don't conform they will be persecuted.'

'Persecuted by whom?' asked Makana.

'By society,' Sami's glasses glinted with defiance. 'The point is not about whether or not I am a Muslim, but whether you have the right to call yourself a better Muslim than me.'

All of this was beginning to sound a little too familiar. 'I met someone today,' Makana said, setting down his glass. 'The wife of Ridwan Hilal.'

'You met her?' Rania's eyes widened. 'How?'

'She's connected to a case I'm working on.'

'Now that's enough, *habibti*. He can't talk about his work. He would have to kill you.'

They all laughed. Sami, leaning forward to scoop a handful of peanuts up from the bowl on the table, went on. 'His wife has reason to be worried. Sheikh Waheed recently repeated his statement about Hilal being an apostate. That lot won't be happy until he is dead or in exile.'

'Sheikh Waheed, the television imam?' asked Makana. 'I remember it as a disagreement about theology.'

'It was nothing to do with theology,' Rania corrected him. 'It was much more simple than that. It's about personal jealousy.'

'You see how we agree about everything?' Sami grinned.

'Ridwan Hilal applied for the post of Professor of Arabic Studies at the university,' Rania explained. 'He had to submit his work to a faculty board for approval. Well, two of the board recommended him for promotion, but the third was Professor Serhan, who turned down the request. The decision had to be unanimous. Nobody understood. Hilal was highly respected and clearly deserved the post. He protested the decision and the matter was referred to another seven-man committee. By then the story had gone public. The television got hold of Sheikh Waheed and decided to stir things up.'

Sheikh Waheed was a controversial imam with the following of a pop star. The media loved him for his provocative declarations. Waheed enjoyed shocking people. It made for good viewing.

'Waheed is a government man,' said Sami. 'He makes them look like they are more Islamic than the fanatics. With him on their side no one can accuse them of not being religious enough.'

Rania continued the story: 'When Waheed pronounced his verdict in his televised sermon one Friday afternoon after prayers, that was pretty much the end of it. Nobody dared go up against someone like Waheed. Not even government ministers disagree with him, and certainly not the university committee, which naturally voted to deny Hilal the post.'

'Waheed then filed a civil case against Hilal,' Sami went on, 'accusing him of apostasy and of turning his back on Islam to marry a Christian woman. It was not just the end of his career, it was almost the end of his life.'

'Once they smell blood, they go in for the kill,' Rania concluded.

'It was what you might call a lynching,' offered Sami. 'Hilal was a specialist and widely regarded as quite brilliant in the field of Arabic studies.' His voice trailed away as he went into the kitchen to fetch more beer.

Makana thought about Meera and her clandestine existence at Blue Ibis Tours. Every day she carried with her the memory of how her husband was made an outcast and how their marriage was condemned publicly. No wonder she wanted to keep her identity secret. It also explained the horror she must have felt on opening those letters for the first time. Naturally she assumed those words were meant for her.

'No one dared stand up for Hilal,' Sami was saying. 'He was tried by silent complicity.'

There was a ring at the door announcing the arrival of their food. A young man in a baseball cap appeared. While Sami paid him, Rania carried it through to the kitchen and unpacked it onto plates. In the old days, Sami would have served it directly from the boxes it came in, but times had changed and plates were now in order. Soon a small feast was arrayed before them on the low table. Roast chicken, *kibba* and *taamiya* rissoles, along with a range of salads. For a time the talk was restricted to comments on the food, and the merits of one takeaway service versus another. It was a conversation Sami and Rania appeared to have had before.

'Hilal's work is very important,' Rania said, continuing their conversation. 'He published a book about ten years ago, *The Quran and its Context*. At the time no one paid much attention, but it argued that any written text is a product of the age in which it is written. So in order to understand the consequences of the Quran fully it has to be studied in relation to society at the time.'

'He was careful,' Sami interjected. 'He didn't dispute the eternal nature of Allah's word, just the historical setting in which it was interpreted.'

'We still interpret the Quran according to what was written fourteen hundred years ago.'

'Hilal's point,' Sami went on, 'is that he believes we must protect religion from being distorted by those who wish to turn it to their own ideological purposes.'

'And that put him on a collision course with Sheikh Waheed.'

'Exactly,' they both said in unison. Sami and Rania looked at one another and simultaneously broke into spontaneous laughter.

'We've been arguing about this guy for years,' Sami explained.

Makana realised how long it had been since he had spent an evening with friends. When he wasn't working he tended to withdraw from the world into a kind of seclusion, rather like a monk.

'I'm telling you,' Sami said as they began to clear up the remains of their meal, 'I love this country as much as anyone, but I am seriously considering leaving.'

'Don't be silly,' Rania chastised him. 'Where would we go?'

'Who knows? Just as long as we don't have to deal with all this bullshit any more.'

'I never counted you as one who gave up that easily,' said Makana.

Sami wagged his head ruefully. 'I'm telling you, this is not a battle you can win.'

His wife punched him gently on the arm. 'He's right, you're not the kind to give up.'

'Maybe I'm getting old,' Sami laughed, but the look in his eye said he wasn't joking.

When Makana finally took his leave, it was long past midnight and everyone was beginning to yawn. Sami walked him down to the street to find a taxi.

'You were getting pretty serious there,' Makana said.

'Well, it gets me down. Sometimes I can't see anything in this country ever changing.'

'I saw your story on the murders in Imbaba.'

'Street kids. No one wants to talk about the subject, which is one reason the police are doing so little. They run away, usually because they are abused at home, which is another taboo subject. They come to the city, where they fall prey to unscrupulous people.'

'What about all this talk about ritual killings?'

'Nonsense being stirred up by, among others, our friend Sheikh Waheed. It's a smokescreen, the same old method of pretending nothing is wrong with our society. It's all external forces. In this case the Copts.' Sami sighed. 'It's all part of the plan.'

'What plan is that?'

'The one to keep us all occupied, fighting amongst ourselves. Muslim against Christian. Poor against poor. So we don't notice that the government is screwing us all.' Sami raised a hand as a lone taxi trundled by and squeaked slowly to a halt. The driver stared at them sullenly through the windscreen.

'If you want to know more, I'm going to visit Father Macarius on Friday. He runs the church over there.'

'Sounds good. I'd also like to take a look at this Sheikh Waheed.'

'He'll be there, giving another of his hate sermons.' Sami opened the car door and held out his hand. 'Don't leave it so long next time. Rania thinks I should invite more decent people around.'

'I'll take that as a compliment.'

Sami's laughter echoed in his head all the way across the river.

Chapter Seven

The boy behind the counter was about twelve years old by Makana's reckoning. He was wondering to himself how he had come to be running this café by himself and was about to ask when he saw Meera walking towards him up through the gloomy arcade. Now that he knew who she was, it occurred to him as strange that nobody had noticed how out of place she was in the Blue Ibis offices. She carried herself with poise and Makana was forced to remind himself that she was a married woman and that they were meeting for a purpose. She, too, seemed eager to stress the nature of their meeting and handed him a large brown envelope as she sat down.

'I knew they were meant for me ever since I saw the first one. I don't know why, I just stuffed them into my bag.' Her eyes narrowed, then she sat back and regarded him for a moment. Her hair was different today, as if she had come out in a hurry and it hung loosely around her face. She didn't look any the worse for it, in fact the opposite. Makana stirred his coffee. Outside in the arcade an old man was sweeping, moving along the cracked tiles with a broom over which a dirty rag had been draped. It slid back and forth like a strange undersea creature swimming through muddy water.

'At first I thought it was some sort of cruel practical joke. I was ashamed, to tell the truth, and felt I should keep it secret. I didn't tell anyone.' Her fingernails tapped at the warped Formica at the edge of the table.

'And now you've changed your mind?'

'One letter might be a joke, but three? Somebody is trying to tell me something.'

'And you haven't talked about this to anyone?'

'Not until now, no.'

Makana noticed the boy behind the counter lifting his head. The eyes widened enough to take a long look at Meera.

'If someone does really mean you harm, perhaps you should consider varying your habits. How you travel, what time you come to work, that kind of thing.'

'Ridwan and I have grown used to threats over the years. A few years ago someone tried to stab him in the street. The dangerous ones are the ones who give no warning. Now, have you thought about my invitation?'

'Of course, I would be delighted to meet your husband.'

'Then that's settled. How about Sunday evening?'

'Fine.'

As she was getting to her feet the boy came round from behind the counter. He was clutching a wet rag in his hands and stood there looking at her until she noticed.

'Madame,' he said. Meera turned and smiled.

'Eissa? Is that you? What are you doing here?'

'Oh, it's just for a week or two, to help out for a friend.'

'Eissa used to be one of my students, didn't you? I used to teach him English.'

'At the university?' asked Makana.

'No,' laughed Meera. 'And now you've found work here?'

The boy nodded his head, embarrassed in some way. Meera seemed to have a certain effect on men of any age, it seemed.

'So I expect we'll be seeing a lot of each other in the next few weeks.'

'I'd like that,' said the boy. He followed her to the door and watched her walk away. When he returned to the counter his head was bowed.

'Can you get me some cigarettes?' Makana called.

'Sure,' the boy nodded without looking up. 'What kind?'

'Cleopatra.'

As the boy disappeared through a back door, Makana noticed a pair of battered boxing gloves hanging from a nail hammered into the wall. He opened up the envelope Meera had given him. It was similar to the others. The typeset, the faint splatters of ink around some of the letters. An old-fashioned printing press. The paper was also the same cheap quality, roughly torn off at the ends, as if cut from a roll. Uneven and full of imperfections. The envelope was of the same poor quality, the edges coming unstuck. There was no address other than the words 'Blue Ibis'. As for the text, Makana was fairly certain that it came from the same source:

Give no heed, then, to those who ignore Our warning and seek only the life of this world. This is the sum of their knowledge. You Lord best knows who have strayed from His path, and who are rightly guided.

'Poetry for the lady?'

Makana looked up to see the boy leaning over his shoulder.

'I couldn't write poetry even if I wanted to.' He took the cigarettes and tore open the packet. 'So, tell me where you know her from. Where did you have these lessons?'

'Oh, she used to come to the church school and teach us.'

'You're a Christian?'

'Me? No way,' said the boy quickly. 'No, they have a gym and everything. They even give you food.'

'Sounds wonderful. How much are the cigarettes?'

'Half price. I can get you a whole carton if you like.'

'Where do you get cigarettes that cheaply?'

Eissa shrugged. A shout came from the door. The *bawab*, Abu Salem, the building's porter, stood there clutching the arm of a scrawny boy of about ten. 'This one says he's with you.'

'And what of it?' retorted Eissa, back to his usual self. 'He helps in the kitchen.'

'The kitchen? This one still has mother's milk on his face!'

Eissa put his arm around the younger boy's shoulder and led him through behind the counter.

'I don't know what the world's coming to,' the old porter muttered to Makana. 'They come and go as if they own the place and not a man between them.' He raised his voice. 'If this goes on I shall have to speak to Yousef.'

'Yousef?' echoed Makana.

'He's a friend of the owner, who has another place he runs across town. Yousef takes care of business for him.'

Yousef appeared to have a hand in everything. He certainly seemed to take an interest in Makana. No sooner had he sat down to work than Yousef turned up. Pushing heaps of folders to one side, he perched himself on the corner of the desk and stretched a rubber band between two fingers.

'Tell me again why you went to prison.'

Makana glanced round, as if worried about being overheard. 'I told you. It was a misunderstanding.'

This amused Yousef. He chuckled and slapped Makana on the shoulder.

'Come on, let's take a drive and do some real work.'

'I am supposed to be trying to help the company.'

'Believe me, that can wait.'

Twenty minutes later they were bumping along Sharia al-Muizz, in the area known as Bayn al-Qasrayn, which once lay between two Fatimid palaces. They passed the tomb of Saliq al-Ayubi, the man who created the Mamluks, a cadre of imported slaves. Slaves were considered reliable because as foreigners they would never aspire to rule the country. Al-Ayubi was wrong. By the time of his death the Mamluks were so powerful that his widow was forced to make a pact with them. Known by the alluring name of Tree of Pearls, *Shagarat al-Durr*, she tried to keep her husband's death a secret. The deception didn't last long and eventually she conceded permission for her son to be murdered so as to remain on the throne herself. Finally, she married the Mamluk leader and so the country passed into the hands of its former slaves, where it remained for three hundred years. Makana wondered if this was where the distrust of foreigners stemmed from.

They came to a halt near the tomb of al-Qalaun. A large pool of muddy water swirled from a burst drain.

'What a stink,' Yousef said, screwing up his face. 'You wait here, I won't be long.'

Makana watched him disappear into a narrow opening between two buildings. He let a couple of minutes pass before he got out. Nearby, a child squatted on a heap of pebbles.

'Where did all this water come from?'

'You didn't hear?' the boy replied. 'The president decided to take a piss. Three days it's been like this. We're still waiting for him to finish.'

'Watch your mouth!' yelled an old man going by, leading an exhausted donkey.

'You see that car?' Makana handed the boy a banknote. 'You keep an eye on it and you get another of those when I get back.' The money vanished from sight in the blink of an eye.

Makana crossed the street and descended a few steps. The narrow passage, barely wide enough for two people to squeeze by one another, vanished into the shadows between the buildings. A few minutes later an archway to his right opened onto an irregular square enclosed on three sides by colonnades of stone pillars. In the far corner he glimpsed Yousef disappearing through a doorway. Makana crossed the square. The door carried no name or number, but the heavy wood was decorated by a distinctive pattern of birds fashioned from wrought iron. Makana stepped back and looked up at the big house behind the wall.

'Looking for someone?'

A passer-by in a grubby gelabiya had stopped to peer at him.

'I was just wondering who lived here.'

'So why don't you knock and ask?' The man regarded Makana with a sceptical eye. Over his shoulder he carried a dirty white sack out of which pieces of charcoal poked like tiny charred limbs.

'It's all right, I'll come back later.'

The man had obviously decided he didn't trust Makana and stood his ground until he was sure he was on his way. Retracing his steps, Makana returned to the car and waited. Ten minutes later, Yousef appeared in the narrow cut. He looked left and right before stepping out of the alleyway and crossing the street. As he got in Makana made to start the engine.

'Hold on a minute.' Yousef opened the briefcase on his lap and reached inside for a thick manilla envelope. 'I don't know why, but I have a good feeling about you.' Unwrapping a thick wad of dollars wrapped in newspaper he peeled off a handful and held them out.

'What's that for?'

'Your share.'

'My share of what? I haven't done anything.'

Yousef winked. 'You drive me here, you keep your mouth shut. That's something. Call it an advance. Later, I might want you to do a bit more.'

'I don't take money for something I haven't done.'

'An honest man, eh? Well, fine, I'll hold onto it for you until you are ready. Just don't wait too long. I'm not known for being a patient man. Next time I'll introduce you to the old man. Now let's get out of here, this place stinks worse than my mother-in-law.'

There was a knock on the window. The boy who had been watching the car stood there rubbing his fingers together. Makana wound down the glass and handed out a note. When he turned back he saw a look of disgust on Yousef's face.

'Keep giving it away like that and you'll need more money than I can give you.'

Chapter Eight

The mosque was within walking distance of the *awama*. On Friday morning traffic along Al Nil Street was a fraction of what it was on a working day. The riverbank recovered some of its natural state. It took him fifteen minutes, first he walked along the river towards Midan Kit Kat and then turned west and walked inland. The relaxed mood extended through the narrow streets. Proud men strolled along leading their young children. Onlookers gathered around a minibus that had been stripped to a skeleton and observed one man hammering it mercilessly. Finding the mosque became a matter of following the crowd. It was a large construction that looked as though it had not been finished. A basic rectangle of grey breeze blocks fenced out the area. Inside, a structure of newly set raw concrete rose up out of the ground topped by a wide dome. Alongside it the minaret seemed out of proportion and uneven as it climbed crookedly towards the sky. Wooden scaffolding was still in place on one side and jagged metal spikes stuck out of the sides, presumably to hold the final outer layer of cladding, when someone got around to finishing off the building. Along the front, metal poles supported a strip of corrugated plastic sheets that provided some shade. Beneath this was a row of simple taps and a drainage gutter where the faithful could perform their ritual ablutions before entering. Around the sides a skirt of scuffed bare ground divided the mosque from the surrounding wall and the road. The street and grounds were packed with people milling about. He looked around for Sami, but without luck. They should perhaps have arranged to meet elsewhere beforehand. To one side of the entrance he spotted a group of what looked like Central Security Forces heavyweights surveying the crowd. Pushing through, Makana made it as far as the shelter where he had a view of the interior through a barred window.

Fans revolved overhead while on a raised dais at the far end of the room, resplendent in white robes, sat the compelling figure of Sheikh Waheed. In his mid-fifties, he wore a wispy beard. His head was covered by a simple turban. An enormous leather-bound Quran rested on a sandalwood stand before him.

'He is the Lord of the heavens and the earth and all that is in between them. Worship Him, then, and be patient in his service.' Sheikh Waheed paused and raised his eyes above his reading glasses to look out at the crowd. Speakers attached to the outside walls made sure his words were carried to those standing in the grounds and the street beyond.

'What greater suffering to inflict upon a parent but the bloody slaughter of a child? Is there one among you who cannot feel the pain of losing a son? Imagine the torment they must endure!'

There was a collective sigh of sympathy from the crowd. Around him Makana could hear people muttering angrily. A scuffle broke out to his right. The heavies from the front entrance moved in to drag the troublemakers away. Everyone fell silent as the sheikh began to speak again.

'A ruthless murderer is amongst us. Is it any wonder, I ask

myself, that people speak of these murders as an evil ritual? Who would dare, in this day and age, to sacrifice children? I ask myself, have we gone back to the Jahiliyya, the days of ignorance before the light of Islam touched mankind?' A murmur of dissent passed through the audience like a restless pulse. 'The bodies of innocent creatures, slaughtered like wild beasts.' The sheikh's voice trembled, his lips quivering with barely restrained fury. 'Such deeds cannot go unpunished, surely?'

'Revenge!' someone shouted from Makana's right.

'Kill them all!' came another.

'Let them feel our pain.'

There were other voices, voices urging restraint, calm, but these were swamped by the flood. The men by the gate were grinning to one another.

Up on the podium the sheikh raised his hands for calm.

'Patience.' His voice shook. There was a touch of theatricality to him as he surveyed the flock gathered at his feet, crammed together shoulder to shoulder, kneeling or sitting on the carpets spread over the hard concrete floor.

'Did the Prophet, May Allah bestow His blessings upon him, not spend twenty-three years awaiting the full revelation of the sacred text?' he asked, tapping the book in front of him. 'Then who are we not to heed the lessons of patience?' The sheikh's tone hardened. 'Those who ask for restraint should know that injustice can be suffered only for so long.' He held the crowd in his hands now. His voice rose, the little body rocked back and forth on the dais as if trying to wear its way down into the earth below.

'When the fateful day arrives, woe to the unbelievers! Know that we send down to the unbelievers devils who incite them to evil. Therefore have patience: their days are numbered.'

Cries of 'Allahu akbar' resounded as the sheikh got to his feet. He moved with the speed of a much older man, bowing to allow his most fervent supporters to kiss him on both cheeks before vanishing through a gap in the crowd.

As the men poured out of the mosque into the street, their anger filled the air. Makana recognised the same Central Security Forces thugs he had seen earlier, huddled together around the entrance. Then he was swept along in the rush of men being herded around the gate. He followed along as they moved off, first in one direction and then another, as if unable to decide which way to go. Then the indecision seemed to resolve itself and the crowd began to move, led by the same small group of instigators. People tagged along, with young boys running alongside, others leaping on top of cars and shouting. The route twisted and turned, cutting down short, narrow streets. Their destination became apparent as they emerged into an open square and the high walls of a church came into view. Unlike the newly built mosque they had just left, this building was old and crumbling. Deep cracks zigzagged up the front wall. The yellowing paint and plaster had come away in large gouts.

Outside the church a dark blue police pickup was parked. Uniformed men stood around it armed with riot sticks and shields as they eyed the approaching mob. A sergeant with a thick moustache stood with his hands on his hips.

'Go on with you. We don't want trouble here.'

'There's no trouble here,' one man said, advancing on the sergeant. 'The trouble is there,' he said, pointing at the church. Then, as if released by a secret signal, the mob broke loose. Stones and bottles flew overhead. A tree nearby shook as it was stripped of a few handy branches that were waved in the air. Glass shattered. The policemen were nervously backing away, stopped only by the sergeant who had retreated behind them, where he remained, arms folded, cautioning them to stand firm. They were easily outnumbered ten to one. The mob seethed, hurling their anger at the church in a rain of bricks and bottles that shattered against the walls. As Makana skirted along the edge he caught sight of Sami, waving to him from the next corner beyond the church.

'I didn't think you would make it.'

'Is it always like this?' Makana asked.

'It's become regular Friday entertainment. They come in from all over the city to hear the sheikh speak, and it's always provocative.'

Father Macarius was waiting for them nervously beside a large metal door that led into a walled compound adjoining the church. He ushered them quickly inside and bolted the gate behind them. Macarius was an impressive figure. Dressed in a black cassock that stretched down to his sandals, he was a tall, broad-chested man with a square jaw that looked as if it had been etched in the stone of his greying beard. According to Sami, he was a bit of a maverick. There was some long story about a scandal behind him. Apparently, he had been expelled from the church at one point, and then reinstated.

'This is not the first time we have been attacked. It has become a form of diversion for young people. It is not their fault, in my opinion, but they are frustrated and easily led astray.'

Makana and Sami had to make an effort to keep up with the priest, who moved with lithe, athletic grace.

'You can't blame people for being concerned,' Sami said to his back. 'These murders have created an atmosphere of panic.'

'That is exactly my point.' Father Macarius spun on his heel to face them. 'There is a need for calm thinking, rationality, but the government is taking a back seat. It is almost as if this unrest is of no concern to them.'

Sami was scribbling furiously in his notebook. 'Are you accusing the government of turning a blind eye to the persecution of Christians in this country?'

Father Macarius smiled. 'I said nothing of the kind, so please do not quote me as having said that. I merely ask the question of why nothing more is being done to catch the person responsible for these murders.'

'And if the murderer is a Christian?'

Father Macarius turned his gaze on Makana. 'The law must apply to all, regardless of their beliefs.'

The interior of the church was dark and cool. Bands of sunlight spilled through the hatched screens that covered the upper windows. A high gallery ran along both sides of the walls, culminating in a square tower that rose up at the far end. The air was laden with dust. The building was in a state of collapse by the look of it. Held together by heavy wooden scaffolding, timbers, rope, nails and a good deal of faith.

The noise of the crowd outside was diminishing.

'They are growing bored,' said Father Macarius. 'Now their minds turn to other things. Their stomachs are hungry and a glass of tea would be nice after all that shouting.'

'A lot of people would not take being attacked in such a good-natured way,' said Sami.

'I refuse to be bullied into retreating to the dark ages.' Macarius gestured about him. 'I built this church from a ruin. That was my promise to Pope Shenouda. Give me a place to stand, I said, and I shall build a tower to God. I did that and I shall defend it with my life.'

A large wooden screen ran along one wall. On it a series of

small panels gleamed darkly like pearls inset in the brown, smoky wood. Icons. Flashes of gold paint, light and varnish brought the religious images alive.

'We have been here for centuries,' said the priest. 'The Coptic church is living history, a connection to the ancient world of the pharaohs.'

Sami nodded and pointed. 'What's this one?'

'Saint Anthony.'

The air carried the tarry smell of old wood, death and stale perspiration. The whitewashed walls bore the smudges of passing hands. Even the light seemed somehow to have arrived here from another century. The priest led the way along the display, pointing out the figures in the paintings.

'Saint Nilus of Sinai, who prophesised the apocalypse; St Amun, named of course after the Egyptian God; St John the Small; St Shenouda.' He ticked them off with a finger as they moved.

'All of them were hermits, weren't they?'

Father Macarius spoke over his shoulder without looking in Makana's direction.

'This church is dedicated to those who took themselves off into the desert in order to commune with God. It is the tradition to which I belong.'

'You are a monk, then? Which monastery?'

'It's of no consequence,' shrugged Father Macarius as he turned, his eyes lingering on Makana for a moment. 'Wadi Nikeiba. It no longer exists.'

They moved on until they came to the last wooden panel in the display. The paintings seemed to merge, blending into a constellation of suffering. It made Makana tired just to think of all that pain. But this last one intrigued him. Two figures shared a frame the colour of blood.

'My namesake,' explained the priest tersely. 'Macarius the Great.'

'What about the figure next to him?'

'Ah . . . that is the Seraph.' Macarius studied Makana carefully. 'You are not a religious man.' It wasn't a question.

'Does it matter?' Makana glanced at the priest and noted a faint gleam of satisfaction.

'You are sure that God does not exist?'

'He may well exist, but I'd like to see evidence of his goodness.'

A smile played on the priest's lips. 'You would like to believe in a benevolent God?'

'I don't believe I am a bad person, Father. I try to be good, at least. I suppose I don't see why God, assuming He exists, shouldn't be satisfied with that.'

'We are not children, but grown men, with responsibilities. Why should we expect God to be simple and straightforward?'

'With all due respect, Father, that doesn't prove anything.'

'Do you not believe that God wishes to make us become better people by facing the difficulties He places before us?'

'I think killing people in cold blood is a funny way of testing us.'

'You are speaking of the murders,' Macarius nodded. 'Perhaps you came to this church to find out if we killed these boys in some kind of secret ritual?'

'I don't believe that nonsense, Father, but I would be interested in hearing your opinion. Do you think God is trying to teach us something by killing these children?'

Sami laughed nervously. 'You'll have to forgive my friend, Father. He has rather a singular way of expressing himself.'

The priest ignored Sami, his eyes remaining fixed on Makana.

'Whoever is killing these boys will one day stand before God to answer for his crimes.'

'That may be a little late for some,' said Makana.

They had reached the end of the central nave. A set of stairs led upwards, the wood creaking as they climbed. The gallery led towards the back of the church while a ladder led up into the tower.

Macarius moved along carefully, examining the big windows for damage. From where they stood they could look down into the street in front of the church. The crowd had more or less dispersed. The police officers were removing their helmets and lighting cigarettes. From here they could also look down over the compound adjoining the church which contained a low, single-storey building along two sides. The roof was covered in tin sheeting that was patched up in places. Father Macarius led the way back downstairs. Through a curtain a doorway led into the building next door. A long, open space. The windows facing the street were all shuttered. Along the sides ran long trestles fashioned roughly from wood. On some of these mattresses had been rolled up.

'This is our little boarding house. We take in children who have nowhere to go, or who cannot go home. We give them a place to sleep, clean water and clothes as well as food.'

'Do you run this place by yourself?' Makana asked.

'We have volunteers to help with most things, including teaching.'

Father Macarius was already on the other side of the long, dark room, exiting through a doorway out into the compound. The high walls were topped with iron stakes and strands of wire whose barbs gleamed like silver teeth and made it look more like a fort than a place of worship. An ancient bus was parked against one wall, the word Delta just visible on its side through the sun-bleached paint. On the far side an open garage door admitted them to the other building, from which they could now hear excited shouts.

'Twenty years ago there was a shoe factory here. When it became cheaper to import than to make them it was closed down. The family refused to sell and the place fell into ruin until I came along.'

'They were Christians?'

'Does that make a difference?' The square jaw tilted like a rocky crag as a dark look clouded the priest's face. 'We must help one another in difficult times. If not . . .' He left the sentence hanging.

Makana and Sami stepped in through the doorway to find themselves in a long, gloomy hangar. The only light entered through opaque sheets of corrugated plastic which alternated in places with the rusty tin of the roof. At the centre was a boxing ring, the ropes hanging slackly. The canvas stretched across its surface was scarred by zigzag sutures where rips had been sewn up by a clumsy surgeon. At the far end of the room were a couple of punchbags that sagged like paunchy old men; beyond that rows of shelves and benches were arranged along the walls. The whole place reeked of decades of sweat. It oozed from the walls and might have been painted on the floor in thick layers. A sign proudly read: Seraph Sporting Club. Below this an angel with flames for wings flew across the wall. Makana recognised the figure from the painting inside the church. The image was pock-marked in places where the plaster had fallen away, and the intensity of the colours had also faded with time to dull browns and reds. The face floated like a pale moon over a speckled desert landscape, which also contained a building tucked into a rocky hillside. Palm trees peeped over the white walls. It looked like a monastery. Perhaps the one Macarius had mentioned. Wadi Nikeiba. Underneath were letters from an alphabet Makana could not read.

'We are at war, Mr Makana. It is as simple as that. A minority act, but it is the silence of the majority which is the real crime.'

'Is that what this is about,' Makana asked, 'preparing people for war?'

'I tell young people to be careful when they go outside. Our women have to put up with insults when they walk in the streets. They have their hair pulled, the crosses torn from their necks. Such barbarism. Where is the merciful and compassionate Islam that history has taught us?'

'I'm afraid I'm not the right person to answer that question, Father.'

'This is my proudest achievement, a gym for boys of all ages. We do not discriminate. People can train no matter if they are Muslims or Christians, or anything else for that matter.'

Makana recalled Eissa, the boy from the café under the Blue Ibis offices. A group of young men were sparring, shadow-boxing, moving back and forth, throwing punches, ducking and weaving. Father Macarius was speaking again.

'Children run away because they have no choice. The home becomes a prison in which all kinds of abuse takes place. No one can protect you from your family. They spend their days wandering the streets, and sleeping rough at night. We give them a place to stay, and food to eat.'

Makana's attention was drawn to the wall where a row of photographs hung. The older ones were in cheap frames. Others were simply pasted to the grubby plaster. Some were clippings from newspapers, frayed and yellowed with age. One of these showed a young Father Macarius, barely recognisable in singlet and shorts, gloved fists raised in front of him as if taking aim at the photographer. There were pictures of boys young and old. Championships. Pictures of the church in better days, gleaming white with old horse-drawn carriages, a policeman in a tarboosh. There were other pictures, of picnics and riverboat outings. A catalogue of young men who had passed through this shed on their way to adulthood.

'Ah, Antun,' Father Macarius said. 'Are those for tomorrow's fight?'

'Yes, uh . . . Father.' A diminutive young man of about nine-teen with haunted eyes. He seemed to have some difficulty speaking. He paused to set down a plastic basket filled with laundry. On the top lay a stack of flyers. Macarius held one out to Makana. It was simply done. The logo of the club ran along the top and underneath it read: Under 16s Championship.

'We hold these from time to time. It gives the kids something to look forward to.'

Antun picked up his basket and moved off, glancing over his shoulder as he went.

'You didn't finish telling me about the Seraph.' Makana tapped the logo on the flyer which was a reproduction of the angel mural on the wall.

'The Seraph?' The big priest frowned, unclasped his hands behind his back and folded his arms over his broad chest. Makana wondered if priests were allowed to play sports. There didn't seem to be any real reason why not.

'The word means, *Those Who Burn*. The seraph is a creature that lives in heaven, close to God. They have eyes all over their bodies and are said to be like dragons, or snakes, with six wings. Amongst the angels they rank most highly.'

'What are those?' Sami pointed at the wooden figures suspended from the girders supporting the roof.

'Oh, yes, they are quite unique,' said Macarius. 'You can read their names: Hassan, Safwat, Ali and Kamal. I am afraid that Antun has not finished carving the latest victim, Amir.'

Following his gaze, Makana spotted the boy who had been carrying the laundry. He was now seated in the far corner, whittling away at a lump of wood.

'You mean, these figures are angels representing the boys who were murdered?'

'You may have heard that there has been something of a miracle here recently. The sighting of an angel?'

'It was in the papers,' said Sami.

'You mean, people really believe there is an angel floating around up there?' Makana asked.

'It brings comfort to a lot of people,' said Father Macarius.

It made as much sense as anything, thought Makana, as he reached for his cigarettes. He wondered what the implications were of murdered Muslim children being turned into Christian angels. His old distaste for religious belief rose in him. Angels and demons seemed a perfect excuse to keep people on their knees with their eyes shut and their hands clasped together in the dark.

'Not in here, please,' Macarius shook a finger in front of Makana's nose. 'I try to discourage the boys from such habits.'

Makana watched a young boy pummelling a punchbag. He was skinny, a collarbone sticking out through the arms of his worn singlet as sharply as a knife.

'Earlier you said the police haven't paid much attention to these murders,' said Makana.

'None at all,' said Father Macarius. 'It's as if they don't care. If it was their children things would be different.'

'I'm sure,' nodded Makana. 'Did some of the victims stay here?'

'All of them, as far as I know, passed through at some time.'

'Do you think these killings could in some way be directed at the church?'

'A way of paying us back for trying to help? Yes, it is possible. Everyone is afraid. Muslim and Christian. This is not a good time. This whole area could explode at any moment and when it does, God help us all.' Father Macarius shook his head in dismay. 'I understand your point of view, Mr Makana, perhaps better than you think. I too, ask myself why the Almighty puts these terrible trials before us, and the only answer I have is that it is to test us, to make us ask ourselves what kind of men we are.' The fierce gaze bored into Makana as he shook his hand. 'That is the only question that matters: what kind of man are you?'

Chapter Nine

The ghostly outline of the *Binbashi* was lit up by strings of coloured lights, making the steamer resemble a sketch by an artist with an unsteady hand. Like Makana's *awama*, it was more a floating building than a ship. The entrance was reinforced by a wall and a gate complete with a collection of doormen deep in earnest discussion who duly ignored Makana as he entered. A path led down to a short gangway that brought him into a lobby, gaudily decorated with coloured tinsel, mirrors and a revolving glass ball hanging from the ceiling. Music played over speakers everywhere you went, providing a non-stop soundtrack to your experience. Makana counted the names of four restaurants, but he had an idea there were more of them hidden around the vessel somewhere. He followed the signs to the upper deck and entered a long stately room with low lighting.

Talal had managed to exchange his customary T-shirt for something with a collar, and he was even wearing a jacket that looked as if it had been through a grain thresher and was at least two sizes too small for him. The sleeves came up to his forearms. They were sitting at a table on the riverside. Through the window the city lights swam like luminous fish in the black water. The woman of his dreams had a high bust and creamy skin. She wore a tight blue dress covered in ribbons and bows that emphasised her full figure. She looked as though she would eat Talal alive.

'Thank you for coming,' he said. 'Bunny, this is the man you've heard so much about.'

'He really doesn't stop talking about you,' she said, holding out a limpid hand. There was a playful lilt to her voice and her eyes lingered for a moment on Makana.

'Please sit,' Talal urged, as jumpy as a scalded cat.

'Thank you,' Makana said.

'Actually,' she giggled, 'I hear your name all the time now that you are helping my father.'

'Yes, how is that coming along?' Talal chimed in.

'It's too early to say.'

The place was almost empty and they seemed to be surrounded by a swarm of beefy waiters, snapping their fingers, holding out chairs, lifting up and setting down cutlery, handing out menus. Makana reached for his cigarettes.

Bunny prompted, 'Talal.'

'Oh,' Talal said, looking up from his menu, which was big enough to hide a family of four. 'If you don't mind. Bunny doesn't like smoke.'

'No problem.' Makana replaced the cigarette in the packet, put the packet back in his pocket and instead took the menu that was thrust under his nose. After staring at it for a time he realised it made no sense to him. The dishes all had foreign names. He took another look around. Low lighting was generally a bad sign in any restaurant. It implied you were not meant to be able to see what you were eating. The empty tables seemed to encourage this line of thinking. Eating was a serious pastime in this country. Not that such trivia affected the happy couple. As Bunny chattered on, Makana realised this was Talal's idea of trying to impress her. He tried to put his doubts aside. By the sound of it they were planning to taste every available dish. Bunny was running down the menu ticking off one after another as a distracted waiter tried to take note. Makana had a feeling this was going to be a long evening.

'What about you?' Talal asked.

'Oh, why don't you order for me?'

It was the right thing to say, and allowed Bunny to spend some time playfully measuring him up with her eye to decide what he might like. She clearly liked attention, particularly the male kind. While the young couple chattered between themselves, discussing the merits of one dish over another, the waiter stood tapping his pen against his pad impatiently as if he had a hundred customers waiting for him elsewhere. Makana was about to excuse himself to go outside and have a cigarette, when a shadow crossed before him and another man pulled up the chair opposite.

'So there you are, we were beginning to get worried.'

The newcomer was around the same age as Makana, in his forties. He wore a colourful African shirt and a broad smile. As he sat down he placed not one but two large mobile telephones on the table and reached into the air to snap his fingers for the waiter. If a moment ago Makana had had good reasons for wanting to leave, they had just multiplied.

Once upon a time Mohammed Damazeen was an artist, a painter with a sideline in the import–export business to keep him in fancy shirts. Makana observed the look of complicity that passed between Damazeen and Talal, whose face was a picture of carefree innocence. A senior waiter in a black jacket appeared, cheerless and balding, and with a look of disdain on his face that had been perfected by years of waiting on tables.

'You two know each other, of course,' said Talal.

'Oh, we have known each other for years,' smiled Damazeen, before turning to the waiter and demanding wine be brought.

'I'm sorry, sir.' A cold sneer creased the waiter's face. 'We only serve alcohol to non-Muslims.'

'It's all right,' protested Bunny. 'It really doesn't matter.' The idea of wine clearly scandalised her. She gave Talal a hard stare, but he had an absent look on his face that Makana had seen before and also appeared to have lost the ability to speak.

'Look,' Damazeen summoned the waiter closer. 'I'm a friend of the owner. Call Ayad Zafrani and ask his permission. *Yallah*, go! Tell him, Mo Damazeen asked for wine.' He turned his back on him in a gesture of contempt. The waiter, clearly uncomfortable with the idea of disturbing his boss with such a trivial matter, tugged nervously at the cuffs of his jacket. He addressed the back of Damazeen's head.

'I'm sure there is no problem, *ya basha*. If you wish for wine, I shall bring it personally.' He spun on his heels and clapped his hands, causing four other waiters to start fighting over a bottle of Omar Khayyam, which was passed along from hand to hand with all the care of nitroglycerine. It took a while for them to find a corkscrew. They poured two glasses in the end. One for Damazeen and then, at his insistence, one for Makana, who had no intention of touching it.

'Still stirring up scandal, I see.'

Damazeen let out a laugh, throwing back his head.

'You see how well he knows me?'

Talal grinned, clearly relieved. Across the other side of the room Makana caught a glimpse of a bulky man in a grey suit. He had a shaven head and steel-rimmed glasses that glinted in the light. He glanced in their direction as the head waiter leaned in to whisper in his ear.

'How is it that you are in business with the Zafrani brothers?'

'Oh, you know how it is in my line of work. We meet so many people.' Damazeen's smile fanned out again as he raised his glass. 'Let us drink to the old days. It's been a long time.'

Makana lit a cigarette, ignoring the glare he got from Talal. Bunny was too flustered about the wine to make an issue of it.

Damazeen had never really been Makana's friend. A long time ago he had been part of a circle of artists in Khartoum that his wife Muna had mixed with when she was a student. He recalled long, carefree evenings sitting in one house or another, discussing politics and art. They even had a painting of Damazeen's on the wall of their home. A swirl of blues and greys. A mythical bird accompanied by lines of calligraphy. Makana couldn't pretend to have an understanding of art but Muna liked it. It all seemed so long ago. Damazeen had been the young upcoming artist. Nasra hadn't even been born then. Another time. An age of innocence it seemed now, when everything was what it claimed to be, and there was something called hope.

When he had first landed in Cairo, Makana discovered Damazeen was already part of the exile community. Their paths crossed a couple of times. By then Makana had lost his job, his wife and child, and his home, and he was discovering that no one makes it on their own. It was the nature of exile. With flight you lost your surroundings, the context in which your previous life existed. No matter what you did you could never get that back, but you could meet people in the same situation and that was a help, of sorts.

Eager to put the awkward start behind them, Talal was keen to make amends. 'Mo has been telling us all about the new centre he is planning to build. It's going to be a retreat for international artists from all over the place.'

'Sounds wonderful,' Makana said.

Mo, as he was known in London and Paris, had put on weight. His hair was threaded with whorls of white now and his shirt was tight across an expanded midriff. All of this only added to his sense of his own presence. He carried himself like a celebrity. In the early days he had been something of a firebrand who talked of fighting the regime through art and politics. A charismatic character. The media loved him. In Cairo's cultural circles he had played the ingenuous country bumpkin, the exotic cousin to their Arab reserve. As far as most Cairenes were concerned, Africa was a distant and very dark continent inhabited by savages. The art world was no more enlightened than most. In those days Damazeen could have marched on stage with a leopard-skin over his shoulder and they would have adored him. As the years went by and the regime showed no sign of stepping down, Damazeen began to tone down the act. Murmurs of compromise circled. He talked of longing for home, returning to his roots. From there to fully fledged apologist was but a short skip and a jump. The old regime had abandoned its hard-line beginnings, he claimed. Some believed him. Others had their doubts. Rumours circulated that he was an informer. When the Americans rained cruise missiles down on Khartoum in retaliation for the attacks on US Embassies in East Africa, Damazeen appeared on state television to voice his outrage. It was a public declaration of his ties to the regime.

'What are you doing here?'

'Come on, lighten up!' Damazeen carried himself like a mediocre actor who believed his hour had come. 'We have a duty to encourage talent, which is why Talal has got to attend the Viennese Conservatory.' He patted Talal on the shoulder.

'You're going to fund him?'

'Why not? What better cause is there than nurturing young artists?'

It worried Makana to see them together. Talal was impressionable, and a few stories about how close Damazeen was to his father would go a long way, and this made him uncomfortable. He also wondered what the connection was between Damazeen and the Zafrani brothers? They enjoyed a reputation as one of the most ruthless organised-crime families. The stories of beheadings, of victims being left buried up to their necks in the desert, or pulled apart by horses, sounded like theatrical replays of medieval practices, but Makana knew enough to take them seriously.

A waiter appeared and Bunny nodded. She and Talal got up to go and inspect the grill on the far side of the room, perhaps also to leave the two men alone to work out their differences.

'So, you're here on art business?'

'You never give up, do you?' Damazeen laughed in slow guffaws. 'A man of virtue, convinced that all around him is darkness and corruption. You should take a look at yourself sometime.'

There were rumours of fat commissions on contracts supplying the military with trucks. Damazeen had always denied it, of course, claiming he was simply selling more paintings than anyone else. He had a mysterious buyer in the Gulf. But everyone knew it would take an awful lot of canvas to pay for his new lifestyle. Now that he was friends with the regime he spent his time with entrepreneurs, army men, unsavoury types who met in shabby hotels and drank only when they thought no one was looking, prayed when they thought they were.

'I had doubts, just like you, but things have changed. Now there are opportunities. Great opportunities. The boom has just begun.

There is enough for everybody now that petroleum is finally flowing from the wells. The Chinese are building roads, pipelines, refineries. And they are not the only ones. Malaysians, Indians, Turks. We are on our way to becoming a developed nation.'

'A few people making themselves obscenely rich doesn't make a developed nation.'

Damazeen reached for his glass and twirled the wine around it. 'You should get over yourself, you know? And stop poisoning the boy's mind with all your paranoia. He's talented.'

The sound of Bunny's laughter echoed across the room. The cook had provided her with another appreciative audience. A handsome man in a tall white hat, he seemed to amuse her, flirting openly, wielding a carving knife in the air like a mad dervish.

'Why did you turn against me? I never understood. We were friends once.'

'That was a long time ago. Things change.'

'You don't trust me. I get it. But you can't live here in isolation for ever, like some exiled king awaiting his glorious return home. It's over. The world has moved on. The sooner you accept that, the better for you, believe me.'

'Why are you really here?'

'I told you,' said Damazeen, refilling his glass. 'I'm here to support Talal.'

'That sounds very generous.'

'I like to help people,' Damazeen said. His eyes were tinged with red from the wine. 'What if I said I could help you?'

'I'd tell you to go and peddle your stories elsewhere.'

'You haven't even heard what I am offering.'

'I don't need to hear. And stay away from the boy.'

'What if I told you I can give you your life back?'

But Makana had heard enough. As he pushed back the chair

to get to his feet, Damazeen tried to block his way, putting a hand on his arm to restrain him, which was a mistake. Hassan Saleh, the man who taught Makana self-defence in the police force, had been trained in East Germany. Descended from a long line of wrestlers in the Nuba Mountains, Hassan was short and squat and as hard to budge as a well-oiled boulder. For some reason they had become friends and Makana had been one of his best pupils. One of the first things he taught Makana was to act on instinct. When an opportunity is set before you, don't think, just act. Makana acted. He grasped hold of Damazeen's hand and twisted it in a clockwise direction, pressing outwards. It didn't take much force. Damazeen was off balance to begin with and the wine probably didn't help. He lurched back into the next table, tipped over a chair before tumbling to the ground. The bald waiter raised his eyes to the heavens. All that fuss about wine and see how it ends. Still, it pained Makana to see the disappointment on Talal's face. He patted him on the shoulder and smiled at Bunny, who twirled a ribbon around her finger.

Chapter Ten

Makana was left standing on the pavement in front of the *Binbashi* feeling annoyed with himself as much as anything else. He shouldn't have used violence. It was an unnecessary and vulgar display. He regretted having Talal witness it, but he knew why. Damazeen had triggered an old and deeply buried anger in him. Talal's father, Abdel Aziz, was arrested on returning from a trip to Cairo and charged with conspiring against the government. Makana had always suspected that the person who had tipped off the intelligence services about Abdel Aziz having met with members of the opposition in exile was none other than Damazeen himself.

A taxi was parked up under a large banyan tree and he climbed in without further hesitation and asked the driver to take him downtown. At that hour the traffic was light and in a little more than fifteen minutes he was in Aswani's. The garish white light from the flyspecked neon tubes that buzzed angrily on the walls was a welcome relief after contemplating dinner in a place where you could barely see your hand in front of your face, let alone what was on your plate.

Aswani was busy tending a grill that threw up gouts of flame as if he had a pocket-sized dragon hidden under the bars. Beads of sweat ran down his face as he dextrously flipped dozens of skewers threaded with kebab and kofta. Water hissed, steam rose in clouds, and orders flew left and right as his staff rushed back and forth to do his bidding. He resembled an ancient pagan sorcerer of some description. Makana found Sami sitting at the back at their usual table.

'It's busy tonight.'

'I wasn't expecting you for another hour or so,' Sami tapped his watch.

'Things didn't work out too well.'

'Really?'

'It's a long story.'

There was a plate of stuffed green peppers in front of Sami that he seemed not to have noticed, his nose being firmly tucked into a heap of newspapers spread out in front of him.

'Didn't you order anything else?' Makana asked as he sat down, suddenly hungry.

'I haven't ordered anything. These came by themselves.'

Makana sniffed the *maashi* cautiously. Aswani must be trying out a new dish. Still, he was willing to give it a try. He wiped a fork on a paper napkin and dug it in.

'So, you couldn't stay away from my food any longer, eh?'

Aswani waddled up to the table. His grubby shirt was generously dotted with pools of sweat and he was wiping his face with a dishcloth.

'Try my *maashi*, yet? The best in the city, I can assure you.'

'I'm sure you're right, but I was really looking forward to your kofta.'

'Ask and it shall be served.' Aswani gave a mock bow and wandered to the next table.

'So, what did you make of Father Macarius?' asked Sami.

'He's hiding something.'

'Hiding what? He's fighting to stay afloat.'

'Then what is he hiding?'

'You don't know that he's hiding anything. He's trying to help these kids. Do you have any idea how many there are? They run away, they fall into the hands of unscrupulous men who promise them money and in return abuse them.' Sami dug a fork into one of the stuffed peppers and chewed cautiously. 'And there he is, rebuilding a church that everyone had given up on and taking in kids from the streets. In another country they would give him a medal, but not here.'

A medal for what, Makana wondered. Survival, perhaps, in a hostile environment.

'The church doesn't want him around. He's a trouble maker.' Pushing another forkful of rice and roasted green pepper into his mouth, Sami chewed for a while. 'What makes you think he's hiding something?'

'He's a priest. Priests spend their lives trying to convince people they are telling the truth, which means they are not very good when it comes to telling lies.'

Makana watched Sami polish off the second stuffed pepper. He wasn't convinced this kind of sophistication would ever catch on with Aswani's clientele. People came here for grilled meat. If they wanted something fancy they went elsewhere, dark places with low lighting.

'There's something else I want you to help me with. The other night you told me that Hilal had caused a lot of trouble with his criticism of Islamic banking.'

'What he said was that they were exploiting people's sentiments to make a profit.'

'Why else would people invest their money in an Islamic bank? It makes them feel better.'

'Exactly. So when Hilal went after the Eastern Star Investment Bank a lot of people got very upset. He took them to pieces.'

'Over what?'

'Basically, their accounting was unsound. Hilal alleged there were huge loopholes out of which the directors took sizeable profits while paying investors a pittance.'

'So he upset the directors. Is it possible to get a list of the major shareholders and the management of the bank?' Makana paused. 'What's the matter?'

'I don't know. This country's in a mess. I mean, it feels like we're on the verge of civil war.'

'You really think it is as bad as that?'

'One thing is for sure. This is not happening by itself.'

'You're talking about what, a conspiracy?'

'I'm talking about . . . everything. You saw the crowd in Imbaba. There were agents there.'

'The *Merkezi*?'

'Exactly, Central Security Forces and their thugs. They are stirring it all up. They know it could explode at any moment. Muslim against Christian, and that would suit them fine.'

'Riots in the street. Churches burning down.'

'The whole thing.' Sami leaned in. 'The economy is in serious trouble. The rich are getting richer. The rest of us need two jobs just to get by.'

'You think they might be involved in the murder of these homeless children?'

'Why not?' Sami said. 'We both know how they operate. Who is going to mourn a child in torn clothes that has been sleeping rough, not eating well, probably sniffing glue and smoking *bango*?

All of that adds up to criminal activity. The police are not going to raise a finger.'

'And by killing them, they gain . . . what?'

'Have you seen the newspapers? The television? The country is going mad over this. The whole country is outraged that Christians are murdering little boys in some kind of ancient ritual.'

'Which is nonsense.'

'Sheikh Waheed talks about it, so there must be some truth to it.' Sami wagged a finger in the air. 'Anyway, my editor has quietly asked me to drop the story.'

'Did he say why?'

'He didn't have to. Someone made a phone call. It's like everything else. Besides, I understand perfectly. No editor in his right mind would publish a story claiming that State Security are trying to stir up anti-Christian feeling in order to take people's minds off the economy, right?'

Makana caught the eye of a man at the next table. Was he listening? Informers were notoriously rife. Sami appeared oblivious, and continued unabated.

'Tourists are too scared to come here. We would starve to death without American aid. We can't even grow enough to feed ourselves. Last year's presidential elections were a joke. Now they want to ban opposition parties. Parliament just extended the emergency laws for another three years. We've been living in a state of emergency since 1967. God, I could use a drink right now. A real drink, not these sugary sodas we are forced to consume. They are turning us into helpless children.'

Food was forgotten as cigarettes were lit.

'They talk about democratic reform. Clinton drops by to say a few words about Palestine and everyone shakes hands and smiles for the pictures.' Sami thumped the table with his hand, forgetting his surroundings. A few heads turned in their direction. Aswani waddled over to stand beside the table and set down a pile of kofta.

'Keep your voices down. I don't want to be closed down for running a hotbed of dissent.'

Aswani walked away, sharing a laugh with the man in grey at the next table, who gave Makana a cold, unresponsive stare.

'Did you hear what they did to that poor novelist?'

Makana had lost his appetite. Sami drew quick nervous puffs, the smoke reeling around his head. 'He got a six month suspended sentence for a book that was published eighteen years ago in Lebanon. Blasphemy?' He put his hands to his head. 'This country used to be the cultural centre of the region. We used to read everything. Now university students are banning Mohammed Choukri and all anyone wants is to draw a veil over their wives. I was thinking, maybe you could lend me some money, just for a time.'

'I thought your paper was paying you?'

'You know how it is, marriage is an expensive business. Rania is accustomed to a certain standard of living.'

Makana reached into his pocket for the money Faragalla had given him. 'How about I pay you for the information about this bank.'

'Sounds fair to me. Actually, a friend of mine, Nasser Hikmet, was supposed to be looking into the Eastern Star Investment Bank.'

'That should make it easy.' Makana handed over the banknotes and Sami counted them carefully.

'I take it you're paying for this,' Sami gestured at the food on the table. Makana reached into his pocket again.

Chapter Eleven

The following morning found Makana sitting in the dreary café inside the arcade, contemplating his second cigarette of the day. The coffee cup in front of him was drained but he was actually considering ordering another. Eissa, the boy behind the counter, was eagerly showing him a carton of cigarettes that he was willing to sell for a third of their price.

'You won't get them cheaper anywhere.'

'The question is, where did you get them?'

The boy grumbled something and slouched back behind the counter. When he looked up, Makana spotted Meera stepping in from the street, her figure silhouetted against the light behind her. She was strolling along, deep in thought. Once again, Makana was filled with an inexplicable sense of loss and regret that he couldn't explain to himself. He was, he realised, still thinking about the meeting with Damazeen the previous evening. Somehow it had brought back all the memories of Muna and the life they once had. What he had lost. This was what hurt. Meera was undoubtedly an attractive woman. The kind who could go a long way towards helping you forget your troubles. But all she did was remind him of the love he had once had and lost.

Still, he seemed unable to take his eyes off her and instead followed her progress. Halfway down the arcade she paused to study the window display in the clothes shop with the hijabbed mannequins. There was some irony to that. Her face lifted as someone stopped next to her. Yousef. On his way out, it seemed, pausing to light one of his foul-smelling menthol cigarettes. He lingered, glancing at his watch before walking on. Meera followed him with her eyes as he walked away, a puzzled look on her face, as if he had said something she hadn't quite caught. Later, Makana would play the sequence over and over in his head, trying to reconstruct the order in which it happened.

A man entered the arcade at almost the same moment Yousef exited. A slight figure, even shorter than Yousef, they almost bumped into one another. The man cannoned away quickly, head down. There was something odd about his posture, the way he walked, the fact that he was wearing an old army fatigue jacket. A woollen cap was pulled down over his head and the collar of his jacket was turned up. By now Makana was on his feet. He wasn't sure why, but he found his way blocked. A group of men were trying to get in through the narrow doorway. They were making a lot of noise, laughing amongst themselves. Pushing his way roughly past, Makana ignored the insults. Slowly. Everything seemed to be happening so slowly. The light flooding in through the entrance reduced everyone ahead of him to silhouettes. People passed between them, shadows obscuring his view. The man's face was half covered by a scarf. The distance between them was no more than twenty metres but the arcade seemed like a vast, endless hall. The man was fumbling inside his jacket, tearing at the folds. Meera bumped into the window behind her. The man's hand came free, holding something so big it looked like a toy in his hand. Makana could hear himself yelling a warning. The shots echoed through the enclosed space. Meera spun off balance, stumbling backwards, the glass exploding around her as she fell through into the interior.

It happened so quickly that it seemed to carry on repeating in front of his eyes. A mannequin burst into dust, parts flew into the air, the legs collapsing with tiny puffs of powder and smoke. There were screams now as people ducked, scattering in all directions. Makana was still moving forward. Brass casings clattered onto the cracked tiles. Clothes jerked spasmodically as if tugged by invisible fingers. Then the gun appeared to jam. It clicked a couple of times. The gunman pulled back the slide and released it, glimpsing movement out of the corner of his eye and turning just as Makana crashed into him. The man's yell was truncated as the two of them smashed through the window, a cracked pane of glass giving under them. The man seemed to weigh almost nothing. Makana's momentum knocked him flying as he himself went down. He saw the man roll and land on his side before leaping up lithely. Makana, sprawled on the floor, was looking down the barrel of the gun. The man pulled the trigger twice. Nothing happened. With a cry of fury he threw the gun and Makana put up a hand and felt it bounce off his forearm. He saw the man turn and run, limping away with a long shard of glass protruding from his calf muscle.

Getting to his knees Makana looked towards Meera. Her body twitched. When he turned back towards the entrance he saw onlookers leaping out of the gunman's way as he threw himself between them. Makana heard the high-pitched engine of a motorcycle being revved. He saw the gunman hop down the steps and go straight over the row of cars parked in the street, the soft metal flexing under him as he slid across and fell to the ground on the other side. Makana reached the entrance in time to see the gunman climb up and settle himself on the back of the motorcycle, as his accomplice twisted the throttle and the machine accelerated away.

Makana became aware of the commotion around him. People were shouting and jostling one another. Someone somewhere was wailing hysterically. Meera lay half inside the shattered display window on her back, one hand thrown up casually across her face, as if she might have been turning in her sleep. Her clothes were torn and bloody. All around her dismembered dummies lay scattered bizarrely. An arm here, a torso there. It resembled a massacre. She didn't seem to be breathing. He put out a hand to feel for a pulse in her neck and her hand came down and clung on to his. He looked into her eyes.

'Meera. Help is on the way.'

Her eyes seemed to search his face for something and he felt helpless, not knowing what it was she wanted to say. For a moment she trembled like that, her hand clutching his, and then she went still and her arm fell away.

'That was a brave thing you did. Foolish, but brave.'

Makana looked up to see a man in a brown shirt standing over him.

'An ambulance. Call an ambulance.'

'It's already on the way.' The man was holding a walkie-talkie in one hand. A plain-clothes *Merkezi* agent. 'Did you get a look at him?'

Makana had a vague recollection of a face half covered by a scarf. He wasn't sure he would recognise him if he was standing in front of him.

'Who was she?'

Makana realised his hands were bleeding. There was blood and glass everywhere. He looked down at Meera's broken body.

'She works here, upstairs.'

The man jabbed a finger at him. 'Don't go anywhere, a lot of people are going to want to speak to you.' He moved off, talking into his radio.

The sirens were converging, orders were being shouted. A loud drumming of boots approached as the police sealed off the arcade in their usual heavy-handed manner.

Meera's eyes were wide. Makana leaned over and plucked a piece of glass from her cheek. A trail of ruby-red blood traced itself down her face. In death she seemed somehow younger, as if all the worries had been lifted from her shoulders.

'What are you doing?'

Makana felt himself being hauled to his feet and held suspended between two large uniformed policemen. Blood trickled down from his forehead into his eye. In front of him an officer with brass buttons on his tunic thrust his bulbous nose into his face.

'Is this him? Are you the killer?' he demanded. The man in the brown shirt was busy elsewhere. The officer levelled a finger. 'Hold him well. Don't let him move until I am ready for him.'

Makana was hauled off, his toes dragging along the ground. His hands were wrenched behind his back and he felt handcuffs tightening around his wrists, cutting off the circulation. The policemen smelt of sweat and fear. They pushed him against the wall, forming a cordon around him. The officer came back over to yell at him some more, for no real reason other than he could not think of anything better to do.

'You're making a mistake,' Makana said.

'Who do you think you are talking to?' demanded the officer, prodding Makana in the stomach with his baton. He felt his legs give way and he sank down against the wall behind him.

Abu Salem was in tears. 'Hey, he risked his life. I saw him.'

'You want to join him, old man?'

'I saw the whole thing,' said the man in the brown shirt.

'I am the officer in charge and this man stays here until I say so.'

Everything suddenly changed. Three large black SUVs drew to a halt outside. Makana could see them through the legs of the uniformed men who formed a ring about him. American cars. Jeeps with flashing blue lights on the dashboard. State Security Investigations. Out of the cars came nine men in civilian clothes armed with light machine pistols hanging loosely from their shoulders. They spread out and started ordering people around. Nobody protested. The uniformed officers shuffled aside gamely, watching with their mouths hanging open. The hunchbacked *bawab* had produced a sheet from somewhere. None of the uniformed men had the courage to tell him not to cover the body up.

'It's not decent to leave her lying there like that,' Abu Salem fretted.

'Let him cover her up if he wants to.'

Abu Salem drew the sheet over Meera, leaving her bare right foot exposed. Makana wanted to go over and cover it. He struggled to get up only to be shoved back down again.

The man giving the orders wore a grey suit. He was tall and muscular, his hair shaved close to a hard, knobbly skull. The arcade was cleared. A perimeter was set up and a search instigated. The threat of a bomb had not occurred to the uniformed captain and he was trying hard to make up lost ground, chasing around on the heels of the shaven-headed officer like an obedient puppy.

'I want to know who the victim was, what was her name and what was she doing here?'

'Her name is Meera Hilal,' Makana said from the floor. 'She works at Blue Ibis Tours on the third floor. I told you all this already.'

The men around him cleared and the shaven-headed man peered down at Makana. 'Why is this man handcuffed?'

The captain repeated the same question to his men as if it was an affront to his dignity.

Bewildered, the uniformed men guarding Makana looked around them in confusion.

'I'll take it from here,' said the shaven-headed man.

The captain's flabby jowls flapped soundlessly for a moment. 'This is police business. We have a homicide inspector on the way.'

'Don't be stupid, man. This isn't a case of homicide, this is political.'

Makana found himself being hauled to his feet and thrust through the crowd and into the back of one of the Jeeps which had a section separated from the rest of the car by a wire screen. He was still handcuffed. He was alone, apart from the driver who sat behind the wheel fiddling with the short-wave radio.

'Who is that man?' Makana asked.

'Lieutenant Sharqi? He's the best. Ex-paratrooper.'

So they were a branch of military intelligence. But how and why had they become involved? And how were they alerted so quickly? Through the window Makana saw Yousef standing off to one side, talking to the man in the brown shirt. Were they just chatting, or was there a connection there? The front door of the Jeep opened and Lieutenant Sharqi leaned in.

'So, you see an armed man shooting and you attack him. Do you have military training?'

'I wasn't thinking clearly.' Makana rubbed his wrists.

'No, you weren't. It was a very foolish thing to do. You are lucky you weren't killed.' Sharqi studied Makana for a long moment. 'Also very brave. Did you get a look at him?'

'He had a scarf over his face.'

Someone handed him Makana's identity card.

'So, you are a guest in our country.'

'My papers are in order.'

'I'm sure they are.' Sharqi tapped the identity card against his thumb. 'A Coptic woman is gunned down, and a foreign man is the closest to her. Do you know what that adds up to?'

'No.'

'Neither do I, but I don't like it. Not one little bit.'

A crowd had gathered around the entrance to the building. Onlookers stared and speculated. Vendors slipped through holding up boxes of tissues, fly swats, plastic train sets driven by yellow bears. A police car pulled to a halt and Inspector Wasim Okasha got out, pushing people aside in his usual brusque fashion. Trucks unloaded trains of men with riot shields and batons who stood around looking bored. An ambulance siren played a hesitant ululation as it drew up to the entrance of the shopping arcade. It was obscured by people. The tumult cleared momentarily, the way a gust of wind parts a dust storm, and Makana glimpsed the covered stretcher being lifted unceremoniously over the row of parked cars, swaying anxiously in the air as if it might just slip loose and fly upwards into the sky, before disappearing into the forest of people once more.

II

The Voice of Reason

Chapter Twelve

Okasha's upper lip curled in distaste as his eye ran over the grubby walls of the café in the arcade. It was the most logical place to commandeer but that didn't mean he had to like it. The two of them were alone. One of his men guarded the door.

'How can such a place be allowed to operate? Aren't there laws about these things?'

'You tell me,' said Makana, gratefully lighting a cigarette. 'There's a boy who makes coffee. It's not bad. He'll sell you cigarettes as well, if you ask him nicely.'

'Okay, enough of the small talk. You have about two minutes to tell me how you managed to get mixed up in all this before the sheriff out there decides he can do what he wants.'

Okasha had made an impressive case of exerting his authority over Lieutenant Sharqi's boys. He was pretty good at throwing his weight around when he had to and he cut a powerful figure, but Makana had yet to see him better this performance. Legally within his jurisdiction, he argued, it would be a dereliction of his duty to let the crime go uninvestigated. A political crime, or whatever they wanted to call it, was still a homicide and that meant it was his case. Lieutenant Sharqi had beaten a hasty retreat and was now in his car in conference with persons unknown higher up the chain of command.

'Why are they so keen to take charge of this case?'

'You know what they are like, always barging in, as if the rest of us were just idiots waiting to be told what to do. How's your head?'

'Still in one piece, I think.' Makana touched a finger tenderly to the plaster that had been stuck across the cut on his forehead. 'What do you know about this Sharqi?'

'Oh, I've heard all about him. Bit of a high flyer. He was in the Special Forces Unit 777. They were specially created by Sadat, remember, and responsible for all kinds of cock-ups including that mess in Lanarka airport. Before his time, of course, but they tried to storm a hijacked plane and ended up killing most of the passengers. They were disbanded for a while and then reformed. Well, he's one of the new generation, trained by the Americans and all that.'

'How did he hear about this so fast?'

'You know what it's like. They have informers everywhere. Someone must have got the message back to him. Who knows, maybe he's been having a slow week,' Okasha snorted. 'Anyway, the point is that any minute now he's going to get a phone call giving him official control of the investigation and I'll have no choice but to comply.'

'Why would he want this case?'

'It's political.'

'You think it was intended that way?'

'Of course. Why kill her like that, if not to create a spectacle? Anyway, maybe no aeroplanes have been hijacked recently. Let's get on to what you are doing here, and don't tell me it's

114

to drink coffee. Speaking of which . . . where is this boy of yours?'

As he spoke, Okasha was moving restlessly about the small café, pausing here and there, peering out through the window for any sign of an approaching officer. Moving behind the counter he flicked the pair of boxing gloves on the wall and grimaced at the state of the facilities. There was no sign of Eissa.

'I was hired by a man upstairs – Faragalla. He thought someone was sending him threats.'

'Threats? What kind of threats?'

'A series of letters. Anyway, it turns out they were meant for her.'

'Why would anyone want to kill her?'

'I don't think they did. I think they wanted to scare her.'

'That's fine, except we have a dead woman out there. That's not a threat any more, that's murder. I'll need you to hand these letters over.'

'Her husband is Ridwan Hilal.'

Okasha swore. 'This is going to stir up the press, which means the politicians are going to have their say, which means they are going to make my life hell.'

'There was a man next to me the instant it happened.'

'Coincidence. Could be anything.'

'Coincidence that he had a two-way radio? He's the reason they got here so quickly.'

Okasha lifted a dirty coffee pot and dropped it into the sink. 'You're too paranoid, and I say this as a friend. Why was a woman like that working in a place like this?'

'She lost her job when her husband was thrown out of the university.'

'Why didn't they leave? Life can't have been easy. They both lost their positions.'

'They believed in this country.'

'May Allah bestow His blessings upon them.'

Makana looked down the arcade towards the broken shop window and the people gathered around the spot where Meera had died. He could see one of Sharqi's men being fielded by one of Okasha's officers, who had no doubt been briefed to stall them for as long as possible.

'Okay,' said Okasha, seeing the same thing. 'Time's almost up. This case is going to be out of my hands in about two minutes. I need to see those letters, so do yourself a favour and don't tell him about them.'

'You're asking me not to tell him what I know? Isn't that illegal? And why do you want the letters if he's going to take over the case?'

'Because we both know Sharqi is going to run around and shoot a few people like a good boy and make the minister fall in love with him all over again, but the case is not going to get solved. Then it will get thrown back to me, like you throw a bone to a dog,' Okasha grimaced. 'And it will be up to me to solve the case or lose my job. I speak to you as one policeman to another. I need as much help as I can get and that means it's your turn to do me a favour. He probably won't even bother to question you again.'

Okasha was spelling out his limitations. He would go out of the way to help him so long as there was no conflict with his own orders. It was the one thing about him Makana had never under-stood, Okasha's adherence to the rules, when everything around him reeked of corruption and incompetence.

'Lieutenant Sharqi would like a word with you, sir,' said the plain-clothes man, having made it through Okasha's fence.

116

'Thank you, I'll be right there,' Okasha said.

'What about me?' Makana asked.

The man glanced at him and shrugged. 'You're free to go.'

Okasha raised his eyebrows as if to say, I told you so.

Makana did some shopping on his way home, stocking up on cigarettes from a twelve-year-old on a corner which reminded him of Eissa and his stolen cigarettes. He wondered where he had got to. Some instinct made him stop at a grocery store that was so crowded with goods there was barely room for customers. He had to edge his way up and down the cramped aisles trying to remember what the point of food was and idly picking up a couple of tins, fava beans and stuffed vine leaves, and even recklessly adding Spanish sardines and a packet of pasta made with American wheat. He was standing in line to pay when the whole idea of eating struck him as completely absurd and leaving his goods on the counter he walked straight out.

On the upper deck of the *awama* he slumped back into the old armchair and gazed out over the railings at the river and the distant bridge. The sound of children's laughter drifted across the river from a playground in one of the leisure clubs on the Zamalek side. It made him think of Nasra. His daughter would have been nearly sixteen by now. A feeling of great sadness came over him and the events of ten years ago came back as if they had occurred only yesterday.

Meera's death puzzled him. If the intention was to kill her as a political statement why had the gunman not cried '*Allahu akbar*' or some other religious sentiment? If not religion, then what was the motive? And there was something else, something about the shooter that had lodged awkwardly in his head. He replayed the whole event in his mind over and over.

After a time he realised that thinking made him hungry after all. In the kitchen he found the remains of a pot of koshari he had bought from Abu Siniya's stand under the overpass four days ago. It didn't smell too bad and with a squeeze of lime juice and some hot pepper it was miraculously restored to something edible. He started eating and then thought of something, so he set down the pot and went out onto the lower deck. He moved aft to a point where he lay down against the cold wood and reached down over the side, his hand scrabbling about until he found the narrow chain. He hauled it up carefully, the water trickling over his fingers and wetting his clothes. At the end of the chain a sturdy canvas bag was tied. Unlocking the chain he opened this and reached inside to extract a heavy plastic bag. Retying the canvas and making sure the horseshoe inside it was still there, he dropped it back over the side, hearing the chain paying itself out.

Back upstairs he opened the plastic bag and took out a cloth-wrapped package that was dry. Inside was a 9mm Beretta. Makana spent the next hour or so taking the gun to pieces, cleaning it carefully and oiling it. He didn't like guns, but this seemed like a good moment to become reacquainted with one. Checking the shells in the clip he put the whole thing back together again. He had taken the gun from somebody a few years ago and held onto it since. Officially, he had no licence for it and kept it for emergencies only, which he felt this qualified as.

It was while he was reassembling the gun that he recalled the sight of the gun in the hand of the killer. It had seemed big, more than big. It had made him think of a toy. And there was another thing. When he had crashed into him and brought him down, he had been surprised at how little the man weighed. He set the Beretta down on the table. It hadn't been a man at all, he realised. The killer had been a boy.

Chapter Thirteen

Meera's death sent the country into a state of shock. A Christian woman gunned down in broad daylight. The spectacular nature of the crime triggered a wave of nationwide soul-searching. What does this say about us? The question was repeated in countless variations by a string of columnists and editors, talkshow hosts and taxi drivers. Rumours proliferated and there was no end to the speculation. Conspiracy theory worked overtime, producing a number of scenarios: it was a plot designed to get Christians to leave the country; a secret list had been found of targets, all of them high-profile Copts. According to this theory Meera was targeted because of the controversy generated by her marriage. The more lurid sectors of the press suggested she was an Israeli spy who had been silenced for refusing to betray Egypt any longer. The hot metal of the presses buzzed furiously as one rumour arrived hard on the heels of the next. Everyone had an opinion. And the anger spilled out onto the surface. A family in Mar Girgis were pulled from their car and set upon. The car was torched while bystanders stood idly by. A church in Qena was attacked – two people killed, fourteen sent to hospital. Angry mobs charged through the streets demanding . . . What were they demanding? No one seemed quite sure. Various ministers appeared on television making statements to the effect that justice would be served and the culprits tracked down. No one held their breath. Meera's death was eclipsed by the outrage it had provoked.

'You're a hero, you know.' The little girl held up a grainy picture of what looked like a statue of a poor relation of Ramses II brought up from the bottom of a muddy lake. Where they had managed to get a picture of him he had no idea. Aziza brought the papers up every morning. She sat cross-legged on the floor as she read.

'Who is the mystery man who took his life into his hands? What was his relation to the young and attractive victim?' Aziza looked up. 'You were in love with her?' Makana pulled a face and Umm Ali's little girl went back to her reading. 'Police sources confirm the man is known to them. Does this explain his shyness in coming forward to talk to the press?'

'Aziza! Aziza!'

The girl closed her eyes, silently wishing the voice to go away. It only grew more insistent.

'I'm hungry. You need to go and fetch me my breakfast!'

'Why doesn't he just die?' she asked, then her face brightened. 'Maybe I could poison him?'

'He's your uncle.'

'I'll bet you know all about poisons.'

'Just go,' he said, shooing her on her way. Afterwards, Makana went back to his reading. At noon he decided that enough days had passed for it to be a decent time for him to pay his respects to the family.

He took the riverbus across to Zamalek and walked the rest of the way. It wasn't hard to find the house. Meera had pointed out

120

the tree-lined street on the afternoon when they went to the Alhambra café. Now the narrow entrance was crowded with people and a lorry filled with folding chairs. A faded set of coloured drapes had been put up to fence off the street. A police saloon was parked against the wall. Three officers leered at him as Makana made his way through workers ferrying stacks of chairs only to find his way blocked by a group of young men.

'What's your business here?' the leader asked as he stepped forward.

'I'm here to see Doctor Hilal.'

'Well, you have no business with him if you don't tell us what it's about.'

Makana had seen him before somewhere. He had high cheek-bones that looked like bruises and eyes like wet stones. A stout man with a neck like a *gamous* stepped between them. He looked Makana up and down.

'Don't worry, Ishaq,' he said, 'this one's not going to cause any trouble.'

'You must scare a lot of people talking like that,' said Makana.

He brought his face closer. He smelled vaguely of fish. 'Are *you* scared?'

'Oh, I'm scared all right. I'm shaking so badly I can hardly stand up.'

One of the others giggled and the stout man glared at him.

'I'm not here to cause trouble. I was a friend of Meera's. I was with her when she died.'

'That was you?' The one named Ishaq pushed forward again. Makana noticed that a couple of the young men were wearing T-shirts printed with the logo of the Seraph Sporting Club.

'Does Father Macarius know you are here?'

'You know Father Macarius?' In the right light he might have been considered handsome. He clearly thought he would have made a fine film star on any day of the week. His hair was long, oiled and combed back like a dog's pelt after a heavy rain. He jerked his head indicating Makana could pass.

'Just watch your step.'

'I'll do my best,' said Makana, winking at the bullish one who was breathing hard enough to burst a blood vessel.

The apartment building had a high surrounding wall painted a sandy-brown colour and a metal gate that stood open. It had about it a gentle air of dereliction and more than a hint of long-gone glory. Beyond this was a garden of sorts. A row of heavy plant pots on the steps leading to the entrance contained huge cacti whose leaves flopped around like the flailing hands of mad clocks. In the front hall more men wearing shirts with the eight-winged seraph motif waved him up to the first floor. Around the doorway to the flat, other men stood together speaking in low voices. They stepped aside for him to enter.

The flat was dark and gloomy with death. The narrow hallway was further constricted by the books that covered every available surface: fitted bookcases, hastily put up shelves, crooked tables, all to stem the flood which eventually spilled into heaps on the floor. Directly opposite the front door was a living room where a number of women sat in reverent silence. Others came and went through a side door carrying trays laden with biscuits and cups of tea. Close friends and family, Makana guessed, from young nieces to wizened aunts. Some in headscarves, others wearing crosses, they appeared to hail from both sides of the family.

'Can I help you?'

On turning, Makana found himself facing Meera. A larger, cruder version of the original. Shorter and bulkier, padded in hips and face where the original had been lean and economical. The effect was unsettling.

'I'm here to see Doctor Hilal.'

'We are only welcoming family members at this time.' She wrung her hands together as if squeezing a cake of soap. Her hair was dark like Meera's but combed back in a fierce bun that pulled her eyebrows apart horizontally, like the splayed wings of a dragonfly.

'It is urgent that I speak with him. My name is Makana.'

By now the conversation around them had come to a halt. The assortment of widows, spinsters and aunts had fallen silent. Tea went undrunk, biscuits remained unswallowed. A certain tension had entered the room. All eyes were now on him.

'Can you at least tell me what this concerns?'

'No, I'm afraid I can't.'

The woman's face grew livid. Her cheeks flushed. Behind her, he could hear the women whispering. He knew what they were saying and she said it for them.

'You are not welcome here at this time.'

'Maysoun, please.'

With a heavy sigh, a large figure shuffled forwards in the gloom. Ridwan Hilal was an untidy, overweight man, with a voice like a baritone. The walls rumbled as he approached. Another deeper silence fell over the women in the room. Hilal had thick, fleshy lips and thinning hair that looked as if it might have contained a recently abandoned bird's nest. He was wearing black trousers and a white shirt that was buttoned up to the neck and whose tails had come loose. His face was slick with the sheen of a man who has just awoken from a nightmare to discover it was all true. Breathing hard from his exertions, he stared at Makana.

'Do I know you?'

'My name is Makana. I knew your wife.'

The keen eyes fixed on him as sharp as any bird of prey and there was a brief nod in response.

'Yes, of course.' Hilal pursed his lips. 'You were with her when she died.'

A rustle went through the room. It seemed to shake Ridwan Hilal out of his stupor. He lifted a large paw like a soft lump of dough and gestured.

'Come with me. We cannot talk here.'

Like buzzing insects, the voices of the women scrabbled along the corridor behind them as Makana followed the doctor. At the end of the dark hall was a study. Here, too, the walls were covered with bookshelves. There was a desk next to the window, which was shuttered. Somewhere in the distance the muezzin started his call for the sunset prayer. The smell of stale cigar smoke hung in the air. Ridwan Hilal eased himself down into a padded armchair behind the desk that looked as if someone had beaten the life out of it. He gave an exhausted sigh and passed a hand over his beard before remembering he was not alone. He opened his eyes and gestured at a chair pushed back against the wall. The eyes were dark and buried under thick eyebrows that jutted out from his head. Makana's gaze fell on a photograph of Meera as a young woman. Ridwan Hilal noticed, and leaned forward to lift the frame off the desk.

'She told me about you,' Hilal said. 'She wanted us to talk, you know.'

'Yes, I'm sorry we couldn't meet under more pleasant circumstances.'

'Have you ever been in love?'

'A long time ago.'

'Before I met Meera I knew nothing about love. I read poetry. I studied it, analysed it. I even wrote papers on the stuff. But it was only when I met her that I realised I had never understood a word of it.' He blinked nervously as he spoke. 'Without her I am the same bumbling fool I always was. Perhaps that is the way of things. Love is a brief light that when it fades leaves the world darker than it ever was.' He set down the picture and sat for a moment gazing at it before looking up. 'Why have you come here?'

'I spoke to Meera the day before she died. She believed that she was in danger.' Makana reached into his pocket to produce the copies he had made. He set them down on the desk. 'Have you seen these before?'

Hilal glanced over the sheets in front of him before giving a shake of his head.

'That's probably because she didn't want to worry you. She believed they were a threat meant for her personally.'

Hilal leaned back in the chair, large hands clasped together over his sizeable paunch. 'Are you suggesting that these letters are related to her death?'

'Meera thought so.'

'This is the Sura of *Al-Nejm*. We look to the stars for direction. Stars are not threats, Mr Makana, they are a portent of something bad or evil. A warning.'

'You think someone was trying to warn Meera that she was in danger?'

'That is what I would have said, had she asked my opinion. My wife had a strong sense of drama, which is probably why she interpreted these as a threat.'

'You're sure of that, even now?'

'Certainly. My wife had little time for religious texts. That was my department. She excelled in English literature. She knew them all. Pinter, Bond, Beckett, as well as the classics of course. Marlowe and, naturally, Shakespeare, whom some of our Islamic brothers believe was an Arabic sheikh. Ignorance knows no bounds, Mr Makana.'

Once he got started nothing stopped, or even slowed down Ridwan Hilal. The big hands rested on his large belly and he lowered his head to stare at Makana.

'I repeat my question. Why are you here, Mr Makana?'

'I was hired by Mr Faragalla at the Blue Ibis company. He thought one of the letters were a threat aimed at him. That might still be the case. Meera understood them to be meant for her. She talked to me about them. She wanted me to talk to you.'

'Why would she want you to talk to me?'

'I think she thought I might be able to persuade you to go abroad.'

Hilal was silent for a moment. 'Are you saying that we might have prevented what happened?'

'Meera knew she could never hope to persuade you to go abroad. I don't think she wanted to go herself, but I believe she was considering the idea. She was scared.'

'She was one of the bravest women I ever met.' The big head rolled from side to side like a melon balanced on a stick. His voice was anguished. 'Do you know what a crime it was for her to have to work in that awful place? A travel agency? With her intelligence? Her learning? She could talk to you for hours about Hardy and George Eliot and make you want to run instantly to read them all. She inspired people.' He bit his lip. 'I was against it. I told her it was beneath her, but she insisted. She went out and found the job herself without telling me a word. Your work is the most important thing, she would say.'

There didn't seem to be much to say in response to that, so Makana remained silent. But thinking about his wife seemed to knock the last vestiges of resistance out of Ridwan Hilal and his head bowed with a sigh like a gasp. A drop fell with a loud plop onto the table. With a sniff, he wiped a hand across his nose and looked around for a handkerchief. Makana passed him a box of tissues lying on the desk.

'It's true she didn't want to worry me, Mr Makana. I have a heart condition. The doctor says I am to avoid stress, which in this world is like trying to stop breathing.' Hilal spread his plump fingers in the air. 'Now, I have police protection. Twenty-four hours a day. What good is that, when they have taken the one thing that matters to me? Those bullets were meant for me, and frankly they could not have done a better job. I am as good as dead right now.'

'This was a professional execution. If they were meant for you, they would have hit you instead of her.'

'But why would anyone want to kill her?' Ridwan Hilal was sitting on the edge of his seat now, his hands gripping the armrests. His stomach heaved as he tried to draw breath. Sweat was beginning to form damp patches on his shirt. 'Please,' he wheezed impatiently, 'whatever you have on your mind, I want to hear it.'

'If she was the intended target then there has to be a reason someone wanted her dead.'

A heavy paw lifted and dropped to the armrest. 'Meera's only crime in life was to marry me. She could not offend anyone. Look outside. Her former students have come to guard her home.'

'There was nothing controversial about her work?'

'She taught literature.' Hilal looked pained. 'Shakespeare, Virginia Woolf. Things that are too complicated to offend people. They would need a modicum of intelligence.' His hands still gripped the arms, as if he couldn't decide whether to break the things or fling them across the table.

Makana took a moment to study the man who had been branded an apostate. His detractors claimed he had taken the sacred book and treated it like a historical dissertation that had not aged well. Was it any surprise some people wanted him dead? Another thought occurred to him. Was it possible that Hilal could have arranged to have his wife killed? He would have needed a strong flair for the dramatic to attempt it this way. A man of his intellectual prowess could surely have worked out a dozen quieter ways of getting the job done. Besides, the sad figure before him told its own story. Makana found himself distracted by the question of what had drawn Meera to this man in the first place. An intellectual attraction of like minds? Now that she was gone, Makana found himself wishing he had had a chance to get to know her better.

'Violence marks our complete failure as human beings,' mumbled Hilal. 'Physical brutality makes us no better than dogs.'

'Unfortunately, there are still enough dogs about to complicate matters for the rest of us.'

The professor gave a brief, concessionary nod. He passed a hand over his eyes.

'I'd like your permission to look into her murder.'

The heavy-lidded eyes jerked open. 'Money? Is that what you are after?'

'I don't need your money. I am still employed by Mr Faragalla, which means I am obliged to inform him of what I find. But I would feel better knowing that I had your consent.'

'I can't see what good can come of this. I would prefer Meera to be left to rest in peace. Can you understand that?'

'Certainly. But until we understand why this happened other people might be at risk.'

Hilal's mournful eyes darted around the walls, as if expecting them to cave in on him at any moment. 'Mr Makana, if I understand correctly, you blame yourself in some way for what happened to Meera. I understand. Speaking for myself, I am convinced that you proved your bravery by trying to go to her aid during the attack. You cannot be held responsible for the actions of a mad man.' He handed Makana a card. 'That is my private number,' he said, pointing to the telephone on the desk. Call me at any time, day or night. I am willing to cooperate in any way.'

Makana left him there, holding the picture of his wife in one hand and copies of the letters that might have killed her in the other. A shipwrecked man clinging to the debris of his life. As he made his way back across the city, Makana wondered if Hilal was right, if maybe he was taking Meera's death too personally. It was one of those questions to which he had no particular interest in finding an answer.

Chapter Fourteen

'I don't know why I came in today. Allah knows there isn't any work to do.'

Surprisingly, it was Arwa, the headscarf-wearing, gum-chewing sceptic who appeared to have been most touched by Meera's death.

Meera's desk was now buried under a small hill of flowers. They had arrived from people in the office, the building and even beyond, from the entire city even, judging by the cards and little messages that had been delivered. Strangers turned up at the door holding fancy cellophane-wrapped bundles. Others strode in carrying wilting handfuls of grey roses, plucked from an exhausted roadside park nearby. The desk had otherwise been completely cleared. No files, folders, even the computer had been unplugged and disconnected. Arwa gave another loud sniff.

'My husband says they all should go. The country would be purer without them, but he is an idiot and doesn't even say his prayers regularly.'

'Where are her things?'

'Yousef cleared it all out. He enjoyed that.' She dabbed at her eyes. 'That dog was glad to see her go. She was the only one who took the work seriously and they couldn't wait to get rid of her. Does that make any sense?'

'It looks like someone cared for her.'

'This is an Egyptian thing,' she said, pointing at the heap of flowers. 'Those crazy bearded men tell you it's wrong. That this is all pagan tradition, nothing to do with Islam. Who cares what it is, it's beautiful to see how people decorate the graves of their loved ones, right? We're not animals.' Another loud sniff followed by a vigorous rub of her bulbous nose. 'I feel bad about some of the things I said to her. We're all Egyptians, *mush kedda*? I mean, at the end of the day that's what it's all about. I should never have come in today.'

'It's probably good to keep yourself busy.'

'Busy? In this place? That's a laugh. There's hardly enough to keep one of us occupied.'

Makana watched her as she pottered about, sniffing and sobbing, arranging the flowers on Meera's desk, pausing to dab her eyes.

'The sad thing is I barely knew her. She never talked about herself. Wild horses wouldn't drag words out of her.' Arwa broke off to lift a telephone that was ringing and barked into the receiver. 'Who? No, he's not here. We are not working today. Why? Don't you read the newspapers, you donkey?' She slammed the phone down and sniffed. 'Even if she was married to that terrible man, so what? What can we do about the men we marry? If my husband was as smart as he thinks he is, we would be living in a palace instead of a hovel fit only for six-legged creatures. He said her husband lost his job because he was a blasphemer. I don't believe it. She was a smart woman. Imagine, she could have been teaching at university, but here she was, working with us. That tells you a lot. She never looked down her nose at any of us, which is more than can be said for some. You know why people say those things? Because they can't stand the idea of a woman making something of herself. Even my stupid husband. All men are the same.'

'She never talked about being in trouble?'

'She kept to herself. Well, except for Ramy.'

'Ramy? You mean Faragalla's nephew?'

'They were friends for a time. Of course, that got everyone talking. People have evil tongues.' Arwa raised an eyebrow. 'What do we know about anyone, right? I mean, here am I talking to you like I've known you all my life, but I don't even know that it's true about you being here to help us.'

'Why shouldn't it be?'

'You don't look like an accountant. They have flat heads and narrow eyes.' She twirled a length of red twine that had come loose from a bouquet of orchids. 'My husband says you are probably with the police.'

'Why would he say something like that?'

'And that's the other thing,' Arwa jabbed a stubby finger at him. 'You always answer a question with another question.'

'It's a bad habit, I'm sorry. You said she was close to Ramy?'

'Like I said, there were a lot of malicious whispers.' She gave another sniff. 'Not that I had anything to do with that.'

'Of course not.'

'No, she was a decent person. Worked harder than anyone else. She was in here first thing in the morning and didn't leave until last.'

'What exactly did Ramy do to be sent away?'

'Oh, he's not a bad person, but he's young and not too good about keeping away from trouble.' She picked at a thread on her sleeve, as if absenting herself from this conversation for a moment, before bouncing back. 'It's that Rocky from downstairs.'

'Rocky?'

'You know, like the film? Honestly, anyone would think you had been living in a cave. I don't know why they call him that, but everyone does. He's the one who runs the *'ahwa* downstairs. He's up to all kinds of mischief that one.' Arwa lowered her voice to a whisper. 'If you ask me, that's why she was killed.'

'Because of Rocky?'

'No.' Arwa glanced around her briskly. 'Hashish.'

'Hashish?'

'Rocky sells it and Ramy smokes it 'til it comes out of his ears.' She nodded as she spoke as if agreeing with herself. 'Also I heard he was messing with some of the clients. Women.'

'Women? Tourists, you mean?'

'I mean the kind young men have shameful thoughts about.'

'How do you know this?'

'Because men are all the same. No better than animals, most of them.'

'No, I mean about Ramy being involved with them.'

'I hear a lot of things,' Arwa said confidently. 'So did Meera. Maybe she told Faragalla. You think that's why she was killed? That's the other thing you do. Either you answer a question with a question or you go all silent. Where's the fun in that?'

Before Makana could manage to process what Arwa had just told him, Yousef swept in. As usual, wearing his leather jacket and carrying the briefcase that seemed to go everywhere with him.

'I thought we were going to clear this out?' he snapped, staring at the heap of flowers.

'Spoken like a man with a stone for a heart.'

133

Yousef turned to her. He looked as though he were about to say something, but then changed his mind.

'We just had a tragedy here, a real tragedy,' she went on, fiddling with the flowers.

'That's no reason for the whole world to stop, is it? Tragedies happen every day.' Yousef marched over to his desk, shrugged off his jacket and began rolling up his shirt sleeves. 'Unless you happened not to notice, this company is fighting for its survival. Now, I advise you to stop thinking about the past and concentrate on your future, because without this company you don't have one.'

Arwa stared at Yousef's back for a time and then idly started turning sheets of paper over. She exchanged a long glance with Makana, as if to say, this is how I pretend to be working.

Faragalla appeared and summoned Makana into his office immediately, closing the door quickly behind him.

'You see now what I told you?'

Makana watched him trying to slide himself behind the desk, dislodging another avalanche of folders and papers, which fell to the floor and were instantly forgotten. The heavy bags under the sunken eyes seemed more swollen. Faragalla leaned his hands on the desk.

'I was right. It was a warning.'

'What are you talking about?'

'This, the killing. They shot that woman as a warning to me.' Faragalla straightened up and moved over to peer out through the dirty, broken wooden shutters. 'We have no idea who they are, or what they look like.'

'I don't think we need to panic.'

'Oh, you don't, eh? Then what should I do? I mean, have you found anything?'

'It's too early to say. The counter-terrorism unit are onto it, under a Lieutenant Sharqi.'

'I know all that. That's not why I am paying you. They'll never find anything. You know what they are like. Like anyone working for the government, they do the least they can without getting fired. I hired you to get to the bottom of all this.'

'I can tell you that there were more letters.'

'More?' Faragalla seemed to stagger. He put a hand to the desk to steady himself. 'More of the same you mean? Where were they? Why didn't I know about this?'

'Meera thought they were meant for her.'

'Poor woman. She didn't deserve to die like that. I regret talking badly about the dead, but she should have told me who she was. I mean, imagine not telling me who her husband was.'

'She was afraid you would fire her if you knew.'

'Really? Well that's just . . .' He sank down into his chair with a thoughtful expression on his face and reached for his pipe. 'She should have come to me about these letters.'

'When you hired me I asked if you could think of anyone who might have an interest in seeing this company ruined. Have you had any further thoughts on the subject?'

'Are you joking? All my rivals are sending me messages of sympathy. We all have to stand together, they say. If one of us goes down it's only a matter of time before all of us do. Secretly, of course, they are hoping this will finish me off and they can close in and pick up my business.' Faragalla puffed away nervously. 'Who knows, maybe there is some way of turning this to our advantage. I'm calling a press conference this afternoon. Put a determined face on it. Let them know that we don't scare easily. We have a tradition to defend. In my grandfather's day there was respect for our profession.'

'So, I take it you want me to carry on with the investigation?'

'Why do you think I am paying you? Get to the bottom of this. And I want to be informed of any progress you make. Anything at all, you understand?'

When he came out of the office Yousef was waiting for him. He nodded for Makana to follow him out. As they walked down the stairs, Yousef paused to flick his cigarette through a window with no glass.

'What did the old man want?'

'He's worried. This whole thing has shaken everybody.'

'You turned out quite the hero,' smiled Yousef.

'The papers exaggerate, it's their business.'

'No, I heard you really did go for the gunman. That takes guts, or was it something else?'

'What are you talking about?'

'I don't know,' Yousef said with a sly look. 'I saw the way you watched her.'

'You see what you want to see.'

'Come on, I'm joking. You were in the army, weren't you?'

'So what if I was?'

'Nothing. We have to look out for one another, that's all.' Yousef reached into his jacket and came up with an envelope which he handed over. 'I need you to run an errand for me.'

'What kind of errand?' The envelope was full of cash.

'The kind that makes you lots of money. Go back to the place we went to the other day.' A map sketched on the back of the envelope showed the route to the House of Birds. 'The old man will give you a package which you bring straight back to me. Think you can manage that? Tell him there won't be more work for a while. We need to lay low until all this fuss blows over.'

Life in the arcade was slowly returning to normal. Broken windows had been covered with flattened cardboard boxes held together with adhesive tape on which Mickey Mouse and his friends gambolled jauntily along. Two police officers stood by the street entrance and a third sat on a chair picking his nose, a scarred AK47 bridged across his knees.

Eissa was back behind the counter. His forearm was wrapped in plaster.

'You've been in the wars. How's the arm?'

'Yeah,' the boy grinned, holding it up. 'It itches.'

'How did you break it?'

'A fight.'

'At the gym?'

'No.' Eissa laughed revealing a set of remarkably dirty teeth.

'You get into a lot of fights, do you?'

'A few. People come looking for trouble . . .'

'You heard about Meera?'

The boy dropped his head to stare into the sink in front of him. He busied himself with washing the dirty glasses.

'You knew her quite well, didn't you?' Makana said. There was no reply. After a time he realised the boy was no longer stirring the dishes. He was just looking at them.

'She was a good person,' said the boy without lifting his head. 'She didn't deserve to die.'

'No, she didn't.'

After a time Eissa resumed his washing up.

'About those cigarettes.'

Eissa sniffed and wiped his bare arm over his face. 'You want me to get you some? How about a couple of cartons?' He still had his back to Makana.

'Can you get me that many? Or do you need to ask Rocky?'

'I don't need to ask Rocky anything.'

'Okay, well, I'd still like to know where they come from.'

'What difference does it make?' he said, turning to face Makana. 'They're the same cigarettes you buy in the street, but half the price.' Eissa picked up a rag and began drying his hands. 'So, you want them or not?'

'If you think you can get them by yourself.'

'I just said I would,' snapped the boy, turning away again. 'Come back tomorrow.'

Half an hour later, Makana was retracing his steps from the day when he had followed Yousef. The square with arches around three sides looked much the same except the colonnades were now filled with deep shadows. A rat squeaked somewhere underfoot. In the centre of the square a stone pedestal housed a circular well that had long since been filled in. The square was so perfectly sealed it appeared as if the walls had closed in behind him, obscuring the way in and out. He reached the wooden door decorated with iron birds. An old Ottoman-style house that had once been a caravanserai, a resting place for merchants who had travelled for weeks at a time, carrying ivory and gold from the interior of the continent, incense and silk from Syria and Baghdad. In the Middle Ages, Cairo was larger than Venice, a vast city of legend, and anyone with an interest in trade had to come here. The door had a heavy iron grille in the middle. A handle was set into the stone wall beside it. On pulling this Makana was rewarded with the tinkle of a bell somewhere far off. After a time footsteps approached and the door creaked open to reveal a young boy of around fourteen wearing a blue gelabiya and a red tarboosh.

'Is the master of the house in?'

Without a word, the boy stepped aside, bowing for him to

enter. Makana felt as though he was stepping into another age. The narrow yard was well tended with flowers and grass, which gave it the aspect of a verdant oasis in the midst of the city. A path led to a small archway and a stone staircase. Beyond were buildings that once were stables, kitchens and stores.

The boy led the way up the stairs which wound about a stone pillar scarred by centuries, rubbed smooth by countless hands. A gallery led through the building, past a window alcove that jutted out over the garden and was decorated by an elaborate carved *mashrabiya*. Traditionally, these window screens allowed the women of the house to observe visitors discreetly, without being seen themselves. In the gallery dozens of birdcages were hanging on long chains from the rafters high above. They were a variety of shapes and sizes and were suspended at different heights. Large, small, round, square, some made of wood, others of iron. There were even some made of ornate silver and gold. The birds they contained displayed an astonishing array of colours and types. Makana was no ornithologist. He might claim to know the difference between a chicken and a pigeon if they were on a plate in front of him, but that was about the size of it. But even he recognised that these creatures were remarkable. The overall effect was like looking at a wall of living flame going from orange to green, to red and yellow, through every brilliant shade of the spectrum.

Another open doorway and three steps led into a circular room lined with books. A few small birds (or were they bats?) fluttered about high above, flitting from one side to the other. It was as Makana might have imagined the library of a wise king. Perched high on a ladder on one of the walls of paper was an old knot of a man wearing dark glasses.

'Hello, Yunis.'

The two men had met some years ago. In those days, Yunis had run his forgery business from inside an old junk shop in the bazaar. Now the old man climbed carefully down and clucked his tongue when he looked at Makana. Without a word Old Yunis led the way back through the gallery of birds to the enclosed balcony where a cool breeze came in through the wooden lattice. He sat down on the carpet and crossed his legs. Makana followed suit.

'You look well.'

'The doctor says these help to keep the cataracts under control,' Yunis removed the dark glasses. 'But I don't think he knows what he's talking about. I can hardly see a thing.' The beady eyes flickered with fury. The years had not dulled his edge. The hollow face had the texture of old wood. He reached into the pocket of his black gelabiya and produced a packet of cigarettes.

'My other doctor tells me I should smoke because my blood pressure is too low.' He struck a match and champed his lips around the filter. 'He too is a fool, but his advice amuses me.'

'I like the birds.'

'Our Lord never misses an opportunity to teach us a lesson in humility. I dreamed all my life of having a collection of beautiful birds. And now that I have them I can barely see them. I can hear them, though, which is some consolation.'

'Do you know why I am here?'

'Your conscience tells you that you have ignored your old friends for far too long?'

Makana was secretly touched that he should qualify as a friend.

'I was here the other day, or rather, I waited outside while Yousef came to pay you a visit.'

'Ah, yes, the elusive Mr Yousef. Since when have you started working for such lowlife?'

'Yousef thinks he can trust me and I'd like to keep it that way for a while.' Makana passed him the envelope.

'You never come to visit me and now you need my help.' Yunis opened the envelope and flipped through the stack of banknotes before putting it to one side. Then he turned to an elaborate chest, made of polished mahogany with a mother of pearl inlay, set against the wall. Pressing a secret panel, he folded back two doors to reveal rows of compartments. From one of these Yunis produced an envelope. It contained a collection of European passports: three Spanish, one French, one Italian, two British. Makana turned the pages slowly. Stamps showed they had arrived at Cairo airport less than a week ago.

'Good work, don't you think?'

'I'm no expert,' said Makana, rubbing the paper. Which might have been true, but unlike ornithology, he had some experience in assessing the validity of documents. As fakes went these were very good. He wouldn't have expected less from the old man.

'Your work?'

'Save your praise, my eyes aren't good enough for this kind of detail, and besides, most of it is done by machines nowadays. But people come to me and since I have a reputation to maintain I became a middleman.'

'I don't understand, why go to the trouble of forging a tourist's passport?'

'Because that leaves us with one genuine passport. All we have to do then is change the name and the picture. You know how much a European passport will fetch nowadays?'

'You mean, you sell them to Egyptians?'

'Not just Egyptians. This city is full of people, including some of your compatriots I should add, who are desperate to find a way to the good life in the West.'

'So Yousef takes these off his tourists and they travel back to Europe with false passports?'

'Whoever heard of immigration suspecting a Frenchman arriving back with his family and a suntan? They wave them through with barely a glance. The Spanish are easier. As for the Italians . . .'

'Somehow, I find it hard to credit Yousef with an idea like this.'

'You're right, he doesn't have the brains.'

Makana had come to the last passport in the batch. Idly flipping it open he stared at the photograph. It took a moment to place the face: Ghalib Samsara. It seemed like an odd coincidence.

'You know him?'

'I did some work for his father a couple of years ago. And I met him again the other day. It probably doesn't mean anything.'

'There is no such thing as coincidence,' said Yunis, rolling his lips over his toothless gums before inserting another cigarette and lighting it.

The boy appeared carrying a waterpipe which he set down beside his master. The next few minutes passed with Yunis sucking on the stem until the aromatic smoke was flowing smoothly.

'Watch out with Yousef. He's small time, but I hear he can be dangerous. He gained a bad reputation in the army.'

'Who is he working for?'

'He has his finger in a lot of bowls. He's a hired thug who does favours for a lot of people including national security. He works both sides of the fence. Have you ever come across the Zafrani brothers on your travels?'

It was the second time that name had come up in a week.

'What do you know of them?' asked Makana.

'Our paths have crossed in the past. I hear they are trying to become respectable.'

'And you think Yousef might be working for them?'

'It's hard to say, but something like this,' Yunis tapped the passports, 'would take somebody with a lot of influence.'

'The Zafrani brothers have that kind of influence?'

'Oh, they certainly do. Some say they are building an empire within. There is even talk they might go into politics.'

'Why would they be interested in false passports?'

'Perhaps it is not the passports they are interested in, but in controlling who gets them.'

'Still, it's a risky business. A cautious tourist might notice something.'

'They take only new passports. The owners are barely familiar with them. They might collect them days before they travel and throw them into a drawer as soon as they get home.' Yunis had a contemplative expression on his gnarled face as he puffed away. 'You'd be surprised how many holes there are in the system. Most of them due to human error. In time that factor will be removed.'

'I have something to show you,' said Makana, producing the letters from his pocket.

Yunis glanced swiftly through them. 'They come from a printing press. The old-fashioned kind. There are a few of them dotted around. I can make you a list.'

'What can you tell me about this star?'

'*Kawkab al-Shiara* – the leading star.'

'Have you ever heard of a group identifying with it?'

Yunis shook his head. 'In the Jahiliyya, before the coming of

Islam, the Arabs used to worship stones and stars. In the days of the pharaohs it was associated with Isis. Its disappearance from the sky was believed to coincide with the passage of Isis and Osiris through the Underworld. It reappears after seventy days and marks the start of the annual floods.'

'So why would a religious zealot choose this reference?'

'Most of them are barely literate. They pick what is close to hand.'

The old man winced with pain as he stretched his stiffened legs and got to his feet. Age had begun to tighten its grip on his body like an invisible spider's web.

'You don't need an excuse, you know. To visit, I mean.' With that, Yunis gave a little bow and turned away. Makana watched the figure disappear between the dangling cages. He looked out of the window. Down below, the boy was spraying the plants along the wall with a hosepipe, the water a silvery peacock fan.

Chapter Fifteen

When he closed his eyes he felt his body jerk in response to the snap of automatic rounds. He heard glass shattering around him and Meera's body falling, falling. Over and over again. A bell was ringing. He was trying to reach her, and knew he would never get there in time. When he opened his eyes in the dark he realised the phone was ringing.

'Hello?'

He was about to put the receiver down, thinking there was nobody there, when he heard breathing. The long silence ended when a voice said, 'Is this Mr Makana?'

'Who is this?'

'I . . . I'm sorry,' said the caller abruptly. 'This is a mistake.' The line went dead. Makana stared at the receiver. A man. Not young. In his sixties perhaps. Educated. He replaced the receiver and sat there staring at it for a time, willing it to ring again. To his surprise it did. He let it ring a couple of times before lifting it.

'Look, this would be a lot easier if you tell me what it's about.'

'All I am asking for is a chance to do just that,' chuckled Mohammed Damazeen, as if summoned from the dark recesses of his mind. 'Do you always answer your telephone in such a strange manner?'

'How did you get this number?'

'Talal wants us to be friends and I am willing to forgive your behaviour the other night.'

'What do you want?'

'I said I could help you and I meant it.'

Makana laughed. 'What on earth could you offer me that I would be interested in?'

'Something that is more valuable to you than life itself. Think about it.'

There was a click, and Makana was left holding the receiver. Music played a hysterical electro-beat off in the distance where the coloured lights on the little pleasure boats flew back and forth across the river like exotic fireflies. He rubbed his eyes and looked at his watch. Leaning down he undid the catch on the locker that was hidden under the big desk. Reaching in he removed the Beretta and weighed it in his hand, trying to decide whether to take it with him. In the end he put it back and closed the locker. Carrying a gun around was usually more trouble than it was worth.

The Seraph Sporting Club was crowded that evening. Light spilled out through the open doors into the poorly lit street. Youngsters pooled around the opening. Inside the big hall the air was damp with perspiration and excitement. The walls might once have been a pistachio-green colour. In time they had faded to a grubby ochre, speckled with crushed flies and smeared mosquito blood, along with all manner of encrusted bodily fluids deposited over the course of the years. The floor was littered with trampled paper flyers and roasted melon seeds glistening with spit. Boys and men, no women in sight. The noisy chatter of teenagers working one another up into a frenzy. The sound of a bell ringing brought attention back to the ring in the centre. Makana recognised the skinny, odd boy called Antun. The heavy brass bell looked big enough to rip his frail arm off as he walked the ring swinging it. The crowd moved closer as the fighters and their respective trainers climbed under the ropes.

'Please give a warm welcome to our next contestants!' Father Macarius bellowed with no need of a megaphone as he stood in the middle of the ring. The contestants were two boys, as dark and lean as racing dogs, their singlets hanging loosely from bony shoulders. They touched gloves and backed away. The crowd began cheering them on.

'So now you're interested in boxing, I see.'

Makana turned to see Ishaq, the young man who had tried to prevent him seeing Ridwan Hilal. He wasn't alone. Behind him stood three of his friends, and further back he spotted a couple more of the same type, all wearing the club T-shirt.

'Actually, I was looking for you.'

'For me?' Ishaq sounded surprised, but not displeased.

'I have been asked to look into the circumstances of Meera's death.'

A cheer went up as the two fighters in the ring started circling one another. The dull thud of them trading blows punctuated the roars of the boys and men around them. Ishaq spoke without taking his eyes off the match.

'What has that got to do with me?'

'I understand you were her student.'

'So what?' snapped Ishaq. 'Are you police?'

'No, this is a private matter.'

'Hilal asked you?' Ishaq spared Makana a fleeting glance. 'Why do you come to me?'

147

'Maybe it would help if you answered my questions first.'

'I studied literature at the university. She taught some of the classes.'

'Was she a good teacher?'

The question seemed to catch Ishaq off balance. 'Good? Yes, of course . . . she was the best.'

Ishaq's eyes were fixed on the ring. It was hard to make out the fighters in the weak light. The long hall floated in a submarine glow seeping from neon strips that appeared to be fixed to the roofing girders by a network of cobwebs and dust. Half of them were out. One blinked as if it couldn't make up its mind.

'Why do you ask about that?'

'Because I'm looking for people who might have had a motive to kill her,' said Makana.

'What has that got to do with being her student?'

'It could have a lot to do with it.'

'How?' Ishaq had given up pretending to be interested in the boxing.

'Well, say a student falls in love with his teacher. And say he asked her to leave her husband for him, and she refused. Don't you think that might make someone kill?'

Ishaq laughed. 'Are you serious?'

'You were a little bit in love with her, though, weren't you?'

Ishaq laughed mirthlessly again, then prodded Makana hard in the chest. 'You should watch out who you are accusing,' he snarled as he pushed by.

Mentally, Makana crossed the idea off as a dead end. You can't be right about everything, he told himself as he watched the boy walk away. The match was turning out to be somewhat one-sided. The larger of the two boys was pummelling the smaller, who could do nothing but hold his gloves up in front of his face in defence as he was pressed back against the ropes. Father Macarius stroked his beard as though considering how long to wait before intervening. Makana made his way through the crowd. Ishaq had disappeared but some of the others were standing together over on the far side by the wall of photographs. Hanging lopsided in a flimsy wooden frame, a clipping from a newspaper showed a row of coffins embedded in a crowd of onlookers. Makana felt the unhurried breathing on his neck.

'Those are the Kosheh Martyrs. Murdered just over a year ago.'

Makana turned to see the bullish boy with a stout neck who had blocked his way outside Ridwan Hilal's home the other day. He did vaguely recall the case. A dispute between a shopowner who happened to be Coptic and a customer who happened to be Muslim sparked off a riot in which hundreds of shops and houses in a town in Upper Egypt were burned to the ground. Twenty-one people were killed.

'They never caught the culprits, did they?'

'Who can expect justice when the police themselves took part?'

The bell was ringing to announce the end of the round. Not just the round, but the whole bout. Blood was pouring from the loser's nose and mouth. Father Macarius held up the hand of the victor, who looked hungry enough to take on another six opponents before calling it a day.

'You shouldn't come round here with all your snooping about.'

'That's exactly the kind of thing a guilty man might say.'

'Guilty, me?' he reared back.

'What's your name?' Makana moved along studying the pictures pasted to the wall.

'Me? I'm Botrous.'

Makana paused, his eye drawn to a particular face. It was the face of a younger man. The lopsided eye was less pronounced, but there was something nasty about that face which was unmistakable. He tapped the picture.

'So, Botrous. This man here. What can you tell me about him?'

'That's Rocky. Everybody knows Rocky,' he grunted. 'Ahmed Rakuba. You don't want to have anything to do with him. Believe me.'

'Is he from round here?'

Botrous thought about this for a moment. 'No,' he said. 'He used to help out. I remember him from when I was a boy. He used to work with Father Macarius. Then he disappeared.'

'How do I find him?'

Botrous laughed. 'You don't look for someone like Rocky. If he wants you, he'll find you, but you'd better pray that he doesn't.'

Makana watched the heavyset young man as he moved away to join the rest of the gang. They looked as if they had their work cut out making the world a better place. Others fell aside to give them a wide berth. Ishaq had vanished.

Coming towards him, weighed down under a sheet of folded canvas, was the nervous boy Makana had seen with Father Macarius on his previous visit. His eyes widened when he stepped into his path, despite the smile Makana had hoped would put him at ease.

'Antun, maybe you can help me,' Makana said.

The boy's eyes roved about the room as if he had just fallen out of an alien spacecraft and had no idea where he was. He tried to speak, failed, and then backed away, still stuttering, until

'He's an investigator,' explained Father Macarius. 'He's here to help.'

The priest's authority again seemed to carry weight. Makana found himself in the unusual position of having privileged first access to the victim. It was something of an honour, he reflected. Once upon a time, in what he had come to think of as his previous life, this had been his work. It was ten years now since he had been an inspector of the Criminal Investigation Department. Most of the crimes he had dealt with back then were straightforward batterings. Murderers were not as sophisticated as their fictional counterparts liked to make out. People killed their wives and husbands, their brothers and in-laws, and they did it wildly and without much forethought or planning. Blunt instruments, broken bottles, kitchen knives and rat poison being the weapons of choice. Taking a torch from the man in the checked shirt, Makana stepped closer and leaned in over the body. The man waved people back.

'Give him room to work!'

Touching a hand to the forearm, Makana estimated that rigor mortis, the stiffness that sets in when oxygen no longer flows through the body, had barely begun. The boy was taller than he had expected and older, perhaps thirteen years old, or more. He had been dead less than three or four hours. He had been bludgeoned with a hammer or some other instrument. Identifying him by his features would be impossible. Makana moved slowly around the body. There was a strong smell of kerosene, the body was doused in it.

'Who found the body?' he asked over his shoulder.

The man in the check shirt seemed to exercise some sort of authority.

the canvas fell from his arms and he turned and darted off. As Makana watched him go a voice behind him spoke.

'Ah, there you are. I was hoping you might show up.' Father Macarius, still buzzing from the excitement around him. 'We need all the support we can get. It's hard to drum up interest in something so crude as boxing, yet what else could be more suitable?'

The evening's bouts were over and the audience was slowly making its way out into the street. As they shook hands, Makana nodded at the departing figure.

'He seems to help out a lot.'

'Antun is very special. He was left in our charge as a baby. The church is all he knows.' Macarius gestured at the walls around them. 'He is a very talented artist. He paints and does wood carvings. The angels up there.'

'They are very good.'

Macarius took hold of Makana's arm and led him outside through the open doorway into the yard where the air was cooler. 'Where is your reporter friend? I was hoping he would write a story about our situation.'

'I came alone. Father, I understand Meera used to help out here.'

'That's right. After she lost her job at the university she would come here to give the children classes in English and Mathematics. Basic skills. The boys were very fond of her.' Father Macarius shook his head. 'Such a good woman. It's a tragedy for all of us.'

'I didn't know she was a religious woman.'

'The truth is she wasn't, not really.' Father Macarius smiled. 'You don't have to be religious to want to help disadvantaged children. She came here because she believed we do good work.'

Makana nodded. 'I understand you basically built this church up from ruins.'

'Well, not quite ruins. But it's true, when I came here the church was in a very bad state. We had no funds of course and no materials, but we managed. That was twelve long years ago.'

'That must take a lot of courage, taking on a task like that.'

'Well,' Father Macarius stared down at the floor. 'I made a mistake. I was given a second chance and I wanted to do my best.' He looked up at the church that gleamed before them in the moonlight. 'It has not been easy, but I think we have achieved something.'

'I'm sure.'

'It is a tragedy about Meera. I cannot tell you how sad we all are.'

'Did she ever talk to you about threats she had received? Some letters?'

'Meera knew about threats.' Father Macarius fixed Makana with a stony gaze. 'We all do.'

'You mean, because of her husband?'

'I mean, because of her faith, which I believe prepared her for the difficulties she was to encounter with her husband.'

'How do you feel about the fact that she married outside her faith?'

'If a person decides to marry outside their faith it is no business of mine.' Father Macarius had the even smile of a man to whom such questions were not new. 'She was a Copt, first and foremost. The rest is' – a philosophical shrug – 'formalities.'

There was a commotion by the door behind them and a group of boys burst into sight with Antun at their head.

'*Abouna, Abouna!*'

'What is it Antun?'

The frail boy's face was flushed. 'They've found another one.'

Chapter Sixteen

By the time they arrived, the alleyway was already choke with people. Makana stuck close to Father Macarius cut straight through the crowd. But even his authority enough in the end. Macarius had to physically throw into the fray until people grudgingly stepped aside.

The house was nothing more than a shell. Th long gone and the walls were crumbling, d windows only gaping mouths. There was little in this part of town and the alley was narr only by a faint lamp fixed to a wall at looped through the air overhead. Peopl the dark, jostling for a better view. The and uneven, slick with centuries of r now resembled the hide of a strar warm, thick stench.

'Did someone call the police?'

A large man in a checked s dirty their shoes round here.

'Who is he, Abouna Makana.

'My son, Emad, he stepped in here . . . to answer a call of nature.'

'It's disgusting!' someone yelled out. 'They use this place like a common toilet.'

'He's just a boy.' The man defended his offspring.

'And who taught him to behave like that?'

'Where is your son?' Makana interjected, before it degenerated into a fully fledged brawl.

'I sent him home. This is no place for a child.'

'Very thoughtful of you, but I shall need to speak to him.'

'Of course, *Effendi*, I shall summon him immediately.'

Makana turned his attention back to the corpse. He wondered how long it would be before someone asked to see his credentials.

'Can you tell anything?' Macarius seemed eager for Makana to prove his abilities.

'It's hard to tell without a forensic investigation, but it looks as though he died from the beating he took.' Makana ran the beam of light over the ground around the boy's body but it had been so firmly trampled that any evidence left by the killer would have disappeared by now. He turned his attention back to the body.

'The bruises indicate that he was still alive when these blows were administered. My guess is that he choked on his own blood.'

Makana examined the underside of the body. It looked as though he had been killed on the spot. He moved in closer, fanning away the flies that clogged the boy's nose and mouth. Behind him he could hear more shouting coming from the street. A scuffle that had been going on for some time, he realised, was growing in intensity. He pushed it from his mind and concentrated on the body again. The boy's clothes were relatively clean.

He was wearing jeans and a ragged coat. His hands were filthy. Not just from the place he was lying, but dirt was engrained in the skin, under his broken nails. The beam of light traced the length of the body and Makana's eyes were drawn to the wrists. There was evidence of old scarring, as if he had been tied up for long periods. But not recently.

'He was held against his will somewhere,' said Makana. 'And then he was released.'

The torch beam stopped on a spot halfway up the boy's calf. Makana leaned closer and touched the torn fabric.

'May God have mercy on his soul!' Father Macarius instinctively crossed himself. The gesture provoked an angry response.

'Hey! What do you think you're doing?'

A group of burly men were now clustered tightly around the entrance to the ruined building. Makana recognised a couple of faces who were outside the mosque protecting Sheikh Waheed. Their progress was hampered by the people inside the building who pushed back instinctively, not seeing who was trying to get by them. For a time there was confusion and it wasn't clear what was going on. Father Macarius tried to make amends.

'I meant nothing by it.'

'Keep your rituals for inside your church.'

'Don't let him speak!' yelled one irate man from further back.

'They want to close our eyes to the truth!' added another.

Everyone seemed eager to get involved in the fight. Faces peered out of the gloom, like miners trapped deep inside the earth's crust. The light from torches and hurricane lamps grazed their eyes as if from an approaching storm, lighting up their fear.

'Don't talk about things you know nothing about.' Makana regretted speaking the moment the words were out of his mouth. The burly men turned their attention to him.

'What kind of an investigator are you exactly?'

'The kind that can recognise insolence when he hears it.'

'What unit are you attached to?'

These were the same men he had seen outside the mosque, or at least some of them. He was sure of it. More than likely they were local men, thugs attached to the *Merkezi*, the Central Security Forces, by some obscure, loosely defined bond. They would be reluctant to reveal their identity, although probably everyone around here knew who they were and what they did.

'This area must be secured for the scientific unit. Instead of spouting nonsense about religious sacrifices, why don't you make yourselves useful?'

'Who are you to give us orders?'

'I don't have time for this.' Makana stepped boldly forward until he was standing in front of the one he took to be the leader. A large man with a moustache. He had, as far as he could tell, nothing to lose. 'I never forget a face,' he said quietly.

'Me neither,' replied the other.

It seemed like a good moment to move on, so Makana turned to make sure Father Macarius was right behind him before leading the way out into the narrow alleyway. The crowd made way for them and the burly men took it upon themselves to secure the crime scene. Somewhere in the distance sirens could be heard drawing nearer. Any minute now the riot squad would come charging through waving batons and beating back the crowds.

'It's better to be gone,' he whispered. Father Macarius, his confidence shaken, agreed with a simple nod. As they reached the end of the alleyway the man in the checked shirt appeared.

'Let me take you to my son.'

'Where is he?' Makana asked.

'My shop, just around the corner.'

It seemed like a good idea. Two minutes later they were sitting in the back of a small grocery shop surrounded by sacks of rice and heaps of red onions. The boy had a defiant look in his eyes.

'Are you Emad?' Makana asked. 'Tell me what happened.'

'There's nothing to tell,' the boy said. 'I often go in there, if I have to.'

'You were alone?'

Another nod. 'I didn't see him at first. I mean, I had my back to him. You know, I was facing the wall. But I heard it moving around.'

'Heard what moving around?'

'That would be a cat or maybe a rat,' the father offered helpfully.

'No, no!' The boy's eyes widened. 'It was the angel.'

'What angel?' Makana was confused.

'The Angel of Imbaba,' said Father Macarius. 'Everyone knows about it. Go on, my son.'

'Well, I started to take a piss and then suddenly I heard it moving and I nearly died. I swear it flew right past me over my head!'

This earned him a swift cuff around the ear from his father.

'Don't lie! I told you about that.' He shrugged at his visitors. 'He's generally an honest boy. Ask anyone. He takes care of the shop when I have business to see to.'

Outside helmeted policemen were milling about in the alley. Batons lifted and fell as they cut a swathe through the crowd. Makana glimpsed the thugs around the entrance. One of them was pointing in their direction.

'We should probably move swiftly along, Father. You must tell me about this angel.'

'Yes of course,' said Father Macarius as they hurried back towards the church. 'And there is something else about these killings, something that happened a long time ago.'

They had just reached the main road when an unmarked car cut them off and two men jumped out and grabbed hold of Makana, one on either side.

'Inside,' they said, and bundled him into the rear of the car.

Chapter Seventeen

'What do I do with you?'

Okasha sat in the back of the car, hidden from the view of the pedestrians outside by curtains along the windows.

'Since when did you begin to travel like a minister?'

'These are dangerous times. I need to take precautions. And don't change the subject. We were talking about you.'

'Forgive me, I don't find the subject particularly interesting.'

'Why are you here, Makana? What is your involvement with this case and how did you manage to arrive before the investigating team?'

'I just happened to be nearby.'

'Coincidence? You're asking me to believe in coincidence?' Okasha barked at the man behind the wheel who started off like a racing driver who has just seen the flag go up.

'Where are we going?' Makana asked.

'Nowhere, but it's easier to talk like this, on the move. Less chance of being disturbed.'

'I thought you weren't interested in these murders?'

'I had a phone call this afternoon.'

'Who from?'

'Who is not your concern. All you need to know is that someone high up in the order Allah imposed on this world wants me to oversee what is happening here, and what is the first thing I find?'

The driver was weaving the car through the traffic as if he had a death wish. Makana clutched the armrest on the door which naturally came away in his hand. Okasha didn't seem to notice. There was a distracted air about him.

'Does he have to drive this fast?'

Okasha ignored the question. 'This is not coincidence? I'll tell you what it is, it's a bad sign, you showing up like this. First the shooting of that woman and now this.'

'Are you being transferred to this from Meera's case?'

'Meera's case is still in the hands of the so-called Counter-terrorist Unit. We have to wait for Sharqi to get bored before he hands it over.'

'In the meantime, you are on these child murders? Are you supposed to solve them or keep things quiet?'

'You're walking a fine line, Makana. We have serious problems in this neighbourhood. A lot of tensions.'

'Which are being increased by people like Sheikh Waheed and his men.'

'You have no interest in Sheikh Waheed, and I tell you this as a friend. He is not someone you want to trouble.'

'Are you saying he is not trying to stir up bad feelings towards the Christians?'

'What is this? Conspiracy theory?' Okasha circled his hand in the air. 'Is that what you want to hear? Someone is trying to create chaos inside the country to take our minds off the political problems? You have been spending too much time with your dissident friends.'

The car lurched sideways across three lanes of traffic to come to halt with a screech centimetres from a lorry loaded with sacks of cement that was creeping along at a snail's pace. Okasha was jerked forward in his seat and then back again.

'Do you have to drive like a madman!? Can you not drive like a decent human being?'

'A thousand apologies, *ya basha*.'

'Where do they find these people? I have no idea.' Okasha straightened his tunic. 'I am advising you not to get involved in this case.'

'Advising me or warning me?'

'Listen to me, put your conspiracies aside. In this case it is pure common sense. We need to avoid a conflict.'

'What about Meera?'

'I told you. We have to be patient. When Sharqi and his men get tired of running around they will throw it back to me in the hope that I will fail. In the meantime' – Okasha could not suppress a smile – 'the motorcycle has been found.' From a pouch, Okasha produced a thin folder which he opened to read: 'Suzuki 350cc. Expensive machine. About ten years old. Off-roader model with reinforced frame. Somebody pushed it into a ditch. The plates are missing, and somebody was clever enough to file the serial number off the engine, only they didn't do a very good job of it.' Okasha beamed at Makana. 'Always rely on the criminal mind to make mistakes. So we have a partial number and considering the rarity of the model we may have a chance of tracking it down.'

'And you're not thinking of sharing this information with Lieutenant Sharqi?'

'He has informants everywhere, so I don't doubt he will find out sooner or later. Probably later than sooner though, wouldn't you think?'

'And you don't think it was political?'

'A Christian woman married to a prominent intellectual and all-round controversial figure? Very possible. You can say what you like in this country, most people have heard it before, but this is not Europe where they are free to burn holy books and crucifixes as they please. Start insulting the Quran and you are touching people in a very private place.'

'So his wife deserves to be shot?'

'I didn't say that. Consider the possibility that she had a lover.' Okasha's thick fingers dug into the upholstery as they swerved yet again. The interior of the car was olive green, probably passed on from the army who were never short of funds or equipment thanks to the Americans.

'You're not saying the husband carried this out? Then what, a jilted lover?'

'The criminal mind is a twisted thing, Makana. You ought to know that.'

'What about the weapon?'

'Ah, now that is interesting. We have shell casings. Nine millimetre.' Okasha looked thoughtful for a moment. 'Sharqi's men didn't get all of them. It seems one of them fell into the pocket of a uniformed officer.'

Makana tried lighting a cigarette just as they went over a deep rut. It snapped in two, leaving the filter between his lips and the rest in his fingers. Tight-lipped, the driver said nothing. He clung to the wheel like a jockey with a runaway camel beneath him.

'Now, listen to me. Sharqi will come to you and ask you to help him.'

Makana tossed the filter out of the window and lit the raggedy end of the cigarette. Flakes of burning tobacco launched themselves into the air.

'Why would he need my help?'

'He's being groomed by Colonel Serrag of State Security Investigations. They are forming a new elite unit. High profile, playing to the crowd. Slow down before you kill us!' Okasha snapped, brushing embers from his trousers as they were tossed ungainly up and down by yet another bump. The driver remained silent but he did manage to slow to a semi-normal pace. 'Whatever he tells you, be careful. I can't help you against someone like Sharqi, and he only cares about getting ahead, up where the air is sweet. So, whatever he promises you, don't trust him.'

'What if I give you something Sharqi would kill to know?'

'Something like what?' Okasha frowned.

'The dead boy back there was older than most of the others. About fourteen. And he had a hole cut in his leg by a sharp object.'

'He cut himself shaving.'

Makana ignored Okasha's attempt at humour. 'I think that wound was made by a sliver of window glass that he picked up when I fell over him.'

'Which means . . . ?'

'Which means I think he's the one who shot Meera.'

Chapter Eighteen

When they arrived back at the *awama*, miraculously in one piece, a car Makana had never seen before was parked under the big eucalyptus tree.

'You have visitors,' Okasha observed. 'Bear in mind what I said. Remember who your friends are.'

Makana watched the police car do a U-turn and race back the way it had come.

He made his way down through the vegetable patch to find Mohammed Damazeen waiting impatiently. Mo wore western-style jeans, tan slip-on shoes with little leather tassels instead of laces, and a Midnight Blue raw-silk shirt with a Chinese collar. It made him look like a waiter in a nightclub, or a conjuror about to shake white doves from his sleeves. The car and driver were his. Damazeen, it seemed, had his own ways and means and enough money to sponsor the lifestyle he was accustomed to these days. The only question Makana cared about was what he was doing here, strolling around the deck as if he was planning to buy the *awama* on a whim. Makana rested against the front of the big wooden desk that constituted his office and observed warily as Damazeen cast a rueful eye over the cardboard boxes full of folders and old newspaper clippings – his archives, as it were. A large stain shaped like a frog in the middle of the floor marked the place where water came in through the roof when it rained.

'You really do live like an old-time sultan,' mused Damazeen, smiling his crocodile grin, showing enough teeth to make you keep your distance. 'The sultan of a crumbling empire, whose glory days are behind him, perhaps. Still, you have style, I've always said that.'

Makana tried to think of an occasion when he might have said such a thing and failed.

'I've had a long day. What's this about?'

'Yes, of course, straight to business. I understand, you are a busy man.' Sarcasm came naturally to a man whose career, in Makana's view, was rather cynically built on his skill at promoting himself rather than his artistic abilities. Early on he had discovered a talent for paying compliments and asking favours – another reason most serious painters seemed to hold him in contempt. Soon he was flitting from one biennale to the next, picking up interest from galleries in Europe and wealthy buyers in the Gulf along the way. The West was looking for icons, emblems of their own benevolence. Damazeen was only too happy to oblige. He turned himself into a one-man Africa, flying here and there, shamelessly promoting himself wherever his feet touched the ground. Perhaps his greatest artwork was himself. Most of the people who bought his paintings had no idea that the same elegant man with whom they rubbed shoulders at champagne receptions was picking up fat commissions on military supply contracts in his spare time. Lorries, jeeps, armoured personnel carriers, and eventually arms. The government was fighting a hopeless war in south Sudan at a cost of some three million dollars a day. Plenty of scope for a resourceful man.

'I need your help. That is what you do, isn't it, help people?'

'Why would you need my help? I thought you had plenty of contacts in this town.'

'It's true I have substantial business interests in this country, but this matter is of a slightly more delicate nature.'

'Which is why you came to me?'

With a flourish Damazeen produced a packet of Dunhills, the gold lighter flashing as he lit a cigarette. Makana inhaled the rich smell of expensive imported tobacco. Reaching for his Cleopatras was almost an expression of pride, or humility. He couldn't decide which.

'We were friends once.'

'Were we? I seem to remember you turning your back on your friends in order to go home and make a profit out of war.'

'I mean before that.' The smile hadn't wavered. 'When I was at the Faculty of Fine Arts at Khartoum University, I used to see a lot of Muna. This was before she was your wife, naturally.'

Makana watched him move out onto the open deck at the back and blow smoke at the stars.

'Did you know she considered dropping biology and switching to studying arts? No? We had long talks on the subject. We were very close for a time.'

'That doesn't change what I said, you and I were never friends.'

'That's because you looked down on me. You don't understand art. It doesn't fit into your world where everything has to make sense. Well, that's the point. Sometimes two and two don't add up to four. They don't add up at all.'

'If you came here to give me a lesson in art, you're wasting your time.'

'I came here to ask for your help, for old times' sake.'

'And I told you, the old times didn't do you any favours. It's over and done with, so why don't you get off my boat?'

Damazeen was leaning on the railing. He studied Makana for a moment. 'What if I was to tell you this was your chance to get back at Mek Nimr.'

'What do you know about Mek Nimr?'

'Quite a lot as it happens.' Damazeen smiled. He knew he had Makana's attention now. 'We were partners at one time, in a business venture. You probably still think of him as an upstart. A man who was once your adjutant, a plodding sergeant in heavy boots. Well, you would be surprised. There is more to him than meets the eye. Did you know he attended Khartoum University? No? He never graduated, of course, he was suspended for political activities. But he was an activist for the Brotherhood. Before that he spent two years studying veterinary science. A farmer, can you imagine?' Damazeen's laughter spilled happily across the water. 'He hails from a remote village in Kordofan, where his father was the sheikh at the local mosque. In another age he would have been educated abroad and brought up to enter the diplomatic service. Perhaps that is why he developed such resentment for those who were more fortunate than him in life.'

'I'm having trouble seeing how any of this is relevant.'

Damazeen smiled. 'You have to remember, the days of national salvation are over. This is the new age of pragmatism. You wouldn't recognise the country. Things have changed. The new oil money has made everyone rich. When I went back I soon found myself swept into the highest circles, among the military men and politicians who are running the country. The

Chinese and Malaysians are busy exploiting the petrol and it flows through the hands of these men. They are greedy and they know it will not last for ever.'

'So you're making a lot of money, *mabrouk*, now you can leave.'

'She was a very special woman, Muna. You must miss her a lot, up here in your splendid exile.' Damazeen's face was half in shadow, but Makana could tell he was smiling. He was enjoying this. 'When she first started seeing you we used to tease her. A police officer? What on earth could you have in common? She felt sorry for you. A man whose dedication to his work was all he had to believe in. She thought she could save you from yourself.'

When he went to pick her up at the university he used to change into civilian clothes, but she used to insist that he was handsome in his uniform, that he made the country proud. He never understood what that meant until she said it. He could barely remember her face, all he could recall was her, the way she was.

'Why have you come here?'

'I told you, I need your help.'

'You have a funny way of asking. Right now I'm more inclined to throw you into the water.'

'We are fighting a war in the south that we cannot win. The soldiers are disillusioned. They don't know the bush. They just want to go home. To distract people's minds from the fact the government is calling it a jihad, a holy war. The young men who die in it are martyrs. The president visits the homes of the fallen and calls for a celebration, telling distraught parents their son is now married to *houris* in heaven. Nobody believes that nonsense any more, except a small group of fanatics, like Mek Nimr.'

Makana recalled the hapless figure of his NCO. Underneath the meek exterior lay a shrewd and very dangerous man, as Makana was to find out at his own cost. He made sure that when Makana's course collided with that of the regime's new order, his career would be over. Makana was lucky to get away with his life but in the process he lost Muna and his daughter Nasra.

'Mek Nimr will never be satisfied until you are dead,' Damazeen went on. 'He let you get away that night on the bridge, but it is as if he carries you inside him and can never be rid of you.'

Three years ago Makana had run into a dangerous man named Daud Bulatt, who Mek Nimr had sent to kill him. In the end it hadn't worked out that way, but it was proof that he had not forgotten about Makana. Damazeen was talking again.

'A large consignment of arms is about to exchange hands. The buyer is a middleman from central Africa. A smart, ruthless and very dangerous man by the name of Assani. The deal is being facilitated by Mek Nimr. He thinks the arms are going to Palestinian freedom fighters. Actually they are being re-routed to the SPLA in south Sudan.'

'You're going to double-cross Mek Nimr?'

'He doesn't like me. Once he has set his mind against you it is only a matter of time. Better to strike first. The scandal will destroy him. The pious man calling for sacrifice, making money out of the blood of martyrs? He will be finished.'

'You'd better be sure of what you are doing.'

'I am, but I need someone along that I can trust. Not just anyone. Someone who understands my motives, someone who has a stake.'

'I don't get it. What's my stake in this?'

'I said I would give you your life back.' The gold lighter

stuttered as Damazeen again bowed his head to the flame and exhaled slowly. 'I know you are not interested in my money.'

'Then what?'

'Nasra.'

'My daughter?' Makana's heart slowed to a halt. 'She's dead.'

'No.' Damazeen's voice had dropped to a whisper. 'That night on the bridge, when you were trying to escape, the car crashed through the railings and fell into the water.'

Makana saw it as if it had happened yesterday. The car careering across the bridge, away from the army lorry. The jolt as it hit the side and he was thrown clear. Reaching out to try and pull Muna clear, and watching as the car tipped and slowly fell away into the water below.

'Somehow a pocket of air was trapped inside,' Damazeen went on. 'The car landed upside down on a sandbank. The water isn't too deep there and it didn't take long for them to drag the car out. Nasra was unconscious, but alive.'

Makana couldn't bring himself to speak. The wind rustled through the trees. The traffic receded to the point where Makana could hear the water rising and falling. Finally, he said, 'What happened to her?'

'I told you Mek Nimr was obsessed. He took her into his home. He brought her up as his own daughter.'

'I don't believe it,' Makana snorted. 'How?'

'I have to say, this is one of the nicest spots in this city and you pay what, a pittance?' Damazeen peered down over the railings into the water. 'Still, I suppose you never know if you are going to drown in your sleep.'

Makana cleared his throat. 'What proof do you have she's alive?'

'Proof? What would you like? A lock of hair, a photograph?

You haven't seen her for ten years. You wouldn't recognise her if she was standing in front of you.'

Makana watched from the railings as Damazeen made his way up the crooked path to the embankment and the road above, taking cautious steps to avoid getting mud on his shoes. He wished there was something he believed in strongly enough to pray to.

Chapter Nineteen

The night passed in turmoil with Makana tossing and turning restlessly, finally wrenching himself free by getting out of bed to lean on the rails. He watched the electric light toiling on the water as he smoked his way through every cigarette he could lay his hands on, including the remains of a packet that he discovered behind the old moth-eaten divan in the downstairs room. The tobacco was so dry he had to hold the cigarette at an angle to stop it falling out. It tasted like ashes.

As the river softened from gleaming obsidian to the warm embers of early morning, Makana had lost count of the number of times he had gone over the events of that night ten years ago in his head. Why had he made the decision to take them with him when he ran? Some protective instinct? He remembered running, though. Running down the long arc of the bridge. Running into darkness and the desert beyond where nothing but blackness awaited him.

Muna and Nasra had left him with an empty void where his heart was. How do you recover from that? He had never seen their bodies, never buried them, and never truly forgiven himself. Was this what Damazeen was offering? A chance to end it, after all these years? Exhausted, he finally fell back into the old wicker armchair and felt his eyes closing. A moment later, or so it seemed, the telephone rang.

'Hello?' The light hurt his eyes. The sun was already high in the sky and the daily racket of the traffic across the bridge in full swing. He must have slept for at least two hours.

At first he thought there was no one there. It took a while for him to hear the uneven breathing coming down the line.

'Is that you again? Won't you tell me who you are?'

'There are things you need to know.'

'I'm listening,' Makana yawned. There was a long pause and he thought his caller had gone.

'Not . . . on the telephone.'

'Don't you think I need to know who I'm talking to before we meet?'

'The Fish Gardens in Zamalek, tomorrow night at sunset.'

The line clicked dead. Makana stared at the receiver for a long time. His mysterious caller had gained the courage to speak. Progress. From the way he spoke and his accent, Makana guessed he was an educated man. Not young, but not old either. It was a voice he did not know.

Umm Ali's brother, Bassam, was lying in wait for him on the path up to the road. He opened his mouth as if to say something about the rent, but Makana cut him off with a breezy *sabah al-kheir*, which forced a response and by then he was past him and up on the road looking for Sindbad.

'I swear you look more like a ghost every day.'

'Thank you, and I trust the family is well?'

'*Alhamdoulilah!* The children eat like horses. I swear we will have to move into a bigger flat soon. Though I have no idea how I shall ever be able to afford it, prices being what they are.'

'Allah will provide.'

'*Inshallah.*'

Having dealt with the formalities, they now contemplated the traffic, which by some miracle was good that morning. It took less than twenty minutes to get downtown. Their first port of call was the Blue Ibis offices which were closed and shuttered. Either Faragalla was supremely confident about his company's prospects, or he did not care.

Downstairs in the arcade a sombre air hung over the place. The windows had been repaired and the mannequins replaced. They stood now with their lifeless gaze fixed on some distant point. A man in a striped gelabiyya was using a bucket and a long dirty rag to wash the floor, drawing it back and forth in slow, patient strokes. It seemed like an endless task and as Makana went by the man straightened up and put a hand to his back before wringing a dirty reddish-brown liquid into a plastic bucket. There was a loud wet slap as the rag was dropped back to the tiles, and silently the man bent once more to his work. The shutters on the café, tucked into the far corner, were half lifted. Makana ducked underneath to find the place deserted. He walked slowly round behind the counter and peered through into the little room at the back. A single naked lightbulb hanging from the ceiling pushed back the gloom. Makana could feel a soft, cool breeze in his face and he wondered where it came from. On the far side of the room was a cupboard that had been pulled back to reveal a hole in the wall. It had been roughly broken with a hammer, and was barely large enough for an adult. Makana squatted down and stuck his head through and found a narrow passageway that seemed to extend in both directions, running along some kind of gap between this building and the next. He felt something cold and hard press against his throat. A carving knife that was long and sharp. An arm covered in plaster tightened around his neck.

'What do you think you are doing?'

'I came about the cigarettes we talked about.'

'I haven't got them,' said Eissa. 'Why are you sneaking about in here?'

'Take the knife away before we have an accident.'

'You'll do what I say or end up bleeding like a headless chicken.'

'I can't talk like this. Let me up. I'm not going to hurt you.'

There was a moment's hesitation and then Eissa stepped back. Makana got to his feet and rubbed his throat which stung faintly where the blade had cut the skin. The knife was a big one and it was pointed at Makana's stomach.

'You don't need that.'

'What are you doing in here?' The boy's eyes were red, as if he had been crying.

'I told you. I came for my cigarettes. You weren't out there so I looked in here.'

'Are you police?'

'No. I'm a friend of Meera's, remember?'

'You tried to help her. That was really stupid.'

'I thought you liked her.'

Eissa shifted his grip on the knife, as if his hand was growing tired. He had just opened his mouth to say something when a shout came from the café.

'Eissa! Eissa!'

The boy froze. His whole body tensed. He gestured with the blade for Makana to move to the side, while holding a finger to his lips.

'If you say a word,' he whispered, 'I'll kill you. I swear. Stay here and be quiet.'

Makana stood just behind the door, out of sight. The boy looked at him and then turned and went out into the café.

'What were you doing back there?' asked the voice.

'Just tidying up.'

'Well stop wasting your time. This place should be open already. Have you been crying?'

'No.'

'Well what's that on your face? You look disgusting. Wipe it off before anyone sees you.'

There came the sound of running water. The tone of the other speaker softened. Makana thought it could be Rocky, but he wasn't sure.

'I'll get him. I promise you. Didn't I promise you? I'll get the retard.'

Makana edged closer and peered through the crack between the half-open door and the frame. Rocky stood with his back to him. From this angle it was easy to see that he had been a boxer. The broad shoulders and neck. He saw Eissa shy away as Rocky lifted a hand to slowly caress the back of his neck.

'You don't have to cry, you know. I'm not going to hurt you. I told you that. You're special. Not like the others. You're my lieutenant, right?' There was a pause. 'I'll get the retard who killed him. Don't worry about that.'

'But why? Why did he do it?'

'Because he's retarded. I just told you. Now get this place cleaned up, okay? Otherwise that old man out there will start asking questions.'

When Rocky was gone Makana stepped out of the storeroom. Eissa stared at him.

'Is he the one who did that?' Makana indicated the plaster cast. Eissa turned away.

'He didn't mean it.' The boy stared down at the floor. 'He gets carried away.'

'Stay away from him, Eissa,' said Makana. 'He's a dangerous man.'

'What do you care?' demanded Eissa, then his face brightened. 'I can still get those cigarettes, if you're interested?'

'Sure,' said Makana. 'Then we can all smoke ourselves to death.'

Makana's mind was still in turmoil. The thought of Nasra having been alive all of these years struck him as absurd. How could it be? He felt as if his whole world had been turned upside down. It was a short walk to Amir Medani's office. The lawyer was buried, as usual, beneath a thick layer of stale tobacco smoke and a wall of yellowing paper heaped up around the desk; a maze of human rights abuses and war crimes that came to rest in this shabby little room like malevolent spirits. Amir Medani was a genial, slightly overweight man with a weary face. A deeply political animal who was incapable of keeping his mouth shut. It had landed him in prison when Makana was a police officer and Medani a simple criminal lawyer, and it had eventually landed him here, in this office in Cairo, fighting the good fight. He gave Makana the same advice Makana had just given Eissa.

'Take my advice and stay away from Damazeen. He's a dangerous man.'

'But what if it's true?'

'Listen to me, don't spend any time thinking about it. You'll only torture yourself. Why would Mek Nimr bring her up as his own? It makes no sense.'

In a way it did make a strange kind of sense. Here was Mek Nimr's ultimate revenge: taking over Makana's life, or what was left of it. Nasra became his daughter. She probably had little or no recollection of her early life. The problem, Makana realised, was that a part of him *wanted* to believe Damazeen. He stared out through the window at the elevated overpass and the constant stream of traffic flying over it. Immediately across from him a cart piled high with huge bundles wrapped in burlap was holding up traffic. Between the shafts, in place of a horse or donkey, was a man trying to move it along. It was a superhuman task, a sight that defied belief as he struggled beneath the towering objects above him.

'And why does he want you in on this arms deal?' Amir Medani demanded. 'He's setting up a trap and if you are not careful you'll fall right in the middle of it.'

'But why would he be setting a trap? What does he want from me?'

'Who knows. But I don't trust him and neither should you. Stay away from him. Meanwhile, I'll make some enquiries. We'll find out soon enough if there's any truth to this.'

Across the way, the man leaned all his weight forward, straining to place one foot in front of the other like a man trying to walk on the bottom of the sea. Behind him a bleating flock of vehicles scrabbled to try and get past him.

'How easy is it to sell arms?'

'Easy enough,' shrugged Amir Medani. 'It's all quite legal. You can sell weapons to anyone you like. All you need is what they call an end-user's certificate. And remember, we have had a civil war in our country for almost twenty years. Seventy per cent of the annual budget goes on arms. There are lots of guns. When was the last time you ate?' Amir Medani looked at his watch. 'Listen to me, you have to be very careful with this. You're not thinking straight.'

'I need to know if it's true, if Nasra is really alive.'

'Just leave it with me. Don't think about it. Let me make some calls. If Damazeen is planning a weapons deal in this town you can bet that our friends in State Security know all about it. Nothing happens here without them getting their cut.' Amir Medani rubbed his temples as if he had a headache. 'I have a bad feeling about this. Promise me you won't do anything until you hear from me? I'm sure this is a trap.'

Makana looked at him. He wondered what choice he had.

Chapter Twenty

On the way to Ridwan Hilal's place Makana noticed that a small motorcycle seemed to be following them. It hung back, always three or four cars behind. A couple of times it actually passed them. The bike was an old Java, in good condition, running smoothly and producing little exhaust. The rider was a man in his forties, slightly overweight, with thinning hair, unshaven, chin flecked with grey, wearing a brown flannel shirt and a pair of soft shoes with split seams. A television set was strapped to the baggage rack. It seemed like an unlikely amount of trouble to take to make him look convincing. He didn't turn his head and after a time Makana decided he must have been wrong.

There were other distractions. A long and turbulent stream of rustic philosophy churned its way from Sindbad's mind and out into the world.

'It's not as if I have anything against them, *ya bey*,' he laboured, trying to explain himself. 'I am a simple man and if Our Lord says they are *ahl-al-kitab*, well, that's good enough for me.'

The People of the Book. The notion that all three monotheistic religions derived from the same written source, drank from the same well as it were, and therefore were deserving of mutual respect. It was a nice idea in theory.

The mourning area had gone, leaving the narrow street quieter and devoid of drapes and chairs, though it was still occupied by Ishaq and his boys. There was a discipline about them that was reminiscent of a trained military unit. They nodded and exchanged whispered commands as he approached. Ishaq stared at him sullenly and nodded for him to be waved through.

Inside nothing appeared to have moved since his last visit. The door was answered by the same sister although dressed more informally in a black gelabiya with gold embroidery, her hand on her plump hip as she peered at him. Maysoun. Her name came to him as she led the way down the hall.

Ridwan Hilal was sitting in exactly the same position as Makana had left him, as though he had taken up living behind his desk in his study. He wore blue pyjamas that he appeared to have been wearing for days. The top buttons were undone, exposing a large expanse of white undervest covering an expansive midriff. A bottle of Johnnie Walker Red Label that had almost been drained of its contents stood on the desk in front of him. Maysoun rolled her eyes as she left them alone. 'As you can see,' Hilal wheezed, 'I find solace in the evils of man. Can I offer you a drink?'

'No, thank you,' Makana produced his cigarettes and placed one in his mouth to light.

'Now you see, there is one of the great contradictions of our age. The Holy Quran.' Hilal bowed forward until his head was almost touching the desktop. He remained like that as if he had lost his train of thought. Then he sat up and fished about in the plastic bowl for ice that wasn't there.

'Maysoun! Maysoun!'

Makana wondered how long he had been in this state. A strand of hair had come free and hung lankly down the doctor's forehead. He brushed at it absently.

'Now, where was I? Ah, yes. Sura 4, Verse 43 of the Holy Quran tells us: *Believers, do not approach your prayers when you are drunk, but wait until you can grasp the meaning of your words.*' He chuckled and sipped his warm whisky before going on. 'How reasonable that sounds. To ask that you are sincere in your worship. What does it mean? I shall tell you. It means that alcohol and faith are not mutually exclusive. It demands only sincerity in the act of devotion. Isn't that beautiful?' He thumped a hand on the desk which made pens and papers jump. 'Now, my point is this.' His eyes were glazed buttons behind the thick lenses. 'Why can these men who try to bore us to death with their Islam not show the same reason and tolerance as their own sacred text? Are you a religious man, Mr Makana?'

'That depends on who's doing the asking.'

'Of course. Of course. Now take that cigarette you so casually lit. Naturally, you are aware of the hazards to which you expose yourself, yet as a grown man you take responsibility for your actions. Had cigarettes been around in the sixth century, you realise, there is little doubt they would have been banned. We happily pontificate about alcohol while placing between our lips something which Doctor Freud would call a substitute for our mother's nipple. Do you imagine I could stand up in public in Attaba Square and explain that without being lynched?'

Makana was examining his cigarette in this new light as Maysoun entered the room carrying a bowl of ice cubes. She placed it quietly down and left the room.

'I accepted her offer to stay on and help,' Hilal sighed, reaching for the bottle. 'And with every clumsy gesture she reminds me of how unique my beloved Meera was. Now let me continue my lecture on the abuses of religion. You are familiar, of course, with the famous Sheikh Waheed. Infamous, I should perhaps say.'

'I witnessed him speaking the other day.'

'Good for you. My question is this: why is Sheikh Waheed spreading rumours that these children are being sacrificed in some kind of Christian ritual? You're familiar with these murders in Imbaba of course.'

'A little.'

'How easily people are swayed by rumour. The papers are talking about the Angel of Imbaba, a strange apparition that some believe is evil and others benevolent. Anyway, clearly there is a maniac at large who should be apprehended. Sheikh Waheed is well aware that he is talking nonsense.' Hilal drank thirstily and refilled the glass, ice cubes skittering across the table. 'I heard him myself on the television telling the world that these children are being sacrificed in rituals conducted by Christians. Blood libel was an accusation raised for centuries against the Jews, not the Christians. The Protocols of Zion. You are familiar with them?'

'I've heard of them,' Makana muttered, trying to hold on to the man's logic.

'That is where you will find such fairy tales. Sheikh Waheed is not a fool, he is much more dangerous than that. He is a knowledgeable fool. And while we are at it, let us ask, why is the government supporting him?' Ridwan Hilal sat back like an elder statesman, hands folded across his paunch, his eyes closing for a moment. 'I don't have to tell you the answer to that.'

'I understand Meera used to teach the boys English at Father Macarius' church.'

The eyes opened and Hilal poured the remaining dregs into his glass, setting down the empty bottle with a sigh.

'It was one of Meera's little obsessions. She always said that if she ever had the chance, and the money, she would start a charity. Well, she never did, but she did help Father Macarius with his little youth club. She volunteered there. She taught the boys to read. She wanted to do good.'

'Have you had any further thoughts on what appears in those letters?'

Hilal sat up and straightened his glasses, suddenly alert. 'You understand that the verses of the Quran can be divided into those which are precise in meaning and those which are ambiguous, yes? The *ayat muhkamat* and the *ayat mutashabihaat*. There is some implication that those whose hearts are troubled by doubt follow the ambiguous parts. In other words, these encourage dissent.'

'And the Sura of The Star is one of the ambiguous ones?'

'Precisely, which supports the theory that they were not meant as a threat at all.'

'You mean, it was some kind of warning? For whom?'

'For me, of course.' Hilal's voice dropped to a whisper. 'Why didn't she show it to me?'

'Meera knew you would think she was trying to persuade you to leave the country. She knew you wouldn't leave, because of your work.'

'She told you that?' Hilal pondered for a moment. 'What do you know about the nature of my work? The history of Islam?' Hilal brushed his own question aside impatiently. 'Have you at least heard of the Mu'tazilites?'

'The group of medieval philosophers?'

'Very good. The Mu'tazili school of rationalism believed that God is perfect and complete. Man has to be free to make mistakes. To find solutions that will answer the challenges of society, we must apply reason to what is written in the Quran. This type of rational discourse is of course known simply as *kalam* – to talk or debate.'

Ridwan Hilal was transported by the mere act of explaining. This, Makana decided, was the man Meera had fallen in love with.

'Another school of thought emerged around the same time which naturally believed the exact opposite. The Hanbalis. To them adherence to doctrine was everything. But see' – Hilal stretched his big paws across on the table – 'how close we are to Western civilisation in this. The roots of Greek democracy lie in the Athenian agora where citizens gathered to stroll freely and to talk – *kalam*. For Islam to endure, it has to grow, to become, as Ibn Arabi put it so beautifully in the thirteenth century, a religion of comprehensive love.' Ridwan Hilal was like a lost man seeking solace in his mind. 'Ibn Arabi sought to make Islam contemporary, to reconcile it with other faiths. Ideas are the most dangerous thing we have. You can kill a man but his ideas live on.'

Makana stubbed out his cigarette in the overflowing ashtray and stood up. Through the window the view of the street was obscured by a large carob tree. The long, hanging pods dangled like strange worms between the branches. Below, he glimpsed the young seraphs huddled together in conference, perhaps planning to get him when he left the building.

'You're saying you would rather die than give up your ideas. Meera believed in you.'

'I believe she was trying to persuade me to go abroad, if only for a short time.'

'She told me she had the feeling things were about to change.'

'What things?'

'Things,' repeated Makana. 'That's what she said.'

Hilal shook his head. 'That makes no sense to me.'

'Meera was spending a lot of time at the office.'

'She worked hard, yes.' Hilal shrugged. 'There is nothing unusual about that.'

'She stayed late and arrived early, which suggests that she wanted to be alone.'

'What are you getting at?'

'I'm not sure. Maybe she was working on something. Did she ever talk about the Blue Ibis?'

'It was work, nothing more. It kept us alive.' Short of breath, the plump man gave a long sigh and reached for his cigarettes. Placing one between his lips, he flicked the lighter. The flame warmed the pallid face, slick with a thin film of perspiration. 'I wish you would leave this alone. For the dignity of her memory.'

'Other lives may be at stake.'

'What others?'

'We still do not know why she was shot. Until we do know we can't rule anything out.'

'Fine. Fine,' Hilal muttered impatiently. 'If that's what it takes.'

'Tell me about the scandal that lost you your job, and Meera hers.'

'Our lives stopped from one minute to the next, thanks to that charlatan.'

'You mean, Sheikh Waheed?'

Hilal nodded. 'Even you must have noticed the level of education to which our beloved president has managed to lower this country. Graduates who are barely able to spell their own names. Writers who are awarded honours for praising his Highness. Sheikhs are the court jesters.'

'It was a difference of opinion that started it?'

'It was corruption. These new Islamic banks look for figures to endorse them. Sheikh Waheed has a high profile, a lot of followers. If he appears on television to recommend a certain bank they will go with him. It made him a rich man.'

'What about Professor Serhan, was that professional rivalry?'

'Serhan?' Behind the glasses the twin buttons seemed to glow with fury. 'The man is an idiot. His vanity eclipses his stupidity. He steals most of his ideas.' Hilal was working himself into a frenzy. He wheezed and puffed on his cigarette as if determined to choke himself to death on the spot. 'Intellectually, that door you came through is superior to him. He has the brains of a small child and that's being unkind to children.'

'He was instrumental in opposing your professorship. Yet, you were friends when you were students, I understand.'

'When one is young, the putty is still unformed. It is easy to form acquaintances which, in the course of time, prove themselves to be errors.'

'Would it be possible for me to look through Meera's things?'

'Is that really necessary?'

'I think it might help at this stage.'

'Very well. Maysoun will show you.' He raised his voice and the sister appeared in the doorway clutching her hands together. After another long moment's hesitation she turned and led the way to a narrow doorway off the hall. She opened it with an air of cautious ceremony as if half expecting to find her sister still sitting there, working away. It was a simple study. Half the size of her husband's room at the other end of the apartment. It contained bookshelves along one wall and a desk over which hung an old Metro Cinema poster of Laurence Olivier in *Hamlet*.

'Did she ever mention that she was planning to leave the country?'

'Leave?' Tugging a white handkerchief from the sleeve of her dress and burying her nose in it, she said, 'Never. I mean, she talked about it. Who can live in this country?'

'In her place you would have left already?' Makana brought his eyes away from the books to the woman in the doorway.

'If I had the chance I would leave tomorrow.' She sounded a resentful note.

He went back to the shelves in front of him, asking casually, 'How did the family take to her marrying him, I mean, Doctor Hilal being a Muslim?'

'Of course, it's not the same, but it's what happens. Anyway, she always did as she pleased, and expected the world to arrange itself around her.'

'It can't have been easy for you.'

'It wasn't. Many people refused to have anything to do with her, but what can you do? We are a family.'

'Of course.'

Maysoun sniffed. 'His faith was not the problem. It was politics. For years we begged her to get him to moderate his views. You cannot reason with fanatics. What's the point of antagonising them? He lost his job. Her career was ruined.' She buried her nose in the handkerchief and blew hard. 'I asked her to tell him to apologise. He refused. Too proud. And now look.'

'You blame him for her death, but Meera believed in him. She supported his ideas.'

'Ideas!' Maysoun clutched her handkerchief fiercely. 'What do ideas matter? They are nothing but the fruit of man's vanity.'

With that she spun on her heels and disappeared down the hall. Makana turned his thoughts on the person who used to inhabit this room. It was the study of a dedicated academic. Meera had obviously read widely, in English, Arabic and French. There were shelves weighed down with theory and others crammed with dog-eared novels. They were used up like old rags that had been through the ringer too many times, corners bent and pages yellowed, spines cracked open to reveal the wonders they contained. The mystery that was Meera threaded its way through all of this. He flipped through some of the books on the shelf finding her name in journals and anthologies, the author of papers on Thomas Hardy and George Eliot. A wave of sudden familiarity washed over him as he recalled Muna's study at home, and that in turn brought back Damazeen. Could he be telling the truth? Could Nasra still be alive?

His concentration broken, Makana returned the book he was holding to its place and turned his attention to the desk. An antique writing bureau with a carved back. It had a number of small drawers and cubbyholes. It wasn't in mint condition. Was anything in this tired city? Everything seemed exhausted and on its last legs. The varnish was scratched and in a couple of places the elegance of an arch was curtailed abruptly where a mishap of some kind had chipped off a corner. Scars in the base showed that the tabletop, now fixed roughly in place with a couple of hasty screws, had once been a folding leaf. Its faded style hinted at the elegance of another age and he wondered if it had once belonged to the grandfather she had spoken of.

The chair creaked comfortably as he settled himself into it. For a long moment he remained motionless, taking in everything in sight. He was aware that he had barely glimpsed the surface of who or what Meera had been, and that the key to her death lay in somehow managing to see through her eyes. A tray inlaid with mother-of-pearl contained pens and pencils. Objects she chose with care. On the right side a series of shelves contained sheets of paper and envelopes of various sizes, shapes and colours, all stacked in order. He went through these slowly and meticulously, opening old bills and leafing through receipts. The drawers were cluttered with things she did not much care for but could not bring herself to throw out. A tangle of ribbons, Sellotape, thumbtacks, a bottle of Chinese ink for an old-fashioned fountain pen. The pen itself was a bulky German thing. A man's pen. The name Graf von Faber-Castell engraved on the side. The left-hand side of the desk was taken up by a stack of three little drawers. Each with a heart-shaped piece of ivory inset around a tiny keyhole. One of them was missing its little ebony handle. None of them was locked. The first was stuffed with more outdated receipts: a watch-repair shop, Madbouli's bookshop, a stationer's in Sharia al-Kasr, a pharmacy in Zamalek. He sifted through and replaced them. The second contained bits of jewellery, odd earrings, a pair of spectacles with a cracked lens, old coins and notes from Syria, Greece, French Francs, Italian Lira, Spanish Pesetas. The watch and the glasses belonged to a man, mementoes perhaps of her father. As he was stuffing them all back the drawer snagged and refused to close fully. Pulling it all the way out he peered into the cavity and saw that something had been caught at the back. It must have slipped down or been stuffed there. Scrabbling about with his fingers he eventually managed to free it: a photograph of three men in military uniforms. It appeared to have been taken in a desert somewhere. He studied the barrenness behind them and wondered where it could be. Then he turned his attention to the faces. He immediately recognised two of them: Rocky was at the back, his left eye drooping. Second from the left was Ramy, Faragalla's nephew. Makana remembered him from the picture of the excursion at the Blue Ibis offices. The third man he hadn't seen before. Makana turned the picture over, but nothing was written on the back. After a moment he tucked it into his pocket. As he turned to leave, Makana paused in the doorway and wondered what he wasn't seeing. Maysoun was standing by the front door, her head bowed.

'Thank you,' he said, as she opened the door for him. She said nothing. It looked as though she had been crying.

Chapter Twenty-One

It was almost eleven o'clock by the time Makana reached the uneven streets of the Mouski and stepped into the narrow gap beside the old silversmith's shop. At this hour of the evening the metal shutters were down along the shopfronts and the streets were deserted. The odd naked lightbulb spilled watery pools of illumination over the shadows. Cats stepped daintily through the garbage left from the day's market like queens from a forgotten age. The hiss of an oil lamp marked the progress of a man trundling his cart homeward, his back bowed with weariness. The cart was laden with heaps of peanuts and roasted melon seeds, wayward horns of paper cones curled skyward like model towers in a fantastical city.

The air felt muggy and humid, as if it might rain. The narrow cut looked dark and uninviting. Makana picked his way carefully. Once his eyes had adjusted to the gloom he found the faint city glow filtering over the rooftops was enough for him to see by. Despite the late hour and the silence, as he cut across the square Makana had the impression he was being observed. When he tugged the bell there was again a long pause before the quiet slap of slippers could be heard approaching. The bolt was drawn and the door swung open to reveal the same small boy in his red tarboosh. Once again, as he crossed the threshold, Makana felt the modern world fall away and his mood lift as he climbed the spiral staircase, one hand on the bone-smooth stone. The hall of bird cages was dark and still, each cage now veiled by a sheet of white cloth. Makana recognised the sprightly figure of Yunis waiting for him at the far end. His silhouette stark against the glow on the other side of the open doorway.

'Ah!' He removed his dark glasses to get a better look at Makana. 'You look tired. What's the matter, you're not sleeping well?'

'I was up late.'

'You need to get married again. You're still young. Soon it won't be that easy. You'll get used to solitude, the sound of your own voice.'

'I could always start collecting birds.'

'A poor substitute for a wife. Take my word for it.' His skin looked as pale and translucent as onionskin paper, an exotic species of bird about to be blown away.

'I wondered if you had had any thoughts about printers.'

They sat in the protruding alcove, overlooking the garden. He allowed the solitude to transport him momentarily to another age, when caravans stopped for the night and the yard below would fill with the shuffle of camels and pack-horses being watered and fed, having borne ice from distant mountains, or animal skins laden with salt across the desert.

'Do you think he suspects you?'

'Yousef?' Makana reached for a cigarette. 'I really don't know. There's more to him than I thought.'

He reached into the pocket of his gelabiya and handed over a list of some fifteen names.

'These printers are the kind you are looking for. Simple establishments, old machines falling into disrepair.' He produced a half-smoked cigarette from another pocket and lit it. The old man's cheeks seemed to hollow impossibly as he drew smoke into his lungs. 'The letters show a lack of attention to detail which means laziness. Which then cut the list further in my mind.' He spoke over his shoulder as he led the way into the circular library to pluck a book from a shelf.

'Statistics In Comparative Human Development: A Case Study.' Makana looked up. 'Sounds fascinating.'

'Examine the first page. Look closely at the places I have marked.' Yunis held up one of the letters Makana had given him. 'Do you see it?'

'They were printed on the same machine?'

Yunis took the book from Makana and turned it over so that he could read the printer's name: Mereekh Academic Publishers Egypt. 'They do a lot of work for Cairo University.'

'Thank you,' Makana said.

'Don't mention it.' Yunis examined him. 'Your mind is elsewhere this evening. What is bothering you?'

'Ghosts. Things I thought I had put behind me for ever.'

'We never put the past behind us, not really. We just put it aside for a while.' Yunis led the way through to the next room and along a narrow passageway. The walls were bare and there was only a fragment of light to see by. A bend brought them to the top of a staircase that descended into darkness. 'You can leave by the rear entrance. Mind how you go.' Yunis paused. 'I'm sorry.'

'For what?' Makana asked, but the old man had already gone. He turned his attention to getting down the staircase, trying not to break a leg. He felt cautiously with his feet, stepping down slowly, moving one foot at time. Then he was in a narrow alcove. Suffocating in the dust and with cobwebs clinging to his face, he felt with his hand to find a heavy old door. Light filtered through cracks in the wood. A rusty bolt finally gave with a snap and the door swung inwards. As he stepped out into the street a shadow rose over him. He tried to duck the blow, but managed only to deflect it as it struck him high on the cheekbone and sent him staggering and down on one knee. An arm closed around his neck and jerked him back up, until he felt his feet leave the ground. His air supply was cut off and he felt himself becoming light-headed. One arm was pinned to his side so he thrashed about with the other, his feet pedalling in the air, trying to find a purchase. Whoever was behind him was big and incredibly strong and smelt of aftershave. Was this to be the last thing he knew of this life: cheap cologne? The street was deserted at that hour. To take his mind off his problems, the second man stepped up and punched him heavily in the stomach, hard enough to expel whatever air was left inside his lungs. Then he was hanging limply from the tree branch that was wrapped across his windpipe. A glitter of light brought the hot glow of a blade closer. Behind it was a short, ugly man with a wispy coil of a beard framing his face. A thinning mat of hair rested across the top of his head. His beard and hair were dyed with henna.

'You feel this?' A low rasp as he pressed the blade to Makana's throat.

There was an absurdity to the situation. The little man resembled something out of a fable. *Ali Baba and the Forty Thieves* maybe. And the question ignored the fact that Makana could not have answered him with all the will in the world. He was immobilised and barely conscious. The ugly man leaned closer.

'Keep your nose out of Zafrani business,' he whispered, pressing the tip of the blade to Makana's ear. He flicked the tip as he stepped back with a swift nod to his accomplice. Makana slid to the ground gasping for breath. His neck was wet and he put a hand to his ear to stem the bleeding. When he looked up again the two men had disappeared like smoke into the night air.

Chapter Twenty-Two

Makana woke up in pain the next day. His body ached and his neck felt as though it had been stretched on a rack. The bedsheet was stained with blood. A quick glance in the cracked mirror confirmed that he had a bruise the size of an egg swelling on his left cheek and a nasty gash on his ear. By the time he reached the Hourriya Café, Sami was already there drinking beer, which seemed a reckless proposal at any time of the day. Makana stuck with tea. An old man at the next table licked his lips like a cat as he watched Sami pouring foaming Stella into his glass. A shoeshine boy went from table to table looking for anyone who still cared about the state of their shoes. Around the sides of the bare, unkempt room sat ageing men in various states of decrepitude. They played chess, read newspapers and smoked their cigarettes. Most of all they just stared into space, remembering times gone by, glory days, as distant as the pharaohs. Sami liked to make out they were poets or literary critics, but to Makana they just looked like sad old men whose lives had been played out.

'You look a lot worse than I feel, which actually makes me feel better,' said Sami.

The atmosphere in here, the sense of resignation, all added to Makana's melancholy mood. 'Does Rania know you drink in the middle of the day?'

'Oh, don't start that.' Sami raised both hands in protest. 'Don't you ever feel that the whole thing is just so hopeless?'

'Everything?'

'Everything. The despair. Don't you feel that sometimes? What happened to you by the way? It's getting to the point where I'm not sure I want to be seen with you in public.'

'Always nice to know you can count on your friends.'

'I hear you and Macarius were out finding bodies the other night.'

'Another homeless boy. Do you know if they have identified him yet?'

'What do you think? Do you know how many homeless kids live in this city? Conservative estimates put the figure at fifty thousand. Boys and girls trying to escape a life of abuse. Most of them disappear, melting into cracks in the pavement. They are the symptom of serious social breakdown. Families that are under such pressure, no money, no jobs, no food, that they start to tear one another apart, like wild animals.' Sami slapped the side of the table, causing an old man snoozing nearby to jump. Sami apologised. '*Maalish, ya ammu.*'

'Can't you go and solve the world's problems somewhere else?' the man grumbled.

'There is some connection here that I can't really see,' said Makana, leaning his elbows on the table. He pushed the photograph across. Sami looked at it.

'Three soldiers. Who are they?'

'This is Ramy, Faragalla's nephew, and the one with the eye is Ahmed Rakuba, Rocky. The third one I don't know.'

'Where did you get it?'

'Meera's study.'

'And you think this means . . . what?'

'I'm not sure,' Makana looked vague.

'You seem distracted. Has something happened?'

Makana looked at him and decided he wasn't ready yet to start talking about Nasra.

'Perhaps I should go to Luxor and have a talk with Ramy.'

Sami watched him as he took a long swallow of beer, his Adam's apple bobbing up and down like a man trying to drown himself. He finally came up for air and began to top up the glass.

'Have you had any more thoughts on what Father Macarius might be hiding?'

'Only the obvious.' Makana recalled the wooden angels floating over the boxing ring and the strange mute who had carved them.

'Which is?'

'That the killer might actually turn out to be connected to the church or the gym. They would shut him down if that was the case.'

'They would burn him to the ground, more like.'

'*Yallah ya shabab*,' muttered the man dozing at the next table. In the middle of the floor, a cat arched its back, stretching itself along a pillar of sunlight that fell across the broken black-and-white tiles. The sandwiches arrived and the cat stepped up, twirling its tail in the air. Makana dropped a slice of chicken on the floor and instantly five other cats darted out of the shadows.

Sami poured the last dregs into his glass and raised the bottle of Stella to call for another one. Makana knew his friend would go back to the paper and put his head down on his desk and sleep for an hour or so until the day cooled off and night fell.

Then he would order coffee and start his rounds of the city's receptions and parties. He did most of his work at home and only showed up at the paper every day, he said, because otherwise someone else would steal his desk.

'How did you get on with the Eastern Star bank?'

'I read Ridwan Hilal's book on the subject. He talks about some of the crooked schemes the banks get up to. One of them involves siphoning funds through small companies with a lot of turnover, particularly of foreign currency.'

'You mean, like travel agents?'

'Perhaps,' said Sami. 'It seems the government set up their own committee of investigation. They published a report.'

'Clearing the bank of all charges.'

'You should be reading fortunes. You'd make a good living. I had an aunt who read coffee grounds. She never made a milliem, always giving it away. Generosity is a flaw in my family.'

'So that's it, the bank was cleared?'

'It gets worse. Remember I told you I had a friend who was working on the story?' Sami slid a folded newspaper across the table and tapped his finger on a small item that appeared at the bottom of an inside page and Makana read: Journalist Nasser Hikmet falls from hotel room window in Ismailia. 'They're calling it suicide.'

'Falling out of windows is an occupational hazard for journalists.'

'Nasser was a good man. He deserved better.' Sami gave a long sigh. 'You know what our problem is? We can't decide what we want. Do we want West or East, Islam or the joys of secularism? We think we can have it all.'

It struck Makana that he was surrounded by people who had made great sacrifice, who had laid down their lives on a battlefield in a war that was undeclared. Meera, Nasser Hikmet, the tortured boy lying in the ruins of a house in Imbaba. Further back, there were people like Talal's father, and of course Muna and Nasra. What was it all for? What cause did their deaths serve? His thoughts seemed to follow an eccentric orbit that kept leading him round, circling what he had managed to keep at bay all these years. What would he do if she was alive?

'Rania is the best thing that ever happened to me.' The beer had made Sami sentimental. 'Was it like that with you and Muna? I never met her, but I feel I have been around her for a few years now. Not that you ever talk about her all that much.'

'We should get moving,' said Makana, glancing at his watch.

'Sure, sure.' Sami got to his feet and grabbed for his jacket which caught, tipping over the chair. It hit the floor with a loud crash, waking everyone from their quiet slumber.

'Okay, *khalas*, it's all right. You can go back to writing your reports now. I'm leaving,' Sami called out as he backed out of the door. He glanced about the room, lowering his voice. 'You ever wonder how many people in here are in the pay of the government?'

'Married life is making you paranoid,' said Makana as he led the way out into the street. He hailed a taxi and pushed Sami inside. He saw the driver flinch and mutter '*Astaghfirullah*' under his breath, his face screwing up in disapproval as he caught the smell of booze.

Oblivious, Sami hung his head out of the window, curly hair blowing in the slipstream, and waved back at Makana like a wild child, delighted with his own bad behaviour.

Chapter Twenty-Three

The punchbags hung limply on chains, as if exhausted and waiting for the next beating. In one corner two men were working out earnestly with home-made weights resourcefully devised from iron cogs salvaged or stolen from some kind of large machinery. Elsewhere, one boy sheltered behind a pad held to his side while a young man threw a barrage of kicks at it, emitting a piercing cry with each blow. So not just boxing then. An odour of rotting drains came accompanied by the steady trill of running water from an open doorway at the far end, indicating changing rooms and a leaky toilet. Makana was almost touching the ropes of the ring at the centre of the room before he realised the man bouncing about inside it was none other than Father Macarius. He wore blue shorts and a white singlet and was trading blows with a hard little brown button of a man who appeared to be made of rock. He attacked with a relentless flurry of punches, arms like stout branches blowing in a hurricane. The priest put up a good show, ducking and weaving and generally tiring out his opponent who must have been at least twenty years younger than him. Makana joined the crowd of young men skirting the ring and watched as Father

Macarius jabbed a blow home between the other man's defences. There was something old-fashioned about his style, but he moved with natural fluidity, hips low, the weight in his shoulders. His legs were sinewy pale springs that sent him bouncing out of harm's way. The little slugger advanced steadily, but Father Macarius stayed on his toes, circling just out of reach. The boys around the side were clad in a variety of ill-fitting, worn-out clothes. Trousers and singlets whose colours were faded to a uniform grey. They ranged in age from their mid-twenties to as young as seven or eight. With each flurry of leather against skin, a cheer went up. A bell rang and the two fighters slapped gloves and stepped away from each other. Grimy furrows of silvery sweat divided Father Macarius' lined face as he sagged on the ropes. Makana recognised Antun as the boy who began to unlace his gloves. He noticed the affectionate way Macarius ruffled the boy's shaved head. Raising a weary hand in greeting, he said:

'Feel like going a few rounds?'

'With you? I'm not sure how wise that would be, Father.'

Macarius laughed as he ducked out of the ring and dropped to the floor. The boots he wore had been scuffed so raw the worn leather appeared to be sprouting hairs. 'You look as though you might benefit from a few lessons.' He indicated the bruise on Makana's cheek.

Father Macarius wrapped a towel around his neck and wiped his face. Over by the wall was a plastic water barrel whose blue colour had been softened by years in the sunlight. Lifting an aluminium mug he dipped it inside and drained it in one go, his Adam's apple straining like a bird trying to get out of a sack. Makana recognised the fighter throwing the kicks on the far side of the room as Ishaq, the sharp-faced young man who had been outside Meera's house. He looked quite good. Makana made a mental note to remember this.

'I saw a couple of your boys guarding Ridwan Hilal's home the other day,' he said.

'They aren't my boys, as you put it,' said Father Macarius, his annoyance evident. 'They make their own decisions. They have taken it upon themselves to form a cadre to protect us. I cannot fault them for that, although I do not encourage violence outside the ring.' He brought down a black cassock hanging on the wall and pulled it over his head. A long string of wooden beads swung on a nail. Kissing the wooden crucifix, he hung it over his head.

Outside, the walls of the white church reflected the light so much it was hard to look at. A couple of young palm trees had been planted in circular plots. A younger man in a cassock was watering these with a hosepipe. Makana recognised him as the sturdy fighter who had just been in the ring with Father Macarius.

'You told me Meera used to help out here, teaching the boys to read.'

'She was a charitable woman and will be sorely missed.' Father Macarius pulled up suddenly and turned to Makana. 'I don't want the church drawn into this.'

'The church is not only drawn into this, Father, it's right at the centre of it. The murder of these boys is directly linked to your church and to Meera's death.'

'We can't allow this. They will close us down.'

'They are already closing you down.' Makana paused. 'Father, the other day you wanted to tell me something. What was that?'

'Oh, I'm such a fool,' the priest chastised himself.

'I'm not the police, Father. It doesn't have to go any further than me.'

'I wish I could believe that.' Father Macarius took a step away and then he turned back to face Makana. 'It all happened a long time ago.'

'Is it connected to the murders?'

'I'm not sure, but I think it might be. I can't tell you any more. Not yet. I need time.'

Makana watched him walk away, disappearing into the church with his athletic walk, the swaying black robes melting into the shadows. Back inside the gym, Makana found Antun mopping the floor by the entrance to the toilets. He looked up, his eyes wide. There was a strange, other-worldly quality to Antun.

'Do you know this man they call Rocky?'

'Rocky?' Antun echoed.

'Yes, Rocky. He used to box here.' Across the room Makana caught sight of Ishaq scowling at him from behind a punchbag as one of the others hit it over and over. As he watched him, Ishaq let go of the bag and came towards him.

'What do you want from Antun?'

'This doesn't concern you.'

'Antun concerns us.' Ishaq smiled. 'What happened to your face? Did someone take offence to your sticking your nose in everywhere?'

There was a snigger of laughter and Makana realised that four of Ishaq's friends had also moved to form a loose ring around him.

'I go for *Abouna*,' Antun muttered.

'Leave Macarius alone,' Ishaq ordered. 'We can deal with this.' Stepping closer, he said, 'Why do you keep coming round here?'

'I'm looking for Rocky.'

'Oh yeah, a friend of yours, is he?'

'I just want to talk to him.'

'You're wasting your time.'

'What can you tell me about him?'

Ishaq shrugged. 'He used to turn up here to box, about five years ago. He was in the army. He likes young boys. Now he runs a group of beggar kids. I swear some of them are not more than ten years old. He picks them up off the street and uses them like dogs. I wouldn't stand for it. I swear, any man who tried to do that to me, I'd take a knife and cut his throat.'

'Why do you say I'm wasting my time?'

'He has protection.'

'What kind of protection?'

'The kind that makes you immune to stupid questions,' said Ishaq as he brushed by, making sure his shoulder knocked into Makana's. The others followed behind him.

There didn't seem to be much more to be gained here. As he left he heard someone calling him and turned to see the shop-keeper from the other night hurrying after him.

'Is there any news, I mean about that poor boy we found?'

'No, no news,' said Makana. 'Have you spoken to the police?'

'The police took the body away and left.' The man glanced over his shoulder. 'After that we haven't seen them. Everybody is scared. I am afraid. For my family, for my business. One of these days . . .' He shook his head in anticipation of the worst.

'There is somebody I am trying to find. Maybe you can help me?'

'Who is it? Just tell me. I know everyone in this neighbourhood.'

'He used to box. People call him Rocky.'

The man drew back. 'What do you want with him?'

'What can you tell me about him?'

'Nothing,' said the man, his eyes cold. 'I can tell you nothing. I have a family. You understand? I have children. Little boys.'

'I understand.'

'No. No, you don't.' The man made to move away when something made him stop. He was clearly scared, but he turned and led the way, and five minutes later they came to the corner of a narrow street. The man pointed at a building.

'That's where you will find him,' he said.

When Makana looked back he was already walking away. A scattering of used coffee grounds had turned the sandy ground into a muddy tongue the colour of molasses. The café was nothing more than a doorway, an opening in the wall, metal doors flung wide in a space that might once have been a garage for a small car. Roughly hammered together wooden benches rested against either side. These were deserted except for one man who sat upright with his back against the wall. Makana sat down opposite him and called for coffee. After a time he became aware that the man, a heavy, unshaven man with a handlebar moustache that looked as though it had escaped from the tomb of some pasha of old, as if it ought to be hanging in a frame, was staring at him.

'I look at you, and the first thing I think is police.'

'We all make mistakes.'

He was a self-styled *Omda*, a neighbourhood leader who spent his life watching the street go by, making other people's lives his business. Air bubbled through the waterpipe as he exuded a cloud of aromatic smoke.

'Around here we take care of our things our own way. We don't need the police.'

'I'm not police.'

Behind the counter a young boy no more than twelve fussed with a small brass kerosene stove set on the counter. He snapped a lighter. The flickering blue flame turned the place into a little cave of wonders. 'I don't mean to tell you your business,' said the man stroking the back of his hand along his moustaches as if they were a pair of plump doves, 'but you're wasting your time here.'

'All I want to do is drink my coffee in peace.'

The boy kept his eyes studiously on the battered pot he was stirring with a spoon. The smell of coffee filled the confined space.

Makana took his time to study his surroundings. The walls were scarred with the usual graffiti: Down with the Americans. Down with Israel. Down with the government. Down with everything and everyone because the rest of the world was better off, and this was as far down as you wanted to go. Who was this Rocky? Why did Meera have a picture of him stuffed behind her desk? The boy avoided his gaze as he set down the coffee on the table at his knees. The man opposite stared at him as he puffed his waterpipe. Makana sipped the coffee slowly as people came and went past the entrance of the building opposite. A little girl leading a small boy by the hand went by, a green plastic bag banging against her legs, heavy with warm round loaves of bread. A tall man with a beard, wearing thick-framed spectacles and a white gelabiya put a hand to his nose and hawked up a mouthful of phlegm which he spat on the ground before stepping out and moving away along the street.

As he got to his feet Makana reached into his pocket for some money. He found a rather worn ten-pound note, with a tear in one side. Far too much for a simple coffee. He folded it carefully and tucked it under the cup out of sight. If he came back some time it might be helpful to be able to talk to the boy. He had been planning to cross the street for a closer look, but found his way barred. Three young men stood blocking the entrance.

'You have no business here,' said the man on the bench behind him. Makana turned to look at him. The man circled the long pipe stem in the air. 'Go away and don't come back.'

Chapter Twenty-Four

The day was fading fast as Makana made his way through the gates into the Fish Garden. Shadows seeped from the base of the banyan trees like flowing ink. Birds chattered excitedly at the last rays of light draining from the sky. Makana hurried, not wanting to be late for his appointment with his mystery caller.

The Khedive Ismail inherited his fierce dislike of the British along with a love for all things French, including the roulette wheel, from his grandfather Mohammed Ali Pasha. A poor gambler, his extravagant tastes and poor judgement bankrupted the country, dropping it neatly into the laps of the European powers in 1879. The Ottoman court relieved him of his post in a telegram addressed to the 'former Khedive'. Ismail had dared to dream of Parisian boulevards and zoological gardens packed with marvellous exotica. His grandiose plans ran out like water in a desert, leaving a few quaint touches such as the Fish Garden, a fossilised relic of a long-dead age. Today it was in a sad state of dereliction, although anything that brought a touch of greenery to the grey cityscape was a welcome addition. A crumbling testament to the desire to carve out a European empire on this continent, it also delivered a stern warning about the perils of trying to impose oneself on a city that wriggled out of any definition you cared to throw at it.

At the heart of the little park was a mound that contained the grotto itself. The air in there was cool and damp. Tanks set into cavities in the rock were built to hold every manner of tropical fish brought from the coral reefs of the Red Sea. Most of these now appeared to be devoid not only of life but even of water. In one tank, painted with a green film of rotting algae, lay a cupful of murky, rust-coloured fluid in which an unremarkable colourless creature was flapping its last. There was no one about. The tunnels of the grotto, never filled with light, were at this hour of the day gloomy and damp. A stooped figure appeared silhouetted in the arch behind him.

'Are you alone?'

'Just as we agreed,' said Makana.

'Yes, but are you alone?' the other man insisted. He was in his late fifties with a dark complexion and tight greying curls shorn close to his skull. The brown suit he had on seemed to have been worn down by nervous energy. The flesh of his face looked slack, overcooked and falling off the bone, hanging in heavy pouches under the eyes. He was clearly afraid, twisting his hands together and looking round.

'It's good to finally meet, Professor Serhan. After all those unfinished phone calls I was beginning to wonder.'

'How do you know who I am?'

'I've seen photographs of you.'

Serhan looked scared enough to bolt like a rabbit at any moment. 'I called because I have information.'

'What kind of information?'

The exasperated handwringing began again. 'Look, the point

is that you can't investigate this matter if you don't have all the facts.'

'What facts?'

They were locked in a strange dance, with Serhan edging backwards and Makana trying to head him off. When he reached the wall of the grotto the professor peered out at the quickening shadows. The smooth trunks of the palms stood out from the rest of the trees like white bones. They stood there for a while. Serhan lowered his voice to a whisper.

'You're the one who was with her when she died, aren't you?'

'Yes.'

'She didn't deserve to die like that.' Professor Serhan took a moment to examine Makana more carefully. 'I knew her, a long time ago.' The professor's courage seemed to waver. Then he rallied himself. 'Let's walk a bit. I don't like staying in the same place for too long.'

Makana followed as the professor led the way up a narrow path, moving unevenly, but quickly. They were soon lost in the twists and turns. The gardens were a popular venue for courting couples who popped up at every bend in the narrow footpaths that wound like string around the artificial mound above the grotto itself. They sat on the benches, surreptitiously holding hands, the young and the not so young, seeking out an elusive moment of privacy. Serhan walked with a determined stride around the little hillock until he came to a bench. They sat side by side like clandestine lovers. He removed his glasses and wiped a handkerchief across his face.

'You need to understand that Meera's death has upset me. I can't help thinking about it.'

'You said you knew her.'

'A long time ago. When we were . . . young.'

'This is before she married Ridwan Hilal?'

'Long before that. We were students. I was older, of course, writing my doctorate.' Serhan sat upright, staring down at his small hands resting on his knees. 'It was a different time. We were young and foolish.' He paused, the spectacles glinting in the fading light. 'There was talk of marriage.'

'Is that why you tried to warn her, by sending the letters?'

Serhan's eyes were deep wells of sadness. His head dipped. 'I knew he would get it. I thought anything else would be too much. If the letter was intercepted. If someone else saw them. But I knew he would understand.'

'Only somehow he didn't.'

'I'm afraid I overestimated his powers.'

'You had access to a printing press.'

'Yes, at the university. They all know me there. I told them it was for a course I was doing.'

'And the references to the Dogstar?'

'I needed some reference that he would understand. I couldn't risk anything more direct. When we were students some of us used to write modernist poetry. We called ourselves the Dogstar Poets. You have to remember, this was the 1980s. Sadat had just been murdered by radicals in the name of jihad. There were great debates among the students about the ideas of fundamentalists like al-Banna, Shukri and Sayyid Qutb, who felt that not only our rulers, but the entire Egyptian society, was living in a state of Jahiliyya. To them, we had all been corrupted by the West.'

Makana was familiar with the thinking of those who believed that Islam had been polluted by popular tradition. Their logic was simple: drop it all and go back to basics, restore Islam to its former glory. The ignorance of modern times was compared to that in the time before the coming of the Prophet. Violence was justified as a means of restoring the country.

'We admired the writers of the early twentieth century, the modernists in what we called the *Nahda*, the Egyptian Renaissance. We questioned tradition and were fascinated, for example, by the poets of the Jahiliyya who were writing before the Prophet Muhammed. We believed that the true nature of this country lay in embracing our past, all of it. Not just Islam.'

'Is this why you hounded Ridwan Hilal out of his job?'

Serhan floundered like a fish out of water. 'That was an unfortunate business, but let me explain. When you are young, changing the world is a simple matter. You are invincible. You can clearly see the errors made by previous generations. As you get older . . .' The professor bowed his head momentarily. 'Well, the thing about compromise is that it starts with something simple, hardly noticeable, but gradually it becomes more serious, until you no longer recognise who you are.'

'You accused Hilal of apostasy. You declared his marriage null and void. Are you trying to say this had nothing to do with your feelings for Meera?'

'No, well . . . I don't know.' The professor looked pained. 'Look, the matter simply got out of hand. Certain people took advantage. It was wrong of me, and believe me, not a day goes by when I don't think of what I did. I . . . I loved her. I would never have done anything to hurt her.' Serhan stared at the ground, wringing his hands together. There was something touching and rather pathetic about seeing a man of great knowledge being reduced to the uncertainties of a lovesick teenager.

'Those were different times. We wore our hair long. There were rock concerts at the pyramids. Imagine that. American bands came all the way from California to play for us. We wanted to embrace this new way of life. To shake off the old ways.' His voice tapered off into a sigh. Then he seemed to have trouble starting up again. 'We thought of ourselves as intellectuals. The women smoked cigarettes and talked about Simone de Beauvoir. I wanted to love a woman like that, a woman who gave herself to me because she chose to, not because society obliged her. You understand?'

'But things changed.'

Serhan nodded sadly. 'There are times when you realise you are not as strong as you thought you were. Marrying a Christian would have devastated my family. We would have been outcasts. Our children, if we ever had any, would be strangers in their own land.'

'So you let her go, but you didn't forget her. When she married Hilal you were jealous. Is that why you tried to destroy him?'

'I told you, people took advantage of me. I was weak. But I also disagreed with Doctor Hilal's thesis. Fundamentally. It is a profound issue. I am a religious man and . . .' He paused, as if seeking a way to convince himself. 'What he did was wrong. You can't treat the word of Allah like some cheap novel you buy in the street. It's just wrong.'

Makana was beginning to get a sense of the differences between the two men. Both were unquestionably devout. Intellectually, Hilal was clearly more agile. He wanted to believe, not only in his heart but also with his quite substantial intellectual powers. Serhan on the other hand was bound by conventions, still struggling to find the courage of his own convictions. He seemed to be no longer sure what he believed, or why he acted the way he did.

'As you probably know, my situation improved somewhat

216

after that whole business.' He threw Makana a wide-eyed look of alarm. 'That wasn't why I did it, of course.'

'Of course not, but you did make a good profit.'

'In a certain way, perhaps I did.' He was squeezing his palms together like he was wringing out wet laundry. 'I went up in the world. But that all came later. I didn't need to be told that what Ridwan had published was wrong.' Serhan licked his lips and stared at a spot somewhere in the distance. 'I began to move in certain circles, among influential people. Powerful men of industry, military officers.' The shadows were lengthening as the last flickers of light were snuffed out.

'One last thing. What prompted you to send those letters?'

'A couple of months ago I happened to overhear a conversation. It was at a shareholders' meeting at the bank.'

'The Eastern Star?'

Serhan nodded. 'There is a general meeting once a year that you are obliged to attend. I generally go along to show my face and leave as soon as I can. I was sitting at the back and there were two men standing behind me. I overheard them talking about having taken care of something. I wouldn't have paid much attention except I caught Meera's name. They also mentioned someone else, a journalist. Again, I would probably have dismissed the incident from my mind but the following morning I read in the paper about a journalist, a man named Hikmet. He had thrown himself from a window. I knew immediately that I had overheard his executioners. I realised they were talking about killing Meera.'

'Who were these men?'

'I don't know. I didn't dare turn around. But it was the way they were talking. They mentioned her by name, and the place where she worked. I didn't know she was working in a travel agency, but I know that things were hard for them after . . . well, you know. I couldn't approach her, for obvious reasons. So I decided to write.'

A groundsman wandered up the path in green overalls and big rubber boots, his feet heavy as if he was wading through thick black molasses, telling people the garden was closing.

'This is a terrible mistake,' said Serhan, leaping to his feet. 'I should never have come here.'

Makana hurried after Serhan, who was rushing down the path at great speed. He grabbed hold of his arm.

'Why send three letters? Why not just one?'

'When the first one didn't work I sent another, and then another. I couldn't understand why he didn't respond.' Serhan's lips moved soundlessly as if worrying at a rag. 'It's no good. I shouldn't have come. You mustn't try to contact me.'

And with that he was gone, melting into the thickening shadows that sprang up all around. Makana considered chasing after him but he had a feeling there was no point. Serhan was scared out of his wits. The only reason he had talked at all was because he had managed to lull himself into a state of false security remembering the old days when everyone had been young and he and Meera had been in love. With a sigh, Makana lit another cigarette. He wondered if Serhan had chosen this place because they used to come here back then. The groundsman appeared again clumping towards him, his boots making sucking noises, opening and closing like black eels clamped around his legs. His eyes were dull white orbs floating in the gloom.

'We're closing.'

Makana took himself off without waiting to be asked again.

Chapter Twenty-Five

It was late when Makana finally arrived home. The river road was silent and empty. The big eucalyptus tree hung down over the riverbank like an unanswered question mark.

Umm Ali's precarious little shack was dark and silent. This, while being unusual, was not out of the ordinary. Although he often wondered at the way she and the children managed to stay up long into the early hours watching some raucous melo-drama on television and still be up at the crack of daybreak, there were exceptions. Perhaps the machine was broken, or it might even have been possible that the good-for-nothing brother had decided to take them all off on a treat. Miracles still happened, Makana had to remind himself, even if they were few and far between. It was only when he reached the end of the narrow path that he began to feel uneasy. He paused to listen to the sound of the water slopping against the sides of the hull and wished he had the gun with him. It was altogether too quiet. Carrying a gun had always seemed to him a good way to get yourself killed, but right now he would have liked the reassur-ance of one in his hand. The Beretta was concealed in the locker behind his desk. To get it he would have to climb to the upper deck. He listened some more before deciding that nothing would be achieved by waiting. The gangplank sagged and creaked as he stepped onto it, making enough noise to announce the arrival of a baby elephant. The staircase amidships he could climb in the dark blindfolded. He paused halfway up to calm his breathing and listen again. This time he could hear something. Faint and distant. Scratching. What it was he could not say, but it was not right. As he lifted his foot to move on he heard it again. A soft mewing sound that could have been a cat. Cats, of course, had been strolling along these banks since the days of Isis and Osiris, protected by superstition and belief, and he could have done with one to keep the water rats away. Instinct told him this was not a cat. Stretching out a hand he found the panel set into the wall under his desk, inserted a finger into the hole and released the catch. Lowering the flap he reached inside. The Beretta was wrapped in an oily rag. He began to feel better about things.

The sound came again, barely distinguishable above the soft beat of the water, and this time he knew it was human. His heart stopped for a moment. Then he moved quickly, stepping up onto the deck in a crouch. The faint light of the crescent moon fell between the dark outlines of the tall buildings across the river. A pleasure boat went by bringing with it a passing jingle of music and laughter, a spotlight played across the *awama* as the passengers enjoyed themselves picking out sights of interest on their cruise. The river glinted like quicksilver through the wooden railings. On the open rear deck an object lay on the floor. At first he thought it was a trick of the light. And then it moved and Makana felt a cold tremor run through his body.

Sami was splayed out on the wooden deck, arms and legs stretched wide. Setting the gun down, Makana knelt and bent close to be rewarded with a faint, tortured hiss of air. The mewing sound he had heard. Sami's face and chest gleamed in the moonlight. His shirt was flayed into ribbons, the cloth soaked with blood that leaked off his chest, trailing from his arms and legs in long rivulets to find the gaps in the wooden deckboards.

'Can you hear me, Sami?'

There was no response. The uneven rising and falling of the chest. He was alive, just. Makana noticed there was something awkward about the way his body lay. When he tried to move an arm, thinking he would make his friend more comfortable, it refused to move: each hand and foot had been nailed to the deck. A guttural cry came from somewhere deep down inside Sami's chest. He was trembling all over as if an electric charge were running through him. The nails were large and square, carpenter's nails that had been hammered through the centre of each palm, crushing bones and parting flesh before embedding themselves deeply in the wood.

Sami thrashed about faintly and then went limp. Makana went to the telephone and called Sindbad – calling for an ambulance might entail a wait of an hour or more. It took ten rings before he answered. He sounded asleep.

'Get here as fast as you can.'

In the meantime, Makana found a hammer and a pair of pliers and set about trying to dig the nails out. It wasn't easy. He started with the left hand. The worn teeth slipped, blood spread over his hands, making the tool even more slippery to grasp. He grabbed the bedsheet and tore it into strips, wrapping them round his hands. Sweat dripped from his brow. Finally, he felt the first nail begin to give. Each fraction that it moved seemed to touch a nerve inside Sami. He rocked back and forth as if in the grip of a nightmare. The pliers were sliding all over the place.

Makana let them drop to the deck and set to work with his fingers. He squeezed until the edges of the nail dug into his flesh. Nothing. He tried again. This time he felt it give. The pain in his fingers made him want to scream. He gave a cry as it came free of the wood and he managed to slip it out of Sami's palm. Sami appeared to lose consciousness. A piece of paper, now soaked in blood, had been stuck to his hand with the nail. Makana slipped it into his pocket as he set to work on the second one. There was a shout from below as Sindbad came down the narrow path, moving with a speed and agility that belied his bulk. When he saw what was waiting on the upper deck, he gave a cry.

'*Ya satyr, ya rub!* Who did such a thing?'

'Help me,' Makana handed him the pliers. Sindbad removed the remaining nails with less difficulty than if they had been pins stuck in cardboard. Then Makana set about using more strips of sheet to bandage the wounds as best he could.

'We must get him to the hospital.'

'*Effendim.*' Sindbad hauled Sami up onto his shoulder and the two of them made their way up the bank to the road. Sindbad drove like a man possessed.

'Why would anyone do something like that?' he asked. 'I thought only Christians did that.'

'They were sending a message.'

'A message?' echoed Sindbad. 'Who for?'

'For anyone still looking for an excuse to hate Christians.'

III

The Nile Star

Chapter Twenty-Six

Makana called Rania from the hospital. Okasha, when he got hold of him, said he would send a squad car to bring her straight to the hospital. A stretcher went by with an unconscious boy of about twelve on it, accompanied by two orderlies trying to steer their way through the crowd and fight off the hysterical relatives at the same time. The boy's mother was screaming and slapping her face.

'We must keep the details secret,' said Okasha. 'This could start a riot.'

'It's too late for that. I have a feeling the news will already have been leaked.'

'Save your paranoia, please,' Okasha groaned.

'A crucifixion. You don't think that's a clear message?'

'We don't know that for sure.'

'You should listen to yourself sometimes. What does it look like to you?'

A young man with red eyes and the look of someone who had not slept for days appeared.

'What can you tell us, doctor?' Okasha asked.

'He has lost a lot of blood, but we believe we have stabilised him. He needs to rest. It's hard to say how much damage was done. The hands and feet are complex. A lot of delicate bones, ligaments, nerves. Whoever did this wanted him to suffer.'

'Then they didn't want to kill him?' Okasha pressed.

'Oh, yes, he would have bled to death eventually, but it would have taken a long time.'

'You think they might have mistaken him for you?' Okasha followed Makana outside to smoke a cigarette.

'It's possible. If they were watching the *awama* and knew I would turn up at some stage. It was dark. They saw a man arrive and go down onto the boat. They thought it was me.'

They stood in the dark as people hurried by to attend to one emergency or another.

'If you're right, then maybe you should disappear for a while.'

'And go where exactly?'

Okasha looked pained. 'Well, at least try and clean yourself up, you look like you just came from a slaughterhouse.'

Makana found a bathroom, which offered a thin trickle of water from a solitary tap, and cleaned himself up as best he could. He buttoned the remains of his shirt and jacket and tried to clear off some of the dark smears he knew were Sami's blood. His face looked a mess. Along with the collection of cuts and bruises, he had acquired the haunted look of a man who hasn't slept for weeks.

In the corridor Makana found a free space on a bench along-side an older woman who gave off an acrid smell. She looked as if she had spent days sleeping in this spot. Her bare feet, gnarled and dry like muddy roots, stuck out in front of her as she snored softly to herself. After a time he closed his own eyes and miracu-lously managed to sleep.

When he gently pushed open the door to peer into the room,

Makana found Rania sitting by Sami's bedside with her head bowed. He thought she was sleeping and was about to turn and leave quietly, when she stirred and raised her head. Her eyes were swollen and red from crying.

'Rania, I'm so sorry about this.'

They stood on opposite sides of the bed, staring down at the inert figure between them. Sami's hands and feet were bandaged and he was under heavy sedation.

'I couldn't understand where he had got to,' Rania murmured. 'I made supper and sat down and waited. I must have fallen asleep. I tried to call him. I wasn't worried. Sami's always forgetting to charge his phone . . .' Her voice cracked and she put a hand up to stifle her sobs. 'They don't know if he will ever be able to walk again,' she cried. 'What will we do?'

'He's strong, Rania, and stubborn. He'll pull through. You'll see.'

'And even if he does, will he ever be able to write again? Did you see his hands?'

'He'll be all right.' Makana recalled the memory of the nail as it grated against broken bone while he tried to pull it free.

'How could this happen?' She looked up from Sami. 'I want to know everything.'

'I don't think they intended to hurt him. I think it was me they were after.'

Dawn was breaking when he got home to find Umm Ali standing by the road surrounded by a small crowd of neighbours. She gave a cry when she caught sight of him and rushed over.

'What a night! I swear by the father of my children I hope I never live to see another like it.'

'How are you, Umm Ali? How are the children?'

'*Al-hamdoulilah*, the Lord saw fit to preserve our lives from those devils.' She paused to wail a little and then told her story. Around sunset three men, their faces covered, had appeared in the doorway of the little shack. After tying them up and gagging them, they left them all lying on the bed together, which is where the police had found them. As they went by the little shack he caught a glimpse of Aziza and her brother standing in the doorway, holding themselves back in the shadows.

'Where was Bassam?'

'That useless donkey? He went out in the afternoon and we've seen no sign of him yet, probably out gambling with his friends, just when we needed a man to protect us. We could have been slaughtered like chickens.' Umm Ali clutched a hand to her throat and wailed some more. 'Is it true what they did to *ustaz* Sami? The policeman told me. These Christian devils? None of us is safe.'

'We don't know who did it yet, or why.'

But Umm Ali's remark told him that by now the story would be eating its way through the city from one end to the other. Twenty-four hours. That was all it would take, probably a lot less, before the story was on the lips of every newscaster and front page in the country.

'May Allah guide you in finding the guilty ones. How is *ustaz* Sami, *ya basha*?'

'He suffered, but he will recover, *inshallah*.' It always surprised him how the words came naturally to him. *If God wills it*. Did he really believe that God was anything more than an alibi, a licence to do violence? It was a reflex that had not been worked out of his system yet. Umm Ali began wailing again and tearing at her hair when she saw the upper deck.

The blood had thickened into stringy patterns along the cracks in the old, dry planks, spreading out in a spiderweb across the deck. Had they found their intended target Makana knew he might have spent all night in agony before being found. He wasn't expecting anyone and assuming nobody dropped by . . . Even if Umm Ali's useless brother had returned to find his sister and her children tied up, how long would it have taken for them to discover him? His eye caught something fluttering in the breeze. Gently he detached a scrap of paper stuck to the deck with Sami's blood. The same note he had left in the café opposite the building where Rocky lived.

There was a commotion down below and he went over to the railing to see two men in casual clothes trying to make their way past Aziza. Slight in build she was far from defenceless. A furious Amazon defending her territory. Her mother called down to ask what was going on, but she coolly ignored her. The two men tried charm, then bribery, and then threats. Aziza stood her ground. Finally they retreated, tails between their legs. The girl beamed with delight.

'They've been trying to get up here all night,' Umm Ali moaned as she dragged a bucket of soapy water up the stairs. She began to scrub at the floorboards.

'Who are they?'

'They want to take pictures. Imagine that? May Our Lord lead them all to damnation.'

The telephone disturbed his thoughts. It was Damazeen. His voice full of cheery bluster despite the early hour.

'Have you considered my offer?'

'I'm not sure I trust you any more than I can stand the sight of you.'

'Put your pride to one side. Think of what I am offering you. What I said is true. I can give you your life back.'

'Does Talal know that you were the one who betrayed his father?'

'He's a talented boy. I can help him.'

'That won't make what you did right.'

There was a long pause. 'I have told you a good deal of my plans. Perhaps that was foolish of me, but I did it as a mark of trust. I need to know you will help me.'

'Now that sounds like a threat. Why do I have no trouble believing you mean that?'

'This offer does not stay open indefinitely. I need your answer, Makana. Remember what I said. I am your only link. Without me Nasra stays dead.'

After Damazeen had hung up Makana stared at the receiver in his hand. He dialled Amir Medani's office and it was answered immediately.

'Did you find out anything?'

Makana heard the lawyer sigh, which wasn't good. It sounded like he had someone in the office with him as he lowered his voice to a whisper, muting it, as if he were cupping the receiver in his hand.

'I made some calls. There is no record of either of them having survived the accident, but that is only to be expected. The militias could do what they wanted back then and they answered to nobody. Then I called a cousin of mine, a journalist. It seems that Mek Nimr has an extensive family – three daughters and two sons. One of the girls is said to be adopted, apparently from his wife's family.'

'So, Damazeen is telling the truth.'

'We don't know that, but yes, there is a possibility she is alive.' There was a long pause, then Amir Medani said, 'I know this is difficult for you, but you must not get involved with Damazeen. Even if it was true, I still think this could be a trap.'

Makana thanked Amir and rang off. After that he took a shower and dressed in fresh clothes, which made him feel a little more human. When he arrived back at the hospital he found Rania asleep on a simple bench in the corridor, her head resting against the wall, a veil of dark hair covering her face. When he sat down beside her she jerked awake with a cry.

'What? Did something happen?'

'Don't you think you ought to go home and get some rest?'

She yawned and rubbed her hands over her face. 'I must look awful.'

'Here,' he said. 'I brought you coffee from the place you like in Zamalek. Latté, right?'

'How did you know about that?' she frowned, taking the paper beaker and removing the lid.

'Sami told me.' Makana recalled the afternoon with Meera in the café.

'And I also brought you some food,' he said, handing over the paper bag.

'I can't think of food at a time like this,' she said, opening the bag to sniff. 'What is it?'

'Cheese fiteer and fried chicken.'

'I'll get as fat as a duck,' she fretted, but nevertheless reached inside to begin tearing strips of savoury pancake off and stuffing them into her mouth. 'I haven't eaten since yesterday.' Rania leaned back in her chair and chewed for a while, the bag in her hand forgotten. She stopped and tears flooded her eyes. 'I keep thinking that if only he hadn't talked so much.'

'How do you mean?'

'I mean, all his big ideas.' She sniffed, found a paper napkin in the bag and wiped her nose. Then she took a deep breath and tried again. 'You know how he's always talking about revolution and changing the world, and all those crazy things that come into his head.'

'That had nothing to do with what happened.'

She stared at him and her eyes filled with tears.

'Eat,' he encouraged gently. 'He needs you to be strong.'

'I just don't understand how anyone could do such a thing,' she said, staring into space, then she stopped again, her hand halfway to her mouth. 'I mean the *way* they did it.'

'The Romans crucified slaves, pirates and thieves. Early Christians adopted it as a form of martyrdom, a symbol of their struggle to be allowed to practise their religion.'

'You're saying someone wanted to make it look like Christians had done it? That's horrible.'

Closing her eyes, Rania sipped her coffee, holding the cup in both hands to breathe in the aroma. Watching her drink took Makana back to that now distant afternoon in the Alhambra café with Meera. Rania spoke without turning to him. 'We don't really know each other, do we?'

'Well . . .'

'I mean, without Sami there to bounce around between us.'

'I suppose there's some truth in that.'

'He admires you, you know. Calls you his moral compass.'

'I'm not sure what that means.'

'I suppose it means that whenever he is in doubt he asks himself what you would do.' Her eyes remained fixed on the cup in her hands.

'He's going to be all right, Rania. I'm sure of it.'

Now her eyes came up to meet his. 'What if he can't walk again, or write, what kind of life will he have? How will we manage?' Her whole body began to tremble and she pressed a hand to her eyes as if to blot out the world. Makana sat quietly.

A moment passed. The hospital seemed quiet at that time. Somewhere in the distance a child was crying. A telephone began to ring. A door slammed and a voice called for help. A nurse went by and eventually the crying stopped.

Chapter Twenty-Seven

Makana found Faragalla on his feet behind the desk in his office. He was busy going through the drawers, dumping things into the briefcase that lay open before him. He seemed agitated and jumped when Makana appeared in the doorway.

'Oh, it's you. I was wondering when you would show up.'

'Are you going somewhere?'

The tall man straightened up awkwardly, one hand going to the small of his back. He regarded Makana with the usual expression of disdain.

'Well, I'm not staying here. It's madness. One minute people are being shot right on your doorstep and now this journalist. He was nailed to the floor. Can you imagine?'

'I was there.'

'Yes, of course you were.' Faragalla gave the matter a moment's pause. 'Well, I'm off anyway. I shall spend a couple of weeks in Beirut until things settle down.'

'What about the business?'

'The business can take care of itself.'

'I suppose it's done so for centuries. A couple of weeks won't make a difference, right?'

Faragalla's face tightened. 'I don't like you, Makana. Right from the moment I set eyes on you, I said to myself there is something bad about that man. I suppose I owe you some money.' He moved to the filing cabinet and opened one of the drawers using a key from a ring that was attached to his belt by a chain. 'Did you find out about the letters?'

'They were intended as a warning.'

'A warning? To me?'

'To Meera. An old friend of hers thought she was in danger and sent her a rather obscure message.'

'Obscure is right.' Faragalla placed a small petty-cash box on the desk and spent a moment selecting another key to unlock it. He stopped. 'But there's more to it than that. I mean, why kill her, and why here?'

'Well, that's where you come into it.'

'Me?' Faragalla sank down into the chair behind the desk. 'So it *has* got something to do with me?' The money forgotten, he reached absently for the pipe which lay in the ashtray before him.

'Do you remember when you hired Meera? Do you remember why?'

Faragalla frowned. 'She was smart, smarter than most people in here. Not unpleasant to look at. I thought she would be a great asset, and I was right. She cleared up the administrative system, did remarkable things.'

'She was friendly with your nephew Ramy.'

'And what of it?' Faragalla peered at Makana over the rim of his spectacles as he reached out a crabbed hand for his lighter. It clicked like an angry insect.

'Meera was here to conduct her own little investigation into your financial transactions. Ramy helped her.'

'He's an ungrateful little whelp.'

'You didn't send him to Luxor, did you?'

'What?' The flame trembled over the bowl of Faragalla's pipe.

'Ramy went all by himself. He did what you are doing now, running away. It must be a family trait.'

Makana moved about the room, his eye falling on a poster hanging on the wall – a picture of the gigantic pillars of the temple at Karnak. Faragalla set down his pipe and lighter with a sigh.

'He just vanished, with no warning. There was an incident with a woman, one of our guests.'

'This happened just before he vanished?'

'Around that time. I didn't want to punish the boy but he disappeared all by himself. I'd been trying to get him to go to Luxor for some time. I wanted someone to keep an eye on operations down there. One day I got a call from him saying he was already there. I assumed he felt ashamed by what had happened. He's not a bad kid but he's a real loser. This is the thanks I get for trying to help family.'

'You just let it be known that you had sent him there, as punishment for the business with that woman.'

'One has to maintain authority, everyone knows that.' Faragalla fiddled with his lighter.

'How much trouble are you actually in?'

'I'm sorry?' The clicking stopped.

'I mean financially,' Makana said. 'Yousef goes around the hotels bribing the managers to give you special rates. Most of the people employed out there can barely bring themselves to turn up for work. The number of tourists passing through your books is hardly enough to sustain a company this size.'

'You see, this is what I was talking about. Your insolence!

What gives you the right to start asking me questions? I'm the one who hired you, remember?' He reached for the steel box and took out a bundle of notes which he tossed across the desk. 'Here you are. This is what you came for isn't it?'

'Are you paying me to go away?'

'You and that stupid kid.' Faragalla's jowls shook with fury. 'How I ever got involved with you, I'll never understand. And do me a favour, tell him to stay away from my daughter.'

'Talal has nothing to do with this. You asked me to find out if there was a threat against you or your business. It turns out the threat was aimed at one of your employees, who might have been killed because of something she uncovered here.'

'That is ridiculous nonsense and I have a good mind to throw you out on your ear.'

'Did you know Yousef is running a little sideline in forged passports? One phone call from me and you will not only be out of business, you will probably find yourself in prison.'

Faragalla licked his lips, then he reached into the petty-cash box and tossed another bundle of cash onto the pile.

'I don't want any trouble. Take that and get out. Consider our arrangement terminated.'

'It's not as easy as that.' Makana left the money where it was.

'I hired you to look into the threats, nothing else. What business of yours is any of this?'

'Who exactly is running this company, you or Yousef?'

'Okay, fine. I'll tell you, but then you have to promise to leave me alone. All this is in confidence. I'm your client remember?'

'I thought you just terminated our contract?'

A weariness came over Faragalla's slack face, causing it to look even more shapeless. His eyes dropped until they were fixed on the bowl of his pipe.

'About ten years ago I was in a spot of trouble. Business was slow. You remember what the country was like then? Maybe you don't. Anyway, after Saddam invaded Kuwait the foreign workers fled and our economy sank. No more dutiful husbands sending money home. And the war scared the tourists away. Then we had the crazy fanatics. Remember the killings in Luxor? Well, that pretty much destroyed us.' Faragalla gazed into the bowl of his pipe. 'Anyway, one day I get a visit. Old army types. You can spot them a mile away. They are dressed in civilian clothes but their spines are as straight as spears. They said they had a financial proposition for me. They were interested in the tourist business. *Marhaba*, I said, you're welcome. You could probably buy up the whole country for a song. These people have no sense of humour. They told me they represented a private fund that wanted to invest in the company. It was the answer to my prayers.'

'Where does Yousef come into it?'

'Well, all was fine for a time and then they started to get nervous and insisted they put their own man into the office, just to keep an eye on their interests. I wasn't too keen on the idea. On the other hand, what choice did I have?'

'So he came to work for you.'

'Exactly. And if you let him know I told you this, I'll be the next dead person you see.'

'Your grandfather would have been proud of you.'

'You can sneer if you like, but I had no choice.' Faragalla set his pipe down. 'They promised me that they would increase their investment, that in time I would see the company grow. But they don't care about the company. They are just using me.'

'And Yousef takes care of business for them.'

'Money flows right past my door, but none of it stops here.'

As Makana got to his feet Faragalla reached over and slid the pile of cash towards him.

'I'm not going to forget what I know.'

'It's not a bribe,' said Faragalla quietly. 'You earned it. Not many people have the nerve to tell me the truth. You told me a few things I would rather not hear.' The dull eyes lifted from the desk as Makana picked up the bundle of money. 'You still haven't asked me the name of this investment company. Aren't you curious to know?'

'I think I already do,' said Makana. 'The Eastern Star Investment Bank.'

Chapter Twenty-Eight

Sindbad had the radio on in the car as they drove to Giza. It was tuned to a phone-in show discussing the murders in Imbaba. Several callers were eager to comment on a newspaper story which carried an interview with someone who claimed to know who the killer was.

'I don't believe a word of it,' said the first man. 'This is just fairy tales for small children. They make them up to sell papers. And you're doing the same thing right now. *Haram aleyk*.'

The next caller added his support for this view. 'It's a shame people are making money out of the murder of these children.'

'These aren't children,' said the following speaker, a woman, 'they are animals. They live in the street. We should applaud this killer for cleaning up the city of these vermin.'

This was too much for the host of the programme. 'Please, everyone. Let's try to keep this dignified.' He cut to an expert, or at least as close to one as he could get. A senior journalist with a state-run paper who provided the conservative view.

'As we have seen recently with the brutal attack on our colleague Sami Barakat, there appears to be a team of senseless killers preying on innocent people. And as the honourable Sheikh

Waheed has pointed out, a man who is much more knowledge-able on these matters than myself, there is a tradition for such ritual slaughter in certain religious beliefs, such as the Jews, and the Christians.'

'Shame on you for broadcasting such nonsense,' said the next speaker, quite irate. 'We have to ask who benefits from us killing one another. Ask your esteemed studio guest that question. Who benefits? While we are all fighting amongst ourselves, his friends are stealing this country from under our very eyes.'

The point was disputed of course and for a time it went back and forth until Makana, unable to bear any more, reached over and switched off the radio.

'He was right though,' said Sindbad. 'That last one. They wouldn't let him speak, but it's true what he said. We have to stick together. One thing is for sure, *ya basha*. You couldn't pick a better time to leave. Let's hope the city is still here when you get back.'

'We can only hope.'

The platform at Giza station was gloomy under the faint glow of a few sparse lights. It was almost deserted at that hour. Makana wandered along the open platform among the odd figures stand-ing around in the shadows. Most passengers went into Ramses main station, leaving only a few stragglers waiting here on the city's southern edge. He lit a cigarette and looked up at the stars. In the narrow gully of the tracks the light was thin enough to allow a glimpse of the heavens. The longer he stared upwards the more seemed to appear, as if seeing them was more a matter of faith, of believing they were really up there.

The darkness moaned, long and low, announcing the train's approach. At the last minute a portly woman came scurrying through the narrow station building from the street accompanied by a taxi driver weighed down under enough luggage to slow a small elephant. He set down one trunk after another, wiped the sweat from his brow, then went back out for the next lot. The woman counted the items of luggage repeatedly, as if afraid they might sprout legs and run away. The other passengers were mostly single men. A newly married couple heading home after a honeymoon in the city of lights. The bride still wore her new clothes, the palms of her hands were decorated with whorls and flowers painted in henna. Three pinpricks of light grew steadily as the big flat-nosed locomotive rumbled out of the gloom from under a flyover with a heavy, reassuring grumble. A plaintive cry sounded as it rolled by like a wounded beast.

Makana carried a small holdall with a change of clothes. His provisions consisted of two packs of Cleopatra and a cone of peanuts wrapped in newspaper stuffed into the pocket of his jacket. He hauled himself up the steps and shuffled past the eager passengers until he found a compartment that was empty. Choosing a seat by the window, he settled himself down in the upright seat.

Whenever he left this city a part of him wondered if he would ever return, as if it was not real at all, but simply a figment of his imagination. Perhaps he would find a new life for himself in Upper Egypt – land of his forefathers. Nubia, the fabled kingdom, straddled the borderline. Not that he was sentimental about such things.

When he closed his eyes he saw the orange glow of the lights on the bridge, felt the thump of the car as it hit the railings and the slow, tortured screech of the metal as it gave way and the car began to tumble, ever so slowly, down into the dark water. Surely Nasra could not have survived that fall? Makana fell asleep, his mind feverish with the events of the past few days. It felt a relief to be moving, as if all that was being left behind him, as if the train's purpose was to distance him from a troubled world, when in actual fact it was supposed to be the opposite.

When he opened his eyes he realised he was not alone. The compartment was dark save for the light of the moon which infused it with an indigo glow. A man sat diagonally opposite him, facing the other way, close to the door. He appeared to be asleep, sitting stiffly upright. An innocent passenger, or something more? A State Security agent perhaps, sent to keep him company? Or something more dangerous? The Beretta was wrapped in a shirt at the bottom of the bag that his foot rested on. Makana wriggled upright and looked out at the rural landscape that shuffled past the window. Fields flew by to be replaced by more fields. They changed in length and breadth, in the placement of the little square buildings on them, but otherwise little. Here and there a crack of light split the darkness as a window shot by affording a fleeting glimpse of domestic life, or the flicker of a fire, embers shooting into the starry sky to vanish without trace. Whether it was the gentle lulling of the train, or the sense of being in motion, Makana fell into a fitful sleep. When he opened his eyes again the sky was lightening and a family was spread out on the seats facing him: father, mother and three children all nodding soundly in sleep.

Makana stepped out into the corridor and pulled open a window to let the air in. He chewed peanuts and watched scraps of stray paper turning over lazily in the air until he realised they were herons. When you looked at these fields it was hard not to think that little had changed since the days of Hatshepsut. Less than an hour later they were ticking through the points on the outskirts of Luxor, the train juddering from side to side.

As he walked through the sleepy town towards the river, Makana recalled coming here years ago with Muna. In the time before Nasra's birth. The trip had been a wedding gift from her father. A man Makana still recalled with some affection. Unlike some in the family, including Muna's mother, he had never voiced disapproval of his daughter's choice. Perhaps she should have listened more closely to her mother. His daughter might still be alive and married to a banker or businessman. Who would want their daughter to marry a police officer? Not even Makana's father wanted him to join the force. He had not done badly in school. There were other options open to him. Makana grew up with the privilege and the curse of having a teacher for a father. Privilege because it got him out of the government schools and into one of the best schools in Khartoum for a fraction of the price. And a curse because, well, if your father was a teacher what could you expect but the regular taunts and occasional beatings? It was his father's dream for his son to attend university, something he himself never had the opportunity to do. So he stood in front of the blackboard day after day and stared out of the window listening to fifty boys repeating their times table and imagined his son an engineer or doctor. A father should be allowed to dream.

The market was coming slowly to life. Merchants yawned as they greeted one another. In a few hours it would be crowded with people trawling up and down for the loofahs that hung in strings like desiccated fruits; tubs of spices heaped like miniature hills; peppery vermilion, coppery turmeric and dusty cumin, little brown pearls of coriander and heaps of dates, of which there was an encyclopaedic variety. These were separated by other stores packed with items shipped in by container from distant continents; brightly coloured plastic tubs, upright fans and plastic slippers, huge underpants flapping in the breeze like flags, towers of shiny metal bowls. On and on it went.

When he reached the Corniche, the air lifted and the palm trees bobbed gracefully in greeting. A battered and faded metal sign announced Blue Ibis Tours with a handpainted version of the strange bird logo he knew from the Cairo offices. Their centre of operations comprised two rusty boats shackled in parallel. In the gully between the two hulls golden ripples of sunlight on water outlined a man perched on a wooden bosun's seat refreshing the paint on the name, *Nile Star*. His dark skin stood out against the oversized grubby white vest he was wearing. The brush hovered in mid-air as his eyes followed Makana crossing the gangway above him.

In the centre of a lobby area with a low ceiling, a large vase stuffed with plastic roses stood on a circular table. The colours were faded and dusty, proving that even artificial flowers had a finite lifespan. In one corner of the room was a high counter with the word *Reception* above it. There was no one behind it. Doors opened to left and right. He had no idea where they led. The sound of voices drew him to a sign marked *Dining Room* where he observed tourists having their breakfast. He was about to go in when a voice behind him said:

'Can I help you?'

Makana turned to find a small woman in a dark suit clutching a clipboard. The very image of efficiency. Pinned to the breast of her nylon jacket was a silver badge with the name Dena on it.

'I'm looking for Ramy.'

'And you are?'

'Makana. Faragalla was supposed to inform you of my arrival.'

'Well,' she frowned, 'we've heard nothing.'

'That's very strange. He gave me his word he would arrange everything.'

'I would have sent a car to the airport.'

'I came by train,' Makana said, although it didn't seem important.

Dena held up a finger as a herd of tourists swept through. They seemed a very mixed bag. Some Asians. The majority being middle-aged Europeans suitably clad for an expedition into deepest, darkest Africa. Their outfits resembled military fatigues, with heavy boots, belts and straps everywhere. Each carried a small rucksack and several had water bottles clipped to their swelling waists. Faces broke into smiles when they caught sight of Dena. They waved and smiled and bowed. For her part she managed to flit effortlessly between half-a-dozen languages. Makana picked up French, Spanish and English.

'*Arigato, arigato. Hai.*'

Four small women bobbed their heads in return as they marched off up the gangway towards the Corniche and the waiting tour buses.

'Full ship?'

'Not exactly. We are carrying about thirty per cent of our full capacity. For some of them this is the trip of a lifetime. They spend years dreaming of coming here. Imagine their disappointment.' The way she studied his rumpled appearance and creased clothes suggested they were not the only ones to be disappointed. 'It's odd that Mr Faragalla didn't tell me about you.'

'He has a lot on his mind these days.'

'Yes, of course, the shooting. That poor woman. I think I might even have met her once.'

'I'd like to see Ramy as soon as possible.'

'Oh,' Dena's face fell. 'I thought Mr Faragalla would have explained.'

'Explained?'

'Ramy is not here. He had to inspect our Aswan offices.'

'When was this?'

'Oh, late last night.' Her teeth gleamed impossibly white as she smiled. 'Can I ask what this is regarding?'

'It's confidential, and rather urgent.'

'I understand. Well, I can only offer to give you a cabin. The *Nile Star* will be sailing tonight. We shall be in Aswan the day after tomorrow.'

'Can't we get there any faster?'

Dena laughed. 'The whole idea is for the tourists to relax and see a bit of the country. Maybe you could do with a bit of a rest yourself.'

Makana was reminded that he was not at his best. Dena led the way down a narrow staircase to a corridor running the length of the vessel. Halfway along she produced a key to unlock a cabin door, which turned out to be a rather cramped office with a bank of grey filing cabinets and shelves along one side and a desk that was almost as wide as the cabin. Compared to Faragalla's office in Cairo this was a model of efficiency – everything was neatly set in place. She cleared the surface of the desk of everything save a telephone and some pencils. Motioning him towards a chair she went behind the desk and sat down. Clasping her hands together on top of the blotter she studied him for a moment.

'Do you mind if I smoke?' she asked, reaching into a drawer for a packet of cigarettes and an ashtray before he could answer.

'Not at all,' he replied.

'We're not supposed to smoke in front of the customers. It gives a bad impression.' She struck a match and lit hers and then leaned across to light his. 'Some cultures frown on women smoking almost as much as ours.'

'We can take some comfort in that, I suppose,' he smiled. 'How long have you worked for the company?'

'Oh, only six months. But I really like it.' She nodded enthusiastically. She was in her twenties he reckoned. This was probably her first job after finishing her studies.

'And how is it working out with Ramy down here all the time?'

Dena regarded him cautiously. 'Is that why you're here? To assess his work?'

'I can't really discuss that.'

'What exactly do you do for Mr Faragalla, if you don't mind me asking?'

'Management consultancy. I look for ways of improving the company.'

'This is because he hasn't been back to Cairo, isn't it?'

'I'm not sure what you mean?'

'I tried to persuade him to go back, just for a bit, but he refused.' Dena stubbed out her cigarette in the glass ashtray with hard stabs. 'I knew this would happen.'

'It sounds like you and he are quite close.'

Her eyes flicked up, quick and sharp. 'We work together, that's all.'

'Still, you must have been happy to hear that he was moving down here full-time.'

'Well, naturally, it makes my job a lot easier.' Everything was already neatly in place on the desk but still, she shifted a pencil as if it held some deep significance.

'Really? Because it looks like you have things pretty much under control,' Makana smiled. 'You must have been used to taking care of everything before. How often did he come down here?'

'Once a fortnight. Sometimes more often.' She got to her feet abruptly and smoothed down her jacket, suddenly bored with his company. 'You must be tired. It's a long journey by train. I'm surprised you didn't fly down.'

'I'm not here to create problems for you,' he said as he stood up. 'All I want to do is talk to him.'

It was plain that she didn't trust him. She had made up her mind that he was a threat and she would do everything she could, he was sure, to prevent him speaking to Ramy.

'As I explained, there was business in Aswan for him to attend to.' Dena stopped short and glanced at her watch. 'I have to get back to work.' She ushered him out of the office, locking the door carefully behind her. 'I shall arrange for a cabin to be made up for you. You can wait upstairs. Have you eaten breakfast?'

'No.' Breakfast sounded appealing. If he was going to be stranded on this vessel for days he might as well make himself comfortable.

The dining room had just been vacated by the tourists. A couple of waiters were trying to tidy up. The buffet table formed an island of white cloth in the middle of the room out of which popped outcrops of plastic flowers and steel food dispensers. As he helped himself to what the tourists had not managed to finish, Makana wondered idly how much it cost to fly halfway around the globe to get here. It seemed like a long way to come for such unremarkable food.

After eating he walked around the deck, breathing in the clear air, listening to the cars honking along the riverbank, the clatter of a horse-drawn *hantour* going by, harness and bells ringing. As the caleche disappeared along the Corniche, a thumping noise to his left brought his attention back to the boat. In the prow a plank of wood and a pot of paint stood alongside a coil of rope. A heavily built man climbed over the railings with the slow, deliberate pace of someone who has learned from painful experience that accidents are caused by sudden movements.

'Your work is never finished on these old ships, I imagine?'

'Oh, they're not too bad.' The man had large, doleful eyes, weighed down by weary pouches. He patted the railings with affection. 'There is nothing you can't do to them.' At first he had taken him for an old man, but on closer inspection he realised that he was younger, perhaps not much more than Makana himself, although he carried himself like someone many years his senior. His skin was darkened from long hours spent in the sun. His chin resembled an iron brush, thick with grey bristles. 'Are you the one they sent from Cairo?'

'And you are . . . ?'

'Adam. Everyone knows me.' A bead of sweat ran down his chest and disappeared into the open neck of the overalls he wore. His hands were gnarled paws that seemed permanently curled into claws. He squinted at Makana. 'You don't look like you belong in Cairo.'

'Actually, my family are originally from the village of Shallal.'

'Shallal? I know the place. It's gone now, of course. They drowned it when they raised the first dam.'

'The price of progress.'

'The people who lived there saw it differently.' Adam took the cigarette Makana offered. The tips of his fingers were dried and cracked.

'Can I ask you a couple of questions?'

'That's what you came here for, isn't it?' The beady eyes held his.

'Yes.'

'Then you'd better ask what you want. Of course, I don't really know anything.'

'It's about Mr Ramy.'

'An unlucky man.'

'Why do you say that?'

'I don't know. It just came to me.' Adam smoked slowly, savouring the taste, staring off at somewhere over Makana's shoulder. 'I don't know anything about anything. Doors get stuck, pipes are blocked. Then they call Adam.'

'But you hear things.'

'Yes, I do.' There was a black mark on his cheek where some mishap had left a scar.

'Mr Makana?' Dena was waving from the rear deck. 'Your cabin is ready.'

As Makana turned, Adam moved silently away.

'I have spoken to Mr Ramy,' Dena said when he reached her. 'He informed me that I am to co-operate fully with you.' She looked him over carefully. 'In fact he insisted that you might be more comfortable staying in his cabin.'

'What happens when he gets back?'

'We will find a solution.' She smiled as though this wasn't going to be a problem.

'When do I get to see him?' Makana called as she crossed the lobby in long strides. She couldn't wait to get away from him.

'Tomorrow,' she called over her shoulder. 'He'll be there when we arrive in Kom Ombo. You'll have time to talk there.'

A nameless man, whose teeth were stained brown from tobacco, led him along the downstairs corridor to a cabin in the bow of the boat. It was quieter there, away from the engines, the man explained. He wore a waiter's uniform of black trousers, short jacket, white shirt, green tie and cummerbund. He led the way into the room and stood waiting for a tip, tossing the key in his hand. Makana handed him a crumpled note which he unfolded carefully before sniffing in disappointment and leaving, dropping the key unceremoniously onto the bedside table as he went.

Whoever had cleaned up the cabin had certainly done a thorough job. The bed was made, the bathroom bare. A tomb robber would have left more. In the wardrobe a pair of shoes had been overlooked on a top shelf. Other than that there was no trace of Ramy. The chair squeaked unhappily as Makana settled into it and turned his attention to the table against the wall. A large map of the country was spread over it. Pins and stickers marked where Blue Ibis was operating. Felt-tip lines in red, green and blue marked various routes on their little mystery tours through the land of the pharaohs. Alongside the map was a simple chart. Across the top was a calendar of dates and for each week there were figures and names marked in squares. These appeared to correspond to the number of people and which company they belonged to. Blue Ibis worked with firms in Europe, North America and Asia which sent them visitors. To someone to whom the idea of taking a holiday seemed quite alien, Makana thought it remarkable how extensive the tourist business really was.

Makana unscrewed the window hatch to let some air into the fetid room. As if set there by the Ministry of Tourism, a fisherman floated into view, poised barefoot on the prow of his felucca to cast a net out over the water. The loop widened in the air, spreading gently before it settled, just kissing the surface. Ripples spread out as the net sank, then he started hauling the line in, arm over arm, with the steady, even rhythm of a man who has been making the same movements all his life. From somewhere close by Makana could hear the click of camera shutters accompanied by cooing sounds of amazement in a variety of languages from the passengers on the deck above him.

Alongside the desk was a shelf of books. Makana ran an eye over the titles. He thumbed through the index of an English guide book, finding references to Dengue fever and advice for lesbian travellers. There were books on Egyptian history, ancient and modern, on the pharaohs, and the exploits of various European explorers. One title leapt out at him: *The Winged Seraph*. On the cover a subtitle was added: *The History of Wadi Nikeiba Monastery*, by Father G. Macarius. It was a fairly humble production, the paper rough and spattered with stray ink from the printing press, held together with thick staples. A younger version of the pugilist priest stared moodily back from a scarred photograph on the back cover. The monastery had been originally constructed in the ninth century but had been abandoned after an outbreak of cholera in the early eighteenth century. The book told the story of how the monastery was rebuilt by a small group of dedicated monks, among them Father Macarius. Makana lay on the bed and closed his eyes and in moments had fallen into the deepest, most profound sleep he had had for months.

Chapter Twenty-Nine

W hen he opened his eyes the room was dark and he was completely disoriented. He thought he was dead, floating in the darkness under the earth.

'Nasra?' he called out.

When he sat up he realised that the woman he had been pursuing in his dream was not his daughter, but Dena, the girl who was running the boat in Ramy's absence.

The boat filled him with a strange calm, as if he was at home. Had Ramy been banished here to protect him in some way? What was the connection between Ramy and Rocky? They had been in the army together, but there had to be something. He took out the photograph he had found in Meera's desk and clicked on the bedside light to examine it again. Three men in army fatigues standing in the desert somewhere. Ramy, Rocky and a third man he had never seen before. Where had they been stationed? Ramy was young enough to have been doing his national service. Faragalla had mentioned that he had given Ramy a job when he got out of the army.

After a time he became aware that the throbbing feeling that was coming through the deck was not the engine. It had a different rhythm. The music cut in again just above his head and he lost his concentration. He decided he wasn't going to do much more thinking after that and instead closed and locked the cabin before following the music upstairs to a large open saloon called *The Ball Room*, complete with upholstered couches and low tables that ran around the walls. These were occupied by passengers who, having eaten their supper, were now settling down for the evening's entertainment. The thumping music came from large speakers set against the wall. On the small stage a man was yelling something unintelligible into a microphone while waving his free hand in the air in some kind of universal signal which the guests appeared to understand. They got to their feet and began shuffling round. Crew members herded them into crocodiles that went waltzing around the room. Everyone placed their hands on the shoulders of the person in front of them. Makana had to admit this was a facet of existence he had never glimpsed before. Next was a dance in which they broke into couples. Here they had to wiggle their hips provocatively while holding a rod between them at waist height in what seemed like an exercise in group humiliation – for tourists and crew members alike. Despite this, they all loved it. A whirling dervish leapt onto the stage and spun round with more enthusiasm than skill, removing his skirts to whip them around his head like a flying *siniya* before folding the cloth into the shape of a swaddling baby. The symbolism of this was lost on Makana, although the Germans next to him applauded ferociously, sighing, '*wie süss*' to one another, whatever that meant. For the finale a man in a loin cloth performed a crude evocation of savage Africa, a reminder perhaps of the continent into which even now they were drifting in darkness. He jumped and stamped his feet, stuck out his tongue and widened his eyes in a clumsy mime. Most Africans would have run screaming at the sight of this display of obvious insanity but the Japanese adored it, clapping their hands to their faces in rapturous delight. With the floor show over, a band took to the stage. More torture. This time inflicted by a keyboard player who seemed incapable of using more than two fingers. The singer warbled like an off-key muezzin. What he was trying to sing, or even what language it was, remained indecipherable. Makana marvelled at this collective ability to inflict and endure indignity and humiliation. The passengers had paid for the experience of a lifetime, and the crew were there because they were being paid. There was some lesson to be learned here. It was a form of foreign domination that made you yearn for Suez again, for revolt of any kind, to free the country of this subservience. In despair, Makana took himself up on deck where he could be alone.

The lights along the shore threaded the dark water with silvery beads as the *Nile Star* eased southwards. The lights gave way to complete and utter darkness. The moon had not yet risen and the landscape was so utterly dark that it appeared as if they were floating through liquid blackness. And finally, there were the stars. The sheer number of which astonished him, so many it was impossible to count. No wonder the Ancient Egyptians saw some great mystery in the heavens. Down here, the *Nile Star*, with its tinny music and the odd peal of laughter from the confines of the ballroom, seemed foolishly small.

'They remain unchanged in thousands of years.'

Makana turned to make out the shadow of a figure leaning on the railings further along – Adam, the handyman who repaired everything. 'We look up and think they are moving, but it is we who move. We see the stars from different angles and draw our own conclusions.'

'So you're an expert on astronomy as well.'

'I've looked at these stars every night for half a century. That ought to count for something, but I feel the same mixture of wonder and ignorance as I did as a child.'

Makana held out the Cleopatras and waited for the thick, oily fingers to fish one out of the packet. Adam held it under his nose as if savouring a Cuban cigar. Reaching into his pocket Makana produced the book he had found in Ramy's cabin.

'Do you know anything about this place?'

Adam held the book under a deck lamp and stared at the cover long enough for Makana to realise that he couldn't read. It didn't matter. He seemed to recognise the picture. Rubbing a flattened thumb over it the taciturn mechanic said:

'Wadi Nikeiba. They closed down the monastery years ago.'

'Do you remember why?'

'They were running a brothel out there.'

'In the desert?'

It seemed an unlikely story, a kind of modern folklore driven by what people wanted to hear.

'I don't recall the details. They went out to the desert to look for God, maybe they found something else.' Adam broke into hoarse laughter, his grin revealing the complete absence of teeth in his upper gums. After a time he grew tired of laughing and his face became serious again. 'Actually, I don't think it was a brothel. I seem to remember someone was killed out there. That's what closed it down.'

'Do you remember when this was?'

'Ten years ago, maybe more.' Adam shrugged and sucked happily at the cigarette.

'You don't remember who was killed?'

'I just remember it was bad. Very bad. A child, something like that.'

'Do you know how to get out there?'

'I can find it. You'd need a car, of course. But what's the point? There's nothing out there but ruins.'

With that Adam tossed the cigarette butt over the side and moved away, leaving Makana alone with his thoughts, suddenly impatient for this voyage to end.

The following day was interminable. For long hours time stopped and there was nothing to do but stare at villages as they went floating by. Makana watched herons perched along the river's edge and hawks turning like leaves buffeted by the warm air. Lean, long-horned *gamous* trampled through muddy green fields. Waterwheels turned as if no technological advances had been heeded in the last two millennia. It was like seeing the world through a telescope looking back over time.

Incredibly, when they finally arrived at Kom Ombo there was a traffic jam, with cruise boats lodged together around the landing dock and continuous herds of people tramping on and off shore. Encouraged by Dena's assurances that Ramy would be waiting for him, Makana went ashore with the mob. A sign in English read: 'Overlooking ancient temple of god Sobek was to worshipped. Refreshments right next toilet.' If the locals had fled before the visitors he wouldn't have been surprised, but instead they ran towards them, knocking one another over in their haste to sell them souvenirs – pocket-sized sphinxes, postcards in long streamers, hats and T-shirts. Makana wandered the ruins of the old temple dedicated to a crocodile god – although Sobek's descendants were no longer to be seen north of the High Dam. Perhaps it was a good thing, progress and living relics of the prehistoric age being mutually exclusive. Or perhaps it was just an illusion of progress. He overheard a guide spreading enlightenment: 'Are you seeing film *Cleopatra* for Richard Burton and Liz Taylor?' The question provoked nods and smiles all round. A teenage girl frowned, whether because she had never heard of the film or could not see the relevance wasn't clear. The guide beamed. 'If you see this film then you are knowing story of Cleopatra,' he explained happily. A short cut through history. The guides seemed to regard their charges with contempt, as if by the very act of coming here and paying handsomely for the experience, they qualified to be treated like idiots. More importantly, here was a chance to assert the superiority of the native culture. The opportunity to bring arrogant westerners to their knees. How better to do it than by throwing Hollywood back at them? Makana, too, felt like a fool as he wandered the island looking for someone who clearly wasn't there. He almost missed the *Nile Star*. When he arrived back, half an hour before the departure time Dena had given him, he found them already casting off. They had to drop the iron gangway back down to let him aboard.

'You nearly got left behind!' laughed Adam. 'You have to pay attention. On a ship you can't afford to be careless.'

'I daresay you're right,' he said, not bothering to explain that either his watch was set to another time zone or someone had planned to leave him behind under Sobek's guardianship. The sister ship had come and gone north, leaving a softly fluttering flag in its wake as the light drained out of the sky over the Western Desert. And not a trace of Ramy.

Dena proved adept at avoiding him. He was sent in every nautical direction imaginable only to discover that she was always at least two steps ahead of him. The crew, ever apologetic, were unable to help him find her. He finally decided to disappear as well and took himself off down to the cabin in the bow to wait. There he discovered that someone had been through his things. His holdall poked out from under the bunk as if it had been kicked there carelessly. An oily rag lay beside it on the floor. He picked it up and held it in his hand. A quick search of the bag revealed that the Beretta which had been wrapped up in it was gone. Nothing else was missing. With a sigh, he threw himself down on the bunk. He seemed to be stuck on a river that was taking him to his doom.

A few hours later, he made his way upstairs to find the evening already in full swing. The noise from the dining room grew steadily in volume and pitch as the combination of plentiful food and wine began to loosen tongues and warm up the guests. The well-fed men and women threw their heads back and howled with laughter. Glasses clinked as the waiters rushed back and forth. The central area was being cleared. Plates were carried away and tables slid aside. The lights dimmed and a moment later the music started up again as the evening's entertainment began. This time a small troupe of three strolled around the room, having changed out of their waiters' uniforms into white gelabiyas, their heads wrapped in matching immas. They rattled their tambourines and thumped their drums and one of them blew a high keening note from his flute.

'They are like children, always playing. They get younger while we just get older.'

Makana turned to find Dena standing in the doorway alongside him. It took him a moment to realise she meant the tourists.

'I'm sorry about earlier,' she said, fumbling with a lighter. 'I understand there was some confusion.'

'You're not helping him, if that's what you think.'

She blew smoke into the air but said nothing.

'Ramy might be in a lot of trouble.'

'And you are here to help him?' A loose strand of hair bobbed around her right ear. Her composure was coming apart. She pushed it back in annoyance and blew smoke in his face. 'How do I know you are not planning to hurt him?'

'If I had wanted to hurt him I would have done this another way.'

She fell silent for a moment, considering her options. 'What is it you want from him?'

'A woman was killed. I think he might know who did it.'

'You mean Meera?' Coming from her the name sounded like an ailment. 'Does it matter who killed her?'

'Perhaps it doesn't, but it's what I am here to do.'

'I understand. I'm sorry about this afternoon.'

'Ramy came here because he was afraid. He knows he's in danger. How long do you think you can protect him?'

'I don't know. Truly. I wish I did, but I don't. He doesn't tell me anything.' Dena inclined her head against the door frame. Beyond her a loop of coloured lights floated out of the darkness past the window. Yet another cruise ship on its way north.

'This is more than a working relationship, isn't it?'

She was silent.

'Is this something new or did it happen before, when he was travelling back and forth from Cairo?'

'These things take time,' she said. 'I care about him.'

'If you do, you must persuade him to talk to me. Sooner or later whoever he is afraid of will find him, and then it may be too late.'

'I understand. Really, I do. And I'll talk to him. Tomorrow, I promise. As soon as we are in Aswan I'll arrange for him to meet you.'

She sounded sincere and Makana decided there was nothing more he could do. He turned his attention back to the spectacle. 'They seem to enjoy themselves,' he said.

The musicians had retreated and now a tumbling ball of colour rolled and gyrated, spilling blues, greens and reds somersaulting around the room. Into this kaleidoscopic cascade leapt a figure in a long robe bound tightly around his waist with a sash. He leapt and whirled and the guests went mad for him. His lean, bony face was handsome in the fierce slashes of light, and he played to the crowd, leaning in over the tables, casting a shawl around the shoulders of one of the Spanish women, flirting outrageously, drawing her into the circle of his dance. The guests were having the time of their lives, whooping their approval. It took on the appearance of a ritual ceremony.

'It's not easy, trying to run an operation like this,' Dena said.

'As a woman, you mean?'

'We think of ourselves as being enlightened, but the same prejudices run through this country as anywhere else in the Arab world. People don't like their daughters to be mixed up in the tourist trade, and certainly not spending the night on a boat full of them.'

'You're the exception.'

'My father used to be in charge of this boat. There was a lot of respect for him. I've been on these boats up and down this stretch of the river since I was a child.'

'So you've known Ramy since you were small.'

'Oh, no. We only really became close in recent years. Ramy didn't come into the family until a few years ago.'

'You mean he didn't come into the business?'

'No,' Dena was adamant. 'I mean, he wasn't part of the family.'

'But he's Faragalla's nephew.'

'Yes, but . . .' Dena frowned. 'I thought you knew.' She turned and walked abruptly out of the room. Makana followed her up on deck. The pulsating beat of the music from below was dampened and punctuated by the occasional shrill scream. Dena stood with her arms crossed in the middle of the forward deck. There was a cool breeze whipping at her hair.

'I shouldn't be telling you this,' she began. Then she took a deep breath and told him anyway. 'Faragalla used to work down here a lot more in the old days. He had a wife and family in Cairo but, as he had to stay here for weeks at a time and, well . . .'

'He became lonely?' offered Makana helpfully.

'He married a local girl informally. There was never any suggestion that she become his official wife. When she became pregnant he paid money to the family and divorced her. The family subsequently disowned her. She killed herself.'

'What became of the child?'

'He was an outcast. The family had disowned the mother and on top of that she had brought more dishonour upon them by killing herself. The child . . . Ramy, was taken into an orphanage run by priests. It was the only place that would take him. Somewhere in the desert.'

'Wadi Nikeiba.'

'Yes, I think that's it.'

'So how did Ramy come to be Faragalla's nephew?'

'Ramy knew who his father was and he went to him. He begged him for a chance to prove his worth. That was all he wanted. He didn't want an inheritance, just a chance to work.'

'So Faragalla took him in and pretended he was his nephew.'

Dena sighed. 'I probably should not have told you, but I am afraid for Ramy. He's in a lot of trouble. He is . . . wounded.'

'You have to trust me, Dena.'

'I know,' she said. Then, with a brief nod she turned and disappeared down below.

Makana turned to face the breeze. The *Nile Star* sailed onwards. There were no lights along the shore. The river filled him with calm. Makana realised this was the closest he had come to home in ten years. He had forgotten what it was like here. How the pace of life was different from the hectic race of Cairo. The moon slipped through the silky black waters beneath his feet like a guilty secret. He could keep going. What was to stop him? The border was only a few hours away. What did borders matter? Lines in the sand drawn by draughtsmen in the pay of emperors and kings. It was the symbolism of it. He was no different from anyone else. The need to belong was perhaps no longer as powerful as it might have been but it was still there, like an appendix, an evolutionary relic that served no real purpose but was lodged in the body as a reminder you had to live with.

Chapter Thirty

The moon was a copper coin tossed into the air. It hung there suspended in the clear sky as if trying to decide their fates. It was so bright it was almost like walking in broad daylight. The felucca was moored along the jetty just beyond the stern of the *Nile Star*. A gnarled figure stood up in the boat as they approached and Makana recognised the hunched outline as Adam. He held up a hand to help Dena step down. She settled herself on one side, arranging a scarf around her head to protect her hair from the cool breeze.

Makana waited until they had cast off. The tall white sail unfurled, fluttered, and then tautened in the wind. The creaking of the mast carried easily over the silent water as the felucca leaned one way and then the other. He moved along the jetty until he found an old rowing boat tied up to a mooring post. Would it bear his weight? It listed badly to one side and silvery water sloshed about in the bottom but there was no other option, the felucca was already slipping away from him, dissolving into the shadows. Stepping down he tripped over a pair of oars. Makana's skill with nautical craft was fairly limited. Still, how difficult could it be? He felt he ought to be able to handle a simple rowing boat. It took him several minutes before he could untie the mooring rope. And then the boat rocked alarmingly as it began to drift away downstream by itself – in the wrong direction. Fighting the urge to panic, he settled himself in the stern and set the oars in place, trying not to make any noise and failing miserably. The distant sail was shrinking like a white tear falling smoothly down a silky obsidian cheek.

He heaved on the oars and promptly tipped over backwards. Righting himself, he set the oars back in place and tried again. They seemed to have little effect, other than splashing water everywhere. As his grip slithered about he peered at the oily looking puddle between his feet and wondered if it was growing. Was it possible he was sinking? The boat was old, heavy and wide. It resisted his efforts to move and seemed to begrudge him every metre it conceded, as if it was rooted to the spot. He forced himself to focus on just lifting and pulling the oars, trying to find a rhythm. It didn't help that he was trying to go against the current. In a matter of minutes he was sweating and his back ached and when he looked over his shoulder the white crack in the darkness that was the sail had all but vanished. He could only just make it out.

He lost track of time as he wrestled with the cumbersome oars which seemed to want to go in any direction but the one he tried to direct them. Whenever he eased up he could feel himself slipping back downstream the way he had come. It wasn't until he was almost level with the felucca that he realised it had stopped moving. How much time had gone by? It felt as though he had been rowing for hours, but a glance at his watch told him it was less than fifteen minutes.

The house was set on the western shore of the river in a broad, flat bay of open ground, trimmed by a thin ribbon of trees. Palm fronds stirred noisily in the breeze, fluttering with silvery light. It stood alone with no other buildings nearby. Just upstream from it lay the rubble of former dwellings whose walls had long since started to crumble into the water. Behind it the land rose in a languorous wave of smooth sand, a hint of the desert that lay beyond to the west. In the moonlight the sand was as flawless as silk. There was no one in sight. The felucca swung in the current, the loose sail flapping like a restless jinn tied in a sack, the wood creaking.

A few lights flickered faintly around the square outline of the house. The nervous flames of oil lamps were vigilant eyes trained on the river. Makana leaned all his weight on the tiller until gradually the boat shifted and conceded to slide in towards the shore. He had been aiming for the ruins, thinking they would afford him some cover, and was unlucky enough to run aground long before the keel struck on the beach. He climbed cautiously over the side and found that the water came up to his knees. He waded up trying not to think of the damage to his clothes. The thick mud sucked him down. His shoes picked up sand, swelling to the size of a clown's flapping feet as he walked. The broken line of withered trees afforded him some cover as he skirted along the incline to approach the house from the upstream side. As the shadows closed in he moved more carefully, more out of fear of disturbing some nocturnal creature. This was a perfect area for snakes and the last thing he wanted at this point was to step on a cobra.

The house was a simple construction. The front walls were plastered and painted and had been decorated with drawings and ornamental clay plates hung here and there according to Nubian tradition. The front gate stood open to a courtyard that was dark. A solitary lamp burned within, throwing shifting shadows across the walls as he stepped inside. It was the kind of place where tourists could stop on their felucca ride to sip something cold. A stuffed crocodile in a lamentable state provided atmosphere. Dried out and cracked in places, it hung at a lopsided angle from loops of rope over the entrance. The main building was shuttered and locked. The bare earth of the yard was dotted with chairs and metal tables. Down a staircase rising along the wall to his left, the faint whisper of voices trickled from the upper floor.

Elongated skulls, also of crocodiles, were set into little recesses along the staircase wall; more atmosphere for the tourists. Halfway up he could see over the walls. The beach was bathed in white moonlight. The river was like oil, dark and glistening with menace. He could make out the felucca Dena had arrived in. He felt disappointed that she had not trusted him.

The upper floor was a terrace where you could sit and look out over the river. There were chairs and tables and grubby divans along the walls. On the far side was a small bar that looked as though it had been knocked together in a day by a blind man. The bricks were uneven and the plaster had been inset haphazardly with angular shards of broken mirror for decoration. Makana stepped up and the voices went silent.

'Hello Ramy.'

They were sitting over in the far corner, in the shadows, against the wall. A single oil lamp rested on the low table in front of them. Neither of them said anything. Dena lowered her head and clenched her fists together. Ramy's face was partially hidden. There was something about it that seemed not quite right. As Makana drew closer Ramy pulled back, further into the shadows.

'You're not an easy man to find.'

'Who are you? What do you want from me?' he hissed.

'It's the man I was telling you about,' said Dena.

'I know that, *ya beleeda*. He followed you here.'

'Why did you come?' she implored. 'Why didn't you give me a chance?'

'You mean, you arranged this?' Ramy was incredulous.

'No, no,' protested Dena.

'I'm not here to harm you,' Makana said as he approached. Ramy was like a nervous horse that could bolt at any moment. 'I just want to ask you a few questions.'

'Questions about what?'

'Well, for a start, what are you doing here?' By now he had reached the corner where they were sitting. Ramy slipped a hand under a cushion and when it reappeared it was holding the Beretta.

'I wondered where that had gone.' Makana glanced at Dena who looked away.

'Did Yousef send you?'

'Yousef?'

As Ramy leaned forwards, the light from the lamp illuminated his face. In the flicker of the flame Makana could make out the curiously twisted surface of the right-hand side of his face. A long, curved welt ran down from his ear, and the flesh around this was covered with a scar that made it scaly and uneven. A gleam of satisfaction came into his eye at Makana's expression.

'Why are you here?'

'I wanted to meet you,' said Makana. 'You're an interesting man. What did you run away from?'

'Who said I was running from anything?'

'You know that Meera is dead.'

Ramy jerked the gun at Makana. 'What have you got to do with Meera?'

'I think you know who killed her.'

'Why would you think a thing like that?'

'I was there when she was shot. I tried to help her,' said Makana quietly, easing himself down into one of the low chairs facing the divan they were sitting on. 'I wasn't fast enough.'

'You're the one who went for the gunman?' Ramy asked. 'And now you are here. Why? What do you gain out of this?'

'Nothing,' said Makana. 'She was a good person. I don't think she deserved to die like that.'

'What has any of this to do with me?'

'I think you know why she was killed. I think you were helping her.'

'You seem to think a lot.' Ramy's hand opened and closed on the butt of the pistol as if it was becoming slippery from sweat.

'You can help me out.' Makana reached into his pocket for the photograph of the three soldiers and placed it on the table between them. 'I found that in Meera's study.'

Ramy leaned forward and peered at the picture. After a moment he began to laugh, the loose, crazy laugh of a man whose mind no longer makes sense to him. Makana and Dena exchanged glances.

'Who is the man in the middle?' Makana asked.

'He was a conscript named Abdallah Hamid. A nobody.' Ramy looked up. 'He's dead. Rocky killed him.'

'Why?'

'Why?' echoed Ramy. 'Because he's insane. Because hurting people is what he does best. No, I'll tell you why, because this man called him a name. A bad name, but nothing worse than you hear any day of the week in the streets. So Rocky killed him with his bare hands. We were in the desert. On a training exercise. There were only three of us. Navigation training. Moving in the night with nothing but a compass and a map. Rocky made me swear not to tell. We made it look like an accident.'

'You didn't tell anyone?'

'I'm not a fool. He would have killed me just as easily.'

'How do you know Rocky?'

Ramy's eyes fell. He scratched his chin. 'I knew him a long time ago. When I was a boy.'

'You were together in the orphanage, at Wadi Nikeiba.'

'My father . . . It's a long story.'

Dena reached for his hand. 'It's all right,' she said gently.

'You told him?' Ramy wrenched his hand free, then after a moment he went on. 'People were already calling him Rocky back then. He was a few years older than most of the boys. He was a bully. He was also a ferocious boxer. One of the priests used to train the boys.'

'Father Macarius,' said Makana.

'Yes. Rocky used to like hurting things, any living thing. He tortured animals, poked the eyes out of a cat once. It was a sickness.'

'But he never hurt you.'

A deep sigh sounded from Ramy. The gun had dropped until it was resting on his knee. He wasn't really aiming it at anyone.

'I was his boy, okay?' He lifted his gaze to meet Makana's. 'Do you understand what that means? I was his boy.' He ignored the whimper that came from Dena.

'He took care of you, in return for certain . . . favours.'

'He took care of me,' mumbled Ramy.

'You never told me any of this,' Dena said. He carried on ignoring her.

'Tell me about Meera. Why did you decide to help her?'

'Why? Why wouldn't I help her? She wanted to expose what that bastard was doing.'

'He's still your father.'

'No,' Ramy laughed bitterly. 'He will never recognise me. He's too ashamed. He has a respectable family. You know what those informal weddings are like, it's just legalised prostitution. My mother was nothing to him but a whore and I am an embarrassment.'

'He took you in. He gave you a job,' Dena implored.

'He gave me a job because he was afraid I would make a fuss. He made me promise that I would never make any claims about inheritance. He's happy for me to work for him, but I always knew that one day he would grow tired of me and that would be the end of it.' He looked up at Makana, as if sure he at least would understand. 'And now it's done.'

'So you helped Meera find the evidence she needed to expose the Eastern Star's actions.'

'I caught her one day going through old files and that made me suspicious. I did some checking on her and guessed what she was up to. She couldn't believe it when I confronted her and told her I had exactly what she was looking for. They had been running money through the company for years. It comes in from one source and goes out to another. They made up the names of hotels, transport firms, caterers. It was all being run by Yousef.' Ramy snorted. 'There's another piece of work. Anyway, Yousef trusted me for some reason. The account numbers were supposed to be destroyed as soon as the transaction was over. But I kept a record,' Ramy smiled. 'I thought, one day this is going to be useful. This is going to be my ticket into the good life.'

'And then what happened?'

'Then Rocky showed up.' Ramy stared into space. 'I couldn't understand how he had found me, but there he was. One day I walked in and he was standing there.'

'Running the café downstairs,' said Makana.

Ramy shook his head. 'Rocky wouldn't hang around in a simple *'ahwa* if there wasn't a reason. No, he was running his band of boys out of there. It was just like the old days, except we were all older. He said he needed my help. I hadn't seen him for five years.' A shudder went through him. 'I couldn't sleep that night. I couldn't eat anything. I threw up. It was as if I couldn't get away from him, no matter what I did or where I went, he would always be there.'

'So that's why Rocky was there, using the café as a front for his activities?'

'Sure, they were stealing stuff all over the place. Downtown is a treasure trove if you know what you are doing. They ran their stolen goods through the café.'

'Cigarettes, for example?' asked Makana.

'Exactly, television sets, radios, things they stole from offices and flats in the neighbourhood. They had a kind of storeroom in the back.'

'What did Rocky want you to help him with?'

Ramy's eyes flicked up to find Makana's. 'Somebody wanted Meera dead. He wouldn't tell me who, but he was going to take care of it, and I was going to help him.'

'You don't know who ordered the killing?'

'No,' Ramy shook his head. 'All he would tell me was that it was going to be a spectacular, headline-grabbing operation. They wanted to use the opportunity to scare people.'

'You have no idea who they were?'

'No, but I got the impression it was personal, to do with who she was, I mean. She was married to some crazy professor. All of that they knew. That was why she had to die.'

Someone from Meera's past, connected to the Eastern Star Bank. Serhan had overheard someone at the shareholders' meeting saying it was time to clear the slate. Was one of those people Sheikh Waheed?

'So, Rocky was there to kill Meera,' said Makana. 'What did you do then?'

'I couldn't deal with it. It was too much. And I liked Meera. I wanted to help her, and now here was this monster that I just couldn't shake off.' Ramy glanced at Dena. 'I thought I'd got away from Rocky. I just wanted to live a normal life.' He laughed bitterly. 'I was so stupid. Some people are born lucky and others, well . . .' He shrugged his shoulders.

'If you wanted to start a new life down here with Dena, why destroy your uncle's company?'

'It wouldn't have destroyed the company. You know what this country is like. These people take care of their own. There would be a scandal and maybe a couple of people would get fined, or even go to prison, maybe even my uncle. But then who would he get to take care of things while he was gone? You see? I was thinking that then he might really need my help.'

'All of this is assuming no one found out you had helped Meera.'

'Yes, well, let's just say things didn't work out the way I expected.' Ramy stared down at the Beretta. He turned it over in his hand as if wondering who had put it there. Makana considered trying to take the automatic away, but decided wrestling with a loaded gun was a bad idea.

'Rocky wanted me back. He said we were fated to be together, that I could never really get rid of him.'

An involuntary sound of disgust escaped Dena. She put a hand to her mouth, but Ramy gave no indication he had heard. If he had, he was beyond caring.

'It was all part of the game. He didn't really care about me. What he wanted was to know that he had me in his control.'

'You could have resisted,' insisted Dena. 'You could have stayed away from him.'

Ramy didn't even look at her. His voice was dead. 'I went to see him. He showed me around. He had a stable of young boys, kids he had picked up off the street. Every now and then he lost control and one of them would die. He didn't care. There were plenty more out there, he said. He locked them up on his roof like animals, living in their own filth, until they were willing to do anything to get out. It brought it all back. The pain and humiliation. The shame of it all.' Ramy's chest heaved as he tried to draw breath. 'I remembered how scared I had once been. Rocky was laughing. I don't know what came over me. I just thought this has to end. I thought I could take him by surprise. It was stupid. He is strong, and very fast.' Ramy's voice dropped to a whisper. 'He beat me, and he held me down and he touched me that way. He said, you'll always belong to me. After this nobody is ever going to want you. And then he poured acid on my face.'

The story seemed to have left him drained. Ramy's head hung down. His body racked with silent sobs. Somewhere in the distance Makana could hear an owl. Dena tried to console him, but Ramy pushed her away. 'Before this,' he gestured at his face, 'I thought there was a chance of starting a new life. But now . . . what does it matter?'

'But it does matter. I don't care how you look,' insisted Dena.

'Well, I do!' he yelled. Then he grabbed hold of her hair and pulled her towards him roughly, pressing her against the burned side of his face. 'How long would it take for you to find this disgusting? Six months? A year? Two years?'

'No, no!' she sobbed. 'I love you.'

Ramy flung her away. 'You should go now,' he mumbled. 'I'm very tired.'

'Yes,' Dena agreed, wiping the tears from her face. 'Maybe we should go.' She got to her feet quietly. 'I'll come back in the morning, before we leave. I'll bring you something to eat.'

Ramy said nothing. Makana had more questions but he could see that he would get no more out of Ramy tonight. He followed Dena down the stairs towards the entrance and out to the beach. A cool breeze was blowing along the river's edge. In the distance the low curve of the felucca could be made out, with Adam outlined beside it, looking out for them.

'It's so sad. I wish there was something I could do,' Dena sniffed.

Makana paused to glance back at the house. The faint glow of light fluttering from within made him uneasy. Ramy had spent his whole life living in fear and when he finally tried to stand up for himself he had paid a terrible price. He had wanted to help Meera, and he had failed at that too. So he fled the city, his face disfigured, and ran to the one person he thought would be able to give him back his dignity. But even that wasn't enough. Makana had come to a halt now. He had turned and started back towards the house when he heard the shot. Then he was running with Dena screaming behind him.

Ramy was slumped against the wall with the ugly, twisted side of his face turned towards the light, his expression one of surprise, his white shirt was spattered with blood and his brains were spattered over the wall behind him. The Beretta was still smoking in his hand.

Chapter Thirty-One

It was dawn by the time Adam delivered him back to the *Nile Star*. Dena had stayed behind to deal with the police, but they had agreed that Makana would not be included in the story. The gun was not registered to anyone, so where it had come from would remain a mystery. Too exhausted to sleep, Makana went up on deck to watch the town come to life. He leaned on the railings and smoked a cigarette while taking in the view.

The Aswan skyline was once dominated by King Farouk's old palace, jutting out over the water, which had been transformed into the luxurious Cataract Hotel and frequented by all manner of royalty and celebrity. Nowadays it was superseded by the grim tower of the Oberoi on Elephantine Island. Twelve concrete pylons rising 30 metres into the air to support a restaurant suspended in mid-air. From a distance it resembled an industrial complex in the shape of a cobra, the ancient royal symbol of Upper Egypt. But it lacked any trace of charm and elegance. The artists of old must have been rolling about in their caskets in indignation. A white rag floated gracefully down overhead and became a heron.

'A sad business.'

Makana looked round to see Adam, his overalls covered in an unusual amount of oil. He had just come from the engine room and carried a monkey wrench and an oily rag. Without a word Makana offered him a cigarette. He tucked the wrench into a pocket and wiped his brow with his greasy forearm.

'He wasn't a bad kid. He worked hard and everyone liked him.' Adam sniffed and rolled the cigarette between his fingers leaving black fingerprints on the white paper. 'It's a shame for the girl, though. She was in love with that boy, would have done anything for him.' He took the cigarette out of his mouth and blew on the tip until it glowed. 'Things have been bad here for a long time. People are worried this is going to finish off the company.'

'You remember I asked you about Wadi Nikeiba?'

'The monastery?' Adam frowned. 'Sure.'

'You said they were running a brothel out there.'

Adam gave a dismissive shrug. 'You know how people are. One story leads into another.'

'Do you think you could find your way out there?'

'I suppose so. I'd need to get hold of a car first.'

'But you can do that, right?'

'I suppose so.' Adam puffed on his cigarette and studied the rivets on the deck. 'Of course, a car is not an easy thing to lay your hands on.'

Makana reached into his pocket for some of Faragalla's money and counted out some notes into the grubby hand. 'I'm sure an old sailor like yourself can get hold of just about anything he sets his mind on.'

'You might just be right about that,' Adam grinned toothlessly.

By noon they had a car. An old Peugeot 504 estate. Five doors and enough room in it to comfortably seat a football team. It might once have been blue but was now a rainbow-coloured history of replacement parts. One door was ruby, the other was ochre, the front wing a battered white. The bulk of it was a faded sky-blue, rubbed clear through to shining steel here and there. The bonnet was military green. Just by looking at it you might be forgiven for wondering if it was capable of moving one more metre, but mechanically it seemed sound. Adam sat grinning behind the wheel. The car belonged to a brother-in-law, he said, who used to drive it as a taxi until his leg was amputated last winter. Smoking. Diabetes. A litany of complaints that kept Adam muttering and rolling his head at the foolishness of man and the cruelty of fate. Such cars were worth their weight in gold according to him and were exchanged for astronomical sums. They were just waiting for the right time to sell. Better not wait too long, thought Makana to himself as he climbed in. The passenger-seat door was held closed with a loop of frayed nylon cord. The rear end seemed to be jacked unnaturally high up in the air and the tyres were smooth enough to write on. To Makana, it resembled a coffin on wheels. The air was warm and once they had managed to negotiate their way through the town's traffic they hit the open road. The green strip of irrigated fields and trees running along opposite banks of the river gave way to dusty emptiness. The open windows blew gusts of hot dry air into Makana's face as he rested his arm on the juddering door, careful not to lean too much of his weight on it.

According to the map in the front of the book, Wadi Nibeika was approximately 20 kilometres away from Aswan to the south-east. They followed a grey ridge that swerved into the distance like the tail fin of an enormous fish whipping through the brown desert. They turned off the narrow strip of road, stones rattling against the underside of the car like a riotous gang of mad drummers. Through a rusty hole between his feet Makana watched the track rolling by beneath him. What did he expect to find? He couldn't say, though he had the feeling that he needed to know this monastery. The big car rocked about on the uneven road as if it was skating on marbles. The dust rolled in through the open windows in waves, so that soon the interior was choking in the stuff and the car and the two occupants looked as though they might have been carved out of the same grey stone of the hills.

The track wound its way slowly up a short ridge, at the top of which the Peugeot stalled and for a few harrowing moments they skittered backwards on bald tyres while Adam struggled to restart the engine. The car coughed respectably and then burst into life. The gearstick was ground into place and they finally crawled over the top to begin the long slide downwards. Here the road was long and straight, broken only by a few gentle curves. It wound its way along the flat bottom of the valley. Tucked into a far corner, shaped like the cupped palm of a hand, lay the whitewashed rectangular walls of the monastery. It swam towards them like something from another age as the car gained speed and tore up a flailing sheet of dust in their wake.

Long before they arrived it became clear that the monastery had been abandoned years ago. There were no vehicles, no people, no signs of life. The walls, on closer inspection, were neglected and cracked. Pigeons flew in and out of a window with a lone wooden shutter that flapped back and forth on its hinges. The big car juddered to a halt just outside the high front gates which stood open, giving way to complete silence that was disturbed only by the hum of the wind and the scratch of sand grains against the metal. A part of the wall had collapsed into a heap of bricks and plaster. The main front gate was closed but a smaller door set into it stood open.

The two men got out of the car and walked through the entrance to find a set of low-roofed, white buildings, now in a state of some disrepair. A path wound its way up towards the hill behind the monastery. As they walked up the shallow slope Makana paused here and there to peer into a building alongside. In places the doors had been locked. The ground was littered with debris, dead branches and leaves from the palm trees, wooden slats from the window shutters, doors, broken bricks, timber, and all of it peppered with a liberal scattering of goat droppings. There was an empty shell of a church with a cracked and blackened dome. Further up the incline were workshops and storage rooms, rough constructions made of adobe bricks and crooked timbers. Makana's eye followed the line of the hill as it rose up to end in the dark mouth of a large cave. He thought he could make out a figure standing in the entrance.

'Can you see someone up there?' he asked, shading his eyes with one hand.

Adam squinted. 'Got to be a crazy man if he's living out here alone.'

Who else would live in a cave in the desert but a madman? Makana wasn't sure his eyes were not deceiving him until the wavering figure began to descend. A prophet, perhaps, out here to commune with the Almighty, or a lunatic? Makana lit a cigarette and waited. A couple of minutes later the small, compact figure was striding towards him. Tufts of white hair stuck out from behind his ears, his beard sweeping down from his chin to his chest. The top of his head was bald and mottled. Thick leather sandals and a grubby cassock completed the outfit.

'You cannot stay here. We do not allow it.'

'We're not planning to stay,' Makana said, wondering who

'we' was. Were there others up there in the cave? A tribe of madmen?

'Then what is your business?'

He was so short his head only came up to Makana's chest but he still cut a ferocious figure. Makana noticed that Adam had taken a couple of steps backwards just in case. He held up the book from the cabin.

'Father Macarius suggested I come by to take a look.'

'Macarius?' The little man stared at the book, his lips moving silently. His chin lifted and dipped. 'The monastery is closed to visitors.'

'I understand there used to be an orphanage here, Father . . . ?'

'Girgis. Yes, but that closed years ago.' The white beard whipped up into his face as the wind changed direction. 'That was the end of it.'

'The orphanage?'

'Yes. What did you think I was talking about?' He frowned. 'Why have you come here?'

It was a question to which Makana could not readily answer.

'I'm curious to know why the monastery was closed.'

'What possible interest could you have in that?' The face cracked like dry pergament.

'One of the boys who was here. I'm interested in one of the boys.'

'A journalist, are you? Here to spin your web of deceit.'

'I'm not a journalist. Father, someone died last night. Do you remember a boy named Ramy who was here at the orphanage?'

His jaw worked silently for a moment. 'I remember a lot of people. I forget their names. We had about thirty-seven boys at one time. How did you say he died?'

'He took his own life.'

The priest winced as though someone had stepped on his toe. 'Maybe I remember him. He was never a particularly happy child.'

'From what he told me that was hardly surprising.'

The white beard twitched as Father Girgis lifted his chin. 'That's all ancient history. Why should you be interested in that now?'

'I thought all human life was sacred.'

A long silence followed disturbed only by Adam clearing his throat, worried perhaps about getting the car back to his legless brother-in-law.

'When we first came here there was nothing much more than that cave up there,' Father Girgis pointed. 'Legend had it that a prophet, Saint Nikeiba, once lived in that cave. He had visions of an angel bearing six wings.'

'The Seraph.'

'Yes, the Seraph.' The pale eyes rolled up towards Makana. 'Macarius told you?'

'He told me that this was a very special place.'

'It was,' sighed Father Girgis. 'We built it together. We worked side by side. After the scandal it fell into disrepair. The government took the children away.'

'What exactly happened?'

Father Girgis gestured for them to walk. 'Let me give you a tour. You know that we are restoring the place finally.'

Again, Makana wondered about this use of the plural. He looked over the little man's head in case a small army of helpers appeared from the cave.

'You had both Christian and Muslim boys here?'

'It's not up to us to distinguish between God's children.' Father

Girgis paused to point out the kiln, the mill where they ground the flour they grew. 'It was a terrible time.' Father Girgis lowered his face and stroked his beard. 'We put our faith in the young, for what else is there? We have to believe that they will carry on after us.' Father Girgis stroked his beard as if he thought it might fly away. 'It's a terrible world we live in.' As Makana reached for a cigarette, the priest stuck out a hand. Makana shook one out for him and produced his lighter. The priest closed his eyes as he sucked the smoke into his lungs. 'Ah,' he sighed, opening his eyes. 'People say memories are only in the head, but some are awakening at this very moment in my body.'

They stood and gazed down over the valley below. The heat was diminishing and colour was gradually returning to the grey landscape. As the sun began to drop, the hills seemed to expand as the shadows deepened, becoming blue tinged with purple.

'Why did they close you down?'

'They said there was a monster in our midst.'

'A monster?'

'Oh, yes,' Father Girgis savoured his cigarette, which had already been smoked down to the butt. The priest's eyes flickered towards Makana. 'Has he killed again?'

'I think so, Father.'

High above in the warm air over the Wadi a buzzard circled in slow, lazy turns. It might have been the wavering light, or a trick of his imagination, but Makana thought he saw a flicker of bitterness in the other man's eyes.

'He ruined us. He turned our dreams to dust.' Father Girgis abruptly began walking down the path, his hands clasped behind his back. Makana had no choice but to follow along. 'It seemed like nothing at first. An unfortunate incident. A lamb went missing and was found torn to pieces in the desert.' Father Girgis spoke in the animated fashion of one who after years of sleeping in a cave had finally awoken. 'We wondered what kind of animal could have done something like that. Jackals? Packs of wild dogs, perhaps? It was dismissed. We forgot about it for a time, but then other things happened.'

'What other things?'

'A cat was nailed to a door, badly mutilated and barely alive. It was horrible. There was a sense that something like pure evil had taken root among us. We were afraid for the boys. Then our worst nightmare was realised. One of the boys went missing.' Father Girgis paused, his eyes focussed on the distant landscape. 'We searched everywhere for him. All day, all night, search parties combed the hills around here, convinced he had had an accident. When we found him it was clear that he had been tortured. Beaten viciously and . . . abused.'

'You went to the police, of course.'

'No,' Father Girgis turned to Makana, his voice grave. 'We discussed it amongst ourselves and took a vote. We knew that the scandal would destroy us.'

Silently, Makana held out the pack of cigarettes and Father Girgis took another.

'None of us was thinking clearly. We were in a state of shock. We thought it would simply go away.'

'But it didn't?'

'No, it did not.' The light was fading fast. Shadows spread like dark wings over the valley. 'When the second victim was found we realised that we had a maniac in our midst.'

'What made you so certain?'

'He was crucified, nailed to a rough cross and left out there in the desert to die. He burned up in the sun before he bled to death. He too had been . . . tortured in the most obscene way.'

They had come to a fork in the path. To the left was a small vegetable patch containing rows of neatly tilled soil divided by rich leafy plants of all kinds. To the right an opening in a low wall marked the entrance to a small cemetery. Here, instead of vegetables, were rows of headstones. These were all fairly simple. With basic inscriptions, some dating back a couple of centuries while others were more regular, clean and bright, the gilt paint on the inscriptions faded. The breeze trickled through the silvery leaves of the olive trees that grew in the cemetery. Sand grains blown on a dry desert wind sounded like a gigantic insect grinding its mandibles. Father Girgis came to a halt at a shady spot where a small stone was set into the earth.

'We buried them here. Macarius and I thought we should try to solve the matter without involving the authorities. We thought we could contain it.'

'You never found the killer?'

'We had thirty-seven boys. Two victims and that left us with thirty-five suspects. Along with the staff of course. There were five priests: Father Macarius and myself, along with Father Basil and Father Elias and three helpers, all of whom we eliminated from our list of suspects.'

'You said there were five monks altogether.'

Father Girgis nodded gravely. 'Father Barsoom was the third victim. He too was crucified. We were sure the murderer had to be an adult. Our suspicions fell on one of the kitchen helpers, a young and violent man. When we confronted him he grew very angry and left. It turned out that he had an alibi that he was keeping to himself. He was stealing our dates to take to a little distillery he had in the mountains. One of his best clients was a local chief of police. So this was how the news leaked to the outside world. There was an outcry. We had tried so hard to keep it secret and now all manner of rumours circulated. It wasn't long before the place was closed down. I stayed, but I could not maintain the place on my own.'

The sky was the colour of a tangerine dipped in ink. Adam was restless when they reached him, clearly eager not to spend more time than necessary in this accursed place.

'None of the boys was suspected?'

'Only one,' Father Girgis said gently. 'But that split us even more. There was one boy who had always been strange. He was disturbed and as a result he was not particularly well liked.'

'Who was that?'

'His name was Antun. He was small and weak but he was seized at times by terrible fits of fury when he could exert great force.'

'Antun is the one you suspected?'

'Yes . . .' Father Girgis gave a deep sigh before going on. 'We were all agreed that we should confront him, all except one, who defended him to the death.'

'Father Macarius?'

Father Girgis nodded. 'It tore us apart. The rest of us were sure Antun was responsible but Macarius refused to see reason. We had to do something, yet we were paralysed by this internal conflict.'

'Father, I take it you haven't heard about the murders in Cairo?'

'Is that why you are here? You think it's the same person?'

'It seems possible.'

'That saddens me,' Father Girgis fretted. 'It means that our failure all those years ago has caused even more suffering.'

'Is it possible that Father Macarius was correct, that maybe one of the other boys was responsible?'

'Which boy?'

'Do you remember Ahmed Rakuba? They used to call him Rocky.'

Father Girgis was studying the cigarettes in Makana's shirt pocket. Makana took them out and offered one, then handed the packet over. Girgis licked his lips, tucking them away in his cassock as if they were made of gold.

'Rocky, you say?'

'Could he have been the killer?'

'I really can't say. There were many boys and my memory is not what it was. I just remember the horror and the sadness. I pray every day for forgiveness, but we cannot bring back the dead. We cannot undo what has happened.'

As he walked away down the hill into the deepening dusk, Makana paused to look back at the spindly figure climbing the hill to his lonely vigil in the cave. The priest's last words echoed in his ears on the long drive home: 'God forgive us.'

IV

Fallen Angels

Chapter Thirty-Two

The train back to Cairo was uneventful. As the old beast lumbered along, dragging its iron belly slowly north along the Nile valley, Makana felt as if he was returning from some forgotten well of ancient history, sliding up the evolutionary scale from the prehistoric era to the present. By the looks of things there wasn't much to be said for progress, except that it was noisy and dirty and tended to block out the sky with high walls and twisted iron. He used the time to think about things and so stared out of the window with a blank gaze as trees and desert and houses passed before him, faces upturned to look at the passing juggernaut as it rolled by.

In Qena, he stepped down onto the platform and stood in the shade of a neem tree to sip a glass of sweet tea. A twelve-year-old with the weary gaze of a man five times his age wandered along the tracks weighed down by a thick armful of headlines. Out of pity for the boy more than anything else, Makana bought the state newspaper, *Al Ahram*. As always, it was a reminder that to read the news in this country was to enter into a fantasy world of fairy tales and deceit, where the rising and setting of the sun each day could not happen without the benevolent presence of the president, *al-Raïs*, whose glorious exploits were plastered across the front pages. In this parallel universe the country was booming and firmly on the road to progress. To understand what was really going on you had to read between the lines: when it said a new hospital had been opened, specialising in kidney transplants, you understood that someone in the president's circle had made a small fortune selling expensive medical equipment to an institution that would function at 20 per cent of its capacity for about six months. After that the machines would mysteriously disappear one by one, to be sold on to an unnamed private facility in the Gulf somewhere. When you read in an editorial that the Americans had personally thanked the president for his role in maintaining stability in the region, it really meant that the annual donations of millions of dollars of free wheat and weapons would arrive unhindered, in exchange for maintaining the status quo and doing nothing to really bring Israel and the Palestinians any closer to lasting peace.

Evening was falling as he came out of the station in Giza to find the battered black-and-white Datsun which looked, as always, as though an elephant had sat on it. Perhaps there was some way of finding a replacement, Makana wondered, before it gave up the ghost. Sindbad was leaning against the side, arms crossed, looking pleased with himself. When he saw Makana emerge from the station building he rushed towards him to relieve him of his bag.

'*Marhaba, marhaba*, welcome back to the city of lights. I trust your journey bore fruits.'

The car lurched violently as they left the kerb and sailed recklessly out into the stream of flowing traffic, oblivious to the horns of protest. Makana felt like a country bumpkin, no longer in tune with the city's ways. He had forgotten the chaos, the urgent sense of encroaching madness. At an intersection a policeman waved his hands frantically in an effort to tame the traffic. You had to admire his tenacity. A supreme act of faith in the face of ridiculous odds. As if trying to hold back the tide, it was like witnessing a small miracle whenever the vehicles actually rolled to a halt obediently and then waited impatiently. Sindbad was eager to explain what he had been up to while Makana was away.

'I did as you asked, *ya basha*,' he said, leaning on the horn to produce a truncated sound from under the bonnet rather like a duck being strangled. 'First, I stayed outside the hotel and waited. For the first two days he did nothing of interest. He went for a walk in the morning. He visited the bank in Kasr al-Nil Street and a number of clothes shops where he made extensive purchases, mostly of shoes and shirts. I have a list.'

Sindbad reached into his shirt pocket and produced a rough sheet of brown paper of the kind that might be used for wrapping fish or ball bearings. It contained a series of hieroglyphics in smudged pencil that Makana could make neither head nor tail of.

'You'll notice that he doesn't settle for the cheap stuff. Some of these places sell shirts for hundreds of pounds.' Sindbad's face betrayed his horror.

'Is that so?'

'Oh yes, and the shoes . . .' A whistle and a shake of the head was all he could summon to convey his shock. 'How can anyone bring themselves to walk along our dirty streets in such shoes?'

Sindbad paused to lean on the horn again, this time startling a skinny waif riding a bicycle, sending him wobbling dangerously across the road, narrowly avoiding being crushed by a large lorry. On his head a long board laden with fresh bread was balanced. It remained steady, bobbing up and down like a diving board as the cyclist fought to regain his balance. It could have been a trick in a circus. They swept on along Sharia Sudan.

'On the fourth day I almost missed him, I have to admit, as Allah is my witness.'

'No more shopping?'

'He stayed in most of the day. I was about to give up and go home.' Sindbad sighed. 'My wife really does not understand the importance of my new responsibilities.'

Makana nodded but said nothing as he suspected this was a ruse to ask for more money.

'Well, anyway. I was about to give in, like I say, and then, around six o'clock, just as the sun was setting, he stepped outside and signals for me. He gets into the back and asks me to take him to the Ramses Hilton. I drive him up the ramp and he tries to short change me. I don't argue because I don't want to draw attention to myself. Between you and me, *ya basha,* for a man who spends on shirts what a family can live on for a month, he should be ashamed to stand before Allah.'

'So, Damazeen went into the hotel. Any idea who he met?'

Sindbad clenched the wheel tensely, caught in the grip of his own tale. 'Well, I had to be careful now because he knew my face. I followed Mr Damazeen into the hotel lobby and observed him from a distance. Naturally, the staff in such palaces regard an ordinary working man such as myself as an undesirable.' Sindbad was smiling broadly, clearly pleased with himself. 'I told them that I was waiting for a client, an eccentric but very wealthy English couple who were terrified of the traffic in the city. I was the only one they trusted, I had no idea why they had settled on me but so it was and I had been given strict instructions to wait for them when they went out to eat. I laid it on a bit thick, but you never know with these slick types. So then they asked me the name of the person I was waiting for and I knew I was a dead man. I saw my life flash before my eyes. Then it came to me, I swear by Allah, just like that.'

'What came to you?'

'Mr Siwan Vista.'

Makana stared at Sindbad. 'And who is this Mr Vista?'

'You don't remember? English matches. Very good. Always light first time.' Sindbad beamed at his own ingenuity.

'And they believed you?'

'I don't mean to insult anyone but many of those people who work in fancy hotels, *ya basha*, they wear nice clothes but they can't tell one end of a stick from another. Of course, I have certain skills in the acting department myself. Did I tell you about my cousin who works in the national theatre? Actually, he's just a *bawab*, but it's in our blood.'

Makana recalled something Adam had said about the stars, about the illusion of them moving, about seeing things from different angles. Was this the reason for the confusion he felt, that he was seeing things from another perspective?

Sindbad was still talking.

'A black man. I mean, excuse me, an African. Perhaps forty years of age. Wearing a striped suit like an English businessman, and with a face like a butcher. I was happy to keep my distance. And your friend didn't seem too happy to be sitting close by him.'

It was an intriguing thought, Damazeen and an African in a striped suit. Was this his middleman?

'He was alone?'

'No. There was a third man. A white man with red hair.' Sindbad stamped on the brakes, skipping around a stalled minibus with only a whisker to spare, a finger still held aloft to emphasise a point. 'This one looked like a military man. Casual clothes, heavy boots.' The wheel was a flimsy ring in Sindbad's paw as he steered. 'Mr Henry Bruin of Cape Town, South Africa.'

Makana had to admit he was impressed. A South African? What was Damazeen doing with these men? All his experience told him that he ought to turn his back on the whole business. But what if Damazeen was telling the truth? What if he could bring Nasra back from the dead? Makana felt his blood swirl in his head, as if he could no longer trust his own judgement.

'Come down with me,' he said when they reached the *awama*, explaining what he needed Sindbad to do. The breeze rustled the dry leaves on the big eucalyptus tree. Umm Ali was pleased to see him. Her brother Bassam was not so happy, and tried to sidle off.

'*Hamdilay salama*,' he muttered nervously when Makana confronted him. 'I trust your journey was a safe one.'

'We need to talk,' said Makana. When he offered his cigarettes, Bassam relaxed, thinking this was some kind of peace offering. Over his shoulder Makana could see Umm Ali watching with interest. He led the way down to the *awama*. Sindbad brought up the rear. On the upper deck Makana signalled and Bassam felt himself lifted off his feet, his arms pinned to his side.

'Now wait a minute,' he protested as Sindbad lifted him high enough to get his legs over the railings. Bassam put up some resistance, but having the air squeezed out of his lungs pacified him. When he was suspended over the side, legs scrabbling for purchase, Makana said:

'If you fall from here it will not kill you, assuming you can swim and that you don't break an arm or a leg, or your neck, Allah forbid, on the way down.'

'They made me promise not to tell.'

'What did you do with the money?'

'I . . . I still have it. Most of it. Let me down. I can show you.'

Sindbad lifted him back over the side and sent him sprawling to the deck. Predictably, he tried to make a break for it. Sindbad put out an arm and Bassam's feet flew into the air and he landed flat on his back.

'All right,' he gasped, when he got his breath back. 'Here, look.' He reached into his back pocket and produced a wad of crumpled notes. 'Take it. Take it.'

Makana took the money and counted it. Less than he had hoped for, but still, not bad.

'Okay, now tell me what happened, and don't leave anything out.'

Bassam nodded obediently, his eyes darting from one to the other.

'Some men came here. I don't know who they are. All I had to do was make a phone call to tell them you were at home and alone.'

'Which you did, naturally.'

'It was a lot of money.' Bassam's eyes were wide, as if he couldn't quite comprehend how such a thing could be held against him.

'So you heard Sami go down the path. You assumed it was me and you called them.'

'That's correct. That's exactly how it happened.' Bassam nodded eagerly. 'I swear I didn't know what they were planning to do.'

'You left your sister and her children to the mercy of strange men?' Sindbad was disgusted.

'I didn't have any choice. I owe some money to some men back home in the *rif*. This money would allow me to go back.'

'And not a moment too soon,' muttered Makana. 'Could you recognise these men?'

'No, *ya basha*. It was dark and my eyesight is not good since the accident.'

'You understand that I am not planning to call the police.'

'That's very kind of you.'

'Not at all. We shall deal with this ourselves. Can you swim?' Makana waved the question aside. 'It doesn't matter. Not many people can swim with a broken neck.'

'A broken . . . Look,' Bassam tried to rise from the floor, but Sindbad shoved him back down.

'The only way you are going to walk off this boat in one piece is if you help me find those men.'

Bassam licked his lips. His eyes darted round until it came to him. 'I can call them. I still have the number.' He fumbled in his pockets to produce a scrap torn from a cigarette packet with a number scrawled on it. Trembling, he held it out. Makana made no effort to take it.

'You're going to call them right now. Tell them you want more money. The police are asking more questions and you're scared.'

'They're not going to believe that.'

'You have to make them believe it. Tell them you need to meet them tonight, quickly, in one hour. You'll come to them. Just ask them where, is that clear?'

Bassam's eyes darted between the scrap of paper and Makana and Sindbad. He had the mournful look of a puppy. After a time he swore and went over to lift the telephone on the desk. He dialled the number and spoke for a while before replacing the receiver.

'Okay, it's done.'

'Where are you supposed to go?' asked Makana, relieving Bassam of the paper with the number on it.

'A place in Imbaba called Al Madina. Can I go now? Only I—'

'You'll go when he says so,' Sindbad cut him off. 'You caused a man to be crucified. We ought to do the same to you.'

Bassam's eyes widened. 'I swear by Allah I never knew—'

'Call Aziza up,' Makana said. 'You're going to give this money to her and then you are going to say goodbye to your sister and lead us to this place. After that we'll drop you off at the station and you can take the bus back to wherever you came from.'

'Of course.' Bassam struggled to his feet. 'I will do exactly what you say.'

The money was handed to a rather astonished Aziza, who said nothing, simply took herself off quietly. They left Bassam to say his goodbyes and pack his things. As they waited in the Datsun Sindbad felt the need to speak his mind.

'Pardon me, *ya basha*, but I swear you let that dog off too easily.'

'Possibly, but if he manages to lead us to the ones who did this it will be worth it.'

The two of them watched as three black SUVs raced towards them out of the darkness, sirens wailing and blue lights flashing. They skidded to a halt around them. Sindbad raised his hands in surrender, the way they do in cowboy films.

Chapter Thirty-Three

'Get rid of the cigarette and get in. Leave the gorilla behind,' said Lieutenant Sharqi.

Makana did as he was told. The car smelled new. Leather and plastic with a weirdly artificial blend of aromas designed to make you think of pine forests in some distant wonderland, but instead put you in mind of a laboratory somewhere underground where they had never seen a tree. Doors clattered shut all around him and they moved off in a smooth convoy, travelling fast. Flashing lights and sirens cleared the way. They raced down to the river-side, shouldering aside an old Russian Volga gushing black smoke like a runaway volcano. The driver was an old man, who ducked his head as they went by. His wife sat rigidly upright, staring ahead of her. Sharqi turned around in the front seat and held up a sleep mask of the type they give you on aeroplanes.

'Put this on.'

'Is this really necessary?'

Sharqi didn't even dignify the question with an answer. He waited until Makana had placed the mask over his eyes before turning around again. With his eyes covered Makana felt the car accelerate. He felt as though he was flying through darkness, towards what he couldn't say, but away from finding the people who had crucified Sami. Bassam would be long gone by the time he got back, which left him with a telephone number and not much else.

With the sirens off they drove for another ten minutes before slowing and coming to a halt. He reckoned they hadn't crossed the river, which meant they were on the outskirts of Dokki somewhere, where exactly he couldn't say. State Security had plenty of clandestine outposts in and around the city. Apartment buildings with no markings or signs to say what they were. Neighbours might see cars coming and going but they would know better than to ask. No one would really know what went on inside. That was part of the problem. Once things had become that secret the line between what was legally sanctioned by the state and what was not dissolved into abstraction. This was the grey zone, a blind spot into which a person could disappear as completely as they might on the dark side of the moon.

The cars came to a halt inside a driveway and the door opened. A hand reached inside to take Makana's elbow. Someone guided him up a flight of stairs and through a series of locked doors. He heard buzzers and bells. The hum of a lift. The sleep mask was removed as the doors slid open and he found himself facing a windowless corridor. A hand propelled him to the right and a man in a light-blue shirt blocked his path and indicated for him to raise his hands.

At the far end another corridor branched left, through a heavily reinforced security door. Sharqi rang a bell and they waited for a guard to emerge from a side door with a key on a chain. They went through an opening in the wall and stepped into the adjacent building. It was a labyrinth constructed in plain sight. From the outside it was two adjacent apartment buildings.

Here were rows of windows with bars across them, presumably to stop anyone jumping out. People came and went, all of them in plain clothes. No uniforms or insignia but faces that you might pass on the street and not think twice about except for the way their eyes followed you. He looked at the faces and tried to imagine them as schoolchildren. When had they discovered they possessed a natural affinity for deception? Inevitably Mek Nimr sprang to mind. Who better to epitomise that combination of envy, hatred, and the desire to inflict pain? Was he being fair, or was he taking liberties with the facts? Since the moment when Damazeen had told him his daughter was alive, Makana had felt something come undone inside him. Where would it lead, this unravelling thread?

The hallway was lined with rooms now converted into offices, interrogation cells, archives full of personal information about the lives of countless men and women, most of whom were blissfully ignorant of the fact they had a file in here. Makana wondered if somewhere in this maze there was a file with his name on it. He saw desks and heavy typewriters, telephones, metal filing cabinets and fax machines. A man came out of a storeroom carrying a tape recorder under one arm. He nodded a greeting to Sharqi as he shut the door behind him and locked it. They arrived at an open-plan area of desks, many of them empty. The few that weren't were occupied by bored-looking men staring at computer screens. They barely looked up as the little procession filed through.

Lieutenant Sharqi's office was small and windowless. On the top of a row of grey cabinets rested a blue baseball cap with the letters FBI stitched onto it in yellow. Behind this on the wall was a framed photograph showing a proud Sharqi wearing a T-shirt bearing the same letters. He was flanked by two men, presumably Americans, dressed similarly. They all wore broad smiles.

'FBI summer training camp,' said Sharqi as he slipped off his jacket and placed it on a wire hanger that hung from a hook on the wall. 'One of the best experiences of my life.'

Makana looked for an ashtray and saw none.

'My brothers all run car franchises, clothes outlets, quality products. My father was appalled when I told him I was staying in the army after doing my military service.' Sharqi went behind the desk and sat down. 'I was good at it. I knew that. I joined the paratroops and scored the highest of any trainee in the last ten years. It took me a long time to persuade my father to accept my choice, but now he says he is proud of me.'

'Patriotism is overrated.'

'How would you know? You're a stateless person. You go back home and they will bury you in a dark hole.'

'I take it there is a point to this touching story of yours?'

Sharqi inclined his head in the direction of the picture of him and the FBI boys. 'When you go to America, you see how things work. The way they think. They love their country, just like we love Egypt. But it's more than that. They believe in the *idea* of America.'

'What idea is that?'

'The idea of freedom and equality, that all men are born equal.'

'And you're worried that it might catch on in this country?'

Sharqi rocked back in his chair. 'You think you're clever, don't you? I know your type. You don't believe in anything.'

'And you do?'

'The point is,' Sharqi said slowly, as if speaking to an idiot, 'that this country is not ready for democracy yet. If elections were held tomorrow who do you think would win?' As he spoke he reached down to unlock a drawer in his desk and produced a clear plastic bag. A strong one, probably standard issue in the FBI, here it was probably reused. It contained an automatic pistol. He set it down on the table between them.

'Our bearded brothers. And what would they do? Overnight, they would take us back to the Middle Ages. I don't need to tell you this because you came here to get away from exactly that in your country. We're on the same side, you and me.'

'And which side is that exactly?'

Sharqi tapped the pistol in front of him. 'Do you know what this is?'

'The gun that murdered Meera Hilal.'

'Very good. Now, try to be a bit more specific.'

Makana took a closer look. It was a Marra. A version of the Czech CZ75 semi-automatic handgun. It was manufactured exclusively at the Military Industry Corporation's centre at the Al-Shagara Industrial Complex, about an hour's drive from Makana's old home in Khartoum. They made all kinds of small arms, based on German or Chinese specifications, using machinery built in Iran. Sharqi leaned towards Makana.

'You follow me, right? The gun which killed Meera Hilal came from a factory just across the border in your home country. Some would say that's quite a coincidence.'

'Some would say it means nothing at all.'

'They might, it's true. So let's look at the facts.'

'If you looked at the facts you would have to drop the idea that this was some kind of terrorist attack and hand the case over to Okasha. Unless, of course, it suits you to keep it that way.'

Sharqi rocked his chair back until his shoulders were touching the wall. 'I have a file on you, Makana, which is full of interesting information, and a lot of gaps.'

'Gaps?'

'Missing pieces. Like, for example, your past. Nobody really knows what you were up to before you came here. We are told you were a police inspector and that you were forced to flee for your life. It's a nice story, only we can't check it. There is no information on exactly what you had to flee from.' Sharqi locked his fingers together behind his head. 'Let's look at the facts we have: two years ago there was an explosion at a resort on the Red Sea. A Russian man named Vronsky and five of his associates were killed. Thirteen people injured, some of them badly. The only person to walk away in one piece was you. I find that interesting, don't you?'

'Fascinating.'

'That bomb was set off by a jihadi terrorist, Daud Bulatt, a veteran of the Afghan war, who has vowed to bring down this government and just happened to be hiding across the border in your home country. Another coincidence? His present whereabouts are unknown, unless you have any ideas? You remember Daud Bulatt, don't you?'

Makana didn't bother to answer. In the wake of the explosion in Vronsky's villa, he had found himself face-to-face with Bulatt. Sharqi wasn't expecting an answer. All Makana was required to do was sit back and maybe applaud.

'And now here you are, a hero according to the newspapers, in the midst of a case that has exposed the religious tensions in this country.'

'Have you considered the possibility that you are looking at this the wrong way round?'

Sharqi stared blankly at Makana, who felt obliged to go on.

'I mean. Perhaps this attack was designed specifically to try and raise tensions. Some people do benefit from this.'

'Who benefits?' A smile appeared on Sharqi's face. 'You mean this is all part of a plot. That actually there is no problem between Muslim and Christian in this country?'

'It's worth considering.' Makana lit a cigarette. He no longer cared about ashtrays. 'It certainly makes more sense than the argument of where the weapon comes from. Would you suspect Americans if a Colt was used? Russians if it was a Klashnikov?'

'You know very well that I am talking about your friend Damazeen's gun running.'

'I know nothing about any such thing.'

'Which is why you ate dinner with him the other night,' said Sharqi. From another drawer he produced a heavy ashtray with 'Quantico, Virginia' embossed in gold letters along the side. 'Look,' he said, leaning forward to rest his elbows on the desk, 'I'm not trying to make your life difficult. I am saying nothing gets done in this country without the right kind of friends.'

'Is that what we are – friends?'

'Someone like you could be very useful to us. And in return, I could be useful to you. Frankly, Okasha's influence is limited.'

'And if I refuse?' Makana tapped ash on the floor.

'That's up to you, but in my humble opinion it would be a mistake. One that might land you on a plane home, or worse.'

'My clients hire me because I'm confidential. If I lose their trust I have nothing.'

'They wouldn't find out.'

'You see, that's why you're on that side of the desk and I'm on this side.'

'The problem with you, Makana, is that you're not seeing clearly. One of these days something bad is going to happen, really bad, and then people like you, the ones who are out there on a limb, will see that we were right all along.' Sharqi hefted the Marra again. 'This is good quality. One of the more reliable nine millimetres on the market.' He turned it this way and that in the light, admiring it before setting it down. 'Smuggling weapons into this country is a serious offence.'

'I know nothing about gun smuggling.'

'Maybe not, but your friend Damazeen knows a lot and he is associated with another old friend of yours.' Sharqi looked Makana in the eye and waited. 'You're still going to maintain you know nothing of what I am talking about?'

'I can't do anything else.'

'Mek Nimr, remember him? A high-ranking officer in National Intelligence and State Security in your home country. Now, we have something of a complex relationship with our southern neighbours, but this man is a direct source of trouble. For years now he has been sowing the seeds of discontent. Weapons are smuggled across the border to militants in this country. There are others like Bulatt, and they are working with Mek Nimr to supply weapons to radical jihadist forces in this country.'

'You think Damazeen is a jihadist?'

'You tell me.'

Makana laughed. 'You really have no idea what is going on, do you?'

Sharqi picked up a pencil and began tapping it against his fingers. 'We know there is a deal being brokered by Damazeen. We think he is working with the Zafrani brothers. Have you heard of them? Fanatics, determined to overthrow the government, but good at keeping their hands clean. I think we can help each other. I need someone inside, someone who can let me know where and when it is going to happen.'

'And what do I need?'

'A friend who can bail him out of awkward situations, such as can arise with a transient figure such as yourself.' Sharqi leaned his elbows on the desk. 'You're a smart man, Makana. You can think for yourself, not like most of the morons around here. But everyone needs a friend. And forget all that nonsense about our countries being brothers. There is a borderline and you could always find yourself on the wrong side of it.' He got to his feet and went over to open the door. 'Help me and I will make sure you don't get thrown out. Work against me and it could be bad for you. Think about it.' He paused, his hand resting on the handle. 'I'll get someone to drive you home.'

Chapter Thirty-Four

Sami had been moved to a private clinic in Garden City at his father-in-law's insistence. Rania's father was an engineer working for a big German company. He wasn't rich but he made a good living, which in this day and age was always remarkable in itself. The clinic was small, clean and surprisingly quiet considering its location. Sami even had a room to himself, with a large window overlooking the river and its own bathroom. He was sitting up, staring at the wall when Makana came in.

'I've decided I'm not leaving,' he said. 'This is better than where I live.'

'You're not paying the bills. This place must cost a fortune.'

'You know the saying: if you're not born with money, then better you marry a rich woman.'

'That particular saying must have escaped me. Anyway, they're not going to let you stay here forever. Eventually, you're going to have to go back to work.'

'You think so?' Sami cast a mournful look at his surroundings. 'Then I'd better enjoy it while it lasts.'

'How are you feeling?'

Sami held up his bandaged hands. 'They have an expert here,

a Bulgarian woman who says I have to try to move my fingers so as not to lose the mobility. The same with my toes.'

'Bulgarian?'

'What can I tell you? The world is wide and full of wonder.' He let his hands drop. 'The truth is I am going out of my mind. Did you get much out of Ramy?'

'Ramy had his own problems.'

'You'd better tell me everything.'

Makana pulled a chair up and they talked for the next hour without stopping.

'So you're saying someone decided that it was convenient to kill Meera, not because of what she represented but because she had found evidence of the bank channelling funds to certain privileged members?'

'Something like that.'

'But we don't know who made the decision, nor who carried out the killing.'

Makana reached into his pocket and placed the bloody ten-pound note in Sami's lap.

'What's this?'

'Whoever nailed you to the deck placed this in your hand first. I left that in a café when I went looking for Rocky. I think this was his answer. It's why they came for me.'

'And found me instead,' Sami said slowly. He turned over the note with his bandaged hands. 'They wanted you to stay away.' Sami fell quiet. He lay back and stared at a spot on the ceiling.

'You probably saved my life,' Makana said softly. 'If I had been there that night I would have bled to death before anyone found me.' By the time he got back to the *awama* the previous night there was no trace of Bassam, just as he had expected. He had taken advantage of the confusion to slip away. The number he had left behind seemed to have been disconnected. Had Bassam warned them, or had he been smart enough to change one of the digits?

'You can thank me when I get out of here and can eat at Aswani's,' Sami said. 'What I don't understand is why Rocky would kill Meera.'

'I don't think he actually did it himself. I think he got his boys to do it. The one that turned up in Imbaba that night. He has a small army of young kids. He trains them. The older ones he runs as his lieutenants.'

'The one who did the shooting and the one on the motorcycle? But why?'

'Somebody wanted her out of the way. Someone who knew that she was about to expose their money-laundering activities.'

'Someone high up. An official. The armed forces?'

'Maybe. Probably not directly, of course, but through an agent of some sort, a hired thug.'

'According to Ramy, Rocky set himself up running the café in the building for his own purposes, which placed him perfectly so his boys could watch Meera and plan their attack.'

'A bit risky, wasn't it? I mean someone might have recognised the killer.'

'There were a number of boys coming and going. Abu Salem the *bawab* couldn't have told them apart. I spoke to one, Eissa, whose arm was broken after the attack.'

'You think he was one of the shooters?'

'The motorcycle crashed into a ditch, maybe that's where he broke his arm. What is it?'

Sami was grinning self-consciously. 'Rania and I put our heads together and started thinking about Nasser Hikmet.'

'And?'

'Whoever killed Nasser took any files he had with him in Ismailia, but we were talking about him and both of us remembered that he was a very cautious person. You could say he bordered on the paranoid. Always seeing conspiracies everywhere. He didn't trust anyone, even close friends.'

'So he was paranoid.' Makana wasn't sure where this was leading.

'He kept copies of everything.'

'Where?'

'The only place he knew was safe. His mother's flat. We like to keep things close to home, you know.'

'Very good. So we need to speak to Hikmet's mother. Will she talk to me?'

'She'll talk to Rania. She's very good at getting people to open up,' Sami grinned. 'She's with her now.'

'Rania went to see her already? How long ago did she leave?'

'A couple of hours ago.'

The look on Makana's face made Sami wince. He lifted a hand and thumped it on the bed, forgetting the wound and crying out in pain.

'I'd better give you the address.'

Nasser Hikmet had lived with his widowed mother in a small flat in Bulaq. A humble building that was nevertheless clean and well kept. A narrow entrance led to an inner courtyard that rose up two floors. Open galleries ran around all four sides, with the doors to the flats facing onto these. Looking up, Makana saw the sky divided neatly by freshly washed sheets hung out to dry on lines that ran on pulleys strung across the yard. Small children in ragged clothes had followed him in from the street and now chased each other around, hopping over a stream of blue, soapy water that drained across the uneven ground. Climbing to the first floor he enquired about the Hikmet family. A woman who was busy hanging out more laundry pointed to a door on the second floor. A small boy of about seven appeared at her side, tugging at her elbow.

'I can show you,' he said, and without waiting for an answer he led the way.

A woman with enormous eyes opened the door on the second floor. In her fifties and small in stature, she held herself back, peering through the narrow opening as if afraid of the light.

'Yes, who is it?'

'My name is Makana. I'm . . .'

The door opened wide and Mrs Hikmet leaned out, looked quickly left and right before grabbing Makana's arm and pulling him inside.

'Quick!' she said. 'Before anyone sees. They are always sticking their noses in my business.'

The interior of the flat was gloomy. The windows were plastered with newspaper for some reason and Makana had trouble not bumping into the furniture. The air was damp and smelled of wet cloth. The little woman moved energetically past, leading the way into the kitchen. A table in the corner was covered with sheets of wilted newspaper on which leaves of cabbage were spread out as if in preparation for some magical ritual. They didn't linger as Mrs Hikmet rushed straight though into a living room and switched on the light. In the weak glow from the low wattage bulb, Makana saw a table and a sofa, one leg of which was propped up on bricks, and a television set. All of these had been pushed back to make space for the object which occupied the middle of the room: a gleaming white washing machine, still wrapped in cardboard and sheets of plastic.

'There it is,' she gestured. 'What do you think?'

'It's very nice,' said Makana tentatively. 'But wouldn't it be better off somewhere else?'

'This is where they left it. I told them I couldn't decide where to put it and they said it would all be taken care of when the engineer arrived.' She folded her arms and smiled at him.

'I'm not the engineer.'

'You're not?' Mrs Hikmet frowned. 'But I thought . . .'

'I'm sorry.'

'But when are they going to send someone?'

'I really can't say. I have nothing to do with washing machines.'

'You don't?'

'No. I'm looking for a friend of mine who may have come to talk to you about your son.'

'A friend?'

'A woman named Rania Barakat. Her husband Sami was a colleague of your son's.'

'Rania? Of course, she was here earlier.' Mrs Hikmet laughed. 'It's strange. Everyone is so interested now. All those years when I had to listen to him complaining that no one cared about his work. He had to fight to get it published, you know?' Mrs Hikmet leaned forward, lowering her voice. 'After the police had been here I had a visit from some other men. Not the kind who wear uniforms, but you can smell them. In the old days the police were on our side, now we are all criminals to them, just for breathing.' Mrs Hikmet glanced at the doorway as if expecting to see her visitors standing there again. 'They went through the whole place, looking everywhere. They took anything with writing on it. Boxes full of papers.'

'How about his computer?'

'Only the big one,' she smiled. 'I don't like security people. I don't trust them.'

'But you trusted Rania?'

Mrs Hikmet nodded. 'I was waiting for her, you see.'

'You were?'

'Of course. I knew that sooner or later, one of his friends would turn up, somebody who cared about the same things he did.' Her voice dropped to a whisper. 'I don't believe a word of it.'

'You don't?'

'Not my son. Not Nasser. My husband died when he was only a small baby. Nasser was all I had. They say he killed himself.' She clutched her hands together. 'They say he fell off the top of a building.' She pointed a finger at the ceiling. 'Why would he do that?'

'Did he go to Ismailia for work?'

'Oh, he never did anything but work. Always travelling, always working.' She broke off to stare at the washing machine again. 'Why did they say someone would come to fix it?'

'I'm sure it just takes time.'

'That's what people always say, but it's not true. Things could be done much quicker. People are lazy, that's the trouble. Nasser was never lazy.' The wrinkles around her eyes deepened as she blinked away tears. 'That's why I was determined his death should not have been in vain. If he died for a story he was working on then I owe it to him to give that story to the world. That's why I gave her the other one.'

'The other one?'

'The computer, of course. It's very small, you see, not much bigger than a box of dates.'

'And you gave it to Rania?'

'I showed her where he kept it.'

Makana gamely traipsed behind her into the kitchen and

squatted down to look into the cupboard under the sink as Mrs Hikmet pulled back a warped sheet of plywood, cracked and rotten in places to reveal a narrow space underneath, now empty. 'It's his secret hiding place.' Mrs Hikmet smiled. 'You lift up the bottom of the cupboard. They never found it.'

'Very clever,' he said, admiringly. 'When exactly was Rania here?'

'This morning. I'm surprised you haven't seen her, if you're such good friends.'

'Well, I'm trying to find her actually. I think she might be in danger.'

'Oh, dear.' Mrs Hikmet put a hand to her throat.

'Did she say anything about where she might go?'

'Oh no. But then they arrived with the washing machine and I had to deal with that.'

Makana was about to straighten up when something caught his eye. Lodged against the side of the cupboard was a scrap of white card. He reached in and plucked it out. It was folded down, trapped between the floor and side of the cupboard.

'What is it?' asked Mrs Hikmet.

'It's a business card,' said Makana, turning it over. There was a telephone number scrawled on the back. A number he had seen before.

Mrs Hikmet was on the move again, talking over her shoulder as she led the way back through to the tiny living room.

'He was a good boy. Always took care of me.' She patted the gleaming white washing machine. 'I told them I couldn't accept it, that an old woman like myself could never pay for such a thing, but they said he had arranged it all,' she beamed like someone who had won the lottery. 'The neighbours will be very jealous.'

Makana examined the machine with renewed interest, for some clue as to what might have happened to Rania. On the side he found a label which gave the address of an outlet in Mohandeseen and the name of the company: Beit Zafrani.

Chapter Thirty-Five

Whbile many establishments settled for upbeat music to lull potential customers into a relaxed state of mind and thereby trigger an unrestrained spending spree, Beit Zafrani preferred to use the sound system to fill their stores with edifying religious readings. Young boys sung the sacred verses through Chinese speakers fitted into the ceiling. The ground floor of the Zafrani brothers' flagship enterprise on Shihab Street was a brightly lit space dedicated to domestic appliances: washing machines, refrigerators, air conditioners. The floor space was taken up by rows of rectilinear white units all lined up to suggest some kind of order. The few people in sight, mostly wide-eyed couples, wandered through this maze of marvels, their faces set with expressions of awe more akin to visitors at a museum displaying the treasures of past civilisations. Here instead was a museum of modern life. Evidence that Egyptian women were no longer prepared to stand up to their knees in the river scrubbing their clothes on a flat stone. Now they lifted lids and opened doors to marvel, peering cautiously inside as if expecting a djinn to reach out and drag them down inside. Men frowned at the prices and at specifications that might have been written in hieroglyphics for all they understood.

What Makana knew of the Zafrani brothers was little more than rumour and hearsay. Between protection rackets, smuggling, prostitution and a string of other enterprises, they presided over a small empire, descended from an extended family of small-time criminals and dealers in contraband. In prison, legend had it they had undergone a religious conversion. Seeing the error of their ways they vowed to dedicate themselves to furthering the Islamic cause. This didn't mean that they entirely abandoned their criminal ways overnight, simply that they determined to straighten themselves out. The chain of white goods and clothing stores was the most vivid manifestation of this will to go legitimate. The straight side was run by the younger of the two, the clean-living Zayed, while Ayad, generally took care of the less palatable business.

Makana was greeted by the gently undulating tones of a young boy singing the sacred verses of the Quran. The religious tones seemed to sit well with the clientele. Men whose faces were lost in long, straggly beards and women wrapped in conservative long sleeves and skirts, their hair bundled under scarves bound tightly under their chins. Their clothes were simple, in plain dark colours. Some of the women wore long coats that buttoned from chin to ankle while others had their faces veiled, sweeping through the room in their black robes like vengeful spirits among the white metal appliances. Children of all shapes and sizes ran about with wild abandon. Parents and children alike remaining oblivious to the frowns of the shop assistants, who in turn stared blankly at Makana when he told them the purpose of his visit.

'Tell Zafrani that Mr Makana is here to see him.'

'To which Mr Zafrani do you refer?'

'It doesn't matter which.'

With a look of disdain the assistant, a slim man with a neatly

319

trimmed beard, disappeared and five minutes later two others appeared. One of them looked familiar. An old man with a hennaed beard. Last time Makana saw him he had his hand wrapped around his throat.

'Come with us.'

The assistant dropped his eyes to the counter in front of him as if Makana had instantly performed the miracle of becoming invisible. A staircase with chrome railings and glass sides led up to the first floor and Ladies Apparel. Women pored through the racks impatiently with gloved hands. The second floor was the men's department, deserted but for a couple of bearded assistants who stood around idly as if waiting for a train to come by. Makana's guides led him word-lessly to a black door with a chromed porthole in the middle of it. The bald head that bobbed up to fill this nodded in recognition at Makana's companions and the door clicked open. On the other side was an empty corridor. They walked down to the end in silence. A turn brought them to an open doorway and a room furnished with carpets. Two sofas against the wall. There were no windows.

'Sit,' said the hennaed man, without elaborating. Makana sat. When he reached for his cigarettes the man clicked his tongue and shook his head. Makana sat and stared at the walls as the two guards took up positions on either side of the doorway.

He didn't have long to wait. The two thugs exited discreetly. The first man to enter the room resembled a school teacher; bespectacled and with the obligatory beard, neatly trimmed. He was slim and delicate in appearance, clad in a pristine white gelabiya with a high collar that buttoned under a prominent Adam's apple. He stood in the doorway and blinked. The other was short and hefty, with a shaven head. Makana had glimpsed him aboard the *Binbashi* that night with Talal and Bunny. The man who gave his permission for wine to be served. Makana guessed this was Ayad Zafrani, the elder of the two brothers. The slim version was Zayed. He did the talking.

'How generous of you to pay us a visit, Mr Makana. We were just discussing you.'

'I'm honoured.'

'Indeed. All roads seem to lead back to you.' Zayed Zafrani had a quirky smile on his face. His brother scowled at the floor. 'People fall around you, friends, associates, and yet you' – he made a movement like a fish with the flat of his hand –'find your way through unharmed. Why is that?'

'Luck?' ventured Makana.

'Oh, come now, it has to be more than sheer luck. Why are you here?'

'I'm looking for Rania Barakat.'

'And what makes you think we know where she is?'

'Your associates delivered a washing machine just before she disappeared.'

Zayed Zafrani's smile deepened. 'You mistake an act of kindness for an aggression.'

'Maybe. I happen to believe you have taken an interest in Nasser Hikmet's work.'

'Indeed. We believe his work is of great value to us.'

'Which is why you tried to bribe his grieving mother?'

'Merely a gift, to show our benevolent nature.' Zayed Zafrani bowed.

'But you still don't have what you are looking for.'

'We are confident it will come to us, one way or another.'

'Is that what your boys were doing when they helped Hikmet out of a window in Ismailia?'

'Watch yourself. Now you're jumping to conclusions,' growled Ayad.

Makana recalled hearing a story about one of the brothers tearing a man limb from limb, dislocating shoulders, cracking ribs, reducing him to a bloody sack of broken bones with his bare hands. It would have to be Ayad. Hard to imagine the smooth Zayed tearing a roasted pigeon apart.

'You're saying you didn't kill him?'

'If that was the case then why should we be interested in Mrs Hikmet?'

Makana considered the facts. It was possible the Zafranis were telling the truth. But if they didn't kill Hikmet then who did, and why? Whoever it was they must have discovered the existence of the laptop after he was dead. They also knew that the police had not found the laptop. Which pointed towards someone with contacts inside the security services. Had they been watching Mrs Hikmet's flat when Rania showed up and left carrying the laptop?

'Just so we are clear. I don't wish to interfere in your business dealings, passports or otherwise.'

Zayed Zafrani threw an uncomfortable glance at his brother, who in turn lifted his eyes heavenwards. 'That was a minor affair we were reluctant to get involved in and which has now been terminated.'

'And Ghalib Samsara, what is your interest in him?'

'I don't know that name,' Zayed Zafrani shook his head.

'Let's start again. Why are you so interested in the information on that computer?'

Zafrani thought for a moment before going on. 'It contains details of certain transactions concerning the operations of a certain bank.'

'The Eastern Star Investment Bank.'

'Frankly, Mr Makana, your knowledge of our dealings concerns me.'

'Like I said, I'm not interested in your affairs.'

'Are we supposed to believe that when you are working with Lieutenant Sharqi?'

Makana recalled the motorcyclist with the television set who had been following him and felt a grudging respect for the Zafranis.

'Sharqi wants me to help him out. He says I need a friend.'

'Such a friend could be very useful to a man like you.'

'Everything has a price.' Makana glanced at Ayad Zafrani who opened and closed his fists as if he anticipated using them soon. 'Why don't you answer the question? Why are you interested in information about a bank you helped set up?'

Zayed Zafrani tilted his head to one side. 'To do that I would have to explain our strategy.'

'Your strategy?'

'In the long term we believe the current regime will have to go. It is corrupt and works against the good of the people.'

'And you hope to hasten that change?'

'Encourage it,' Zayed Zafrani smiled.

'Did you order Meera Hilal to be killed?'

'An unfortunate incident. Very clumsy. When people get nervous about Islamist fanatics sooner or later they start pointing in our direction. We would like to avoid that.'

'Are you saying you didn't kill her?'

'Yes, of course. Why would we kill her?'

'You wanted to suppress the information she had dug up.'

'We want to know who that information concerns. Names.' Zayed Zafrani paused. 'Are you planning to take this to Lieutenant Sharqi?'

'All I care about right now is Rania. Why is the bank so important?'

'We have invested a great deal in transforming our assets into legal ones.' Zayed Zafrani gestured at their surroundings. 'The Eastern Star was a part of that move.'

'So let me see if I understand,' said Makana. 'You set up the bank as part of your legitimate operations. A way to accumulate a solid foothold in the country's economy, and to make yourselves known to the people. You managed to get the endorsement of your friend Sheikh Waheed. Then things started to go wrong. A group of people inside the armed forces started to take a personal interest. They bought into the bank and began using it for their own purposes. Large sums of money were moved around using small companies like Blue Ibis. The money comes in, stays for a few days and then goes out again, perhaps in two or three directions, and all trace of it disappears.'

'Armed forces people,' grunted Ayad. 'They think they can do what they like.'

'If you know something about us then you will know that we spent long periods in prison. At first this was because of our . . . activities. But this was all part of our fate. I am a religious man,' Zayed Zafrani said moodily. 'I've suffered for my beliefs. We both have. I have had my bones broken. I have been tortured. We don't like to be taken advantage of, particularly by people like Sheikh Waheed, who, by the way, is not a friend. He represents everything that we wish to see the end of.'

'Waheed is where it all went wrong. He brought in his government friends. Yet you brought him in to endorse your bank.'

'It was a mistake, but even snakes have their uses sometimes. Waheed is a puppet, feeding his friends and doing their bidding.'

'Stirring up animosity towards Christians, for example?'

'A distraction. We are not interested in distractions. We want people to wake up, to see how badly this country is being run.'

'And then what, they rise up and take to the streets?'

Zayed Zafrani lifted his shoulders in a careless shrug. 'The details are not important. The point is that change is inevitable. You cannot suppress seventy million people forever. We started this bank in order to bring people back to the idea that Islam can be used to run the state.'

'Because you believe Islam is the solution to this country's problems.'

'The people, the *shaab*, have been cast into a long sleep for many decades. But one day soon, *inshallah*, they will awaken.'

'Shall I tell you what I think?' asked Makana, lighting a cigarette. 'I think some part of your masterplan has gone awry. You've lost control. In a word, one key piece is out of your hands, or to put it another way, somebody you trust has betrayed you.'

'Go on,' said Zayed Zafrani quietly.

'This person is playing both sides to his own advantage. You expected to get the information you needed in Ismailia. It wasn't there. You thought Hikmet's mother had it, but Rania beat you to it. Now you say you don't know where she is, and perhaps I'm wrong, but I just might believe you. Maybe somebody else has her, the same person who set up Meera's killing without your asking. He made it look spectacular, which was exactly what you don't need. The case passed from the police to a special counter-terrorist unit and Lieutenant Sharqi, who is going to come knocking at your door one of these days.'

'And you think you can help us to take care of this person?' murmured Zayed Zafrani.

'I think I might be able to.'

'And what do you get in return for doing us this favour?'

'Well, there is one matter of great importance to me that I think you can help me with.'

'Please, speak freely.'

'I need to know about your business with Mohammed Damazeen.'

Zayed Zafrani was silent. Ayad muttered something to himself and stared at his feet.

'I was right about you,' said Zayed Zafrani after a time. 'You are an interesting man.'

Chapter Thirty-Six

On the way across town, Makana stopped to call the hospital. By some miracle he managed to get through to the right nurse who told him that no, Mrs Barakat was not with her husband. He insisted that he needed to speak to Sami, that it was a matter of life and death. Eventually, after much complaining, a line was connected and somebody presumably held the receiver to Sami's ear. He was desperate and had heard nothing from Rania. Makana hung up and made more phone calls. He was trying to eliminate possibilities. Eventually, only one would remain, the one he feared the most. He called their apartment where there was no reply, then her office and finally her parents. Nobody had seen her.

The police presence had been reduced to one dark-blue pick-up which slumped under shot suspension parked on the corner of the street. Two uniformed men sitting in the back watched Makana with a mixture of indifference and sullen resentment. The acned face of the young man who stepped up to block his path was unfamiliar. Like the others he wore a shirt emblazoned with the image of the many-winged angel on it: the Seraph. He smelled of hair oil and was carrying a short iron bar. He clearly knew who Makana was.

'Our hero returns,' he sneered.

'Where's Ishaq?'

'He's not here,' he replied helpfully. The others began to crowd round, breathing in quick, shallow gasps, like fighters gearing themselves up before plunging into the ring. 'He's at the gym.'

'Tell him I need to speak to him,' Makana said, pushing his way through. There was resistance, but no one seriously tried to stop him going inside. They might not have liked him but they weren't going to assault him in front of the police. They would have to wait.

As he walked up the stairs into the building he heard a television playing somewhere. A chirpy jingle selling something nauseating and completely lacking in nutritional value. It seemed to sum up the age. The door to the apartment was opened by Meera's sister, Maysoun, who looked him over with the same mixture of distrust and resentment as the boys on guard duty outside. She lifted a hand to stop him, but Makana pushed her aside.

'Where is he?'

Maysoun shook her head speechlessly. She wore a plain black dress with a high neck and long sleeves. She examined her nails.

'He's not good. He drinks too much and gets depressed. Then he doesn't sleep. His nerves have never been good.'

'Is he asleep now?'

'The doctor gave him a sedative. He needs rest.' She stared down the hall, gloomy and dark even in daytime. 'My sister married him. This is still her home. Out of respect for her I cannot abandon him in his hour of need.'

'It's an admirable attitude. A lot of people would not go to such lengths.'

Her eyes pinned themselves sharply on him. 'Did you find out who murdered her?'

'That's why I'm here. I need to ask the doctor a few more questions.'

'I don't like to disturb him.'

'It's too late for that.'

Maysoun again glanced down the hall in the direction of Hilal's study. She turned back to find Makana watching her and finally decided to step aside. She gestured towards the salon.

'Please, wait. I will go and tell him you are here.'

The salon was defended by a couple of old aunts. Dressed in black they sat side by side, perched on a sofa covered with white lace like a pair of tidy crows. They stared at him in silence. A clock ticked loudly somewhere.

After a time Maysoun reappeared and led the way back down the hall to the big study. Ridwan Hilal looked worse. He was dressed in a shirt with stain marks in the armpits and he appeared to be growing a scruffy beard. He sat slumped behind the desk, his head resting on his right hand. The eyes opened and he made an effort to sit up as Makana entered.

'Please, don't hurt him any more,' Maysoun whispered as she went by on her way out.

'So, our investigator returns. And . . . have you found out who killed my wife?'

'I've found out a number of things we need to talk about.'

Hilal waved a weary hand towards a chair. 'Very well. Please speak your mind.'

Makana glanced at the open doorway as he sat down across the desk from Hilal.

'Feel free,' Hilal smiled. 'There are no secrets in this house.'

'As you wish. Do you know why Meera went to work at the Blue Ibis company?'

'I have no idea.'

'Perhaps it will be easier,' Makana smiled, 'if I explain what I think happened and you correct me?'

'Very well.'

'Nasser Hikmet came to you. He said he was working on a story about the Eastern Star Investment Bank. Since you had some expertise on the subject of Islamic banking he thought you might be able to help. He was looking into a number of small companies that he believed were siphoning funds away from the bank into the accounts of private individuals, some quite high-up officials. It was a huge story and not without risk.'

'I thought you were trying to find out who killed my wife?'

Makana ignored this. 'I imagine you dismissed Hikmet as a dabbler. What could a poor journalist understand about the theoretics of Islamic banking? But Meera saw it differently. She persuaded you that this was an opportunity to restore your reputation. She contacted Hikmet and went around the list of companies he had until she found work, at Blue Ibis Tours.'

Hilal stared at Makana in silence, then he got up and went over to close the door.

'Inside the company, Meera made friends with Ramy, Faragalla's unwanted bastard. For his own reasons Ramy decided to help Meera and led her to the documents which demonstrated how money was being re-routed from the bank. And that brings us to the letters.'

'What about the letters?'

'The letters were meant as a personal warning, to you, from an old friend, Professor Serhan. He overheard Hikmet's name mentioned in connection with Meera. When Hikmet fell out of

a hotel window Serhan suspected she was in danger. For sentimental reasons perhaps, he decided to warn her, to warn both of
you, in fact. But there was a problem, he couldn't contact Meera
directly. He was on the side of respectability now, and she was
your wife. He would have died of shame if the story had come
out and besides, he was probably still a little bit in love with her.
Being a professor he came up with an obscure and roundabout
way of trying to warn you. He sent the Dogstar letters to her
anonymously. He thought you would understand.'

'How would I know they were a warning?'

'I think you did. When I spoke to Professor Serhan I asked
him why he had sent three letters. Surely one would have been
sufficient? He thought so too. He couldn't understand why you
didn't respond to the first one. He was counting on you recognis-
ing the Sura, since as students the two of you had been young
poets, part of a movement that revered those texts. The ambiguous Suras, as you explained to me. The first time I showed you
the letters I asked if you had seen them before. You said no. You
lied to me. Why?'

'None of what you are saying makes any sense,' said Hilal.

'Let's go on. When Meera found out why Faragalla was hiring
me she decided she had to talk to me. She told me about the
other letters. Faragalla had only seen one. She was worried I
might discover what she had found in the office records and that
her plan would be exposed. Meera was a cautious person. You
had told her not to worry about the letters, but she wasn't
convinced.'

'This is all pure speculation.'

'I think it was pride that stopped you from responding to
Serhan's warning, but there was another reason you lied to me
about the letters. You told Meera there was nothing to worry

about. You didn't want anything to deflect her from her task. This was your chance to be vindicated, to expose the people who destroyed you as charlatans prepared to subvert the law to make some money. You would have a chance to make your case again. You might even be reinstated.'

'You are simply making this up. You have no evidence for any of this.'

'I don't need evidence, because all I'm doing is telling a story.' Makana tossed onto the table the business card he had found underneath Mrs Hikmet's sink. Hilal reached over to pick it up.

'Where did you get this?'

'I found it in Hikmet's flat. It's identical to the one you gave me, remember? It has your name on it and your private line.' Makana pointed at the telephone sitting on the desk. 'Despite your assurances, the letters still managed to scare her. Meera knew that the information she had would blow the roof off the Eastern Star Bank and take a number of prominent people with it. But she also knew she was dealing with dangerous people. Army officers, State Security officials. Going after them would be like kicking over a basket full of snakes. She decided it was too dangerous to proceed.' Makana got to his feet and moved over to the window. 'That's when you decided to take matters into your own hands. The chance of getting your name back was too strong. You called Hikmet and arranged to meet. You gave him the information he was looking for. Your pride and vanity was more important than your wife's safety.'

Ridwan Hilal groaned and bowed his head.

'You asked me who killed Meera,' said Makana. 'Whoever killed Hikmet found evidence of where the information had come from. They put two and two together and came up with her name.'

Ridwan Hilal pressed his balled fists into his eyes and let out a sob. 'I didn't want to hurt her. I just wanted my life back. I wanted to be let out of this prison. Is that such a crime? To show the world that I was right and they were wrong?' And then, almost as fast as it had started, his fury ebbed away. 'Oh, God,' he sobbed and dropped his face into his hands.

As he made his way out, Makana paused by the open door to the salon and looked in. The two crows stared back impassively. They didn't even blink. Maysoun was waiting by the front door, one hand clutched to her throat. In her other she held a handkerchief; the neck of white cloth twisted like a strangled bird as her fist tightened around it. Neither of them said anything. The sound of Ridwan Hilal's sobs echoed down the lonely hall.

Chapter Thirty-Seven

There was only one person whose name kept surfacing in Makana's thoughts. One man who was always there in the background, just out of focus. Someone who fitted all the requirements. A man who was everywhere and nowhere. Yousef had been running the passport scam if not for the Zafranis then with their blessing. As an ex-Military Police officer he still had contacts inside the security services. He was placed inside the Blue Ibis by the same officials who had turned the Eastern Star Bank to their own purposes. Yousef was everybody's friend and nobody's. He took care of business for himself, first and foremost.

Father Macarius was waiting for him in the big gloomy hall that served as a dormitory and dining room. He was sitting at the far end of the long table, his head resting against the wall. On the table in front of him lay a string of rosary beads and a wooden cross. He looked asleep and it wasn't until Makana was standing over him that he opened his eyes.

'Ah, there you are. I was wondering why we hadn't seen you.'

'I have been away.'

Makana slid onto the bench opposite the priest. Father

Macarius' face looked gaunt, painted in bands of shadow and light coming through the narrow windows high above.

'That must have been nice for you.'

'I went to visit Wadi Nikeiba.'

Father Macarius stared at him.

'Father, I think you tried to tell me about what happened all those years ago.'

'I tried, but I couldn't.' Father Macarius closed his eyes for a second. 'It was too painful. Wadi Nikeiba was a dream for us. It wasn't just about rebuilding the old monastery. We wanted to go back to the old ways, to return to the solitude of the desert, to find the solace of prophets and make our peace with God.'

'It didn't turn out that way.'

'No,' Father Macarius looked up, his eyes dark. 'We harboured a monster in our midst.'

'And you think that monster has followed you here?'

'How else to explain it?' Father Macarius sat up, suddenly alert. 'There are too many similarities for it to be coincidence. The children are roughly of the same age as the victims back then. The nature of the attacks. The brutal disfigurement and torture. The person who committed these murders is inhuman.'

'You think you were wrong about Antun?'

'I . . . I don't know. I believe he is a good boy by nature. He was too small, too frail to have done those things back then.'

'Father Girgis told me he was seized by terrible fits of anger.'

'He has a nervous condition, but I don't . . . I can't believe he is capable of such cruelty.'

'But now you're not sure.'

Father Macarius lowered his head. After a time he nodded.

'I was protective of Antun, it's true. Perhaps more so than the others. Why? I cannot say. He was vulnerable and weak. I developed a particular bond with him.' Macarius reached for his rosary beads. 'To me, he was always very special. I tried to protect him. I fed him stories.' Macarius' voice echoed through the gloom. 'He possessed a powerful imagination. He wasn't like other children. He wanted to know where he came from. I told him that an angel had brought him to us.' There was another lengthy silence as the priest seemed to lose his way again.

'But the other monks suspected him.'

'They were . . . suspicious of everyone. They couldn't understand our relationship. We had something special, Antun and myself. A loyalty, an understanding. Nothing more.'

'So, when the time came you offered to take him away with you.'

Father Macarius nodded slowly. 'In the end, when they came and closed us down it was a relief in a way. The distrust between us was unbearable. None of us knew if the others were killers.' Macarius' voice cracked. 'I took the boy with me. I brought him here. Oh, Lord forgive me, I brought him here.'

'Father, do you have any evidence that Antun is responsible for these recent killings?'

'I haven't been able to stop thinking about it.' Unable to sit still, Macarius got to his feet and started pacing. 'Imagine if it is true, if I have protected him, all these years. My God, what have I done?' Father Macarius faced the crucifix hanging on the wall above his head and closed his eyes. 'I caused the death of those children.'

'No!'

The anguished cry echoed from the dark recesses on the far side of the room. Makana turned in time to see a shadow dart from where he had been hiding and head for the door.

'Antun!' Macarius cried. 'Quick! We must catch him. He must have heard everything.'

They made it out into the yard in time to see the figure vanish through the doorway on the far side leading to the darkened gym. The priest hurried over, pulling open the door and disappearing into the blackness within. Makana felt he was chasing a shadow.

'That's his room up there.'

An enclosed storage space made of warped plywood ran along the far end of the room just under the roof, suspended over the punchbags and weights. A staircase materialised out of the gloom. Steps creaked ominously as they climbed. It led to a square hole. Makana stuck his head through and found himself inside a small room.

'There used to be a bulb up here, but it seems to have gone.' Father Macarius' voice echoed out of the darkness. Makana stared hard in the direction it had come from. He could have been standing with his nose almost touching the wall and he wouldn't have known. There was some scuffling and then the sound of a match being struck. Father Macarius' face surfaced briefly in the halo of light from a candle. Then he turned and disappeared like a fish swimming into black water.

Makana realised he had been standing next to a window of sorts, a hole cut into the plywood wall. In the turgid gloom below punchbags dangled like hanged men. The patched and grubby canvas ring stood out as an outcrop of dull ivory against all that darkness. The snap of wings made him look up sharply. Something. A pigeon? A bat?

Father Macarius was moving deeper into the gloom. The stuttering flame cut ahead of them like a dying star. Makana felt the floor creak beneath him and realised that the whole structure around him was made of rotting old wood. The watery light picked out shadows scattered around the walls. Close up they resembled people huddled on the ground, then he realised they were old sacks stuffed with equipment, ripped gloves, torn singlets, stacks of paper flyers. Makana made his way over carefully, following Father Macarius' voice, his heart stopping with each crack the floor gave, like brittle ice. There was no reply from within. The sides around the entrance were grubby from people's hands. The light narrowed as the priest squeezed through another gap.

'He's been living up here for years . . . No one else ever comes up here.' The voice tailed off.

The next room was low and dark. Here, faint light filtered through an arched window at knee level which faced onto the street. Opaque glass covered with patches of old newspaper. A heavy musty smell in the air reminded him of a cow shed. The floor was cluttered with all manner of junk, bits and pieces that appeared to have been salvaged from the street. Out of the gloom floated wooden crates, milk churns, wheel rims, hubcaps, a soapstone sphinx minus its head, electric cables, car batteries, a heavy wooden tiller, and across one wall an array of bird cages awkwardly shaped from chicken wire and whittled struts. Makana was put in mind of Old Yunis' rather more exotic menagerie. These birds were in a much poorer state and looked wretched for the most part: brown turtledoves, sharp-eyed pigeons with twisted wings, a yellow canary that stood out like a tiny sun floating in the darkness. There was an old mattress slung in one corner. A few cardboard boxes that seemed to contain Antun's clothes. How could they let him live like this? More than sheltering the boy, Makana suspected that Macarius was hiding him from the world.

'Oh, my God!' Father Macarius uttered the words in a low whisper, staring past him.

Makana turned to look back. The wall through which they had just passed was covered with symbols and letters. The words were written in what he knew was Coptic. The stark images were like a religious vision. They appeared to have accumulated over many years. Painted onto the wood in such thick layers they resembled the icons Makana had seen in the church. Even in the low light he could make out vivid ochres and reds. Angels floated around the ceiling with golden wings and halos circling their heads. The images seemed to make up some kind of biblical mural. At the centre was the large figure Makana had seen before. A face surrounded by what appeared to be wings or flames. They tapered into points above and below. The angel with eight wings. The Seraph.

Father Macarius gasped. He touched a hand to the wall gently. 'Saint Macarius and the Seraph. Only here it is the winged angel alone. Antun identifies strongly with it. Here' – he leaned closer – 'you can see that it has Antun's face.'

Makana drew closer to the flame and the features of the slight, retiring boy he had seen in the gym floated out of the gleaming dark wood into the light.

'He has lost his mind,' said Father Macarius quietly, almost to himself. 'All these years I have tried to protect him.'

'What does the rest of this mean?' Makana turned back to the mural. Father Macarius stirred himself from his thoughts and lifted the candle stub again. His hand was covered with melted wax.

'This is the Book of Daniel. The angel precedes the coming of the apocalypse.'

'The end of the world?'

'*Apo-kalypto* in Greek signifies the lifting of the veil. The world is cleansed by fire. Truth is revealed. The age of dishonesty ended.' Father Macarius leaned back, his eyes slowly reading the words scrawled on the walls. 'The poor child sees himself as the angel heralding the apocalypse.' Father Macarius stepped closer to the wall, raising his free hand as if to touch the angel floating above him. 'And so he turned himself into the Seraph, the highest of the orders of angels, the Burning One.'

'What does that mean?'

'He will cleanse the world with his flame. I still can't believe he would kill anyone.'

Makana lifted something from the floor. A cape of some sort. 'Do you know what this is?'

'Some of the fighters wear them to keep warm before they enter the ring in a tournament.'

Something had been sewn onto the inside of the lining.

'Feathers?' asked Father Macarius incredulously.

'Pigeon feathers by the look of it.' They had been sewn into the cloth in bunches. Makana turned the cape around in the air. Tiny flashes of light revealed strips of silver foil, coils of tin that bobbed gently as if they were living creatures. The whole cape was covered in feathers, sewn with great care into a pattern.

'The wings of an angel,' murmured Father Macarius. 'The Angel of Imbaba.'

'And this?'

Makana drew the priest's attention to another figure which appeared to dominate one corner of the mural. It was drawn in charcoal and was the face of a man, with horns.

'Satan. The devil.'

It struck Makana that the drawing was more than that. In fact, it seemed to him that the face was actually a depiction of someone specific. A mixture of the mythological and the real. A focus for the pain that Antun had carried with him for years. The features were precise. Makana stepped back to get a better look.

'You recognise who it is?'

'Of course,' muttered Father Macarius, his jaw hanging slack. 'It's Rocky.'

Chapter Thirty-Eight

Makana felt as though events were taking their own course. All he could do was follow the sequence set out for him. As he came out of the gym, he found himself surrounded by Ishaq and his boys. There seemed to be more of them this time and a number of them were carrying what looked like weapons: chains, sticks, iron bars.

'What is going on?'

'Why are you asking for me?' Ishaq asked in response.

'I need your help,' Makana said. 'Antun may have gone after Rocky. He might be in danger.'

'Rocky? Why should we help him?'

'Antun is the one who is in danger,' said Makana.

'You think Antun killed those children?'

'I don't think so. I think it was Rocky.' Makana looked the others over. 'Also, I think he knows where a friend of mine is.'

'You want us to go after Rocky?'

'You know where to find him?'

'We can't go there. There are not enough of us.'

Ishaq fell silent. Makana could feel the other boys twitching around him.

'There's a café called Al Madina, that's where you'll find him. If you go over there,' Ishaq warned, 'you'll be in their territory. We can't go into that area.'

Al Madina? The same name that Bassam had mentioned. 'Who are they?' he asked. Suddenly all of them were talking at once.

'They are the ones who are fighting us.'

'They want to drive us out of here and burn the church to the ground.'

'They have protection.'

'The police won't touch them.'

'Just as they won't touch Rocky.'

'He's one of them.'

It added to the theory that the violence towards the Copts was being coordinated in some way. If Rocky was on the payroll of the security forces as a hired thug that would explain why he was given free rein to act with impunity. He was a small cog in a much larger wheel. By turning a blind eye to his activities they were ensuring that the terror continued. In the frenetic agitation he felt around him Makana sensed that something was about to break.

'You're preparing for an attack?' Makana asked.

'They said they would come tonight.'

'They are saying Antun is the one who killed those boys,' explained Ishaq. 'It's just an excuse. They are coming for the church.'

'I still need to find Rocky,' Makana insisted. Heads were being shaken and eyes turned away. They were so wrapped up in their own fury nothing else could deflect them. It put him in mind of Ghalib Samsara. Where did that fury come from? Makana thought about the dogstar's long journey through the darkness, of the desperation and madness that traditionally precedes its reappearance on the horizon.

'You're on your own,' said one. 'We have to stay here.'

'They are blocking the roads,' said another. 'There's no way through from this side.'

'We can go round from the other side by car,' Makana suggested.

Finally, with a reluctant shrug, Ishaq stepped forward.

'I'll show you the way.'

Makana waved Sindbad over. As the battered Datsun ground its way towards him, he thought it was a good idea to get going before Ishaq thought the matter through too carefully and changed his mind, but Ishaq dropped into the back seat and stared idly out at the street.

'It all just got out of hand. These murders . . .' Ishaq shook his head. 'It's a war out there.'

'Why is it people keep talking about war as though it was inevitable?' Makana asked.

'What would you know about it?'

'Watch your mouth, boy!' interjected Sindbad.

'It's all right, Sindbad.'

'*Hadir, ya effendi.*'

'Sindbad,' Ishaq leaned over from the back seat. 'I knew I'd seen your face before. You used to box, didn't you? Heavyweight, right?'

Sindbad mumbled something under his breath.

'Maybe you have all the protection you need, after all,' Ishaq said, sitting back.

'Let's hope so,' said Makana.

They drove back towards the riverside and sank into a mass of dense traffic, as if the wheels were churning through thick

344

mud. At the Kit Kat roundabout they turned in again and the streets grew narrow and more crowded as the number of pedestrians swelled. They flooded across the road, reducing the car's progress to a snail's pace. A camel being led by the nose overtook them. Loping gracefully along, oblivious to the absurdity of its surroundings. Horns beeped in harmonious disarray while figures wandered back and forth through the headlight beams like a herd of sleepwalkers. Ishaq leaned over the front seat and pointed.

'Take the next left. It's on the next corner. You can see it.'

'Take him back to the gym,' Makana said to Sindbad as he got out of the car. 'I'll walk from here, then come back and wait here for me.' To Ishaq he said, 'Try and find Antun. If you do, take him to Father Macarius.'

As the Datsun screeched away, Makana stumbled off over the usual debris of shattered bricks and shredded nylon bags. The street was dark and uneven. A discarded watermelon rind smiled up at him from the dirt. The asphalt, if there ever had been any, had long since been buried beneath layers of mud and rubbish. It had been broken up and ground down by lorries and horse carts and every manner of human transport and footwear, and never replaced. No one really paid much care to an area like this. The politicians and their loved ones didn't live nearby and few tourists ever ventured here. The houses were unadorned. Ragged scraps of light appeared here and there announcing an opening in a wall was a shop of some kind. Children scampered by. A group of boys were kicking an old football about under a solitary lamppost. Spurts of dust flew up around them. An uneven goal had been drawn on the wall with a stick of charcoal. You could barely see the wall, let alone the goal. Training for a generation of blind footballers.

The café was closed. The name was painted in letters so feint you had to look twice to see them. The metal doors were shuttered and bolted, sealed with a heavy padlock. It was the same hole-in-the-wall café where he had left a ten-pound note for the boy. The same torn note that had been nailed to Sami's hand. There was no sign of the Omda with the handlebar moustache.

The building where Rocky lived was right across the street. Could Rania be here? Makana had a sense that he was being watched as he crossed and ducked quickly through the open doorway. The threshold was like a heavy curtain, on the other side of which was pitch blackness. The glow from the street behind him revealed only the foot of the narrow stairwell. Up above him faint threads of light filtered under doorways. It was hot and airless in there. Landlords regularly overstepped the building regulations, discarding common sense as they did so. Thus a four-storey building would be pushed up to seven, nine or eleven floors even, as if trying to push the limits of human stupidity, or break the world record for precarious living. Every now and then the earth would give a slight tremor to remind people of their humble place in the scheme of things. Whole buildings came down, walls crumbling as if they were made of brittle clay. Men, women and children crushed in their beds. There would be the usual cries for justice and the blame would be passed, and gradually things would return to normal and people would sleep peacefully again, until the next tremor. At a small window on the second floor he paused and put his head to the opening and breathed deeply. Outside, an eerie combination of shadows and streetlights painted the street in squares of light and dark. Turning back, Makana flicked the wheel of his disposable lighter to reveal graffiti left by tomb raiders: apartment numbers and the names of occupants scratched on the wall with charcoal. The sounds of the street fell away. The excited chatter of televisions played obliviously behind closed doors. People talking, mothers calling to children, an argument between man and wife.

Above him a door opened and closed abruptly. Makana heard the sound of someone moving upwards in the darkness and then stop. For a time there was nothing but the muted sounds of life from the apartments around him. He waited, sensing that the person above him was waiting for him to do something, but what? Slowly he took a step upwards, and then another, feeling his way as carefully and as quietly as possible. There was no inside edge to the stairwell, nothing to stop him falling if he put a foot wrong. He stopped and pressed himself back against the wall as something swooped down on him. A heavy object struck the edge of the staircase just above his head. There was a crash as it exploded, showering him with bright dust and small chunks of concrete. Then he could hear the sound of someone running upwards and he began to move again, this time with less caution. With one hand scraping along the wall, he felt his way, a blind man racing through a tunnel. His eyes were adjusting to the dark and he could make out a faint glow from high up where he guessed the stairs gave onto the roof. Makana moved quickly, climbing the last three flights as fast as he could, stumbling a couple of times, scraping his hands and banging his knee painfully, until finally the dark enclosed space gave way to the open air.

Breathing heavily, Makana stepped cautiously up onto the roof. It was a relief to be out of the choking confines of the stairwell and out into the cool night air. He looked around him but could see nothing but shadows. There was no light up there save

347

for the faint glow that filtered up from the street and surrounding buildings.

The stairs carried on up into the sky, a hopeful, if crooked chart of the building owner's projected ambitions, aimed at the stars and cut off abruptly in mid-air. He circled around trying to avoid tripping over the clutter of junk: television antennae, buckets and planks of wood, old car wheels, broken bicycles, chicken wire, paint hardened in pots, bags of cement turned to solid rock by the rains. Like a distant oasis the skyline of downtown Cairo glowed in the distance, announcing the eternal life of neon-strip signs championing airline logos, cigarettes, soft drinks. Modern idols begging for worship. Beyond lay the soft domes and lean Ottoman minarets of the citadel which floated above the city in a bowl of light, like a looming spacecraft from another age.

On the far side of the roof he could make out some kind of flimsy construction. It wasn't uncommon for people to build shacks on rooftops. The shortage of housing, funds, available space, forced people to make do. These would not have been out of place in a shanty town. On closer inspection Makana could see that for what they were they were fairly robust. A sound brought him to a halt. Something, or someone, was moving around inside. There was a scrabbling about that made him think of rats at first, but this was bigger. His next thought was a dog. Then it hit him. Moving in closer, he examined the hastily nailed-together planks, sheets of plywood. All the material appeared to have been assembled haphazardly from a variety of sources. It was solid enough though, with a roof of zinc sheeting. At the level of his head a series of openings ran along at regular intervals. As he approached these the stench hit him. Standing on tiptoe he could peer inside. The commotion inside increased in intensity, like animals in distress sensing danger.

'It's all right,' he said softly into the opening. 'I'm going to get you out.'

Easier said than done. The door was reinforced as well as bolted in two places. Makana rattled the heavy padlocks, increasing the alarm within. He would need tools to get it off. Moving around the roof in search of a lever of some kind, Makana discovered there was no perimeter wall around the edge. No doubt the owner had decided it wasn't worth it. When he had the money he would simply construct another floor. Makana peered down into a narrow cut created by the awkward angle between this building and the next. Some miscalculation by a surveyor had left a couple of metres to waste. Or perhaps it had been left on purpose, as a thoroughfare designed by the municipality. In which case another planner had truncated this scheme by placing another building at the far end. As he peered over, sliding one foot carefully towards the edge, he was met by a rotting stench of drains and bad water.

It was as he was turning away that something hit him. Hard. If he hadn't been moving it would have knocked him out cold. Instead, the blow aimed for his head glanced off his shoulder. Still, it was enough to send him staggering back. He could hear a grunting, wordless sound, like a man in pain. The second blow hit his outstretched arm, sending a ringing numbness through his left side. Trying to evade the blows Makana found himself being pushed backwards towards the edge of the roof. He tried to straighten up, but his assailant was too strong. The next blow struck his side. His foot tripped over something and as the other man drew back his weapon, a length of wooden scaffolding, Makana scrabbled about on the ground until his hands found a weapon. An old tin that must have once contained paint that had long since been hardened by rain and sun. It weighed a

349

couple of kilos. He swung it while trying to straighten up, hearing the satisfying crack of the heavy tin hitting home. There was a wild scream, but the man responded by throwing himself at Makana with renewed fury. This time the wooden spar hit him high up in the chest and pushed him backwards. There was no barrier, nothing to stop him. He scrabbled blindly, clutching only handfuls of air. His right foot skidded over the edge. The night spun around him as his arms flailed wildly and he toppled with a cry into the dark void.

Chapter Thirty-Nine

A dead man falling, Makana thought. There were seven floors of empty space beneath him. Lighted windows flared like brief matches as he fell past them. He braced himself for impact, for unimaginable pain. He could hear a voice, vaguely similar to his own, yelling. Nobody falls seven floors and walks away unscathed. Then, before he had time to think any further thoughts, he plunged into a soft, spongy mass. A sticky, moist hand closed around him, then he was sinking, no longer falling. Confused, Makana scrabbled about hopelessly. The stench filled his throat, so strong he could not breathe. Something sharp dug into him. Wet plastic stuck to his face, suffocating him even as it sucked him down, pouring in on top of him, burying him alive. Years of accumulated rubbish, tossed out through kitchen windows without a thought, had produced a layer of decomposing matter – vegetable, animal, mineral – all wrapped in plastic and about two floors deep. Alive, too, by the feel of it. Something was moving about under him. Fighting panic, Makana kicked frantically to roll clear of the mess, to breathe, to stay afloat. He floundered in the dark until eventually he managed to roll himself into a corner where there was a lighted window. He banged on the glass as loudly as he could. It was like floating on soft mud that might at any moment give way, leaving him to plunge even deeper into the bowels of this creature. Something scampered over his leg. He shouted and banged more frantically. A light came on. Shouts of alarm, children crying.

'*Ya Allah!*' a woman implored. '*Iblis*, the devil himself is out there!' The howling children joined in the hysteria. '*Allahuakbar!*' they all chimed together.

Makana was afraid he might pass out from the stench of putrid gases. He was clinging to the window sill to stop himself drowning in the muck.

'Police! Open this window!'

The voice of authority had a sobering effect.

'What did he say?' the woman asked.

'Police. I think he said,' replied her husband.

'Police? How can the police be out there?'

'Do I know? Stand back, woman, let me open it.'

There were cries of alarm as the rot and bits of blackened waste matter tumbled into their kitchen, along with a tidal wave of cockroaches, worms, and finally a strange man smeared in all manner of nasty material fell through the window. Something jumped nimbly off Makana's back and bounded across the floor.

'A rat!'

'Quick, kill it! Where did it go?'

Makana struggled to his feet and stood brushing the rubbish off, checking himself for bites. His whole body itched and he fought the urge to retch. Banana peels, bones, bits of rind, along with all manner of unidentified decomposing matter tumbled off him to the floor. The man and his wife stared at him in horror. The child was busy chasing the rat through the house, hammering the walls with a broom.

'How can you live like this, buried in rubbish?' Makana asked.

'We never open that window,' the man explained.

The woman shrieked as a large black beetle fell into her sink. 'It's the people from upstairs. They are the ones you should question. No respect. They just throw their rubbish out of the window like there is no one in the world except them. Are you really from the police? You can arrest them.'

'Nothing would give me more pleasure,' said Makana honestly. 'But right now I need to use your telephone.'

While he called Okasha the child reappeared holding the dead rat by the tail, two smaller children trailing cheerfully along behind. Makana stepped past them out into the darkened stairwell.

'You know the man who lives on the fourth floor?'

'Everyone knows him. He's a brute. But what can you do? If you say something his friends will come round and break your legs, or worse even.'

'You know what he keeps on the roof?'

The man muttered something and fell silent.

'You're coming with me,' said Makana. 'Have you got any tools?'

Armed with a hammer and a large screwdriver Makana climbed back to the roof. Behind him, the man was finding his tongue.

'He treats them like slaves. It's shameful. They steal, they rob, and he lends them out to other men for even worse things. But what can you do? I have a family. And the people who protect him are too strong.'

Makana peered out over the darkened roof and realised that his legs were shaking, from fear or shock he wasn't certain. Nothing moved.

'I don't want any trouble. I have to live here, you know.'

'Just keep your eyes open in case he comes back.'

Makana pushed the long screwdriver through one of the hasps and leaned his weight on it until it came away with a yawning, wrenching sound. Then he did the same with the second one. As the door swung open a terrible smell hit him.

It took a moment for Makana's vision to adjust to the gloom. He could make out a couple of mattresses on the floor and counted at least three frightened sets of eyes blinking back at him. They were huddled together over by the far wall. The room, more like a hole in the ground or a grubby cave, stank of all manner of human waste and decay.

'It's all right,' he called out. 'He's gone. It's safe.'

Slowly they crept towards the light. One by one, as if afraid it was a trap. Half naked, covered in grimy rags. There were five boys, of varying age. The youngest was not more than six, the eldest around twelve. Where they had come from, what their stories were, he could only imagine. What they shared in common was this little prison and the abuse they had suffered.

'*Ya allah*,' murmured the man from downstairs.

'We're taking them out of here,' Makana said, turning to reassure the boys. 'It's all right,' he said again. None of them had yet spoken a word. They stared at him with wide eyes that seemed to have lost all sense of light. He ushered them towards the stairs.

In the street below he found the bewhiskered Omda stamping his stick indignantly. A crowd had gathered round the entrance to see what the commotion was all about. They closed in on Makana as he came out of the building with his little band of wretches.

'What is going on here?'

'It's all over. The police are already on their way.'

354

The Omda put his hand on Makana's chest, his moustache wrinkling with disgust. 'I told you, we take care of ourselves around here. The police aren't welcome.'

Knowing the state of the traffic, Makana knew that it could be a while before Okasha showed up.

'You're protecting a criminal.'

'These . . . animals,' he wrinkled up his nose, 'are like vermin. They carry disease.'

'They are children.'

The crowd was closing in, and Makana realised that things could get nasty. Several of them, including the old goat with the moustache, were probably accessories. Rocky no doubt paid them off as well as providing some of them with extra services. The boys were beginning to get nervous. He backed towards the entrance to the building thinking it might provide some shelter until help arrived. He scanned the crowd hoping for a sight of Sindbad. Then one of the boys lost his nerve and made a break for it. Running along the side of the building, he triggered off an instinct in the men surrounding them who immediately gave chase. They cornered him, penning him in quickly. The boy darted one way and then the other as the circle closed in on him. Any minute now, Makana thought, and they would all be ripped limb from limb. He was in no doubt that the Omda was not joking when he said they took care of their own.

'There he is!'

All eyes followed the finger pointing upwards, and there, running along the parapet of a building, was a slight figure.

'It's the angel!'

'That crazy Christian boy,' someone else shouted. 'We'll get him this time.'

The Omda thrust his stick into Makana's face. 'There's the

355

one you should be after. He's the one who killed those boys.' And without waiting for a reply he turned and hurried after the mob. Makana felt a certain relief watching them go, although he was concerned about what might happen if they caught up with Antun. As he turned his head back, Makana glimpsed a face retreating quickly into the shadows two doors down. At that moment Sindbad huffed into sight.

'I heard the noise. What is happening?'

'Look after them,' Makana told him, indicating the kids. 'Okasha will be here in a moment.'

'What are you . . . ?' Sindbad's voice trailed off as Makana crossed the street quickly and stepped through another narrow doorway. Rocky had not gone far. He had come back down the stairs and slipped into another building, hoping no doubt to watch them carry Makana's body out. Now he could hear him, breathing heavily as he climbed the stairs above him. Makana was in some pain. The fall had bruised his chest and twisted one leg. He realised he was hobbling up the stairs rather than running. But he was moving, which was something.

The roof of this building was similar to the other and cluttered with all manner of junk. Here, washing lines loaded with sheets flapped in the night air. In the distance he could hear sirens. A shadow popped up and then vanished just as swiftly. He crossed the roof and saw the figure had dropped down and was now running across the top of the next building. Makana swung himself down, scraping the skin on his hand in the process. He moved as quickly as he could, trying not to trip over too many things. Ahead of him he glimpsed Rocky jumping to the next building, showing more athletic prowess than Makana would have given him credit for. When he reached the edge he saw that it was less than two metres across a narrow alley to the next building. He took a run and cleared it easily, falling over an old oil barrel lying in the dark on the other side. By the time he got up, Rocky was already halfway across the next building. Torches burned a trail along the street below, marking the progress of the gathering mob. The flames bobbing along on a tide of angry shouts and upraised hands. The flares lit the faces of onlookers: a flickering portrait of unease.

Makana was now running parallel to them, with Rocky a fleeting shadow ahead of him. They leapt across another street and then another. Below, the road widened and the high white walls of the church loomed out of the darkness. This time they would surely burn it down. Beyond the church the road narrowed again, vanishing once more into a labyrinth of crooked buildings. Rocky was climbing a wall, standing on something and hauling himself up. It slowed him down a bit, but Makana was faced with the same problem when he got there. He stacked up a couple of crates and then threw himself up until he got his fingers over the lip. He felt a nail rip his hand as he scrabbled with his feet, running up the brickwork, trying to find some support.

From up here the city looked like an electric sea tossing in a storm. The hard lines dissolved into darkness and the buildings emerged like tall grey vessels floating out of the gloom. When he straightened up he realised he was now directly opposite the church. But the street separating them was too wide to jump at this point. He watched a fireball spin slowly through the air before exploding, spilling an angry tear down the white wall. Another Molotov cocktail followed the first. There was a tinkling of glass and flame erupted inside. The leaping shadows playing in the high windows in the church's side.

Ahead of him Rocky was getting away, running across the

precarious roofing that spanned the buildings further down. The street narrowed there. He was trying to get across. He was trying to get to the church. What for?

On the other side, Antun appeared in one of the windows of the church tower. He climbed out and ran with sure-footed recklessness along the parapet until he stood directly over the mob gathered in front of the church doors. There he stood and raised his hands above his head. Makana stopped running, spellbound by what he was seeing. Antun seemed to really believe he was some kind of supernatural creature. An angel even. Then Makana saw the shadow rise up at the rear end of the church and begin edging carefully along the narrow parapet. Rocky was heading for the front of the church. If he knocked Antun down no one would accuse him of murder and the crowd would have their killer.

Below, a second group had gathered in front of the church, apparently in an attempt to repel the attack. Ishaq's angry gang. Makana could make him out on the frontline, ahead of his men who carried sticks and bicycle chains. A car exploded into flames as the two groups advanced towards one another. Makana could make out Father Macarius fighting to get between them. A crowd was forming as people gathered to see what was happening. Some shouted excitedly:

'There he is!'

'*Al-malaika!*' someone cried. 'It's the angel.'

'Killer!'

The thin figure standing at the apex of the church tower stood out in stark contrast to the white walls. A silence fell over the crowd below as they caught sight of him again. People were looking up and pointing. If Antun was the devil who was preying on young boys he was also the miracle. The Angel of Imbaba.

Indeed, some had fallen to their knees and were crossing themselves, raising their hands in prayer. The boy seemed not to notice any of this. He was balanced right on the very tip where there couldn't have been more than a few centimetres to stand on. Yet he appeared perfectly stable, as if he had stood on that exact spot many times before.

'Antun!' Makana shouted, waved his arms in warning, but to no avail. Rocky was drawing closer. The slight boy would be no match for him. Antun seemed oblivious. Another car exploded into flames as the sirens drew closer. Rocky disappeared from sight and then reappeared, just on the other side of the church tower. Antun saw him now. He lowered his arms, almost in a gesture of resignation. Makana could see the smile of satisfaction curl across Rocky's upper lip as he closed in. The look on his face changed to one of puzzlement as Antun turned towards him and threw himself into his arms. The expression turned to one of panic as Rocky realised that Antun was not trying to fight him off, but was instead clinging on, his arms wrapped tightly around Rocky's neck. The two figures toppled slowly from the roof. Antun's little cape gave a brief flutter before they hit the ground with a sickening crunch.

Silence fell over the crowd. They drew back from the two bodies which lay there still entwined. In death, Antun's face appeared to be smiling in an odd fashion, as if he had finally found peace. The rest of his body was crushed and broken by the fall. His legs were twisted away to either side at unnatural angles and his chest had collapsed, but his face had somehow managed to remain untouched. All the animosity had gone out of the crowd. As they stood puzzling over the body and why he had jumped, a flare of light rose with a clap into the night sky and everyone turned to look up at the church.

'We can't let it burn!'

'Call the fire brigade.'

'You could die of old age waiting for them to turn up.'

'We have to do it ourselves.'

'Come along, y*allah*, everyone! Maybe we can put it out.'

It was an extraordinary sight. What a moment earlier had been a mob out for blood was now transformed into a united group determined to put out the fire. In a matter of minutes they were organising themselves into teams, their religious differences forgotten. Christians and Muslims together. Some went to fetch buckets and hosepipes, others rallied around the church. A group of women knelt down and gathered Antun up in a white sheet which was wrapped around him like a shroud. Then they lifted him onto their shoulders and held him high as they carried him away.

Chapter Forty

Mo Damazeen was waiting in the lobby of the Gezira Sheraton when Makana walked in the following afternoon. Sombrely dressed, in a sharply cut black linen suit and a crisp white shirt, he paced nervously, fidgeting with his cuffs as Makana watched him from across the wide room. Beyond, large windows looked out on a wide view of the river looking south towards Manial Island. Scruffy palm trees poked at the sky, their crowns waving madly in the dusty breeze.

Makana himself had seen better days. Along with the aches and pains from the previous night's exertions, he had only managed to get a couple of hours' sleep. Okasha had arrived with enough reinforcements to put down a small coup, but they had proved unnecessary. Somehow the deaths of Antun and Rocky had brought a certain calm to the situation. It was almost as if their sacrifices had cleansed the world in some strange way. In Rocky's flat they had discovered an Aladdin's cave of stolen goods comprising everything from televisions and video players to statuettes of Nefertiti, gold and silver amulets, along with a rich haul of various foreign currencies and a handful of passports and other stolen documents. Rocky's boys had been busy. In return they recounted their abuse. They had been bullied and beaten, starved, locked up in the cage on the roof. Now that he was dead it seemed there was no limit to the number of people willing to come forward and testify to his brutality. Okasha was in supreme form, almost crowing with delight, confident that he would find enough forensic evidence to link Rocky to the murders and put Sharqi in his place in the process.

As for Antun, his passing was mourned above all by Father Macarius. The body was laid out in the church, among the debris and ashes, the smoke-charred walls. The structure wasn't too badly damaged, all things considered. The scaffolding had collapsed into a heap of carbonised struts which resembled gigantic burnt-out matches. The floor was soaked in water. A space was cleared for Antun to have a moment's rest. 'He never asked for anything,' Father Macarius said, his voice choked with emotion, 'except a place in the world.' At the end of his quest, Antun's face glowed with a kind of graceful serenity.

As for Rania, they found no trace. Rocky's death had brought that line of investigation to an abrupt stop. Yousef had disappeared. Makana spent what was left of the night trying to track him down, but he appeared to have vanished without trace. Nobody knew or was willing to share what they knew.

And so Makana stumbled into the Sheraton in a state of near exhaustion. The hotel lobby was largely filled with tourists from every corner of the earth. Indian families looked around them, plump with contentment. Japanese men in floppy hats studied their surroundings like anthropologists in uncharted jungle. Stout German women in trousers composed almost entirely of pockets yodelled loudly to one another across the room.

Damazeen was his usual immaculate self, fumbling with a mobile phone so he did not notice Makana's arrival. It was only when Makana sat down opposite him that he looked up and pulled a face.

'Couldn't you at least have made an effort? You look as if you haven't slept in a week.'

'That's about how I feel,' muttered Makana.

Damazeen reached into his pocket for his Dunhills. 'I was beginning to wonder if you were going to turn up at all.' He puffed away gently, regarding Makana. 'You won't regret this, you know. Once Mek Nimr is out of the way you will have a chance to put your case. I told you before, we live in a new age of pragmatism. You could come home, resume your life again instead of living here like a homeless mongrel.'

At the next table an old Chinese man with cameras and bags strapped across his chest like a commando lay slumped back staring at the river, puffing on a cigarette as if he had been starved of tobacco for months.

'I'm not like you. Not many people are. I couldn't live in obscurity like an outcast,' Damazeen continued. 'When I arrived home I was hailed as a returning hero. I became a symbol of the progressive nature of the regime.'

'Doesn't it get tiring being a national hero?'

'We all need a place where we belong. Even you. I don't understand how a man can cut off his roots and make a new life for himself in a foreign land.' A shudder seemed to go through Damazeen. Then he glanced at his watch and got to his feet. 'Let's go. Our guests are already waiting in the suite I am paying for. The sooner this is over the better.'

The Chinese man at the next table had been watching them. Now his attention was distracted by half a dozen of his compatriots, all of them young females who appeared to be talking at the same time. The older man now resembled a kindly emperor surrounded by his concubines. Makana sat back and wished he knew what he was doing here.

'How can I be sure that you are telling the truth? I have no proof that Nasra is alive.'

'You must have faith,' smiled Damazeen. 'You have no choice but to trust me. Shall we?'

The chattering concubines were giggling and pulling their emperor to his feet before leading him away. Reluctantly, Makana followed Damazeen through the lobby. While they were waiting for a lift to arrive he patted down his pockets.

'I think I forgot my cigarettes on the table.'

'We can get more cigarettes,' Damazeen snapped.

'I won't be a moment.'

Damazeen looked at his watch again. 'Be quick!'

Making his way quickly back in the direction of where they had been sitting, Makana stopped by the reception desk.

'I need to make a phone call. Can you charge it to my room?'

'Of course, sir. Your name is?' The receptionist eyed Makana cautiously.

'Mohammed Damazeen, I booked some business associates into suite . . .' He clicked his fingers absently.

The receptionist consulted his screen. 'Suite 1202.'

'Exactly,' Makana smiled. 'Now, where can I make that call?'

There was a row of telephones on a shelf along the wall to which he was directed. He made two phone calls. Both calls lasted less than a minute. Then he took his cigarettes out of his pocket and lit one before strolling back towards the lifts where Damazeen was pacing impatiently.

'Hurry up. I don't want to keep them waiting.'

As they rode up in the lift Makana thought about the decision he had made on the bridge that night ten years ago. A decision that had decided the course of his life from that moment on. If by some miracle he had been able to turn back time, to return to the days when he, Muna and Nasra had been a family, he knew in his heart that he wouldn't have hesitated for a second. That was life and this was . . . what? He wasn't sure. Time, of course, didn't work like that. It was only a continuum in his head, a freely running line that passed back and forth. The truth was much simpler than that. What happened that night on the bridge could not be undone. Or could it? If Nasra was still alive then so much of what he had believed would change. He had lived these last ten years believing it would have been better if he had gone over the side into the river with them, only now to discover there was, perhaps, a reason to go on. Time was the final mystery, the puzzle he would never solve, the door he could never open.

'Seeing as you have come this far, I feel it only fair that I reward you.'

It was Damazeen's tone, rather than his words which made Makana look up. He was holding out a thin envelope. Reluctantly, Makana took it. It contained a photograph of a young woman. Makana would have put her age at about sixteen. Instinctively, he felt a door open deep inside him, felt the cold water rushing in.

'You don't recognise her?'

It was like a spasm that clenched his heart tightly like a muscle cramping. The girl in the picture was familiar and yet at the same time completely alien. How do we recognise people? By particular features, or some undeniable element of their character? he wondered. She stared straight at the camera with purpose and conviction that seemed to demand a response from him. He slumped back against the side of the lift. After ten years he still wasn't prepared. How could one ever be prepared for something like this?

'Is she here?'

'You are getting ahead of yourself,' Damazeen laughed lightly. 'Why would she be here?'

Why indeed? But then again, why not? Makana examined the picture again. Could it be true? Could this young woman be his daughter? Despite himself, despite his racing heart, there remained a tiny flicker of doubt. Was it possible she could have survived? He couldn't allow himself to believe it, not yet, in case it was false. And yet the story had the kind of strange and twisted logic that made an odd sort of sense. He was trying to stay afloat, trying not to allow his feelings to distract his thinking. Ten years was a long time, but the wounds suddenly felt fresh and raw. He examined the picture again. Was there something in her eyes that reminded him of Muna?

As the lift slowed to a halt and the doors slid open, Damazeen said, 'Think of it as a second chance at life. Everyone deserves a second chance, don't you think?'

The white door to Suite 1202 lay at the far end of a discreet corridor. The door opened to reveal a white man in his forties. With broad shoulders and a heavy build, he wore khaki pants and a dark polo shirt. A gun hung in a shoulder holster under his left arm. He didn't say a word, just looked them both up and down before motioning for them to enter. After a quick glance down the corridor to make sure no one else was around he closed the door and flipped the bolt. As he turned to walk by Makana felt his shoulders seized by two powerful hands. His face struck the wall as his jacket was wrenched down, pinning his arms in place. A pair of hands then patted him down quickly and expertly, finding nothing. Damazeen held his hands up meekly for the same treatment.

'Go on in,' said the man in English.

They entered a wide living area. A long sofa and chair arrangement took up one half of the room, facing the windows. Along the rear wall was a long bar of polished black marble, behind which were glass shelves backed by mirrors. The view through the windows was of the river. The baking traffic flowed like molten silver across the bridge far below. To the right, through an archway, was a dining area. To the left another door led elsewhere, probably a bedroom. In front of this door stood another white man, dressed similarly to the first. This would be Mr Henry Bruin of Cape Town, South Africa, the man Sindbad had seen in the lobby of the Ramses Hilton. Older and heavier, his red hair and beard cut to the same short style. Bruin, Makana concluded, was the more dangerous of the two guards.

'They're clean,' said the first.

Bruin turned and rapped on the door behind him. It opened a moment later to reveal a large black man in his fifties. He was taller than anyone else in the room, and moved awkwardly, as if he had back problems. A warlord from somewhere in Central Africa, Makana guessed. He wore a grizzled beard and a pair of reading glasses dangled from a cord that went around his neck, lending him a vaguely academic air.

'*Bonjour messieurs.*'

'Mr Assani,' Damazeen shook the man's hand. 'This is my associate, Mr Makana.'

'Ah, we have many fine names for what we do,' chuckled Assani. He waved a wrist on which a large gold watch rattled. 'These are my *executive* associates, Mr Fitch and Mr Bruin.'

Assani gestured towards the dining room. 'Shall we commence?'

Makana followed Damazeen through and they settled themselves around a lacquered dining table. The walls were painted white and adorned with modern papyrus prints in glass frames.

Assani gave one of his chuckles. 'The Egyptians in my opinion should go back to their old ways and forget all this nonsense about Islam. What do you say, Mr Makana?'

'You might have a hard time persuading them to give up fifteen hundred years of history.'

'You sympathise then, with the *integristes* who wish to return to the days of their prophet?'

'Not exactly.'

'Ah,' he nodded sagely, 'a pragmatist.'

'You can only hold people against their will for so long.'

'Well said, and when the talking is done then we must reach for our weapons, which brings us to today's business.' Assani laughed. 'Interesting associates you have, Mr Damazeen.'

'Mr Makana has his own opinions,' said Damazeen curtly.

Assani snapped his fingers briskly and Bruin came forward with an attaché case which he set on the table. Setting his glasses on his nose Assani spun the tumblers until the latches clicked open. From within he lifted a small black bag of chamois leather which he opened. He spilt the contents into the lid of the briefcase. It looked as though a layer of crushed ice had been spread out before them. Makana heard Damazeen's quick intake of breath.

'We know war, we two,' Assani said softly, his long fingers fanning out over the table. 'Many say that the sacrifices we make in war have no compensation. This, gentlemen, at least goes some of the way to making up for what we have lost.'

'How much is there here?' Damazeen's voice was little more than a hoarse croak.

'Two million US dollars, on today's market,' Assani grinned, 'give or take.'

Makana had never really seen raw, uncut diamonds before. They didn't look like much. It was hard to imagine that they could be worth so much money. Damazeen's eyes were unfocussed, lit up by the strange glow that seemed to issue from the centre of those opaque, oddly shaped lumps that looked as if they belonged on another planet far away. Makana wondered how much he actually knew about diamonds. Turning back to the briefcase, Assani extracted a satellite telephone with a large bar antenna which he unfolded before handing it over.

'Now,' he said, holding out a scrap of paper, 'it is your turn. Here are the coordinates.'

Damazeen took the phone and punched in a series of numbers. A moment later he was speaking in Arabic, reading out the coordinates and urging whoever was on the other end to go ahead as planned. Makana glanced at Bruin, who was standing in the doorway behind him. He felt exposed and unarmed. If Assani decided to renege on the deal and murder both of them once the weapons had been delivered, there wasn't much he or anyone else could do about it.

Assani took back the phone and made his own call, setting his side of the operation in action. Then he set the phone down and glanced at his watch.

'Now all we have to do is wait.'

The diamonds were replaced in their bag. The bag returned to the briefcase and the tumblers spun. They adjourned to the next room. Placing the case on the counter, Assani went behind the bar. 'Now, who would like a drink?'

He produced a bottle of Johnnie Walker and an ice bucket. He poured a large tumblerful for himself. When Damazeen declined he wagged a finger.

'Oh, you people make me laugh. Always playing games.' Assani nodded at Makana. 'You are afraid he will disapprove, *n'est-ce pas?*'

'It's not that,' Damazeen swallowed nervously. 'I just don't want to drink this early in the day.'

'*Comme vous voulez*,' shrugged Assani. He sat down on the sofa and stretched out to rest his long legs on the coffee table. 'Myself, I fly to Paris tonight. My friends keep telling me to move to Dubai, but I can't stand the Arabs. All of them are two-faced, even you who should be African.' He chuckled to himself as he sipped his drink. 'At least in Paris you can get a decent meal.'

It took forty minutes for the call to come through. Assani was dozing on the sofa by then. Neither Damazeen nor Makana had moved a muscle. They remained under the vigilant eye of Bruin and Fitch. Rubbing his eyes, Assani sat up and pressed the phone to his ear. He listened for a few moments and then nodded. Getting to his feet he gave a signal and the mercenaries pulled on jackets and headed for the door. One was out in the corridor while the second held the door.

'Now, gentlemen, I am afraid I must leave you.' Turning to the attaché case, Assani spun the tumblers once more and plucked out the bag of diamonds and handed them over. Damazeen's eyes lit up as he opened the bag and dug his hand inside to let the glittering reward trickle through his fingers.

'Do not attempt to leave this room for the next half an hour,' Assani warned, 'or one of my associates will shoot you. It has been a pleasure doing business. I suggest you lighten up and have a drink. *À la prochaine*.' With a slight bow he headed for the door, briefcase in hand. 'Oh, I almost forgot.' He turned and revealed the silenced pistol he must have taken from the case after extracting the diamonds. 'Your friend, Mek Nimr? He sends his regards.' He fired twice and Damazeen collapsed backwards into the chair he had been sitting on. Two, star-shaped tears appeared in the otherwise pristine white shirt. Assani leaned over and picked up the bag of diamonds from Damazeen's lap. The barrel of the gun swung towards Makana. There was a moment's hesitation and then the pistol sailed from his hand forcing Makana to catch it. With a smile, Assani was gone.

Makana heard the door to the suite click shut and stood for a moment. He stooped over Damazeen and confirmed that he was certainly dead. A diamond fell from his hand as it dropped lifelessly to his side. As Makana went through his pockets quickly to see if there was anything connecting the two of them there came a knock at the door. He went over and carefully turned the bolt to lock it from the inside. As he stepped back he heard Sharqi call out:

'Open up, Makana!'

Makana glanced at his watch. The ever eager Sharqi had arrived earlier than agreed, which Makana now realised he should have taken into his calculations when making his plans. He considered his options. He was locked in a room with a dead man and he was holding the murder weapon. Leaving by any route other than the door was going to be difficult considering this was the twelfth floor. He went over to the window and considered the long drop. Death no longer held the same appeal it once had, now that he knew Nasra might be alive.

'What are you playing at Makana? Open the door before we break it down!'

It wouldn't take long, he knew, for Sharqi to get hold of a pass key or decide to simply forget about the expense and give his men the satisfaction of kicking the door in. Makana wasn't sure how far he could trust Sharqi, but he guessed that expecting him to forgive the murder of his prime source of information was probably too much to ask. Their agreement was that Sharqi would get Assani and Damazeen, after Makana had a chance to

371

talk to Damazeen in private, maybe offer him some clemency in return for Nasra's whereabouts. He looked down at the gun in his hand. Escape seemed out of the question.

Out of the corner of his eye a movement made him look left as a man floated up before him through the air. A miracle, or was his mind playing tricks? The windows facing him looked out over the river and were covered by balconies. The window to the left in the dining area was flat. The face on the other side of this window was one he had seen before. Not exactly pretty, nor what you might expect of an angel or performer of miracles. The last time he had seen this particular face had been in the alleyway behind Yunis' house of birds. Before that it had been riding a motorcycle with a television set strapped behind him. Slightly overweight, his flabby features blurred by grey stubble, the man came to a halt when he was level with the room. Makana went over and opened the window.

'There isn't much time,' the man said calmly. He held out a hand. Tucking the gun into the small of his back, Makana climbed out. The platform started to rise.

'Sorry about last time,' said the man apologetically, as he pulled the window closed.

'Never mind,' said Makana, peering down at the ground and thinking it looked a long way.

'They use these things for cleaning the glass.'

The electric winch whined as it lifted them slowly. High above a metal arm jutted off the roof over which the cables ran. A rubber wheel on either side squeaked along against the side of the building as they rose. Without warning it came to an abrupt stop and for a few moments they hung there, suspended in the air. The man sniffed and fiddled with the buttons on the control panel. Neither of them said anything. Then there was a click and the maintenance platform began to rise again. A couple of floors up the man pulled another lever and they began to move sideways. There was a good deal of swaying as the platform changed direction. In a few moments, however, they had reached the corner of the building. The man pulled a lever back for them to descend and they soon came to a halt outside another window. The man lifted the safety bar and gestured for Makana to step inside. Then he disappeared upwards again towards the roof. Makana pushed through the billowing net curtains into the room to find the slim figure of Zayed Zafrani waiting for him.

'So, Mr Makana, we meet again,' he said, holding out his hand.

'So it appears.'

'I believe you have something for me?'

'If you mean diamonds, I am afraid that Assani took them with him.'

'Ah,' Zafrani took the loss of two million dollars with a philosophical shrug. 'That is unfortunate. This means that they are in the hands of Mr Sharqi and his boss, Colonel Serrag.'

'It looks that way.'

'Well, that can't be helped.' Zafrani gestured towards the room. 'Please, make yourself comfortable. I suggest we wait an hour or so for the excitement to settle down before attempting to leave the hotel. Can I offer you tea?'

'Tea would be nice.'

'And Mr Damazeen?'

'I'm afraid he won't be joining us.'

Zayed nodded as if he expected this. 'Mr Damazeen was playing a dangerous game. What I don't understand is that you were prepared to take such a risk. What was there in it for you?'

'I was trying to get my life back.'

'Ah,' Zayed Zafrani frowned and then smiled as if this was the kind of answer he expected.

Makana felt sick. He felt as though a cold door had been shut in his face and Nasra had once more been condemned to the grave.

'There is a matter we still haven't settled yet,' Makana said, bringing himself back to the present. 'The details of the Eastern Star story are going to have to come out after all this.'

Zayed Zafrani tilted his head to one side. 'Perhaps there is a way in which they could emphasize the role played by Sheikh Waheed?'

'Would you be satisfied with that?'

'It would be a sacrifice,' said Zayed Zafrani, 'but it would be something.'

By the time he got back to the *awama* it was after sunset. His mind was in turmoil, preoccupied with all that had happened, and with what had not. Distracted, he did not register the fact that as he came down the path Umm Ali's little shack was silent and dark. It was only as he came aboard that he realised something was amiss. As he reached the foot of the stairs a voice spoke out of the shadows behind him:

'A man could get tired of waiting for you.'

Makana had half-turned before the blow hit him.

Chapter Forty-One

Makana came to as the smell of kerosene hit him. It made him feel nauseous. It was everywhere, all around him, on his clothes, on his skin. He was drowning in the stuff. When he tried to open his eyes he felt them sting. Where was he? It felt like a bad dream. Fuzzy spiders crawled around inside his head. He knew this place, but somehow he didn't. A moment later he realised he was at home, on the upper deck, in his favourite chair. A sinking feeling told him this was not a dream. He managed to lift his head. There was a ringing pain over his right ear. Someone had hit him. He remembered now. His clothes were wet. He shook his head to clear it and looked around him. When he tried to move he discovered that his hands were tied to the arms of the wicker chair. There was kerosene sloshing about. He turned his head as a large, yellow plastic jerrycan appeared, dousing everything in sight. A face loomed into view.

'Just in time,' said Yousef, setting down the jerrycan.

'What are you doing?' Makana didn't recognise his own voice.

Yousef clicked his tongue. 'You disappoint me, you know. We could have been such a good team. Do you ever ask yourself what the point is, of what you are doing?'

'What I am doing?' Makana followed his eyes across the deck to the bed pushed against the wall. Rania lay there, her hands and feet tied, a gag covering her mouth. Her eyes were wide with fear. 'All of this just to protect Sheikh Waheed?'

'Waheed? Waheed is a fool,' Yousef said. 'I don't care about him. You see, that's the problem. You're always trying to look beneath the surface. Waheed is a clown. What do I care? No, this is about me. That's the way it should always be, right? It could have been about you, too. But then . . .'

'You killed Meera.'

'Rocky killed Meera. It was necessary. If you don't understand why then you are stupider than I thought. People have a right to protect their investments, don't you think?' Yousef squatted in front of Makana.

'You and Rocky?'

'I came across him in my time in the Military Police. I was ordered to arrest him for beating a conscript half to death. I realised that someone like that could be very useful, if directed in the right way. Rocky was an animal. I made sure he got off the charges and he was very grateful. Of course in time he got out of hand. People like that always do. No control.' Yousef bounced to his feet again and carried on splashing kerosene about. 'To tell the truth, it's a relief he's gone. Rocky was a liability. And how do you get rid of someone like that?'

'Meera found out what you were up to, moving money through the Blue Ibis accounts. Nobody noticed because the books were in such a mess, not even Faragalla.'

'Faragalla's an idiot. I mean, why take on a woman like that? Women who think they know something, they're the worst. Like this one.' He went over and stroked Rania's thigh. She squealed and tried to turn away, which only seemed to increase Yousef's enjoyment. 'Women should know their place. In the kitchen . . . or in the bedroom.' He caressed her again, taking his time now. 'Think of how far that would go to solving the world's problems.'

'Let her go, Yousef. She's no threat to you.'

'There, you see, that's where you're wrong.' Yousef came back over. 'She is very much a threat, maybe even more than you. She has the facts. I thought we were finished with all that when Hikmet went out of that window, but no. She had to come along and find his other computer. Who would have that?' Yousef kicked an object lying on the floor. 'Well that's all taken care of now. By the time we've finished here it won't be any use to anyone.'

'Why are you doing all this? For a group of army officers who are making themselves rich. You think they care about you?'

'You see that's where you're wrong.' Yousef had a distant look in his eye. 'These people, Waheed, Serhan, all the other big fish up there, they know they would be nothing without me. Nothing. I make them and I can bring them down any time I want.'

'They could find someone to replace you in an instant.'

'No, you're wrong. It's about commitment. Just like in the military. You have to be prepared to make sacrifices. That's what people respect. This country is made by people like me. No one can claim to love Egypt more than I do. These kids don't understand. Can you imagine what would happen if we handed the place over to them?'

Yousef stood off to one side, looking out, his face in the shadows, lit only in part by the white glow from the buildings across the river.

'The little men. Where do you think all those politicians and businessmen would be without us? Even the president. They all depend on people like me to make things happen.'

'They use you because you are expendable,' said Makana, suddenly weary of this raving lunatic. 'Even the Zafrani brothers. They were already onto you. How much longer did you think it would last?'

Yousef snorted his derision. 'I can't expect someone like you to understand. Like I said, you and I could have made a great team. *Maalish*, you'll have to excuse me now, I have work to do.'

With that he picked up the jerrycan and disappeared down the stairs. The *awama* was as dry as a tinderbox. It wouldn't take much to set it alight. But Yousef obviously wasn't taking any chances. Makana wrestled with his bindings but Yousef had done a good job. He thought about smashing the chair, but although it was old he had the feeling it would still take a lot of punishment before it gave way. He looked over at Rania, who was watching him with a look of terror in her eyes. Her hands were tied behind her back, but perhaps she could untie his knots.

'Try to sit up,' he said. Then he managed to lift himself and shuffle forwards. His feet were untied. He made it in about ten moves, sliding the chair across the deck, trying to make as little noise as possible. By now Rania had managed to turn over on the bed. She twisted until she had her back to him and was almost sitting up, her shoulder against the bedstead. It didn't look like much, but at least she could move her fingers.

It didn't take long to discover that it wasn't going to work. The knots were too tight and Rania couldn't get a proper grip. She tried and tried and then with a cry of frustration she fell back. In her eyes he read resignation; the realisation that death was inevitable. Makana could hear Yousef down below, moving around the lower deck, splashing fuel over everything.

Then a glint of light caught his eye and looking towards the gangway he saw a figure crouched there in the half shadow.

Aziza. The little girl looked around the room carefully and then stepped boldly up and came slowly towards him. In her hand was a nasty-looking curved knife that Umm Ali and her able children used for slicing the stems off artichokes, freeing aubergines from the earth. A general all-purpose tool. It had a rough wooden hilt wrapped tightly with grubby cloth and a blade that was sharpened on a stone. Aziza, despite her young age, handled it like a professional but it still seemed to take ages for her to slice through the ropes holding Makana's left wrist. When it was done he took the knife from her and cut his other hand free, then he released Rania.

'Wait here,' he said. 'Don't forget the computer.' He took the knife and slipped off his shoes, then went down the metal steps as quietly as possible. At the bottom he waved them both down and pointed towards the gangway. He waited until they were ashore. He still had the knife, but there was nothing to indicate where Yousef was. Then he heard a sound that stopped his heart in mid-beat – the faint rasp of a lighter. It came from the stern of the boat. He leaned around the side and saw the figure standing close to the railings at the far end. Yousef's face was briefly illuminated by the glow from one of his cigarettes. A few puffs and then he would casually toss it aside as he stepped ashore to watch the whole thing burn. There wasn't time to think and no way of separating Yousef from the glowing end of his cigarette. So Makana charged, gaining speed with every step. Yousef had time to look up, his face registering surprise as the curved knife buried itself in his shoulder and Makana thudded into him. There was a whoosh and Makana recalled that his clothes were doused in kerosene. He felt the heat flare up around his face, enveloping him in blue flame, but by then his momentum had propelled both of them over the railing and into the water.

The river was a great muddy fish that reached up to swallow them whole. He felt Yousef wriggling in his arms, sinewy and strong, like a powerful reptile that he couldn't contain. A cold current seemed to suck both of them deeper and deeper until finally Makana knew he was going to drown. He was no longer fighting to contain Yousef, but to break free of him. The water was cold, far colder than he had imagined. Beneath the calm surface of the river he knew there were turbulences, stirrings, undercurrents that could whip even a strong swimmer down. Miraculously, Yousef's grip loosened. One arm disabled, he was flailing about like a man who could not swim. Makana felt the creature release its hold and he began to rise just as Yousef was drawn further into darkness. He kicked and clawed his way towards the surface.

Chapter Forty-Two

A swani's was strangely deserted at that hour. They had the place almost to themselves. Okasha arrived late, huffing and puffing, blinking at the odd assortment of strangers gathered around the table wondering who all these people were. In deference to the presence of a lady, Aswani had produced a plastic tablecloth from somewhere. It was red with cartoon drawings of yellow ducks and green puppy dogs. Where he had kept it hidden all these years, Makana could not imagine, let alone why. The cook himself was busy at work behind the counter yelling orders as his assistants ran back and forth to do his bidding.

'At least they have television now,' Talal said, nodding at the set up on the wall. Makana followed his gaze. A set had indeed been perched rather precariously on a lopsided shelf high on one of the pillars. It looked as though it might fall at any minute.

'It won't last,' Makana said. Although it wasn't much of an improvement, he wasn't sure he was right. Talal made no attempt to reply. He seemed subdued. No doubt still mourning the loss of his love. In time, perhaps, he would see that he had been lucky to get out of Bunny's clutches in one piece. Makana still hadn't really said anything to him about Damazeen, but that loss too must clearly have been weighing on the young man's mind. Before they sat down, Makana took him aside. He reached into his pocket and produced the diamond that Damazeen had been clutching in his hand when he died.

'I can give you the name of someone reliable who will buy it off you at a fair price. That should cover a year in Vienna.'

'Yes, but—'

'Don't ask,' Makana said. 'Damazeen would want you to have it.'

After that they all sat down. Sami sent his regards. He was holding a pen this morning, Rania reported, and was busy working on their story. It would appear under joint names, and would no doubt create a small tidal wave of scandal, engulfing numerous people including Sheikh Waheed. Okasha was more than happy with the way things had turned out. He had closed the case of the murders in Imbaba, managing to show up the much more high-profile counter-terrorism unit. He seemed to think his chances of promotion were greatly improved, he said, as he gave them the closing details:

'Eissa, the boy in the café, confessed once he was told Rocky was dead. He was the one who drove the motorcycle. He broke his arm when it crashed.'

'They had tunnelled through the wall, where they kept their stolen goods,' Makana explained. 'That's how he slipped out when the shooting started. But he was fond of Meera.'

'And terrified of Rocky,' Okasha agreed. 'I had the feeling he was just waiting for someone to ask. He felt bad about what he had done.'

'How sad,' said Rania.

'Ahh!' sighed Sindbad, the last member of their curious little party, at the sight of Aswani's assistants making their way across the room with large trays of food. Makana wondered at the wisdom of taking a man like this to a restaurant. He could probably eat the entire contents of the kitchen single-handedly. A silence fell over the table as everyone turned their attention to the business of eating. Plates kept coming. *Ful mudames*, fried kidneys, grilled sausages and eggs and tomatoes, with kebab and roasted lamb to come.

'You're spoiling us,' Makana said to Aswani who oversaw the operation like a general surveying a battlefield.

'Allah alone knows why I bother,' he sighed, rolling his eyes skywards, forever convinced that people never fully appreciated the tenderness and love he put into his cooking.

Makana was almost too tired to eat. What he looked forward to most of all was sleep. The stench of kerosene seemed to have eaten its way through his clothes and the pores of his skin to his very soul. The heady fumes threatened to overwhelm him, flooding his mind with thoughts of Nasra. As he watched everyone begin to help themselves to the food, Makana knew he would not rest until he found out the truth. But perhaps that would have to wait for another day.

'According to Sami,' Rania was saying, 'we are already living in a dreamland. A country that only exists in our imagination. We don't know if we're awake or sleeping. Lights, movies, music. It's all a tune of enchantment, keeping the country asleep. Who is going to wake us up?'

'Be careful what you wish for,' said Okasha, chewing fiercely. 'You have no idea what you might unleash once you let the djinn out of the bottle.'

'That is so true,' Talal replied absently. He wasn't looking at them. Rania followed his gaze until both of them were staring upwards.

'Isn't that New York?' she said.

They all turned to gaze up. A drama was being played out on the screen above their heads that would influence the next decade in ways none of them could yet imagine. Makana would look back on this moment time and again, sitting there in Aswani's. The stunned expressions of confusion and bewilderment, and finally, fear.

'That's a really bad pilot,' Talal said, only half-joking.

'It's not an accident,' Rania said, as the scene was replayed, over and over again even though the tickertape along the bottom of the screen said 'Live'.

In that moment a strange silence seemed to fall over the group, the restaurant, the city, the entire world. It was as if time was standing still. The image of the two dark towers rising into the clear blue sky seemed almost medieval, a throwback to a world of invincible fortresses and impregnable city portals. Out of one corner of the screen the arrowhead that was a jet airliner curved slowly, inevitably, towards its target. At the point of collision there was something incredibly graceful and tragic about its movement, as if this was part of a complex choreography, like the motion of the planets, an errant star that exploded into a ball of flame before their very eyes.

Makana found himself thinking about Ghalib Samsara. He wondered where he was at that moment. But it was Rania who spoke first, whispering the words that were on all of their lips, almost as if she were speaking their thoughts aloud:

'Now there's going to be trouble,' she said.

A NOTE ON THE TYPE

The text of this book is set in Baskerville, named after John Baskerville of Birmingham (1706–1775). The original punches cut by him still survive. His widow sold them to Beaumarchais, from where they passed through several French foundries to Deberney & Peignot in Paris, before finding their way to Cambridge University Press.

Baskerville was the first of the 'transitional romans' between the softer and rounder calligraphic Old Face and the 'Modern' sharp-tooled Bodoni. It does not look very different to the Old Faces, but the thick and thin strokes are more crisply defined, and the serifs on lower-case letters are closer to the horizontal with the stress nearer the vertical. The R in some sizes has the eighteenth-century curled tail, the lower-case w has no middle serif, and the lower-case g has an open tail and a curled ear.

THE GHOST RUNNER

A MAKANA MYSTERY

A question of honour. An eye for eye. The truth cannot stay buried for ever

It is 2002 and as tanks roll into the West Bank and the reverberations of 9/11 echo across the globe, tensions are running high on Cairo's streets. Private Investigator Makana, in exile from his native Sudan and increasingly haunted by memories of the wife and daughter he lost, is shaken out of his grief when a routine surveillance job leads him to the horrific murder of a teenage girl.

Seeking answers, he travels to Siwa, an oasis town on the edge of the great Sahara desert, where the law seems disturbingly far away. As violence follows him through the twisting, sand-blown streets and an old enemy lurks in the shadows, Makana discovers that the truth can be as deadly and as changeable as the desert beneath his feet

'Bilal whisks the reader straight to the dark heart of Cairo ... His prose has a subtlety that is rarely found in crime novels'
ECONOMIST